TRIAL OF FLAME AND WINGS

TRIALS FROM THE GREAT MOTHER
BOOK 1

AMY PROKOPIS

Amy Prokopis

Cover image by Abigail Sins

Edited by Lucia Ferrara

Published by Amy Prokopis

First printing edition 2025

www.amyprokopis.com

For all the strong, independent women kicking ass and taking names.

Part I

THE GREAT MOTHER

EXCERPT FROM THE BOOK OF THE GREAT MOTHER

Our world blossomed from the heart of the Great Mother. Everything we have and all that we are was created by her hand. She first created the air to breath, the land on which to stand, and the sea in which to swim. She was happy with her creation, though so great was it that she grew tired of expanding our world and desired to fill it with creatures that would too stare in awe at her creation.

Rather than fill the world herself, she instead created beings of great power. Each would rule over a different realm of her world and make it their own, creating creatures in their image and whatever else pleased them. Together, they all provided balance for this realm. In harmony, the world would be good, the creatures residing there happily, and the Great Mother's creation would thrive and remain healthy, thanks to their powers.

1

"One day, little bird," Leif said from my right, repeating the words he'd said during all our lessons since I was a little girl. "One day."

I shifted on the rocks and turned away from the sea to look at my teacher. Sir Leif Folee had a long history with my family, a story that was told on the ridges of every scar that marred his body. His dark hair had started to gray at his temples a year ago, but he still carried himself with the valor of the king's knight and was still known as the best among his company. He told me it was his greatest honor to be assigned as my teacher, but I knew that if he hadn't been the best he would've remained among my father's guard much longer. Leif knew that I knew. I didn't need to speak the truth and doing so would make things far more difficult in the long term.

"Let me look at you," he said and extended his hand.

I let out a frustrated sigh and accepted. I slid down the side of the boulder to face him. Before he could reach for my face, I grabbed the waterskin from his hip and used the first mouthful to wash out the blood staining my teeth. After I spat out the ruddy water on the sand, he turned my face to his with a calloused hand.

This was the part I hated, the final assessment of my failures. He rarely drew blood; not because he chose not to but because I'd grown skilled enough a long time ago to avoid those kinds of wounds. I was one of the best, maybe the finest swordsman in the entire castle, and no one knew. That was, no one but the one person who could still kick my ass, the man studying my bruised cheek and wiping the dried blood from my chin while I tried to avoid his gaze.

"I taught you better," he said as he brushed the bruise over my cheekbone.

I flinched away. "I know better."

"You're distracted."

"I turned twenty over a week ago," I said and brushed past him. I walked to the mouth of the cave where I'd shoved the tip of my sword deep in the sand after I lost the last round of sparring. I pulled both our swords free and turned. Leif caught his by the hilt when I tossed it.

"Let's go again," I challenged.

"Your father might have me strung up if I put another mark on that pretty face," he said and sheathed his sword at his hip.

"You know he'd praise you," I scoffed. The comment didn't soften the knight's resolve. On the contrary, it made him appear older. He held out his right hand, palm up for my sword.

"He would ask yet again what you have done to deserve the mark. One bruise, I can assuage his temper with. Two would earn you a beating and you have endured plenty this month," he said and nodded toward his palm.

"I will endure whatever gets me closer to my freedom and yours," I said and circled the tip of the sword around his hand.

"Yes, but you and I both have displeased the king and he made it known he would dismiss me if you continued to disobey. Do you not remember that he said if you were ordered to the post before the trial? It would not be me that holds the whip, Wren."

A small shiver shot down my spine at the memory. Leif had been my mother's guard. After she was executed, I was assigned to his care. He was more than just a teacher. The way my father saw it, Leif was responsible for me and that included my discipline. Leif was always as gentle as allowed, but my first time at the post was not thorough enough for the king.

I held the hilt of my sword to him with a sigh and he relaxed, a small smile pulling at his lips.

"One day, little bird," he said again before tossing the sword into the shadows of the cave. "Come now."

We started the trek along the shore back toward the castle. These walks were always my favorite part of my lessons.

"I need strategy *and* strength to win the trial," I said before he could launch into his usual lecture.

"Yes," he agreed, kicking a seashell in the sand toward me so I could pick it up. "But, you have the upper hand where strategy is concerned. You will be far underestimated. In entering the Trial for Marriage all of the contestants will naturally avoid harming you. They will take care of a lot of the battle for you and leave you alone until the end. You will need to conserve your strength as long as possible to be prepared to kill the final contestant, likely the strongest among them."

"I don't want to win by playing the damsel in distress," I groaned. It wasn't the way I dreamt of the trial. I would fight for my own hand, win my freedom, and be an heir to the crown in my own right. It would clear the way for a rebellion against my father and against my brother after that and spark hope for a tyranny-free Honor Cove.

"The trials themselves will prove challenging enough without facing your opponents. Keep your skill a secret so that it will serve as the strength you need. You will have the upper hand so long as you are underestimated. That's how you will win," Leif said and stopped walking as I bent over for another shell. "Conserve your strength and hide your skill until the end."

I straightened up and laid the shell flat in my palm. The shell was a spiral that tapered to a point at one end. Suddenly, I was a little girl walking barefoot on the beach on a day just like today, a much younger Leif at my side. I had always collected seashells along our walks, but when I was little, he told me a story about unicorns. He said that sometimes they would come to the sea and if you were lucky, you might find one of their horns buried in the sand. I'd only found a shell like this once before and it was on a walk with Leif. I gave it to him as a gift only to get it back on my birthday when he gave me a rocking horse with that seashell glued between its ears.

I looked up and held out my hand to him, the shell sitting in my palm. Instead, he closed my hand around it with a smile, giving my fist a gentle squeeze before letting go.

"You keep this one," he said. "I have plenty."

I looked away when I heard the sound of horns in the distance. After a moment, it started to grow louder until ...

"It's time," I said, my heart thumping in my chest. Something like relief stole my breath and washed all the worry from anticipation away.

"One day," Leif said firmly, pulling my gaze back to his serious expression. I could see the slight fear in his eyes as he gave me a nod. I returned the gesture and focused on the next steps of our plan. I wasn't allowed much time to process before I heard the whinny of a horse ahead.

Four horses carrying castle guards raced toward us as the sound of the horns continued. I shoved the shell into my pocket and Leif took his place a few paces in front of me as they approached, slowing to a stop several feet away. The lead guard dismounted and led his horse forward by the reins.

"Sir Folee," the man greeted with a brief incline of his head. He offered more of a bow in my direction before addressing the knight. "King Elroy has called everyone to court. The suitors have all arrived for the trial and plans are in place to host a welcome feast this evening."

"What are his orders?" Leif asked.

"Her Highness's attendance at the gates. The public has already started to gather. The royal family will be in attendance to welcome the suitors into the castle. Princess Wren must return to the castle to dress in her chambers," the guard said as he handed the reins over to Leif.

"Princess." Leif prompted me to approach by extending the reins to me. I mounted first, settling into place with the reins in hand as Leif climbed into the saddle behind me. Once he was seated, I spurred the horse forward and let the wind take my hair. The feeling of riding like this was freeing, an exhilarating moment that quickly passed when we reached the end of the beach, and the sand met the cobblestone streets.

The guards drew closer as we approached the castle, riding to the stables where a team of people were already waiting to tend to our horses. Leif dismounted first, offering to help me down as he always did despite my never accepting it. I landed easily and started for the castle doors before anyone could join us. Two men with swords at their hips pulled the doors open wide for us for moments before they closed again, and it was just the sound of our boots on the stones.

"Slower," Leif said from behind. "The trial won't be for another few days."

I slowed my pace enough that Leif was able to catch up. We walked together up the stairs and down the long corridor. I wanted nothing more than to just storm the last few yards to my chambers to face whatever ordeal waited for me. He grabbed my hand at the last second. His expression was so serious when I looked back at him that it chilled my skin.

"Be careful who you speak to and what you say. All eyes will be on you. We need to be on good terms with your family through this. Once things are in motion though ..."

I'd be a traitor. Once I entered into the trial, not only would I be directly defying my father, but I would be a challenger to the throne. I was second in line. Waylon wouldn't allow me to stay at court if I won, not that I'd choose to.

"Like you always say," I told him, and reached behind me for my chamber door. "One day."

I pulled it open and stepped inside, looking back to see his encouraging smile before it vanished behind the crack in the door.

2

When I stood from the vanity chair, I shivered as my long brown hair swept across my exposed back. Normally my hair would've been piled high on my head, but I knew my father had asked my lady's maids to keep it loose to hide the scars across my back. The red dress was flowy and eye-catching. No one at court would be wearing such vibrant a color and it ensured that I would be the center of attention like a trophy on a pedestal. Silver was the traditional jewelry worn by nobility since gold could only be found in the mountains where the Fallen reigned. However, gold brought out the natural shine in my brown hair. Plus, my father said it made me look more appealing and overshadowed my dishonorable disposition enough that it was worth me wearing gold and only gold.

Once the room of royal lady's maids had stopped picking at my appearance, I opened the door to the hall and left the team of guards to trail after me. I didn't ask for permission before reaching for the door to the king's council room, but the doorman beat me to the handle just in time to pull the oak door wide for me. I was the last to enter and the room quieted imme-diately.

"You look worthy of the crown on your brow," the king said with just enough of a sour tone to set me on edge.

"Beautiful," Leif said and stepped forward to take my hand and lead me toward the armchair my father sat in.

When my eyes met my father's, my entire body tensed. What little good humor he possessed faded from his expression as he rose to his feet. I kept a straight face despite the throb of my cheek as he pressed a thumb to the bruise.

"How?" he asked, his voice low.

"Me, Your Majesty," Leif said at my side. "Punishment for not being fully prepared for the day's lesson."

"I've been distracted by the trial. It's been over a week since I turned twenty," I said despite knowing that Leif was silently willing me to stay quiet.

My father's shoulders rose with his deep breath, and I swore the entire room braced for the slap. I didn't look away. If he was going to hit me, I was going to take it straight-on. He didn't make a move. After a long pause, he brushed past me. He stopped next to my brother long enough to squeeze his shoulder and then continued past him to the balcony. Two guards flanked him as he stepped to the stone railing with his hands held high, waiting for the cheering to die down before addressing the crowd.

"In a few weeks, you'll be another man's problem," Waylon said.

Rivalry was the only way to describe the relationship between us. It shouldn't have been that way. I was the spare, second in line to the throne after him. But it didn't matter. Waylon saw treason and challengers everywhere and had practically licked our father's boots from the moment he was born. He was our father's prize to the throne and I was merely a pretty jewel to be lorded over the rest of the realm.

Marrying me off would mean upward mobility for the winner of the trial and the highest of blessings from the Goddess Aria.

Win the Trial for Marriage. Be bound to the princess of Honor Cove by the goddess herself. Be added to the line of succession.

Our father ruled with a cold heart. Where he fought to cut down the Fallen in the Dark Realm at every opportunity and enslave those remaining, Waylon was eager to do the same within our realm. Waylon wanted to control every aspect of the kingdom. Those he couldn't control, like me, he would send to Aria's Stone for execution. If Waylon ever took the throne, all would be lost.

"Always yours though, brother," I said, unable to contain my smirk at the hate that turned his cheeks red.

"It's time," Leif said curtly, casting a warning look at me as Waylon turned to the balcony. "Careful," he whispered as I followed my brother into the open air.

"Princess Wren Bellator!" the court herald yelled from the right of the balcony. Cheers erupted as I took my place beside Waylon, putting on a smile and waving to the crowd in a manner I knew I'd be scolded for later. I always did the most to appear sympathetic to our people. I would need their favor in the end.

"Now opens our festivities in honor of the upcoming Trial for Marriage of Princess Wren Bellator. The winner of the trial will be a paragon of persistence, strength, and leadership that may one day lead our realm with honor bestowed by the Great Mother and power blessed by the Goddess Aria herself. Each contestant will enter the trial through a blood offering to Aria's Stone. Those who are accepted by the stone will fight to the death to prove themselves worthy of the crown. Let us now welcome the eager suitors," the man proclaimed.

A horn trumpeted from somewhere below and the first of my opponents was introduced. Each man walked down a red carpet laid across the cobblestone below that led through the front doors beneath our balcony. They all walked with their heads held high, offered a bow in our direction, and were trailed by their excited entourage of guards, attendants, and family members. Most of them were young men of nobility that I'd seen at court a few times before, but I didn't pay much attention to their names until a thickset man with dark hair graying around his face sauntered down the aisle.

"Lord Dallin Vondrelle from Vann Elding!"

Lord Dallin stopped halfway down the carpet to bow. Unlike the others, my father actually acknowledged him with the wave of a hand. In his mid-forties, Dallin would likely be the oldest of the contestants and the most experienced when it came to marriage. His first wife was killed by Fallen soldiers in a raid. His second wife was poisoned, and her assassin was never caught. Of course, my father would favor him. Dallin was terse, crass, and his body was a result of the hard life at sea. As much as I despised the man, at least he had calloused hands.

My father relaxed as Lord Dallin passed and the long procession continued with the usual family names being read. Everyone perked up again, Waylon included, at the mention of a family that hadn't appeared in court in ten years at least; an affluent family with a very coveted heir.

"Lord Beau Renault from Scout Sea!"

Lord Beau was the youngest man so far, not much older than me. He had short blond hair and looked out of place despite his lavish coat and slacks. He paused after his introduction and had to be prodded from behind by his father. Beau took in the crowd first as he walked before looking up at the balcony nervously, like he was looking at his executioner. He recovered quickly and smiled, bending into a bow before walking much quicker toward the entrance.

"Ten years all for the finest family in all the Light Realm to produce that runt," Waylon scoffed. I heard my father scoff in agreement, neither of them paying attention as the final two contestants proceeded down the carpet.

"All contestants are welcome to attend the feast in an hour in honor of Her Highness Princess Wren Bellator!"

"Who's that?" Waylon asked. "Father?"

I turned back toward the courtyard at the same moment many in the crowd noticed him. He was hard to miss. The man had dark hair pulled back at the crown of his head. He was dressed for battle, the shine from his armor worn. He was taller than any man I had ever met, and walked with such purpose that every castle soldier surged forward with their weapons drawn should they need them.

"State your name and intentions!" the court herald yelled.

The man stopped and looked straight up at the balcony.

"My name is Ezra Loreign and I have come to enter the Trial for Marriage."

The courtyard was full of sound and didn't quiet until the king approached the railing to peer down at the soldier.

"On pain of death, what right do you have to spill your common blood for the trial?" he bellowed.

Several guards moved into place, one on each side of the man and another behind, positioning the blade of his sword just underneath the man's left ear. Ezra Loreign did not flinch. He remained straight as he lifted the wooden box from his side and held it between his hands.

"My name is Ezra Loreign and I survived the battle at Notell against the Fallen. I would like to enter the Trial for Marriage because I alone survived against the Bone Breaker of the Mountain himself, the heir to the throne of the Fallen."

"Bone Breaker has not been seen since the battle," said the king. "Those who survived the battle died of their injuries. No survivor has come forward. Why should I believe that you were at the Battle of Notell at all, much less fought Bone Breaker himself?"

"Because I put him in this box," Ezra said and lifted the box. The courtyard was silent. There was a long pause before two castle guards came forward to rip the box from his hands.

"Bring him to me!" Father ordered.

He turned from the balcony and Leif and the rest of the guards quickly ushered us back inside, shutting the doors on the chaos outside.

"No one survived Notell," Waylon said, following our father

to the map table where the battle was still marked with little figurines of soldiers.

"There's no way to be sure," Leif said, stopping on the opposite side of the table.

"That box," I said, gaining my father's reproachful look. He and Waylon talked in hushed voices together, leaving Leif to study the map himself before the doors opened and four guards came in with the man in tow, hands bound together in irons before him. The doors shut behind him and the two guards holding his arms forced him onto his knees while the other two brought in the wooden box. I moved aside as the king and Waylon hurried forward, my father taking the box and tossing the lid aside.

They both stood transfixed. It was like all the air was sucked from the room. In the bottom of that box was a pair of curved horns, the tips each dipped in gold.

"They could be any Fallen's horns," Waylon scoffed.

"Gold is only found at Mount Sollom and here at the castle. What is here is closely monitored," Father said and passed the box to Waylon. He then quickly reached out and pulled a sword from the hip of the closest guard and positioned the point under Ezra's chin. Ezra remained calm, even tipped his chin upward to expose more of his throat to the king.

"Where is the rest of the heir to the Fallen?" my father asked.

"Rotting in that field where I cut him down," Ezra said. The room went silent as the two men kept careful eyes on each other. The king tipped his head to one side, letting his eyes rove over Ezra Loreign's scuffed armor.

"Well," the king said and stepped forward, moving the sword so it rested on Ezra's left shoulder. "From the moment you rise, you will be known as Sir Ezra Loreign, the only surviving knight of the Battle of Notell."

The king handed the sword back to the guard while another quickly removed Ezra's shackles. Ezra was easily the tallest in the room and it was clear now how he was able to defeat Bone

Breaker in a fight. He was thick with muscle that deserved far more than the ill-fitting soldier's armor he wore.

"The sword, Father," Waylon said and pointed to Ezra's hip. The hilt alone was larger than most swords, a beautiful uncut red stone mounted at the pommel. The matching sheath and sword belt were elegant and etched with intricate markings.

"Your Majesty," Ezra said with a bow. "I would like to keep it as a show of valor."

The king let out a laugh. "You kill the only heir to the throne of the Fallen, our greatest enemy, the man they call the Bone Breaker of the Mountain, and you ask only for a sword in return?"

"And a trip to Aria's Stone to enter into the trial," Ezra added.

"You are dismissed, Sir Ezra Loreign," the king said and clapped the knight on the shoulder. "I hope to see you at the feast and standing at the starting line."

"Your Majesty." Ezra gave a final bow, and he left the room.

After seeing those gilded horns, I couldn't help but notice all of the attendants around the hall during the feast. They weren't just attendants. They were slaves, Fallen men and women stripped of their horns and forced into jobs on the castle grounds if they were deemed fit. They didn't look any different from anyone else without their horns. The newer attendants around the castle still had bandages around their heads from where their horns had been cut, but none of those who served in the hall were new. They were all dressed in their black serving uniforms and stayed along the dark walls where I usually didn't notice them.

The woman with a pitcher that served the king's table froze with wide eyes when I thanked her for refilling my cup.

"They're ready to open the floor, Your Majesty," one of the guards said.

I looked toward the corner of the room where the orchestra was. Just to their right was a wall of windows that overlooked the choppy sea. Several ships were moored in the sea and bobbed along the churning water as the sky lit up with the occasional bolt of lightning. Some of the guests were already boisterous from beer and wine. I couldn't imagine what the trip back to their ships tonight would be like after another few hours of drinking.

The king stood from his seat and grabbed my left arm. I ignored the reflex to pull away and allowed him to lead me toward the open floor. It was cue enough for the orchestra to start the night of dancing with one of my father's favorite pieces, an upbeat song that forced me to stay on my toes and prance like an idiot around him when all I wanted to do was sink into a chair by the windows.

A few of the people in the room cheered when I hopped and swooshed my skirt to the left and right. I took my father's hands, spun underneath them, and then we waltzed around the edge of the dancefloor and back to the middle where he held my right hand aloft and spun me toward the crowd, offering me up to the next man brave enough to follow his dance.

Lord Dallin stepped forward with a loud laugh and took my hand before I could pivot away. He pulled me tight enough to his chest so that I could smell the barley on his breath and see the gold tooth where a molar had once been.

"Red suits you, Princess," he said as we danced.

"I'm glad you like it," I said and gripped his wrist tight before his hand could slide any farther down my back. "I'll wear it at your funeral."

Dallin gave a dark laugh and lowered his eyes to my chest before raising them back to my eyes.

"Someday maybe. You'll have to wear it to our wedding first."

"You can't possibly think you can win the trial."

"I spend my days at sea, and I've fought enough beasts to know I can handle any of the soft-skinned bastards here," he scoffed and spun me in a circle.

"You're at least ten years older than these so-called bastards and I happen to know that you took a tumble down the stairs of your ship and your leg hasn't been the same."

He pulled me close again, the humor in his eyes no longer matching the smile on his face.

"And you have lived a very sheltered, untouched life here," he growled into my ear. "You'll thank the Great Mother herself after you've had a taste of my experience."

I pulled away and he didn't try to hold me. He laughed and flashed a wry smile my way.

"How about another dance, Princess?" he asked loud enough for the waiting suitors to hear.

"The next time I dance, it will be on your grave," I said with a curtsy and turned away before any of the other men could approach. I heard several groans of disappointment as I made my way across the dance floor to the windows. I could feel everyone's eyes on me before I was even halfway across the room. My brother watched my every move on a good day. I slowed my pace and approached one of the attendants carrying a tray of glasses.

"Your Highness," she said with a curtsy that set her off balance just enough that she nearly dropped the tray. I grabbed on to the end and with a few adjustments, managed to keep all seven remaining glasses from tipping. All color left the woman's face, and her mouth opened and closed as she tried stuttering an apology, looking from me to the nearest guards who had somehow not noticed the encounter.

"Take the tray and calm yourself if you want to avoid the whip," I whispered and stepped closer. She took the tray from me, brushing a tear from her face with one hand before straightening up.

"Th-thank you. This is my last chance," the girl said with a sob. She squeezed her eyes shut and took a deep breath. God, she was so young. She looked barely of age, maybe seventeen or eighteen. Who the fuck was getting these people and from where?

"What's your name?" I asked.

She gaped back at me again, needing a moment to recover before she could answer.

"Norelli."

I tipped my foot just so, angling the heel of my shoe and shifting all my weight onto it until I felt it snap. I ignored the girl's gasp and pulled the broken shoe from my foot and then removed the other.

"Guard!" I motioned for the nearest armed man to join us and before he could bend into a bow, I used my free hand to push the tray into his arms. "I broke my shoe and fell into this nice girl. I could've broken my ankle if she hadn't stepped in. I want one of your guards to show her to my chambers with my shoes. She is now one of my maids."

Before the guard could object like I knew he would, I handed my shoes to Norelli and told her to bring me a new pair. She curt-sied and hurried toward the door. I took a glass of wine from the tray and held it toward the guard in a toast.

"Thank you," I said and continued toward the windows. I leaned against the sill as another flash of lightning lit the sky, thunder vibrating the stones under my elbows. I took a sip of the wine that turned into a gulp when I noticed the way Lord Dallin was staring at one of the ladies among Lord Renault's entourage.

"Even most commoners would've beaten that girl for the clumsiness," a deep voice said to my left. Ezra kept his eyes on the crowd. He was dressed in a dark jacket with silver detailing along the lapel. Borrowed judging by the snug fit. I doubt there was a nobleman in the castle of close enough build to borrow dress clothes from. His dark hair was pulled in a topknot at the crown of his head, and I could tell from the few inches that poked from the elastic that his hair was long and curly.

I raised the glass to my lips again and looked over the crowd of dancers.

"I am no commoner," I said slowly and drank.

"And not of the usual nobility either," he said with a deep hum. "The king would've had her beheaded."

"Which is why I intervened."

"You added her to your team of maids. You did more than intervene," Ezra said and turned from the crowd. "Why?"

I sat my glass on the windowsill and turned to face him, a little surprised at first by just how big he was now that I was just inches away. He was at least seven feet tall, and wider than most men—his jacket unbuttoned to accommodate the fact. He would be difficult to overpower in the trial if I had to face him. I'd have to use more covert tactics. I could already hear Leif's coaching telling me to focus on my skill over my strength.

"Why do you care that I was nice to one of the Fallen? There are thirteen more in the room and none of them will get a meal tonight judging by how long the party will last." I waited for him to answer and when he just stared curiously back at me, I leaned against the windowsill again and crossed one bare foot over the other.

"The fact that you notice them at all ..." he said under his breath.

I looked up at him to ask what that was supposed to mean before I realized he'd been staring at the wall behind the throne this entire time and not the room. The wall was covered with Fallen horns on mounts. The gilded pair he'd brought earlier today were mounted just above my father's silver throne. Their gold tips made them easy to spot.

"As if it's not enough to bar them from the Light Realm, we have to torture them, enslave them, and mount their horns on the wall like morbid trophies," I said, prepared for the military outrage that never came.

"Be careful who you say that to, Princess," he said with a single laugh.

"Going to turn me in for treason before the trial?"

He gazed at me now with a smile, looking over me with that curious expression that made me feel a little uneasy. I was used to men paying attention to me, but not like this. He wasn't looking at my curves the way men normally did. It felt like a game of cards, like he was looking for the cracks in my façade. I started to worry about his skill in finding them.

"Slavery isn't always marked by chains," he said and raised a hand toward me. My heart skipped in my chest as his fingers came inches from my necklace before he paused and lowered them back to his side. "Sometimes it's dipped in gold."

The words were rough but somehow flowed from his lips like velvet. He didn't meet my gaze again before leaving. I watched him cross the room without drawing much attention for someone his size. I was still staring after him when Norelli came through the doors with a pair of shoes clutched to her chest. I could see her relief across the room when she noticed me and hurried over.

"Your Highness," she said with a dramatic curtsy. Before I could respond she was kneeling at my feet and guiding them into the new heels. This pair was black and added another inch to my height than the first pair. What I wouldn't give for a pair of boots ...

"Norelli," I said as she rose, noticing the way several of the men in the room had taken notice of my replacement shoes. I groaned, knowing it would mean several hours of pretending to be nice.

"Something wrong, Your Highness?"

"Not at all. I want you to go to the kitchen and fill a plate with one of everything from the feast. Stuff the plate full. You understand?"

"Yes, Your Highness."

"Take it back to my chambers, set the table, and then eat it," I said and gathered my skirt in both hands. Norelli stared back at me in awe. "Tell no one."

I sent her a stern gaze that broke as soon as I noticed the humor seep into hers. She fought to hide her smile, but it was there at the corner of her lips and in her shimmering eyes.

"Thank you, Your Highness. I will," she said and hurried back across the room.

I let out a deep sigh and walked back to the dance floor, hoping the remaining suitors would at least act more nobly than Dallin. My assumptions were correct. The next two men who approached me for a dance were kind, though had nothing to talk about aside from how beautiful I looked and what riches they had to offer back home. I focused on the dance and didn't give any reply.

One man and then the next. I danced until my feet started to ache and I noticed the next in line was Dallin, eager for round two.

"I could use another drink," I said loudly as the song ended and I pulled away from my partner. I didn't need to go far to find an attendant with a tray. I lifted the glass and drank, walking through the crowd as I sipped and sipped until the next time I lifted it to my lips it was empty. I sat the glass on the tray of another attendant and turned just as someone stumbled forward. I gasped when I felt the cool liquid spill onto my chest and slide down the front of my dress.

"Shit! Oh, Gods! Forgive me," he blurted, eyes wide and face turning pink.

Finally, a reason to leave.

I pulled the glass from his hands and tipped the remainder of the red wine onto my chest for good measure, gasping loud enough just before to make sure the nearest people would notice.

"I should really be more careful," I said with a groan. "I'll just have to change."

"Your Highness," the man stammered. I recognized him now as Lord Beau Renault. I remembered the way Waylon had talked about him earlier today and felt a little bad that it had been him I used like this.

I handed the empty wine glass to the nearest attendant and started for the doors. I felt suddenly exhausted with each step, my muscles relaxing as I passed through the doors and into the empty hall.

"I am so sorry, Your Highness. I didn't mean it to ruin your dress," Beau said from behind.

I whirled around the face him, and he took a step back, right into the large oak doors. "Leave me the fuck alone."

Beau didn't look at me. He was looking to the right where Norelli stood with a butter knife in her right hand that she had pointed toward him. A shattered plate and the remnants of roast and potatoes littered the floor a few feet behind her.

"You should be back in my chambers by now," I sighed.

"I thought you might need me, Your Highness," she said, adjusting her grip on the butter knife. The entire scene was pathetic, Norelli's vise-like grip on the short knife like it would save her life, and the way Beau stared back at her like she could actually manage to kill him with it.

"She's not going to hurt you," I groaned to Beau. It was like my words pulled him out of a trance and he was suddenly aware of just how ridiculous he looked, because he took another look at Norelli and her knife and relaxed against the door. She lowered the knife and took a step back as Beau adjusted his jacket and moved away from the door.

"Norelli, go get another plate," I said. With a curtsy, she turned and hurried down the hall to the kitchen.

"I am so sorry, Your Highness. I didn't mean to ruin the night."

"I thought I had it made until you followed me out here," I grumbled and pulled at the front of my dress. The wine-soaked front was starting to stick to my skin and grow cold.

"W-wait. What do you mean?" Beau asked and glanced back toward the great hall before looking back at me again. The confused look on his face melted as he put it all together. For a moment I worried that he would tell me off or try convincing me that I was missing out on a great opportunity to meet all the suitors. Instead, he let out a sigh of relief. "If anyone asks, can you please say that I left the ball to help you?"

"Why, so you can tell the entire court that you're some chivalrous prick and that I fell at your feet in gratitude?"

"What? No," Beau scoffed. "I meant so I can leave the party without my family thinking I'm a disgrace. I just want to go to my chamber."

I was stunned by the honesty. It was so honest that I almost laughed.

"I wish I'd snagged a bottle before I left the room though. I want to go to my chamber, but I feel like people would be less likely to ask questions if I at least show up to breakfast hungover," he said under his breath.

Norelli had returned, somehow managing to run with a plate stuffed with food between her hands. I pulled it from her hands and held it to Beau who took it with a furrowed brow.

"Take this and follow me," I told him as I pulled off my shoes, handing them one at a time to Norelli. I turned before anyone could ask questions and started for the stairs.

4

Miraculously, we didn't meet a single guard along the way, not even the man who normally stood outside my chambers. Norelli raced ahead of me to open the door and I walked straight through and passed the table for the cabinet just behind. I pulled down a bottle of wine and three glasses, which I sat on the table along with Norelli's plate of food.

"Allow me, Your Highness," Norelli said and moved to grab the bottle. I took a step back as I twisted the corkscrew in the top and pulled the cork free with a pop. I poured a glass for Beau, who stood with his hand inches from the closed door like he was waiting for the right moment to bolt. I pushed the glass across the table toward the empty seat and motioned for him to sit.

"You said you want to go to breakfast hungover," I said and poured another glass. I sat that one in front of Norelli who looked even more shocked that I'd offered her a place at the table at all. For fuck's sake. I'd rather die in the trial or be caught and executed than live the rest of my life like this.

"Norelli, you should just eat. I know you aren't fed well here, and I won't even ask how you're treated. A meal is the least you're owed," I said, and pulled out the chain in front of me. I plopped down in my chair and looked up at Beau.

"It wouldn't be proper for me to join you," he said with a small bow.

"You found your way into my chambers. Isn't that the whole reason you and the rest of those men are here at all?" I asked with a snort, lifting the glass to my lips.

"I'm not here for you, Princess. I'm not daft enough to believe that I have a shot. I'm entering the trial to make a good death, to bring an honorable end to my noble family line," he blurted, finally approaching the table. He paused with his hand inches from the wine glass before he let out a laugh of disbelief and downed half of it in one go.

Waylon had called him a runt, the runt of the Renault family. It should've dawned on me sooner that his entire purpose here had more to do with bringing some semblance of valor to his family than actually winning.

"I understand," I said.

He scoffed and shook his head. "Do you?"

"I may not be expected to uphold the family name, but I know what it means to be buried by it," I said and sat my glass aside with a clatter.

"At least you have something to offer the trials."

"You bring with you more skill than you realize," I said and pulled the last of the pins free from my hair to alleviate the growing headache. "You're better educated than all of those men."

"I guess I'll just tell the first to attack me during the trials to fuck off in one of the three languages I know, or maybe I'll just use all three. I could read to him from the *Book of the Great Mother* while I'm at it," Beau said and downed the last of his glass.

The tension broke at the abrupt slap of Norelli's fork landing against her empty plate.

"I'm sorry. I didn't mean ... Your Highness."

"My name is Wren Bellator and from now on, whenever we're

in private, I'd like to be called by my name." My muscles relaxed as I said the words. God, I'd wanted to say that my entire life. I wanted at least someone other than Leif to know me as more than just Princess Wren. I was more than some damn title. I *would* be more than a title.

"When I die in the trial and Honor Day comes, what will they call me?" Beau asked.

At first look, he seemed angry. His eyes conveyed something much deeper. Pain. In life and even in death, he would always be this. I'd never been to an Honor Day ceremony, but I'd read about them in our kingdom's history. All the contestants are memorialized for their deaths in the trial and the legacy they left behind. They were all sons of Lord so-and-so and grandsons to whatever noble house.

Lord Beau Renault. Son of Jude and Penelope Renault. Heir to the fortune of the noble house of Renault in Scout Sea. Faced death bravely fighting for the Princess of the Light Realm.

"What would you like to be called?" I asked.

Beau thought for a moment. Finally, he sank into the chair opposite me and turned the empty wine glass in a circle between his hands. I pulled his attention back by filling the glass again. I drank the last of my wine and filled mine as well. The corner of Beau's lips turned upward in a slight smile as he looked at me.

"Beau Renault," he said and lifted his glass to me in a toast. "Good person."

I couldn't help but laugh and was glad when he joined in. I raised my glass to his.

"Wren Bellator," I said, thinking of what I would want to be called. Seconds passed and still I had nothing.

"To Wren Bellator," Beau said and pressed his glass to mine with a clank. We both drank and I noticed that Norelli had lifted her glass to us and was now drinking as though she hadn't had a drop all day. Once she'd finished and sat her empty glass next to her empty plate, she refused my offer for a refill and sat back in her chair to listen as Beau and I took turns talking about our strict upbringings and the subtle ways we rebelled.

What I remembered next was a flash of white light followed by a splitting headache and my stomach twisting so tightly that I thought I might throw up.

I rolled onto my side and realized as my vision adjusted that I was lying in bed. The table near the door was cleaned, not a sign of the late night entertaining that had taken place, and it looked as though the rest of the room had been cleaned more than usual as well. I looked toward the window where the sunlight streamed in and found Norelli pinning the curtains back with an apologetic look on her face.

"I didn't want to wake you, but you've slept as long as possible," she said as she finished tying the curtain and hurried toward the wardrobe in the corner. She opened it and pulled out a blue dress. It was simple with its long skirt and scooped neckline, but the back had a line of gold buttons that told a different story.

"What— How did the night end?" I asked, remembering laughing at the table with Beau Renault and handing him the bottle of wine after I'd taken a pull.

"He tucked you in bed after you nearly fell asleep at the table," Norelli said with a blush on her cheeks. "Then, he took the rest of the bottle and went to his chambers."

Rest of the bottle? I knew we'd finished one. How many had I opened?

"What's with the dress?" I asked, sitting up and accepting the fact that I'd have to make an appearance sometime today.

Norelli laid the dress at the foot of the bed and went back to the wardrobe for a pair of shoes, a pair of black boots that I was thankful for given how sore my feet were from the feast.

"There's the ceremony at Aria's Stone in a few hours. The suitors will offer their blood to Aria," she said.

My heart took off in a sprint and I needed a moment to calm it. Twenty-four hours. This time tomorrow, all the contestants would know if their blood offering had been accepted by Aria. I had until the end of the day to offer my blood or else risk being married to one of these men.

I climbed out of bed, still a little unstable from all the drinking, and moved to the foot of the bed. I stripped off the red dress from the night before and pulled on the blue one, getting it halfway down my torso before Norelli was there to help flatten it out.

"There's time for a bath if you want, Your High— Wren," she said, offering a cautious look. Funnily enough, it sent a jolt of satisfaction through me to hear her call me by my name.

"After the ceremony," I said and stepped into my shoes. "I want to be there early enough to see Leif. You do my hair and I'll do my makeup?"

Norelli followed me to the vanity and started to brush out the knots from my brown hair as I rubbed off the smeared mascara under my eyes. My hand shook as I attempted to do my makeup and I gave up on doing anything fancy and settled for a basic look. I finished swiping on some mascara and added a little color on my cheeks as Norelli tied the end of my hair in a braid.

"It's all I really know how to do," she offered with an apologetic smile in the mirror. The braid was thick, three French braids that met at the crown of my head and trailed down my back. I loved having my hair pulled back, but I rarely wore it this way for these kinds of events. My father liked the feminine look of my hair hanging loose past my shoulders.

"It's perfect," I told her and grabbed her hand on my shoulder before she could remove it. I gave her hand a firm squeeze and felt my nerves melt at her wide smile. It was the happiest I'd ever seen her. "You'll come with me. Bring a few pins and things. If anyone asks, you're there in case I need a touch-up or have an errand."

"Oh. Okay," Norelli said and slowly gathered my makeup and a few hair tools and stuffed it all into a little pouch. A knock came at the door and I rose, adjusting the skirt of my dress as I went to the door before Norelli could.

Leif stood in the hall wearing his best jacket on to escort me, flanked by two guards in full armor. All three of them gave me a bow as I ushered Norelli into the hallway and locked the door behind us.

"Are you ready, my little bird?" Leif asked and took my hand.

"Eager as anyone who has climbed the scaffold," I grumbled.

Leif gave my hand a squeeze and led us down the hallway. The guards clanked behind us, close enough that I knew better than to talk like I normally would with him, but also far away enough to make me a little more relaxed.

"How did you sleep, Princess?" Leif asked, turning his eyes to mine just enough that I could see the warning there.

I let out a deep breath and said, "With no regrets."

"The more you play by the rules, the more of them you can bend."

"I won't pretend that I like any of those men."

"Fine, but don't publicly reject them either," Leif advised and tightened his grip on my arm. I pulled free and moved ahead of him for the stairs, hearing three guards adjust their pace to keep up with me.

"We are late," I called over my shoulder to them.

No one tried to stop me, but I could hear the agitation in the way Leif groaned behind me. The four of them kept just behind me as I walked through the castle halls and out the main doors. Just down the hill where the dirt became sand was the stone arena. Round like the sun that provided light to the world and made of dark stone walls, the arena was a symbol of our realm. Outside of the Light Realm was a world of darkness where magic thrived, and evil waited in the cold and damp shadows. At least, that's what the *Book of The Great Mother* said.

"Your Highness," the guards at the entrance said in unison and dipped into low bows.

The arena had many entrances, a total of six archways that led straight to the sandy floor. At the center on top of a dark stone platform was Aria's Altar. It was a stone so white that it was almost striking to behold against all the darkness around it. It was flat on top and appeared surprisingly smooth considering the number of people who had had their heads hacked off there by the executioner's axe.

"How do you feel?" Leif asked.

I hadn't realized that I'd stopped walking until he stood beside me. I noticed the way many of the nearest people watched us now, eager to see my reaction to the ceremony. They'd all study my face and gossip for the next week at court about which man I had most favored.

"It's fitting that they ask me to begin my marriage at the place so many revolutionaries come to take their final breath," I said. My chest felt heavy as the words settled over me.

"Just as the Goddess Aria is present for the first breaths of life, so is she here for the last," Leif said and took my hand again. This time, it was me squeezing his hand. Then, we continued through the crowd toward the scaffold set up just behind the platform where the king sat on his throne with his precious heir standing next to him.

"Your Majesty," Leif greeted with a bow as he helped me up the final stairs. I took my place to my father's left as he rose. Norelli bent into a curtsy so low that I wondered how she'd ever get back up.

"My maid," I introduced, hoping it would be enough to prompt her to rise. It wasn't and she simply looked up at the king with such a look of terror that I kicked Lief's calf so he would go and help her.

"You appointed Fallen scum as your personal maid?" Waylon questioned, the words slicing the air like a knife.

Leif stopped next to Norelli and subtly nudged her with his knee so she would stand.

"I needed one to prepare for the trial and since one was not appointed to—"

"Your staff were dismissed as a result of your behavior," Waylon snapped.

I took a moment to compose myself. It was all I could do not to launch across our father's lap at him.

"You can't expect me to dress myself for these formal events. How am I supposed to button my dresses?"

"Rumors last night suggest you found someone to at least unbutton them for you," Waylon smirked.

I was distracted by a pinch on my left arm. Leif drew in close, casting me a stern look before he raised a hand to my hair and pretended to smooth it down.

"Perfect, Your Highness," he said and smiled before looking at the king. "It's an exciting day, Your Majesty."

"Not a word," the king said in that gravelly voice that sent chills up my spine, "from anyone." It was the tone he used before losing his temper, the warning that blood would spill if the people around him didn't tread lightly.

I ignored the twisting in my gut from the anger and focused instead on the bleached stone ahead. I ignored the man who read from the *Book of the Great Mother*, telling the story of the first Trial for Marriage and the peril that the contestants may face in a few days. I recounted what I knew about each of the contestants as they took turns climbing the pedestal. Each cut their palm with their sword or dagger and smeared their blood onto the rock and waited, applause filling the air and relief washing over their faces when the blood soaked into the stone and vanished.

It was merely an offering. Aria would give her sign whether they were accepted into the trial or not. Historically, most were. There were never more than a few in each trial who were denied entry to fight to the death. Still, they all celebrated with a raised, scarlet hand or a shout when their blood vanished, as though they'd already won the first test. All except for Ezra.

Ezra was dressed in dark clothing as he strode through the crowd and easily climbed to the top of the pedestal. He looked almost annoyed to be there. He didn't flinch when he dragged the tip of his dagger across his palm and rubbed it against the stone. The blood had barely vanished before he started back toward the crowd where he moved to the back to lean against the dark walls of the arena.

My father let out a single laugh that pulled my attention back to the ceremony. Beau looked small as he climbed the steps and stood before the white stone. He paused with his dagger in his right hand and his left palm open before he looked away and swiped the blade across his palm. Blood pooled in his hand before he pressed it to the stone, leaving behind a red handprint before he wrapped the wound in a handkerchief. He lifted his head, and my stomach sank.

A purple bruise sat just underneath his left eye. I was sure he was looking at me before he turned and started down the steps again, the crowd cheering and one of the guards announcing the end of the ceremony.

PART II

Aria

The Great Mother first created Aria, Goddess of Land, Life, and Death. She bloomed from the earth where Mother planted her. The Great Mother breathed life into her and so her realm was born. Aria planted the trees and flowers first. The Great Mother was so pleased with Aria that she granted the goddess the ability to create life and take it away. With her power, Aria created animals to feed and continue the cycle of the earth. The goddess next created the humans that rule the world now. She gave them the land to rule while she maintained the earth for all of her creatures.

With the Great Mother's permission, Aria, Goddess of Land, Life, and Death spent her days blessing our world with life and ushering in an easy death. It is by Aria's will that we live great lives. It is also by her will that we either suffer the pain of death or experience the comfort of an easy release.

5

There was yet another feast after the ceremony. Just like the night before, I had Norelli collect a plate of turkey, fluffy rolls, and vegetables and take it to my chambers. I ate quietly next to Leif and Waylon, unable to look away from Beau Renault's bruised face farther down the table.

"Have any of the suitors made an appearance in the ring?" I asked, not realizing I had spoken over Waylon until the words left my mouth and the table quieted. The ring was on the outdoor grounds just behind the castle. The castle guards would convene there for training, but until the trial began it would be reserved for the contestants to practice.

"The ring won't be open for the contestants until tomorrow," Leif answered and speared another hunk of turkey with his fork.

"Eager to check out more of your suitors?" Waylon grumbled.

I couldn't help myself. I kicked him under the table, only feeling angrier that it didn't seem to hurt him. He tightened his jaw and glared across the table at me for a moment. I didn't look away. I wouldn't put up with his bullying. I wouldn't let his final memories of me be caving under his threats, not when I might be whisked away without notice for the trial and never see him again.

The thought of the trial was enough to break my attention and make my stomach turn over. I had until sundown to give my blood offering to the stone.

"Your Highness," Leif said across from me, setting aside his glass of water and lifting his fork again. "You look pale. Are you feeling all right?"

I could tell from the subtle look he cast my way that I was to play the part. I let out a sigh and pushed my plate away from me a fraction.

"Um, well, I think I just need to rest," I said and rose from the table.

"We will meet for lessons later today then," Leif said and sliced the last of his turkey in half. "Send your maid to me this afternoon when you are ready."

Leif was always intentional with his words. How no one else at court had ever noticed it, I would never understand. I did, however. He often spoke like this whenever I was around, sending me subtle messages and sometimes explicit instructions. This was the latter.

"Of course," I said before turning from the table. I ignored the many bows and inclined heads of respect as I passed for the hall. My heart raced in my chest for so many reasons that it was overwhelming, so much so that I didn't hear him behind me until I was halfway down the hall for my chambers.

I was shoved against the wall, my head hitting the stone hard enough to blur my vision. Waylon's red face was inches away from mine.

"You may get this precious moment before the goddess, but Aria herself knows you will never sit on the throne!"

I wrapped my arm around his, shoving it away from me and ducking when he took a swing at my head. He looked back at me in shock, and I knew I'd pay for it later.

"I will not have my life dictated by the crown, no matter who wears it!" I knew the implications before I said the words. I'd ached to say them my entire life. I was prepared to die by them and if today was that day, then so be it.

"You are nothing if not *my* sister, the final Bellator, the spare. I could have every man who came here for your hand assassinated, and no one would ever question it," Waylon said, lowering his voice as he stepped closer. I didn't move away. I crossed my arms and kept my head held high, prepared to accept the blow or whatever punishment he planned to unleash. "While you whore yourself across the ballroom, the rest of us have enough respect for the trial to allow fate and Aria to choose your husband. Married or not, I will see to it that you will never add to the line of succession."

It felt like everything had stopped around us. I wasn't at all surprised by his threat. I knew he would do everything to limit my claim to the throne, even if that meant horrendous bloodshed. What had me pinned in place was the way he talked about the goddess, so easily juxtaposed next to his violence.

"When did you beat Lord Renault?" I asked.

"After you bed him."

I shoved him away with both hands, relishing the way he stumbled.

"Married or not, I will accept none of those men into my bed!" I threw my hand back toward the hall behind me. I kept my head high as Waylon slowly walked toward me.

"Once you are married," he said and stopped next to me. "No man will need your invitation."

My skin went cold, though I suppressed the shiver that snaked up my spine. Waylon grabbed my hand and raised it, so it was in front of my face. I stared at the silver band on my ring finger as he ran his thumb across the engraving of our mother's name.

"You are nothing if not my sister," he repeated as I tugged my hand free. "Don't make the mistake of thinking you can be more."

I hated that my words were suppressed by the thickness of

my throat. I hated that all I could see was our mother's eyes burning into mine as she mouthed her final words to me, the only person at the stone she'd acknowledged as she was led up the pedestal. I hated that the most vivid memory I had of her was the moment the guard pressed her chest to the stone and the axe fell, the ring of metal on stone going on and on as my father held my head from behind and forced me to watch as hers rolled away.

Waylon continued past, stopping just a few paces behind to say, "I will bloody who I like and beat who I choose. Careful, Sister. Your behavior has influence."

I stood in the hall until I couldn't hear his footsteps anymore. I twisted my mother's ring around my finger and no matter how badly I wanted to cast it and all the nightmarish memories aside, I did not.

Just as Leif instructed, I sent Norelli to find him after I took a mid-morning nap. She returned an hour later with roses and a get-well note tied around the porcelain vase.

"Sir Folee wanted you to know that he would've sent a dozen, but was short one," Norelli said as she closed the door behind her and moved to the table. She sat the vase in the center and began arranging them so they were even from all sides.

Eleven roses ... as in eleven o'clock? That was pushing things. We would have an hour to sneak out of the castle and make it down to the arena.

"Norelli," I said from the bed. "Go tell the kitchen that I'll need dinner delivered to my chamber tonight."

She moved to curtsy, but stopped herself and offered an awkward wave before hurrying toward the door. As fast as she moved to do everything from fetch, deliver, and piss she'd be back in minutes. I threw the sheets back and ran to the table. I pulled the vase toward me and counted the roses myself. Eleven, just like she'd said. I heard a *thunk* when I shuffled the roses and pushed them to one side to look inside the vase.

A flash of silver caught my eye and I reached into the mouth of the vase for it, surprised when my hand didn't meet water but the cool hilt of a dagger. I pulled it out along with the sheath and strap that came unfurled as soon as it emerged from the vase. It was designed to be fastened around my thigh, the leather crafted well enough to be discreet no matter the attire and sturdy enough to remain in place. A feather design was burnt into the leather sheath; a bird taking flight was etched into the steel of the dagger's hilt.

Quickly, I strapped the weapon to my right thigh before flattening my skirt over it. By the time I rearranged the roses and went back to bed, Norelli came flying through the door.

"They will deliver dinner in an hour, Your High— Wren."

"I won't be mad if it takes you more than a few minutes to run an errand, you know?" I said, glad that she caught on to the joke after a beat. Norelli smiled and after ensuring that the door was locked behind her, moved to the table. "What else did Sir Folee tell you?"

Norelli's expression fell. I could feel her eyes assessing me before she let out a long sigh. I pat a spot on the bed across from me and after a cautious moment, she joined me and sat on the edge of the mattress.

"You should know that I have the utmost respect for you," she said so simply that it almost surprised me. "Sir Leif Folee told me to deliver the vase directly to you and not make any stops at all. He made a mistake by not filling the vase with water. Sure, it would affect the leather, but it would be less noticeable."

Fuck. I froze for a moment, my hand sliding to my thigh beneath the sheets. I'd been trained long enough to know that Norelli noticed the movement, but she didn't change her relaxed demeanor.

"Why respect me? You're here because of the violence my family showed you," I said, keeping my fingers poised.

"I respect you because I know that whatever the reason is that you have a dagger, I know it is not theirs," Norelli said and looked directly at me. "I think the real question is, how much do you trust me?"

I had no reason to trust her. She would kill me, if she was smart. It would make escaping the castle and the Light Realm easier if she knew how to go about it. She already knew more than she should, but she came here to admit the fact despite how I would react. I could kill her and no one would care, even if I did so without a reason. My stomach twisted with disgust at how much satisfaction that would bring my father and brother.

"What if I told you that I could help you get your freedom if you helped me get mine?" I asked, leaning my left arm on the bed. Norelli smiled and cocked her head to one side.

"Why would you help me?"

"Because you don't belong here any more than I do," I hissed. "And I'm tired of these fucking men."

Norelli laughed, a high-pitched sound that burst from her lips before she could clap her hand over them to contain it. I couldn't help but laugh and I was glad when she joined me. It felt good. I couldn't remember the last time I laughed like this.

"I will do whatever you need," Norelli said once we had recovered. She lay across the foot of the bed while I propped myself up against the headboard. "So, Wren Bellator, what is the dagger for?"

I opened my mouth to explain but stopped when Leif's voice came to the front of my mind. He'd tell me to be careful who I trusted and even among those I did, be careful who else might be privy to the conversation.

"I need to switch clothes with you at eleven. Take a nap in my bed with the sheets high enough to hide your hair. If anyone checks, they won't be any the wiser. If I'm not back by midnight, make yourself scarce," I said, watching as the humor melted from her expression. "Can you do that?"

Norelli nodded. "Whatever you need."

The knock came at exactly eleven. Norelli, wearing a simple shift dress, cracked the door for just a moment before she moved back and let Leif slip inside. He looked over the servant's attire I wore, a black long-sleeve dress. Norelli had helped me to contain my long brown hair beneath an entire roll of white bandage she wound around my head. She said I looked exactly like a new Fallen castle servant.

"I thought we could move a little quicker if I had a disguise," I told him.

Leif considered my appearance again before nodding and opening the door.

"The quicker the better, little bird," he said before darting back into the hall.

I knew the lack of guards down the corridor was his doing. Rather than making our way toward the main entrance, we hurried in the opposite direction. We made it down the first two flights of stairs and were nearly at the bottom of the third when Leif reached behind for my hand and guided me after him.

"Stay in my shadow and keep your head down," he whispered. "You're a servant."

I took a few more steps to ensure that I was just behind him, lowering my eyes as we passed two men wearing riding boots. Guards.

"Sir Folee!"

My stomach sank and ice shot through my veins. I took another step closer to Leif, close enough that I could smell the sea on his hair.

"Lord Dallin," Leif said as he prodded my leg from behind. "Has anyone shown you the royal armory?"

When Leif stepped away from me, I hurried toward the nearest corridor. The tightness in my chest eased when I saw the doors at the end of the hall. I slipped through and was greeted with the strong smell of manure and straw.

"Mind yourself!"

Before I could register what the stable hand meant, I turned face-first into a bale of straw dense enough to send me staggering backward. Several people groaned as my left foot slipped underneath me and I sat in the middle of a puddle that I knew immediately wasn't rain or sea water.

The man with the offending bale sat it aside and offered me a hand. "Sorry."

Everyone else at the stables had gone back to their business and for once, the man in front of me didn't gawk or bow. No one on this side of the castle knew what Princess Wren Bellator looked like and even covered in shit and piss, it was a relief.

"Thank you," I said and took his hand. I assessed the damage. The back of the dress was soaked, but I was able to scrape most of the manure off Norelli's boots on a hitching post on my way through the stables. It wasn't until I had gotten over the feeling and smell of my wet skirt that I realized why I needed Leif so much tonight.

The arena was a sacred place, and servants were not allowed in alone. Fallen were not allowed at all. I ignored my racing heart and continued ahead down the path. There were few buildings this way and those that were there had darkened windows. Once I'd trudged several yards, the sound of men and horses was drowned out by the tide to the right. The ships anchored offshore were lit by torches that sent a warm glow flickering over the soft waves. The moon was reflected between two of the ships and I noticed then that I'd slowed my pace to a stroll. Once I'd spilled my blood for the stone, I could sit on my balcony and watch the moon ripple across the tide.

It was late enough that the only guards I saw were stationed on the far left where the arena met the street. I veered right and peeked within the arches before darting inside the arena. The white stone was practically glowing under the moon. It looked like it was floating against the black stone of the pedestal and arena walls.

I hiked up my skirt as I hurried toward the stone, freeing my dagger as I approached the steps. I barely reached the top before I'd sliced my palm, gasping against the pain and wincing when I pressed it to the cold stone. I held it there a long moment for good measure before I stood back and watched the dark streak slowly vanish. My throat tightened and my vision blurred before I could remind myself that there was still the trip back to the castle. I hurried down the steps, blinking back the tears when someone came through the arch just ahead of me.

Rather than hide, I launched myself at him. My arm with the dagger raised was quickly caught in his tight grip and he pulled me closer so I could see his face.

"Did you do it?" Leif asked in a whisper.

I held up my left hand to show the cut across my palm and he immediately fished a handkerchief from his pocket and wrapped it tight around my hand. I burst into tears. I cut off the second sob by holding my breath, fighting the desire to sink to the dark stone and beg Aria herself to accept my offer.

"Put away your blade," Leif said as he finished tying the handkerchief. I gathered my skirt and slid the dagger into the sheath with a shaky hand. When I looked up, Leif cupped the sides of my face and pulled me close enough to press a kiss to my forehead.

"I did it," I said with a sigh.

"The night isn't over yet, little bird," he said, already leading me back down the path.

The trip back through the castle was much easier this time of night. The guards we did pass in the halls didn't pay us much attention as we walked. My door was still unguarded, and I rounded Leif to open it, eager for a hot bath.

"You're back," Norelli said and rose from the bed, getting a few feet across the room before she stopped and raised a hand to her nose. "What happened to you?"

"I need a bath," I said, already stripping the wet fabric off. Norelli rushed to the bathroom as I pulled on my robe. I left her to fill the tub and moved onto the balcony. We were close enough to the shore that the air smelled strongly of salt and the tide was a soothing shush of sound on the sand. I leaned against the stone railing and watched the moonlight ripple over the water, my muscles relaxing until I noticed something in the water. It was getting larger, like it was coming out of the sea. When his shoulders broke the surface and he shook the water from his dark hair I knew exactly who he was.

Ezra walked out of the sea, fully clothed, stretching his arms like he'd just been on a long swim. Maybe he had, but fully dressed? It was strange, but my suspicions were confirmed when he moved across the shore and lifted a towel from the sand, and used it to dry his hair before tying his curly locks at the crown of his head.

"I bet the hot water will feel great after today," Norelli said from behind me.

I turned from the railing and pulled my robe closer around me.

"Yeah. I could use it. Thank you," I said and left her standing on the balcony under the moon.

6

I woke the next morning to the sound of the bells. I went to the balcony, the wind blowing my hair behind me as I leaned my hands on the railing. Several dinghies were rowing to shore from the ships.

"Princess!"

I looked toward the nearest dinghy. Lord Dallin Vondrelle stood in the center between the rowing men. He let out a triumphant laugh and held his left arm in the air, pointing to it like a fisherman would to show off his catch.

I looked down at my forearm and felt my heart skip. An image of a sun was burned into my flesh. I ran a finger over it, expecting it to be sore at least. It was completely healed, as though it had been there for several months and not just a few hours. The gash on my palm was gone. I guess I would have to wear long sleeves or gloves until the trials started.

"A step closer to your freedom," Norelli said. I turned from the railing to face her. She held two mugs of tea and offered one to me.

"When did you figure it out?" I asked and passed her in the

doorway. I sat down at the table and admired the breakfast she'd laid out. There were several different kinds of fruit and pastries.

Norelli shrugged. "I had a hunch pretty early on. You weren't putting up with any of those men and you didn't seem excited at all by the trial, so I made a guess." She sat across from me.

She filled her plate with grapes and croissants. She wore her hair loose aside from a braid at the top of her head and one on each side to keep the curls away from her face. It was the same hairstyle she'd done for me yesterday aside from finishing the braid down her back.

"Where are you from?" I asked, finally reaching for a croissant.

She let out a deep sigh before popping a grape into her mouth. She sat for another moment in silence before she looked down at the plate before her and started her story.

"I haven't been here long. My parents own an inn and tavern in Drach."

"Drach," I said and pulled apart a small piece of a croissant. "You lived in the Mist?"

Norelli looked up at me but didn't say a word. The Mist was the most dangerous area of the whole Dark Realm. It's where the God O'Riah fell and lost his wings. It was nearly void of any light and the Mist alone is where we lost most of our troops.

"How much of our geography do you know?" Norelli asked with a smirk.

"You don't get out much when you're a princess. It leaves a lot of time for reading."

She laughed and popped another grape into her mouth before continuing her story.

"My father used to run the business. My mother and I took turns hunting. That last month, it was mostly me bringing in the game. She started helping out in the inn more after we'd lost a few staff members. The Mist is grim and treacherous, so I didn't think much of their disappearances. One day, when I returned from hunting, the village had been ransacked and most of the people had either fled or been captured. It was too late at that point for me to run. I tried, but there were too many soldiers. They transported us back here and when they figured out that I was proficient with butchering, they put me in the kitchen."

I sat the croissant aside and took a sip of the tea instead, my stomach turning against the warm liquid. I always thought the slaves in the castle were prisoners of war or low-level criminals. I wondered how many of the Fallen within the castle walls were just people stolen from their homes to serve ours.

"How many Fallen came to the castle with you?" I asked.

Norelli scoffed and shook her head. "A couple hundred or so were taken from the village by the soldiers. Some died along the way. There were still over a hundred when we got to Honor Cove. I'd say less than half of us were taken to the castle. I don't know where they took everyone else."

If less than half of them were now serving in the castle, who else could have Fallen slaves? Sometimes they were given as gifts to nobles.

"The contestants were all invited to train in the ring this morning. If you're finished ..." Norelli started, eyeing my croissant anxiously. I knew I should eat something, but the mix of anger and disgust had soured my stomach.

"Sure. Let's go," I said and stood from the table.

"What a show of bravado," Norelli whispered at my side.

There were twelve contestants. Well, thirteen including me. Each contestant but me was represented by a red flag with their name stitched into it and positioned around the top of the ring. Just above the entrance was a banner that displayed all their names together beneath the title *The Trial for Marriage of Princess Wren Bellator*. There were four from the coastal cities: Lord Astor Willow, Lord Dallin Vondrelle, Lord Beau Renault, and Lord Soren Yoder. Seven were from inland cities: Lord Donovan

Merry, Lord Jakob Somerled, Lord Rorik Raust, Lord Nicholas Fenrick, Lord Magnus Ode, Lord Elias Vonhenson, and Lord Milo Bran. There was also Ezra Loreign, wherever he came from, and me.

Now that I had taken stock of the room, Ezra was the only contestant not present. He seemed to keep to himself whenever he could and in truth, that was probably wise. Everyone would be wary of him once the trial started due to his size, but that would be all they knew about him at this rate. Sir Ezra Loreign knew better than to show his hand before he needed to play his card.

"Lord Donovan isn't much of a swordsman," I whispered to Norelli.

"All he's done is talk about his many hunting trips at each meal. He's taken down a moose on his own."

"With a bow," I said and pointed to him down in the ring as Lord Rorik disarmed him with a cheer from the crowd of nobles. "He's right-handed. His right bicep is a bit larger than the left."

"What does that tell you?"

"If you forced him to fight with his left or attacked from that side, he wouldn't be able to defend himself well," I told her and leaned on the railing.

A new pair of contestants strode into the center of the ring, both egging on the cheering crowd as they took their places. I continued to point out their strengths and weaknesses to Norelli. It had become such a fun game that she laughed each time I successfully predicted who would win a fight.

"You're brilliant!" she beamed.

I looked away from the ring to smile at her, noticing how the crowd on the balcony parted behind her. I straightened up just as Waylon joined us with a sly grin. He turned toward the ring to watch Lord Dallin bash at Lord Soren's shield until he knocked him into the dirt. Dallin's triumphant laugh echoed around the ring as he went back to his place on one side and Soren slowly got to his feet with a hand clapped to his right shoulder.

"Well done, Lord Dallin!" Waylon called out, the ring

quieting at his cheer. All sound stopped when he raised his hands. "Gentlemen, how about a bet?" Waylon stood a little straighter at the gasps of anticipation around the room. He flashed that sly smile my way again and my stomach sank. I was a moment too late to intervene. He pulled Norelli away from my side by the front of her bodice and gripped her face with one hand, turning it so she was looking at the men in the ring.

"A night with my sister's maid to the winner of the next dual," Waylon yelled.

Dallin gave a deep laugh that carried over the room. A sour taste filled my mouth at the thought of him alone with her, but he wasn't planning to enter. He clapped Lord Rorik Raust hard on the back twice and whispered something in his ear that made both men laugh before shoving Rorik into the ring. Lord Raust caught his footing and drew his sword, raising it toward the prince and pointing at Norelli.

"Any challengers?" Waylon asked with a laugh.

Lord Beau Renault walked into the ring slowly, eyeing the ring of men before looking up at us. We couldn't hear him over the shouting at first and he waited until the room quieted to speak.

"I will."

"The runt of the Renaults," Waylon said so only Norelli and I could hear.

Beau didn't draw his sword right away. He was focused on the three of us and it wasn't until Rorik said something that he turned his attention to the fight.

"How do you think Lord Rorik will take you, Fallen slave?" Waylon asked Norelli, wrapping an arm around her waist and pulling her closer.

The clang of one sword on another kept me from acting and drew my attention back to the ring. Beau was scrambling to his feet while Rorik showed off for the crowd by flexing a bicep. Beau didn't launch an attack; he stood at the ready with his sword held before him now as Rorik shouted insults his way.

"You really think you can best me? You're half my size!"

The laughter from the crowd didn't get to Beau. He stood firm, eyes focused on his opponent. He dodged when Rorik swung for him and then stepped away when Rorik charged. Rorik turned from the ring of men, getting encouraging pats on the back from Soren and Magnus as he faced Beau.

"Are you going to use that thing or not?" Rorik asked.

Beau held his sword in front of him, scanning the ring around him. He was forced to dodge again when Rorik swung at his head. Beau moved to the left where he dodged another swing for his middle, feigning left again. He took a big step back when Rorik swung across his chest, the crowd gasping as the tip of the blade whizzed inches from his stomach. This time, Beau raised his sword high above him. He launched himself upward, swinging above him and catching one of the ropes that held the banner above the entrance.

The giant swathe of red fabric came down with a whoosh, draping over the top of Rorik. Beau used his sword to free the remaining side of the banner from the wall and then tossed his sword aside as the crowd groaned. He grabbed one of the ropes and began running in circles around Rorik as he flailed for a way out, pulling the fabric tighter and tighter until Rorik fell to the ground. Beau was quick to tie the ropes together and attempted to drag the man to the middle of the ring and only got a foot before he gave up and looked up at us.

"My prize, Your Highness," Beau said, this time loud enough to be heard over the boos of the crowd.

Waylon scoffed, jaw tight and ears turning red.

"Hardly a prize," he called back before shoving Norelli hard enough that she fell over the railing and down toward the ring below.

7

When I made it to the castle's infirmary, Norelli was holding Beau's hand while he lay on a bed next to a doctor. He let out a gasp and his back bowed against the mattress.

"Fuck," he hissed. The doctor sat back far enough that I could see his bare torso. There was a dark red bruise on his left side. Beau sucked in another gasp when the doctor began prodding around the bruising.

"Not one, two fractured ribs," the doctor said, nodding her head toward the man with the clipboard who began jotting down notes.

Beau winced as he took a deep breath and propped himself up against the headboard with Norelli's help. "Thanks."

The doctor promised to be back with a tonic to dull the pain and hurried across the room with the nurse in tow. I moved to the end of the bed, looking from Beau's blanched face to Norelli. The guilt was obvious in her expression, and I opened my mouth to say something, maybe comfort her, anything, when he spoke first.

"You should get looked at," Beau said, turning a fraction to look at Norelli.

"N-No really. I'm fine," she said and crossed her arms over her chest.

"You hit your head pretty hard on my shoulder," Beau said, reaching out to take one of her arms before she could wrap them any tighter around her middle. I noticed the way she glanced toward the door and then the rest of the room.

"My Lord," the doctor said as she rounded the end of the bed and stopped next to me. She held out a small vial with a dropper and gave Beau a serious look. "Take no more than two full droppers at a time. No alcohol. No training. Get more rest, if you can. Come back here if you cough up any blood."

"Thank you," he told her as she filled the dropper with the tonic and approached him. She practically shoved it between his lips before he opened his mouth. Beau wrinkled his nose at the taste while she filled the second.

"Once you're finished with Lord Beau, I have an order for you," I said as she lifted the dropper to his lips again. This time, she was less aggressive.

The doctor sat the tonic on the side table and turned to me.

"Yes, Your Highness," she said and gave a curtsy.

"My maid may have sustained an injury in a fall. Take her into one of the exam rooms and give her a full assessment. Treat her the way you would me. Tell no one."

The woman's mouth parted in awe. After a moment, she caught on that I was serious, and she gave me another curtsy before inviting Norelli to follow her. Norelli rolled her eyes as she left us and went to one of the doors at the back of the room.

The large room of beds with white sheets was mostly empty. The only other patients were asleep farther back in the room. I sat on the edge of the bed and looked at Beau who was leaning against the headboard now, looking much more comfortable than he had moments before. This close, I could see the shadow of the bruise under his eye. First that, now this ... I had to push my brother's words to the back of my mind. He'd received both of these injuries because of me. Despite everything Waylon had said about him, he wasn't entirely defenseless. He'd been cunning enough to beat Rorik, for one. Also, there were curves to his naked torso, rounded biceps, a defined chest, and subtle hills beneath the bruising across his abdomen. There was also a pink scar just above his right hip a couple of inches thick.

"I fell on an anvil trying to get out of a fire in the stables," he said when he noticed me looking.

I lifted my eyes from the mark to his face. He gave me a small smile as though the horrible event was just a fond memory now.

"Your family allowed you to be in the stables?" I asked. The Renaults were the wealthiest family outside of the crown and maybe just as proud. I couldn't imagine his parents letting him near the stables. It would be beneath him.

"I'm not sure they knew that I spent mornings there," he said with a shrug. "The stable hands didn't tell. They taught me a lot about horses and how to care for them. I love animals and I spent as much time as I could riding."

"How did you end up in a fire?"

"My sister used to have a cat until it hissed at our mother one day, and she tossed it out. I found it months later in the stable. The stable hands were glad to have her because she kept the mice away. One day, I noticed four kittens. I told my sister about them and when I got to the stables the next morning, smoke was billowing from one side. I found her inside trying to collect the last of the kittens. She said their mother had spooked her and she dropped a torch. The fire was too high to stop, so she got the last kitten and ran. I opened the stalls for the horses. By the time I got them all out, it was like hell in there. The final horse knocked into me, and I fell on a hot anvil. When I made it out of the stable, I noticed it had burned right through my shirt."

I could tell how the story ended just from the small smirk on his face.

"So, you got burned and took the blame," I said.

"I'm surprised I still don't have marks across my ass from the caning I got," he said with a laugh. He adjusted on the bed so he could sit up more, wincing as he scooted his legs closer.

"So, you do make a habit of displays of chivalry," I said, shifting on the bed so my left leg could lay where his feet had been, and my right could drape off the side.

Beau shook his head with a smile before looking directly at me with those blue eyes, too innocent to be of his namesake.

"I just try to do right by all living things. There's enough cruelty in the realm, especially where women are concerned."

Aria's Choice. Always self-sacrificing for the sake of others. I'd heard the story so many times and I loathed it, though I would never say it aloud. My chest felt suddenly heavy as I looked at the sincerity in Beau's eyes, knowing that he felt the same. He somehow understood that despite it being the goddess's story that was used to smother women, especially women like me, he also rejected the teachings of the book.

"I'm sure a brilliant woman like you has scars she proudly bears," Beau said quietly, his eyes no longer shining with the same humor.

Just like that, I felt heavy for a different reason. I felt a shiver creep up my back, prickle along the ridge of every scar from the whip. I could feel my muscles vibrating against the post as I struggled to keep myself upright. I could hear the way my father's voice filled the hall when I was scooped into Leif's arms, feel the spit fall from my father's lips as he yelled into the knight's face for allowing me to be so disobedient. I could hear Leif asking for forgiveness over my sobs as he dressed my wounds in my chamber.

I jumped at the sound, looking across the room where the doctor had just shut the exam room door and was striding across the floor toward us. I realized then that Beau held my hand and was stroking the back of it gently with his thumb. *Oh, fuck. I can't let this get to me.* I had to move forward with a clear head.

"Your maid has a concussion and bruised her spine in the fall, Your Highness," the doctor said, looking briefly at Beau when she told me the diagnosis. I knew she was matching whatever bruise she'd seen on Norelli's back to Beau's chest. Her gaze was too clinical to be anything more.

"Can she be cared for in my chambers?" I asked, clearing my throat to get rid of the thickness that had developed there.

"Yes, Your Highness," the doctor agreed with a curtsy. "She's well enough to walk there herself. I can send a nurse to check on her this evening."

"Thank you for your discretion, Doctor" I said clearly. She understood the silent threat. The doctor nodded, reminded Beau of the dosage for the tonic, and called for the nurse to bring a clean shirt for him. She gave us another curtsy before starting for the exam room again.

"Wren—"

"It's too early for the trial to start," I said and adjusted the sleeves of my dress, pulling them farther down my wrists. "I'm sure you will be healed before that day comes."

Norelli joined us, giving me an awkward smile. There was a tonic in her hand and a small jar with a powder inside.

"Lord Beau," I said and stood from the bed.

"Your Highness," he returned and inclined his head toward me.

I reached for Norelli and ushered her toward the door. Once we were in the hall, I stayed ahead of her to avoid the conversation I knew she was dying to have. She was smarter than most people assumed and thanks to that, she knew more than she should about the castle and noticed more details than I cared to explain.

When we reached my chambers, she shut the door behind us as I went to the wardrobe for an extra blanket. There was already a fire going in the fireplace, to which I added another log before laying the blanket across the couch. Norelli watched as I worked in silence, not saying a word until I'd finished making her bed and sat out a glass of water on the coffee table for her. She raised her eyebrows in question when I finally looked up at her.

"When are you supposed to take all those medications?" I asked her and pointed to the bottles.

Norelli let out a sigh and sat the tonic on the coffee table next to the water. "I take the tonic before I go to sleep. This one is for you."

I hesitated before I took the jar of powder. Half-buried inside was a little measuring spoon that looked more like it belonged in a dollhouse rather than in anything medicinal.

"She didn't even assess me," I said and moved toward the bathroom.

"You mix a spoonful of the powder into whatever drink you like once a month," Norelli called from the main room, and I went to the sink and unscrewed the lid off the jar. "The doctor thought with your marriage approaching that you might need a *particular* tea."

I stopped with the jar over the sink. In a matter of days, I would be tossed into the trial with twelve men who were more than eager to fight for a right to my body and name. I would disembowel any of them who tried, but still ...

I screwed the lid back on the jar and I tucked it into the cabinet above the sink.

"You're playing it safe," I told Leif after I'd disarmed him for the fourth time.

"You've gotten quicker on your feet."

"I know what you're avoiding," I said and tossed the sword aside with a groan. He hadn't taken any of the same chances when we sparred since the mark appeared on my arm. He claimed that an injury might hinder me in the trial, but I knew it had more to do with my father and whatever he might do if he thought I was challenging him again.

"Tell me again how you're preparing," Leif said, sheathing his sword at his hip.

I looked back at him and watched as he tucked my sword into the shadows of the cave.

"I wear riding clothes and boots to bed. I keep that dagger strapped to my thigh. What I need is to sleep with a sword," I said and swiped my boot across the sand, sending a clump of it raining to my left.

"The trial is still weeks away. I am working on getting a sword to your chambers." Leif stopped at my side, but something else caught my attention. A dark figure emerged from the water just in front of the sunrise. I only knew it was Ezra because of how tall he was as he walked out of the sea and onto the beach. Just like the last time, he was fully clothed. The water washed off of him in rivets, making his pants hang low on his hips.

"Sir Loreign has made himself scarce since the ball," Leif said.

"He doesn't train with the others either, or at all from what I've gathered," I said. I'd made it part of my morning and afternoon walk to stop by the ring and watch the men practice. I'd learned a lot about their combat styles, their strengths, and their weaknesses. Ezra Loreign was the only man I hadn't seen with a sword in his hand. "Is he even marked?"

"His name was brought to the official record. He may not flaunt the mark like the others, but he still bears it the same."

I watched Ezra for a moment. He stared at the castle ahead for a long moment. Then, he went back to the shore where he'd piled his belongings. His sword belt was thicker than most to accommodate the larger-than-average sword sheathed there. He strapped it around his hips and adjusted the sword and the dagger, so they sat just right on his hips. After brushing the sand from his feet, he put his boots back on and turned to face the water. Just when I thought he would turn and walk toward the castle, he launched into a run, feet easily cutting through the shallow water, and dove into an incoming wave.

Leif snorted. I looked at him.

"So, he does train," he said with a smirk on his face.

8

It took Leif another three days before he could sneak a sword into my chambers with Norelli's help. I stored my haul under the bed in an old dress box. Each night, I prepared as though I might wake up in the trial. I dressed in my riding clothes and best boots, the dagger strapped to my thigh. I wore the new sword belt around my hips with the sword in its sheath and a little pouch that held smaller items Leif and I agreed I should take. I had a small first-aid kit, the pointed shell he'd given me the day the horns sounded, the tea from the doctor, and a little vial of a poison Norelli brought me and warned me I should take great care with when using.

Leif and I trained every morning by our cave. Ezra Loreign was always there, fully clothed and dripping wet from his swim as I watched him walk back to the castle from my hiding place behind the boulders on the beach. His sword never left its sheath, and neither did his dagger. It was the only time I ever saw him. Leif and I had begun researching him the best we could and found out that he'd ordered all of his meals to be delivered to his chamber. Other than training sessions, we weren't alone often to discuss the contestants. So, the trip Leif, Norelli, and I took to the docks for the ceremonial blessing by Nex felt more like a business meeting than the lavish trip it likely was for the other contestants.

"Sir Loreign is not a nobleman, so there won't be any records of him here at the castle," Leif said and peered past the curtain of our carriage.

"He killed the Bone Breaker of the Mountain on the battle-field. Would there not be a record of his military service here?" I asked, noticing the subtle way Norelli tensed next to me at the mention of the assassination.

Leif shook his head. "Nothing more than a name and that would even be unlikely considering he was of low rank until now."

I sighed. Our carriage bounced over the cobblestones, prompting me to look outside.

"We missed the turn for the port," I said and looked back at Leif before looking ahead. All of the trial contestants, my brother, and other noble members of the court were heading to the port to board the royal ship. It was tradition to make peace with the waters and honor the God Nex ahead of the trial, seeing as much of it would take place in and around his domain. It meant spending a few days on the ship, which meant I was allowed to bring Norelli to help manage my cabin. A look ahead of our carriage confirmed that the others traveling with us were taking the same detour.

"Hey!" Leif had stuck his head out the window to yell at the driver. After a short moment, he sat back in his seat and pulled the window shut again with a stern look on his face. "The king has ordered everyone to attend his speech before we board the ship."

I groaned. It shouldn't have been a surprise that he would use the opportunity to flaunt his power.

"So, we are heading to the arena first." It was more a state-ment of fact than a question. My father thought so highly of himself that it only made sense he would want to speak on holy ground. No one said a word as we continued to bounce along the cobblestones until we came to such an abrupt stop that I was nearly tossed off my seat.

A guard opened the door to my right before bending into a bow next to his comrade.

"His Majesty would like the prince and princess by his side," the first guard spoke and extended a hand to me. I ignored it and stepped out of the carriage, already several paces ahead before any of them caught up to flank me.

"Easy," Leif whispered from behind before slipping past me to move in front. The crowd of nobles parted with bows and curtsies as we went. Leif led the way through the stone archway and toward the platform where my father stood in front of Aria's stone. Waylon stood behind it just to the right next to two of his guards. The men who'd met us at my carriage led us around to the left side. As I took my place and tried not to look annoyed before the crowd, I glanced at Leif and my entire body went cold.

"N-Norelli?" I whispered as I recovered. I'd seen that expression only a few times before. I knew we weren't here for just any speech.

"I made her stay in the carriage," Leif said quickly, keeping his eyes ahead.

I forced myself to look ahead, as well. People were still coming through the archways at the back of the arena, all dressed in expensive dresses and fine coats for the deck party on the ship later. They looked strange next to the dark stone but didn't seem at all unnerved by it as I felt. They fell silent as the king climbed on top of the stone. My heart sped up as he smiled at Waylon who smiled back triumphantly back. My father stared down at me next, something sinister in his face, a kind of threat and promise to crush any ounce of rebellion in my soul. I saw the humor in his expression before he turned to address the stunned crowd.

No one stood on Aria's Stone. Touching it alone meant baring your soul to her ...

"Just weeks ago, our soldiers faced the largest battle in a decade and the worst slaughter in several more," the king said, his voice echoing off the stone walls. "It was a great loss, a loss that meant our borders were unsafe and our kingdom was at risk of attack. Magic was able to creep out of the Mist and into our farthest villages until what was left of our troops could eradicate it. I thought I would live the rest of my days rebuilding our military presence and our iron hold on protecting the Light Realm until news came that the infamous Bone Breaker of the Mountain, son to the Fallen king and heir to the disgraced god's throne, had been put down on that battlefield."

Cheers erupted from the crowd. I noticed Beau standing with his family to the far left. While his mother and father cheered, he remained tucked behind them with his arms firmly by his side. I looked to the middle of the crowd as the sound died out and the unmistakable looming figure of Ezra Loreign easily moved through the last few rows of people to stand in the front. He wore the same black and silver ensemble he'd worn at the ball, though his presence in the front row made it look more like armor.

"The *Book of the Great Mother* tells us that the God Nex and Goddess Aria reward those who are loyal to them and those who revere their creations. I swore my fealty as king to this realm and protected it with all my power and the goddess has rewarded me by revealing not one, but seven Fallen soldiers who served the Bone Breaker of the Mountain, the last of his company. I will have you all witness their executions and celebrate the destruction of what is left of our enemy!"

The king pointed to the right as the noble houses began cheering again. The Fallen were led out in a row, each with their hands chained behind their back and a guard escorting them toward the platform. Of the seven, four of them were women who wore their hair in plaits that stretched down their backs. The women had been treated worse than the men from the looks of their bruised faces. The woman who stood just a few feet to my right had a broken nose. They were all dressed in black leather. No, not leather. I was close enough to the woman and three men to see the texture of their uniforms. It was almost like snakeskin.

It looked as though someone had stitched together large scales that I was sure felt rough to the touch.

All of them had dark horns near their temples and one of the women and all three of the men had large black wings protruding from their backs. Their wings had been shredded to ribbons that flowed in the wind, useless for flight if they tried to escape.

A man holding the executioner's axe ascended the stairs from behind and the arena was silent as he approached the woman next to Waylon. The soldier that held her kicked the back of her knees and she fell into the stone. Just before the soldier could force her chest to the stone, she looked up at the crowd of noblemen and screamed.

"FOR THE BONE BREAKER OF THE MOUNTAIN!"

The words hung in the air for a second before the axe fell with the thick crunch of bone and clang of metal on stone. Her head rolled toward Waylon who caught it by the hair with a laugh and held it up for the cheering crowd to see. The noise quickly died out as a battle cry replaced it.

"FOR THE BONE BREAKER OF THE MOUNTAIN!"

The remaining six Fallen soldiers cheered in unison, over and over until it echoed off the walls. The executioner nearly slipped on the blood as he stepped over the first woman's body, the large axe making him slow enough that the king turned toward the six guards.

His face was red with anger when he yelled, "Slit their throats!"

"FOR THE BONE BREAKER OF THE MOUNTAIN!"

The guards surged forward, pressing their armored chests to the backs of the Fallen soldiers and gripping their hair.

"FOR THE BONE BREAKER OF THE MOUNTAIN!"

In a matter of seconds, their heads were pulled back, and their bare throats were exposed to the sky.

"FOR THE BONE BREAKER OF THE MOUNTAIN!"

I looked away, keeping my eyes on the top of the arena where I could see the setting sun when I felt the hot spray across my cheek and arm. I watched the sun slip below the top of the wall as the soldier's battle cries were replaced with the bloodthirsty cheers of noblemen. The arena grew dark, a darkness I recognized as one we'd been told permeated the entirety of the Dark Realm. I couldn't imagine a place as hopeless as this, thanking a goddess who was once praised for bringing love and life into our world and was now only celebrated for the death she supposedly brought to the enemies that I couldn't bring myself to hate.

I shifted my weight, feeling just faint enough that I nearly slipped on the slick blood beneath me and it took the firm grasp of Leif's hand on my forearm to steady myself again. The king must have dismissed us because he was climbing down from the stone and Leif tugged on my arm before I remembered the crowd of onlookers and started down the steps and toward the nearest archway.

Leif let go of my arm and I realized as we moved outside that we'd somehow got away without the castle guards in tow. I nearly ran along the side of the building toward the street, slowing as I approached the line of carriages and found ours. I could've sworn I heard sobbing within as I pulled on the door handle.

Norelli's eyes were red and puffy, but she sat straight-backed with a neutral expression when I climbed into the carriage. I hoped she had stayed in the carriage and hadn't seen the executions, but I knew that if it had been me, I would've wanted to be there. I would want to witness my people take their final stand, show them that they aren't alone.

Leif got in the carriage moments later, calling for our driver to head for the dock before he slammed the door shut. We endured the rough cobblestones, listening in silence to the cheers from the arena, for several blocks before the roads grew smoother and the smell of sewage and death was replaced with the salt of the sea.

Without removing my eyes from the royal ship I could see waiting in the harbor, I reached out and took Norelli's hand and gave it a squeeze. The knots in my stomach eased when she gave mine a tight squeeze in return.

9

The three of us stayed in the carriage while the dock hands began to unload our things and carry them aboard. More carriages began arriving and the ramp onto the ship was soon filled with smiling noble families, excited to be a part of a feast and ball. In a few hours, most of them would be drunk and vomiting their guts into Nex's precious sea, the last god we had to beg for protection before we were all thrust into the trial.

"You need to bathe before the deck party, Little Bird," Leif said.

It was hard to ignore the blood that had dried on my skin and soaked into my shoes and hemline. Neither Leif nor Norelli had spoken since leaving the arena. Norelli used his comment as an invitation to procure a handkerchief from her uniform and raise it to my face. I brushed her hand aside and looked away from the window and into Leif's expression. I knew he saw my intentions in mine because his jaw tightened, and his eyes burned into me a plea I didn't consider.

"Go make my cabin ready," I said and pushed open the door. I was halfway out the door when I felt Leif's rough hand grip my forearm. I pulled free and stepped into the street, knowing he wouldn't challenge me in public.

"We will meet you there, Your Highness," he called back, the warning so subtle that I doubt anyone but me noticed. I didn't need long. I just wanted a moment, some air, time to walk off my irritation.

The dockhands bowed and curtsied as I passed. I walked up the ramp and into the middle of the ship. The walls were deep mahogany with gold sconces lighting the way. I went up the stairs and turned toward the sound of laughter at the end of the hall. It opened to the main deck and the closer I got, the more voices I recognized. Men cheered at the pop of a cork as I reached the last sconce along the wall. The door on the right ahead of me opened and Ezra Loreign stepped out, needing to duck under the doorframe. He moved to the opposite wall and watched as I stormed toward him, nearly passing him before he shoved me into his room and closed the door.

I stumbled into the bedframe, nearly bouncing off and onto the floor before I got my footing and remembered the dagger strapped to my calf. I pulled it free and turned, managing to evade his attempt to grab me. I swung for his middle, but he stepped back just far enough that the tip of my blade *whooshed* past, giving him just enough time to surge forward and pin me against the wall. He kinked my wrist hard enough that I dropped my dagger. He pinned both my hands high on the wall above my head, halting my next plan of bashing his nose with my forehead. It wouldn't have worked anyway, considering my forehead only reached his chest. Ezra had me so effectively pinned that I was on my tiptoes to keep from being lifted off my feet and he did so with just a single hand, leaving the other free to push the wisps of curly hair behind his left ear.

"You would go before a party of your suitors, some of the most powerful men of the court, wearing the blood of your enemies in protest?" His voice was deep and rough.

"My father's enemies, not mine, not my kingdom's," I said

and spat in his face. He wasn't fazed. His expression remained like a stone as he wiped the spit off his cheek with his free hand.

"You should watch your words, Princess."

"And you should take your hands off me if you'd like to keep them, Sir Loreign."

I saw the hint of a smile on his lips before he released me. I fell into his broad chest, and he merely grabbed my waist and pushed me onto my heels before I could slap his hands away. He knelt in front of me and picked up my dagger, holding it out. My fingers had no sooner brushed the hilt before he pulled it away again, piercing me with a stern gaze.

"Watch. Your. Words." He offered the dagger again and this time I plucked it from his hand, resisting the urge to put a cut along his firm jaw. "Most of the men here would cut out your treasonous tongue."

"What does someone like you know about men like them?"

"I know men," Ezra said with a snort. "And men with unchecked power eventually abuse it. Men with armies abuse others."

I balanced on my left leg long enough to tuck my dagger back in place, watching as he rose to full height again. I noticed that his sword was still belted around his hips, not at all the way a nobleman would dress for a celebration. If not to swim, did he ever take the damn thing off?

"Why do you swim wearing your clothes and weapons?" I asked. I knew I was giving away a lot. Fuck, he already knew I didn't agree with the king's decision in the arena.

"The same reason you go to your tutor's lessons with a sword instead of a pen," he said and cast me a final warning look before brushing past me for the door. He left it open, a signal that the way was clear. I followed rather than going back down the hall to find my cabin. I didn't care that he was right about sending a message with my bloody attire. They'd either think I reveled in the blood of my enemies or refused to appear as their polished princess. Both were true. It didn't matter.

All of the contestants were on the deck, celebrating with champagne and mugs of ale. It seemed that several were already into their second or third round of drinks from the way they stumbled at the slight lull of the ship. It wasn't until I'd studied them all that I realized who I was looking for.

Waylon wasn't there. His men weren't there. I counted all the castle guards standing watch by the railing. I moved farther onto the deck to get a look at the masts and spotted several archers keeping watch from above. He was supposed to be on the deck. At least, the castle had planned for his absence.

"The jewel has arrived, boys!"

I turned toward Dallin's voice, anger flooding my veins. He leaned against the railing, his eyes roving over my body before finding my face. He took a drink from his mug before letting out a low whistle as I strode toward him.

"The way she walks could trap a man more than any siren's song," he said with a laugh that was echoed by several of the men. I stopped in front of him, just close enough to make my skin crawl. A smirk of satisfaction spread on his face when I took his mug. It was half full. I didn't care for ale, but I drank anyway. The men began to laugh and whisper the longer I drank until I lowered the empty mug from my lips and gripped the metal handle.

The deck filled with gasps when I smashed the mug into Dallin's jaw. It knocked him off balance but didn't seem to maim him like I had planned. Dallin straightened up, leaning on the rail for balance as he stared back at me in shock. I looked at the dented mug and was ready to swing again when I looked up and saw the humor in his eyes. Someone gripped my arm before I could raise it and pulled the mug free.

"And there's Her Highness's royal caretaker," Dallin said. The deck filled with the groans of the men, sad to see the fun end. I turned to face Leif as he tossed the mug onto the deck with a clang, his hand remaining firmly around my arm when I tried to pull free.

"Wren!" Leif snapped, dropping all professionalism just long enough for his cheeks to redden and for him to puff out his chest. Just like that, he was back to playing his part. "Your cabin, Your Highness."

Dallin let out a hum of disapproval as I allowed Leif to practically drag me toward the hall.

"And off he goes to spank the naughty princess," Dallin declared with a hearty laugh. "The lucky bastard."

I caught Leif off guard when I pulled free and turned around again, just enough to make it two steps before Ezra stepped in front of Lord Dallin. He picked him up by the front of his jacket. The entire deck was silent.

"Touch her again and I'm sure she'll do more than dent that fancy cup of yours." Ezra tossed Lord Dallin over the rail and a moment later a splash filled the silence. All but Beau and Ezra scrambled for the railing to peer down at Dallin. Beau didn't come out of his shock until he'd nearly spilled half his ale onto his shoes. Ezra gave me that same stern look from earlier before he went to the nearest servant holding a tray and snagged a mug for himself.

10

Leif's grip only grew tighter as he dragged me down the hall. My cabin was at the very end, the gold door covered in elegant filigree giving away every bit of the luxury within. I did not get to look around at the plush red couches or the grand mahogany table for very long. Leif pulled me into the room and finally released me once he'd sat me on a couch next to Norelli who looked back at me with wide eyes.

"I told you to go to your cabin," Leif said, keeping his voice calm despite the tremble.

"You did not, and I am not a child to be ordered around."

"The king's will allows exactly that!"

"I am of age, and I know that you give as much a fuck as I do about what the king wills!"

Leif slid the gilded coffee table away with his foot so he could stand closer, his finger pointed inches from my chest. I would've told him where to stick it had I not seen the way his eyes glistened. My heart skipped in my chest and suddenly I was a child again.

"I have been your teacher and protector since your birth. I was there at your first breath and held your hand when you took your first steps. The king may have ordered that I take the position to disgrace me, but your mother gifted you to me. In the dead of night, we plotted from the beginning and when she was sentenced to death, she entrusted you to me. I swore on pain of death that I wouldn't allow the king to have you, to subject you to the same prison he kept her in. I raised you to be the woman that she was. I taught you and trained you so you would have the skills she didn't, to fight for yourself, and to demand the freedom that she deserved, the freedom *you* deserve. You have endured too much to allow your emotions to risk all of that. You have worked your entire life for this single event that will grant you your freedom. Don't let your pride and stubbornness ruin everything that your mother died for!"

I bit down on my lower lip hard to keep the sobs at bay. The tears flowed hot down my cheeks regardless, washing away the dried blood and leaving red splotches in my lap where they landed.

"You are strong," Leif said with a much calmer tone. A whimper nearly escaped my lips. I nodded. "Say it."

I sucked in a shaky breath. "I am strong."

Leif stood in front of me a moment longer as I fought against the wave of shame and grief threatening to crush me. Finally, he stepped away and slid the coffee table back into its place.

"Stay here," Leif said from the door.

"Yes."

He left the cabin and I shut my eyes. For once, I welcomed the memories of that day. I went through every detail of my mother being led up the stone steps and kneeling before Aria's Stone. I wanted to scream at the memory. I felt like my chest was caving in, but I endured the pain in silence on that couch. I didn't utter a word, tasting the blood in my mouth from how hard I was biting on my bottom lip.

I endured. Just like I always had. I would endure.

Norelli helped me undress and then left me alone to scrub away the dirt and blood with a rag and bucket of water. She unpacked my things into the wardrobe as I scrubbed until my skin was raw and I was shivering.

"Here." She held out a towel for me. After I tucked it around my chest, she led me toward the vanity chair. She pulled my long hair behind me and began drying it with a towel as my fingers found the raised mark on my left forearm. I traced the sun, wondering how much Ezra knew about my tutoring sessions with Leif. The encounter had revealed one thing, at least. He may be a knight of the king's army, but he was not a supporter.

"You care about the Fallen," Norelli said.

I looked up from my lap to find her in the mirror, eyes focused on my hair as she dragged a comb through it. "I care that my father goes out of his way to inflict pain and spread violence throughout our kingdom unnecessarily."

"You don't see the Fallen as your kingdom's enemy." She finished brushing my hair and began a braid just above my right ear.

"I don't think they are our enemy," I said slowly. It was a complicated history and even my strict education with Leif had shown me that the truth was more to do with power and prejudice than threat and destruction. "I think that we are theirs."

Norelli let out a laugh and I saw a smile pull at the corner of her lip.

"What do you know about our kingdom?"

"I know it's through the Mist and farther away."

"Do you know the name of our ruler?"

"No." I wasn't ashamed to admit it. No one knew the names of the king and queen of the Fallen. They did not take part in battle and their forces knew better than to carry anything with them that would give away that information. What we knew was that the rulers sent their children to the battlefield in their stead, always the leaders of the army, always bearing titles rather than the names they were born with and would rule under. It's why the gilded horns of the Bone Breaker of the Mountain mattered so much to my father.

"I feel like I lose that part of myself with each day that I'm here," Norelli said softly. I watched her braid for a moment. She tied off the section that went over my ear before starting another braid down the center of my head.

"If it wasn't for Leif, I would fight back more than I have," I said. Her hands stilled at the back of my head, and she looked up, our eyes meeting in the reflection of the mirror.

"Your father would beat you for acting out. He would take your tongue for speaking out."

"I know," I scoffed. "I can bear the lash easier than sitting in silence with the truth. But Leif..."

I could see in her expression that she understood. Leif never threatened to punish me, not since that day my father was so specific with his orders.

"Do you not remember what he said if you were ordered to the post before the trial? It would not be me to hold the whip, Wren."

"You ask me to address you by name, like a friend," Norelli said as she started a third braid above my left ear. When I didn't respond, she continued. "May I speak as one?"

"Norelli, you are the closest friend I've ever had," I said in a sigh. My chest felt heavy with the weight of the words. I kept it so tightly bound that it was hard to admit that the tension I felt was so often from loneliness.

"You can't let your feelings for others guide your actions. It will only lead you to your grave," she said, pulling a piece of hair a little tighter than she had before. "Love and friendship are important and may be the only things worth pursuing, but it is also a luxury and a weapon."

They were cold words, but I knew she was right. Compassion got my mother executed. Worry for Norelli's parents got her captured and enslaved. I risked everything I'd trained for to earn my freedom and free my kingdom all because of my outrage for seven soldiers.

"Why the braids?" I asked as she finished tying the last. Three braids which she'd fluffed to make them look fuller.

"They suit you," she said with a small smile.

I admired them for a moment in the mirror. The style wasn't traditional in the Light Realm. No one in Honor Cove wore their hair this way. That was enough.

Norelli fell asleep on the couch with my bloodstained dress across her lap. She'd tried most of the night to scrub out the stains and after deciding to take a break, I looked up from my book at the table to find her eyes closed and looking more peaceful than I'd ever seen her.

My cabin had a large bookshelf filled with books about the sea and sailing. I thought it might be wise to explore the more sinister titles to see what I might need to do to best prepare for the trial. The Trial of Marriage always took part in two phases. Much of it was at sea, where Nex would no doubt put us all through hell. That was the phase I was most nervous about. I rarely spent time on the water. At least, not any farther than a mile from shore. I could only imagine what beasts would be waiting for us in the open ocean.

I looked up from the illustration of several tentacles slinking up the side of a ship when I heard the click of a key and the door opening. Leif paused in the doorway before pulling the door shut and slipping the lock back in place. He glanced at Norelli before removing his weapon's belt and crossing the room toward me. He sat the belt on the table in front of me before sinking into the chair across from me with a sigh. He looked exhausted and I wasn't sure if it was from our fight earlier or from the night of dealing with the drunk men on the deck.

"It's late," Leif said.

"Only two days and all these books ..." I said, turning the page to yet another illustration. This one was of a large snake-like creature that swam under a ship.

I looked up again at the sound of something sliding across the table. It was a scallop shell, the colors almost matching the mahogany table beneath it. I knew he didn't mean for my chest to ache with guilt, but it did all the same, and damn him if I hadn't looked up at his gentle expression before I'd composed myself.

"Don't cry, little bird," he said. "This world isn't worth your tears."

"It's not the world I care about," I said, cursing myself for letting the sob slip past my lips. There it was. Leif was out of his chair and on his knees in front of me. He scooted my chair away from the table as though I wasn't in it at all, turning it so I could face him.

"You and Norelli should leave when we get back to the castle," I said, pulling my hands back before he could reach for them.

"No. We make no other moves until the start of the trial."

"Then you leave with her as soon as it does."

Leif stood up and cast me a serious look. "You will worry about yourself and the trial and nothing else."

"Promise me!"

"Wren!" Leif had my face between his hands. We both froze, not breathing until several moments of silence had passed. Leif closed his eyes and let out a frustrated sigh before lowering his hands from my face. "I've been your royal guardian since your mother's death, though I've considered you a daughter from the moment you were born."

"And I'm not a child anymore," I said, holding his face between my hands this time. "You can't turn me over your knee to make me obey you any more than the king can send me to the post to obey him. I know what I face. I am willingly choosing the executioner's axe over the slavery of a marriage I did not choose, one that would only further serve the king's tyrannical reign. I know what I face, but I can't fight for myself not knowing what I will leave behind for you or Norelli regardless of what happens to me."

Leif gripped my wrists as he shushed me, his forehead now pressed to mine. "And if you remain focused, you will be successful."

"If I'm to focus, I need to know that you have a plan after the trial starts."

"I'll take Norelli west to the Mist. She's familiar with the terrain. It will make the passage easier. I will find you when the time is right. I swear it," Leif said before pressing a kiss to my forehead. "I swear it."

My muscles were sore, and I felt exhaustion creep in as I considered his words. There weren't many major villages from here to the border. It was almost suicidal for anyone to consider the Mist as an option. By the time anyone thought to look for them, they would be halfway to the Mist. By the time anyone thought to consider their plan, they'd be through the Mist and into the Dark Realm. I took a sobering breath and remembered the book on the table. I had a whole journey ahead of me that I knew little about.

"I don't know the first thing about sailing," I said and sat back in my chair.

Leif pulled the chair next to me away from the table and climbed into the seat.

"I taught you how to navigate using the stars. You are a strong swimmer. You can keep track of currents. You are more prepared than you think," he said.

"Fine. What about the beasts in the water?"

"Avoid the teeth," he said and reached across the table to close the book in front of me. "Weapon or not, aim for the eyes or the gills."

I reached for the book, but he slid it to the opposite side of the table where it slowed to a stop at the edge. I ignored the urge to go after it. I opened my mouth to ask how I would manage in a fight against those men, but I knew what he would say. I was quick on my feet in the sand. I'd be quicker on any other surface. He was right about the water. I was a strong swimmer.

"Do you trust me?" Leif asked, pulling my attention away from the book.

It was a stupid question and we both knew it. I had no reason not to trust him. He'd helped my mother. He raised me. He did his best to protect me, even when it meant severe punishments to avoid a worse fate at my father's hands. It was Leif's doing that kept me in the king's mostly good graces.

"I trust you."

"Then know that you're ready for the trial and start acting like it," he said, not cracking a smile until I nodded. "Off to bed, little bird. Get some rest. I'm not going anywhere until you do."

I rose from my seat and took the shell from the table, leaving him in his seat and Norelli curled up on the couch in the main room to go to the sleeping quarters at the back of the cabin. The bed was almost as comfortable as mine back in the castle, but it was getting more difficult to fall asleep these days with a sword strapped to my hip.

PART III

Nex

EXCERPT FROM THE BOOK OF THE GREAT MOTHER

All things were well with the world, but the Great Mother noticed that Aria grew lonely. Her realm was alive and beautiful just as she was, but still she grew sadder with each day. The Great Mother, pleased with everything Aria had done with the realm she had granted her, created a companion for the goddess. The Great Mother, sad for the goddess, cried a tear into the sea with which Nex was created.

The god was given the sea by the Great Mother. Nex used his power over the sea to create creatures that could survive its treacherous waters. Nex sent a tide toward the land, his desire to find another with power to match his. Aria allowed the tide to wash over the land, binding them together and strengthening the world now that their realms were together.

Nex calmed the raging sea and Aria's people used the waters

to navigate their new world. With their realm combined, they were able to expand their homes and create new cities. They could hunt on land and now fish in the sea. All was well in the world. The god and goddess were happy and this pleased the Great Mother.

11

It was a classic Honor Cove morning, gray and cool as we bobbed along the water. We were all back on the main deck, though the mood was much more subdued than the night before, and not just because most of the men were hungover. We were all gathered around a wooden crate, sealed tight with the warning "do not open unless you bear the seal" painted across the top. Present on our trip at sea were: the castle guards; the contestants in the trial; Leif, Norelli, and I; and three priests who had to be nearly ninety years old. The priests were sent from Van Elding where the largest shrine to the God Nex was located and they were here to bless the contestants in the trial. All three of them had the suction cup marks of a tentacle wrapped around their right arms, the marks raised and pink like they'd been burned there. It was Nex's mark, just like the sun burned into my forearm was Aria's.

I leaned closer to Leif. "What's in the crate?"

No response.

The three men hadn't said a word from the time we were all called to assemble on deck. I was told to come dressed in black, so I wore the same dress I'd worn to my mother's execution. When the contestants arrived, one of the silent priests led them all into a room down the hall. They all returned barefoot and wearing the same thick black robes. Beau's robe was so long that it swept along the deck as he followed the line of men out. Ezra was so tall that his thick calves were on full display. Dallin shot me an ornery grin that made me direct my eyes to the deck before I could see how he chose to wear his robe.

We all watched with only the sounds of the sea as the threesome worked to prepare the area. Torches lit the deck, casting a ghostly glow over everything. The youngest of the three priests walked past us with a wooden bucket in one hand. Inside, the dark sand glittered. The remaining two priests began working on the crate, using hammers to wrench the nails free until they could lift the lid off the crate.

It was such a stark contrast from the grim surroundings. Water lapped at the sides of the crate as the ship swayed. The bottom of the crate was covered with gravel and floating in the water along the top were more than a dozen creatures that left me stunned. I wasn't sure what I was looking at, not at first. They were too large to be the tiny creatures that sometimes washed ashore during the warm months, but still ...

"Blue dragons," Leif said under his breath.

Blue dragon sea slugs were as dangerous as they were beautiful and that was when they weren't four times the normal size like these. Each had four legs that looked like dragon wings that could deliver a terrible sting when provoked. I could only imagine what torture they could unleash when they were the size of your palm. As though reading my mind, the priest who had carried the bucket was now dragging a trunk across the deck with a red cross painted on the side. Another priest carried a set of steps and sat them on the end of the crate nearest the line of robed contestants.

The oldest priest spoke. "After magic took hold in the east, the Mist grew darker and more dangerous, and the Goddess Aria abandoned her land and people for the arms of O'Riah, Nex prepared the sea for a great war to bring balance back to the Great

Mother's world." The other two priests had taken their places by his side, one holding the bucket of sand and the other holding a golden bowl in one hand and an unsheathed dagger in the other.

"Nex came to shore on the back of a great blue sea dragon to meet O'Riah and Aria and it was that blue dragon that brought Aria back to her realm, restored the balance between realms, and fulfilled the will of the Great Mother. Blue dragons are sacred and a symbol of protection. Today, we ask the God Nex to protect the contestants through the Trial of Marriage. We ask that he examines each contestant's soul and ensures his intentions are pure and that he is worthy of the hand of a princess and a seat on a throne." After finishing his speech, the old priest turned and walked up the steps to the crate. He lowered himself into the water until it rose nearly to his hips. The blue dragons continued to float at the top of the water, unbothered by his joining them.

"Extend the hand of your choice," the priest with the dagger said as he stepped toward the end of the line where Beau Renault stood.

Beau had barely raised his left hand before the priest reached out and sliced his palm with the dagger. Beau gasped but remained still as the priest held the golden bowl beneath his hand to catch the blood. After a few moments, he continued to move down the line until he'd cut each man's hand, and the bowl had a shallow pool of blood collected at the bottom.

"We offer blood to the gods and goddesses to show what we are willing to sacrifice, to honor the Great Mother for her creation of our realm. In reverence of the Trial of Marriage, the contestants pool their blood together to honor the sacrifice all but one will make," the old priest spoke again, this time from the center of the crate.

The priest with the bowl stood next to the priest with the sand as the first name was called.

"Lord Beau Renault."

Beau stood frozen for a moment, holding his bleeding hand before he slowly approached the two priests at the steps. They stood with solemn expressions, one holding the bowl and the other the sand.

"Disrobe."

Beau cast a brief look my way, his blue eyes making me aware for the first time that the men might all be naked beneath their robes. My stomach clenched and my heart fluttered more than I cared to admit as he slid the robe off his shoulders and let it fall around his feet. Shit. Fuck my stupid heart for the way it pounded now. I was relieved when Beau was left standing on the deck, wearing a pair of briefs. Still, I couldn't calm my heart as my eyes scanned the curves of his muscles.

"Blood of the contestants. May their offering be accepted by Nex."

The priest with the bowl dipped his hand into the red pool and began smearing it along Beau's body. He pressed his fingers to his brow, ran a line down each of his arms, and then painted his chest.

"Sand from the bottom of the sea from which all Nex's creatures arise."

The priest with the sand came forward and slathered handfuls of dark sand along Beau's body until it stuck to the blood. Beau looked like he might collapse when the two priests stepped aside, and he was called to the water. He slowly made his way to the top of the steps and after a deep breath, he lowered himself into the crate. The water rose to his hips, and he moved slowly toward the priest in the middle.

The silence on the deck became low murmurs when the blue dragons slowly converged on the pair. Beau's back tensed as they grew closer until the entire group of slugs was brushing against their legs. The priest whispered to Beau as he touched his arms, then his brow, and finally pressed his hands to his chest before taking a step back and leaving him in the middle of all the blue dragons.

"Wash yourself of the blood of your equals. May Nex's waters bless you and protect you."

Beau sucked in a breath before he submerged himself under the water. When he stood up again, the bloody sand was gone and several blue dragons clung to his skin instead. He let out a gasp of horror before standing still as a statue, eyes raised toward the dark sky. The priest standing in the water just feet away looked like he'd seen Nex himself. I looked to the other contestants who were just as stunned.

"Where are you from?" the priest asked.

"S-Scout Sea," Beau stammered.

The priest nodded as though his answer offered some explanation. "Blessed indeed. You have Nex's favor."

"What?"

"You heard him," Dallin called out and waved a hand for him to move. "You can get out now."

Beau looked back at the priest who just stared at him for a moment. When Beau started for the end of the crate, the blue dragons slid down his body and back into the water. Once he climbed out, they resumed their normal lazy circles in the water.

The ceremony proceeded similarly, although not nearly as dramatically. The blue dragons did not gather around any of the contestants or cling harmlessly to them the way they had to Beau. Dallin was practically seething about the fact when his turn went as uneventfully as the other contestants before him. Ezra was so tall that the priest stepped forward and pushed him under the water to fully submerge him. When he emerged, he was gasping and fell into a coughing fit that didn't subside until he joined the other men in line.

It began raining hard, and the priests gathered at the end of the crate just long enough to wish the contestants well. Everyone immediately headed for cover. Even the priests joined the procession down the hall toward the cabins. Leif closed the door behind us and stopped me with a hand on my shoulder.

"No one will be on deck in a rain like this," he said and turned me around to face the door. "Go ask Nex for his blessing."

I opened my mouth to protest, thinking of the priests all

taking cover in their rooms, but when had I ever worried about formalities? I didn't need a priest to ask on my behalf. I would speak for myself.

I hurried out of the room and braced myself against the rain pouring down on the deck. It took only moments before I was soaked. The priests had left the bucket of sand and the bowl of blood inside the trunk of medical supplies. I took notice of the many vials of purple liquid in case I was unfortunate enough to need one later.

I used my dagger to slice my hand and add my blood to the bowl. In my rush to avoid diluting it with rainwater, I tossed the last of it onto my chest and frantically began scrubbing the wet sand over my skin until I felt raw from the effort. It was too much of a risk to undress and I didn't trust the little amount of time I was sure I had left, so I hurried up the steps of the crate and stepped into the churning water before I could think about what might happen.

"Please let this work," I begged as I sank into the water. I took one last breath before I went under and let my body sink until I felt my butt meet the rocky bottom. Pain shot through my right leg. I gasped, inhaling enough water to make my lungs burn. Before I could push toward the surface, another blue dragon stung my left arm and I thrashed against the pain as though I could fight off the creatures. The water churned around me and my head spun, the pain of the stings radiating through me. I tried reaching for the surface and my hands met rocks instead. I turned over just as someone gripped the front of my dress and hauled me up.

My vision was blurred as my gasp pierced the air. My scream was stolen by my coughs as water caught in my throat. I felt the firm deck at my back, and I rolled to my left side, water pouring past my lips before my stomach rolled and I was vomiting onto the wood. The pain shot through my arm and leg like lightning and as much as I tried, every scream turned into retching until there was nothing left in my stomach.

"Open your mouth," a deep voice said.

I looked up at the sound. I only knew it was Ezra Loreign from the outline of his broad chest and the loose curl that framed his face. I turned away as he reached for me, unable to reach my dagger as I realized he'd pinned me to the deck with a knee to each of my legs.

"Open your fucking mouth!" He hooked a finger in my cheek, and I felt the mouth of a vial shove between my lips. I nearly gagged at the feel of the thick liquid sliding down my throat, but he clapped a hand over my mouth to keep me from spitting it out. When he finally got off of me, I scrambled to my feet, nearly falling as the ship rocked hard to the left. I looked back at him as he pulled the cork from another vial with his teeth and spat it on the deck. He lifted the vial to his lips and drank the entire thing before tossing both empty vials aside to the ground where they shattered.

"You were stung too," I said, looking over him as though it would be obvious where he'd been injured. He was dressed in a pair of pants and a white shirt, his dagger and sword belted around his hips. Most of his hair had come free and was hanging in curls around his shoulders.

"Nothing gets past you, Princess," Ezra said and pushed his hair out of his eyes and started toward the hallway beneath the captain's bridge.

Maybe it was how he addressed me by my cursed title. Maybe it was the fact that Nex didn't keep those damn blue dragons from stinging the hell out of me or the fact that I had no idea how I would be able to kill Ezra Loreign, as massive as he was. Whatever the reason, I was pissed. I was vibrating, I was so angry. For once, I wanted to act. I wanted to do something that would matter.

I shoved him as he passed, using all of my strength against his solid body so that he stumbled into the edge of the crate. It was such a subtle movement, but it took so much out of me, and it felt good. He looked back at me with more annoyance than shock in his face and it only made me hate him more.

"Did you really think Nex would bless you in this trial?" Ezra straightened up to his full height. "Nex waged a war and personally dragged Aria through the sand and sea the moment she tried going after what she wanted."

"Why are you here? What is it that you want from this bloody trial?" I yelled. I didn't care if anyone heard, though I was sure it was impossible through this storm. I didn't budge, even when Ezra's expression grew dark, and his muscles tensed. My heart picked up pace as he drew in close.

"What do you want me to say? I'm not a nobleman, so excuse my manners, Princess. I don't want your fucking kingdom. I don't want the damn title or money. I don't even want your royal cunt like all the men who would gladly slit their own throats for even a chance to look at it. No, I don't want you."

My ass was pressed against the railing. "What do you want?"

Ezra shook his head in disbelief, relaxing a little before he looked back at me. "You can hate me, but you and I aren't that different."

"Fuck you," I said and shoved him again, catching him off guard just enough to put a couple of feet between us. "And fuck Nex and anyone else who actually believes Aria is just the Goddess of Land, Life, and Death. You know what, fuck her too for not fighting harder."

It was strange to see the panic cross his face as I leaned backward over the railing, welcoming the stormy sea below. I sank beneath the surface, the water rough enough that it took a moment longer than I'd expected to kick for the surface. I'd swam in choppy water before, so I knew it would be a rough swim to shore. I hadn't expected the splash from behind. I twisted in the water to face Ezra just as he surfaced, a wave crashing over us before I could prepare for it. We were dragged under and I fought against his arms as he tried grabbing for me.

Once I was free, I swam as fast as I could. My arms and legs felt almost numb from the ache, and I let the current take me the rest of the way to the shore and stayed bent over on my hands and knees as I caught my breath. It was nearly a whole minute later before he came storming out of the water behind me the way I'd seen him do day after day, fully dressed and ready to wage war.

"Did you enter the trial to win your life or to end it?" Ezra yelled.

"You'll never find out," I said and continued walking through the sand. My legs were so damn tired that part of me wanted to duck inside the cave near the castle for a nap.

"Really? Why's that?"

I whirled around to face him, and he nearly walked right into me.

"I'll kill you first. That's why," I said, ignoring the urge to punch him in the teeth when he smiled.

"You really think you can do that?"

"You don't think I can kill you just because I'm half your size?" I challenged.

Ezra wasn't smiling anymore. It made my stomach twist.

"I meant *kill*, Princess. Do you really think you could kill?"

"Men like Dallin Vondrelle? You? I would've done it already if I didn't need you all for the trial first," I said and turned on my heel.

"You'll kill Beau then?"

I'd taken a step toward him again before I realized I reacted. I didn't know why I cared. I should've kept walking. Ezra rolled his eyes.

Fuck.

"Beau is only here because it makes his family look good. He deserves an easy out," I said and started walking again.

"And you'll give that to him? How? Stab him in the back when he doesn't see it coming?"

"Fuck off!" I stared back at him, glad to see that he looked like his normal serious self again. "Leave me alone. Don't talk to me.

The next time you come within five feet of me, we better be in the trial because either way my sword will be in your gut."

He didn't say a word. He didn't react at all to my words. I only realized now as he stared back at me that it had stopped raining, and the sun was shining. All I wanted now was to lie down in my bed and be left alone for as long as possible. I already knew that being alone was asking too much.

The castle wasn't aware that I'd jumped ship until Ezra and I walked through the front doors. I ignored the orders from the guards to alert the king and the armed men who gathered around me as I walked toward the stairs. I ignored them as I continued toward my chambers.

"Stop in the name of the king!"

I ignored the order and continued down the hall and into my chambers. Someone stopped the door behind me before it could slam shut. When I turned around, Waylon shut the door behind him and it was just the two of us in the room.

"Why weren't you on the ship?" I asked. He didn't answer. He walked farther into the room, looking over the kitchenette and running his fingers over the top of the table as he moved.

"Sir Loreign said you fell," he said as he moved to my bed, running his fingers along the fabric of the comforter as he continued toward the balcony doors. "Why were you on the deck at all in that storm?"

"I didn't realize the contestants were the only ones allowed to pray to Nex." My stomach turned as he stopped at my wardrobe and opened the doors to look at my clothes. He shut them and stood in front of the mirrored door for a moment, admiring himself and running his hands through his dark hair so that it was slicked back in that messy way he preferred.

"Finally out of escape plans, are you?"

"If I wanted to die, I'd be dead already," I said as he straightened up from the mirror and moved to the vanity without so much as a look my way.

"I stopped the guards at the doors. I told them I would handle it and not to worry our father with such a small matter." Waylon peeked into the bathroom and when I didn't reply, he finally stopped walking to look at me.

"If you want a thank you, you'll be disappointed," I said. I wanted him to leave so I could change out of my soaked clothes. I was so cold.

He took another step forward with an annoyed sigh.

"I want you to be a good girl and stop harassing the contestants, especially Lord Vondrelle. Stop looking at me with that smug, self-righteous expression," he said before I got a chance to defend myself. "Didn't think anyone would find out? Whose guards did you think were on that ship? Speaking of guards, I've added to yours. You can keep Sir Folee for the little he's worth and your Fallen slut to clean your floors or whatever you have her do. Your new guards will report directly to me. Keep that in mind, dear sister."

"Is it a matter of not trusting me or being threatened by me?" I asked and crossed my arms, smiling at the color that flooded his tight expression.

"When Father dies and the crown is placed on my head, you will lay yours on the executioner's block. That is unless I find you useful through your new marriage. You better hope Vondrelle wins," Waylon said before shoving past me. The door slammed shut behind me and I heard the scuffle of feet as my new guards took their places outside my door.

I didn't meet Leif on the beach. I hadn't spoken to him since I jumped from the ship. I saw his reproachful face in the crack of my chamber door when Norelli joined me for the night. I'd told them I needed her to draw a bath when I really just wanted the company of anyone but a man. I'd been surrounded by men for the past twenty-four hours and I would spend the entire trial that way. The last thing I wanted was to listen to another man, especially not Leif, and his lectures.

Instead, I woke up like normal, had Norelli lace me into my favorite blue dress, and went to the only place in the castle I knew would be empty. There was a kind of peace that always fell over me when I was in the library. I could feel my chest tighten with anticipation as I walked down the hall, my steps echoed by three of Waylon's guards behind me.

"I want to be alone," I told the nearest man.

"I'll do a sweep," he said and ran ahead, ducking into the room at the end of the hall. The fabric around my arms felt itchy and hot as I walked, waiting for the guard to leave the last sanctuary I had. I opened my mouth to order him out just as he walked back into the hall and took his place at the door. I didn't acknowledge any of them before striding into the room, the tightness in my chest only abating once I'd reached the end of the long aisle.

There were dozens of bookshelves so tall that it took ladders to reach the highest shelves. The shelves were so high that when I was little, Leif forbade me from stepping onto the ladders at all. He told me to call for him or ask a maid to climb their heights. I never did and it wasn't until I'd fallen off the ladder when I was six and badly bruised my arm that I was caught. I only remember the event so vividly because it was the only time I'd successfully cried my way out of punishment from Leif. He was every bit as stubborn as I was, and no amount of careful planning or creative negotiation ever worked on him. I'd learned to accept my fate long ago. The only thing that worked, and marginally so, was putting it off. That's what I was doing now. At least, I thought I was until I was standing on the stone floor staring down the rows and rows of shelves that had been there for my favorite memories.

I kicked off my shoes and felt a little more at home as I walked the first aisle with the cold stone beneath my feet. Leif and I used to meet for lessons in the library, just us. When it was clear that I'd sat for too long and could hardly focus on another map or math lesson, he'd tell me to run, and the aisles of books turned into our playground. I'd run barefoot through the aisles and squeal with glee when he'd appear at the end to catch me, turning on my heels and running in the opposite direction.

The library had a wall of windows that opened to the balcony and overlooked the sea. I used to run through the aisles, Leif pretending to be too slow to keep up, winding through each one until I reached the double doors. I'd run outside and to the end of the balcony and look down at the sharp rocks below before turning to face him. He'd say something about having me cornered before snatching me into his arms where I'd shriek, and he'd carry me all the way back through the library and to our table near the front to resume our lesson.

I wasn't quite running, but I found myself winding through the aisles. I took each turn faster, matching my pace to the racing of my heart as I went down aisle after aisle until I knew I was losing it. I was losing control. My brain was a muddle of memories of these books and Leif and this fucking castle and everything I'd endured without so much as a grimace. I still had nightmares of being tied to the post, my back searing as the whip sliced into my skin. The way Leif begged for my forgiveness. He sounded so unlike himself, beside himself, grief-stricken in a way I hadn't seen him even after my mother's execution. Her execution ...

I turned the final corner, relieved to reach the balcony doors and feel the cool air on my hot skin and instead froze at the sight of Beau Renault sitting in an armchair next to the doors looking just as stunned to see me.

"Princess ... Wren," he stammered, pushing himself out of the chair. He bent halfway into a bow before catching the formality and straightened up. Once he gathered himself, the shock in his eyes turned to concern. "What's wrong?"

I surged forward, grabbing the front of his shirt and pulling his chest to mine. My lips met his. He returned the kiss, brushing my hair behind my ear with a gentle hand while the other rested at my hip. I thought my heart might explode when my hands found their way to his waist. I struggled to find the button to his pants and my fingers slipped into his waistband when he broke the kiss with a groan.

"Wren," he breathed and slid his hands to my waist.

"Undo this thing. Get me out of this corset," I said and kissed him again, finally finding the button of his pants when his hands brushed mine away.

"We can't," he said, despite kissing me again and pulling me a fraction closer before turning his head to end the kiss. "We can't."

What was I doing? I was only making this harder on myself. It was just like Leif warned me. Fuck, it was exactly what Ezra said. I would have to kill Beau. I couldn't stand to see him meet anything but a merciful end and I knew the trial wouldn't allow it. I would have to do it myself. This was all so selfish, and it only made my stomach twist with guilt so tight that I thought I might rip in two.

"I'm sorry, Wren. I am. I want to, but your ... Please, don't cry."

Cry? As soon as he'd said it, I felt the moisture on my cheeks. It was all it took to pull me out of whatever moment of weakness this was. He was an escape, something so familiar and yet so different from the harsh reality of this realm and the cold men that controlled it. I knew I was looking for something more than he could ever offer and yet a part of me still wanted to feel every inch of him.

I turned on my heel and hurried down the center aisle. I quickly slipped on my shoes and stalked from the room without uttering a word to the guards, my face dry and my hair smoothed back into place as though nothing had ever happened.

I watched from the second floor of the arena as Dallin Vondrelle and his new posse of fellow contestants squared up below. The rest of the contestants used the other side of the arena to lift bags of sand or practice sparring maneuvers on mannequins. Beau watched from the sidelines. Ezra was absent and for all it's worth, his lack of interest in the trial was proving to be an asset. No one talked about him. No one knew anything about his abilities aside from their assumptions, considering he'd walked into Honor Cove with the Bone Breaker of the Mountain's gilded horns. The contestants who hadn't forgotten about him entirely wouldn't know a thing about his strengths or weaknesses. It was a brilliant strategy if that's what it was. It also meant that I had no better chance against him than any other contestant and that was enough to set me on edge.

I looked away from the ring when I caught movement out of the corner of my eye. One of my new guards had stepped away from the wall to adjust, tugging at his armor and repositioning his sword at his hip before stepping back in line and revealing Leif, whose eyes caught mine before I looked away. Norelli raised her eyebrows, and the gesture alone made me wish I'd stayed in my chamber rather than agreeing to visit the training arena with her after breakfast.

"He's angry, you know," she said.

"I'm sure he is." I knew him better. He was pissed.

"I'm not supposed to tell you," Norelli started and waited until she'd pulled my attention from the ring to finish. "He's going to come to your chamber tomorrow morning. He doesn't trust you to meet him on the beach and he said that if you don't want to train by the sea, he'll kick your ass in your room."

"Why did you tell me?" I asked and looked back down at the

ring where Lord Elias Vonhenson had taken a bow and just sent his first arrow into the forehead of a mannequin on the other side of the ring.

"You're the only person I serve here," Norelli said.

Her words echoed in my head. Such a damn farce that beneath the gods we served anyone. Maybe the gods themselves weren't even worthy of our adoration. I would never say it aloud, but I struggled to relate to Aria. To me, she was just another woman imprisoned by the will of a man. That alone we had in common. I wouldn't be put on a pedestal for it though.

I looked directly at her and said, "When this is all over, you will serve no man or woman." She looked like she might cry for a brief second before giving me a curt nod. "Do Fallen horns grow back?"

She smiled and gave me a single nod.

13

I heard a swishing sound. It reminded me that Beau's screams of pain were just dreams. The resistance I felt was just the sheets wrapped around my hand and as I tried to pull free, I came out of my deep sleep and opened my eyes to the darkness around me. The sheets were wrapped around me like usual and I twisted to free myself, pulling my right arm away when a hand clapped over my mouth.

I heard the hiss of a knife as it sank into the mattress next to me. I thrashed against the sheets holding me in place, freeing myself just as I heard the knife sink into the pillow inches from my left ear. It was too dark to see, so I rolled to the right until I felt the floor knock the air from my lungs. I was on my feet before I'd taken a full breath, pulling the dagger strapped to my leg free and ready to react to what little I could see of the dark shape kneeling at the end of my bed.

It leaped off the mattress and ran at me again. I moved a step to the right and swiped at it with my dagger, spurred to action when I heard the figure gasp in pain. Before I could launch another attack, it ran for the door. I chased after it, throwing myself against it before it could open the door. It fell, pulling me to the ground with it. I rolled so I was straddling the body, and I brought my dagger down hard, ripping it out and plunging down again and again until the attacker had stopped gasping for air. The last time I stabbed the man, the room was flooded with candle-light, and I could see the terror on his lifeless face. The look was enough for me to let go of the hilt of the dagger and scramble off his limp body.

"He's dead. There's no one else here," Norelli confirmed and set the candle on the table next to me before rushing to light the fireplace. I spun around when a pair of arms came down on me from behind.

"Easy, little bird," Leif said, dodging the knife in my right hand before looping his hands under my arms and dragging me several feet back from the man lying dead before the door. "Get a fresh nightgown, Norelli. Quickly!"

Leif tugged the dagger from my grip and quickly wiped the blade clean on his thigh. He slid it back into the sheath at my calf as Norelli knelt next to us with her arms full of fabric.

"Dress her and hide the blood," Leif said and stood up.

I hadn't realized I was covered in blood until Norelli began tugging the riding shirt from my torso. I pushed myself off the floor to make the effort easier, nearly falling over as I peeled off my pants. A wet sound drew my attention toward the door where Leif was stabbing his dagger into the chest of the dead man.

I looked away, allowing Norelli to guide my arms into a clean nightgown. She smoothed the white fabric down my body and stepped back to inspect me before looking down at the discarded clothes that lay in a pool of blood. As soon as she'd turned to toss the bloody clothes into the fireplace, Leif was there, eyes wide with fear as he held my face and then my shoulders, assessing me for any sign of injury.

"It's over. He's dead," I said.

"Are you hurt?" he asked.

"He's dead. I killed him."

"LOOK AT ME!"

His words were like lightning and I stared back at his blue eyes, the fear in them chasing away any other emotion. He was here. I was here. Norelli was fine. The attacker was dead. I'd killed him. I killed. I killed someone.

"Fuck. Gods!" I gasped and glanced toward the body in front of the door, Leif's dagger buried in his chest.

"Listen to me," Leif said and gently slapped the side of my cheek until my eyes were locked on his. "You woke up to a noise. That's all."

"I woke up to a noise," I repeated. "That's all."

"Go sit with Norelli," he said, leading me into her arms.

I'd barely sat on the couch before the fireplace before the door burst open and Waylon's guards flooded the room. Leif was there to explain it all. He told them how he'd heard a strange sound and opened my chamber door. He told them how I pushed the attacker off my bed and onto the floor and how he'd used that moment to strike, subduing the man just as he reached the door.

Not a single guard questioned the story. Two guards began searching the room to determine how the attacker had entered. Two more began assessing the attacker's body, rifling through his pocket for any sign of identification. Once they were happy, Leif guided Norelli and me from the room. He led us down the stairs and through another corridor that I only recognized as the guest wing after we'd stopped outside one of the chambers. He withdrew a set of keys from his pocket and flipped through them until he found the one he was looking for.

The door closed behind us before Leif lit a candle. Warm light flooded the space, and I knew immediately where we were. It was mostly bare. The kitchen was void of fine glassware and there was just a single place setting at the table. A half-empty glass of water sat on the coffee table a few feet away. The bed was just a few more feet past the couch and was still made as though the resident hadn't yet been home. Just above the bed was a window. The moonlight illuminated the marble-like seashells that lined the sill.

"Are you hurt?" Leif asked, turning from the door to look at me. "Tell me."

I shook my head. "No. No, I'm fine."

It felt like I hadn't taken a full breath until he wrapped his arms around me, somehow holding together the last pieces of myself I thought I'd lost in the attack. It was hard not to think about the feel of him beneath me, the resistance beneath my hand as my dagger cut through his flesh.

"Norelli?" I started, looking over Leif's shoulder where I found her setting three glasses on the coffee table with a bottle in one hand.

"I'm here," she said as she poured a shallow amount of dark liquid into each glass. "We are all here."

Leif must have guided me to the bed because I was seated at the edge of his mattress a moment later and Norelli was handing me a glass of amber liquid. I took a deep sobering breath as I swirled the liquid around the glass. I lifted the glass to my lips and drained it in a single drink.

"Did I just kill a man?" I asked, lowering the glass to my knee.

"You just killed your assassin," Leif said and cupped the side of my face. "You did well, little bird. You did well."

"The assassin is dead," Waylon said and stood from the table. "I have increased her guard, again. I don't see why we are still discussing the matter."

"I mean no disrespect, Your Majesty. Your Highness," Leif said and bowed to my father and my brother respectively before addressing everyone gathered in the king's chambers. "Someone made an attempt on your daughter's life ahead of the Trial for Marriage. It's clear the man did not act alone. It is important to her safety that we investigate all parties that may have had a part in the plot."

I held my tongue when I noticed Waylon roll his eyes. I

should've expected as much considering we were sitting in a room of my father and Waylon's guards and advisors. None of them seemed concerned with my well-being, but several did perk up at the mention of the trial.

"I had my men investigate the attacker and all those associated with him. There was no connection. It seemed that he was seeking to ruin the princess in a night of passion," Waylon said.

I shot a warning expression his way, wishing more than anything that the truth could be known. I wanted them all to know that I'd killed the would-be assassin. I suspected that Waylon had ordered the hit and I wanted him to know that I'd taken care of his man myself.

"He did not act alone. Did you not hear?" I asked, glaring directly at my brother.

"Were you expecting *two* men in your bed chamber, sister?"

"A man doesn't attempt to stab a lady before having his way with her."

"Enough!" The king did not raise his voice, but his tone was sharp enough that I knew I'd pushed the boundary as far as he would allow. I worried a little that I might have wasted precious words and what little patience he had on lashing out at Waylon. My father cast us both warning looks before nodding for Leif to continue.

"The attacker was armed with several daggers. The evidence supports that it was an assassination attempt. The man also possessed a note that detailed how to get into the castle and where to find the princess's chambers. The note was written *to* him and not *by* him, meaning that he attacked on someone else's orders," Leif said before looking to Waylon. "Increasing her guard is necessary, but I ask that further investigation is done into who might have ordered the assassination."

No one spoke for a long moment. The king sat, staring at his maps as his expression grew more and more frustrated. He let out a harumph and looked up at Leif.

"This came right before the trial. Killing her would leave no prize for the contestants. Her guard has been increased. We will remain vigilant, and should there be any more threats, stop them before they can reach the princess."

"Your Majesty," Leif continued as the king stood from the table and motioned for everyone to leave. "There may be someone trying to silence your reign and limit your power."

This, of course, caught his attention.

The king froze, eyes wide and face turning a deep shade of red. "Everyone out," he said, his tone low and controlled despite the tension in his shoulders. "If anyone speaks of this again, it better be because they've caught an attacker or have answers. I don't have the time for paranoid musings."

The three of us had taken no more than a few steps toward the door before my father started yelling again. "Get out! Gods help you if I have to address another issue about the trial ..."

Leif hurried me from the room and down the hall, grabbing my wrist when I attempted to turn to face Waylon as we passed.

"Not another word," he hissed as I turned around, retaking our positions so I was securely within the circle of guards next to him. I didn't say anything, but not because he'd asked me to. What I wanted was to push past all the armed soldiers and blaze my own trail down the hall. I held my breath, reminded myself that my time would come, and focused on making it to the trial instead. *Make it to the trial. Survive until the end. Win my own hand. Free the rest of the kingdom and take my place on the throne after my father and brother are gone.* This was about so much more than just me. This was about so much more.

The guards took their positions outside my chamber, Leif holding the door as I entered and following me inside. I barely acknowledged Norelli as she stood at the wardrobe, hanging my clean dresses. I went straight to the cabinets behind the round table and pulled a bottle of wine from the shelf along with a glass and turned when a pair of hands gripped mine.

"I will look into it myself if he won't," Leif said and pulled the bottle from my hands.

I let go of the glass, and it shattered on the floor. I wish I hadn't. I wish I had thrown it on the floor instead of just letting it slip from my fingers like some pathetic …

"If I die, it's one less child he has to offer anything to. My father would cut me out entirely if it wouldn't make a political statement, one that would cause others to question his authority and my place next to him. He is as complicit in this as Waylon is, if not privy to the details."

"Yes. I know that, little bird," Leif said, setting the bottle on the table behind him and holding my face between his hands despite my attempts to pull away. "I know."

I let him hold me, if anything because I knew that the trial had to be close. It had to be. I couldn't stand to think of spending another week like this, so it had to be days away and if it was days away … I knew that Leif was struggling more than I was with all of this. Regardless of what happened, he would lose. It had me frozen in his arms, his gentle hands holding me in place in more ways than just physically.

"I know that it is a political game that I have no way of winning. I know that he won't put any resources into looking for the man behind your assassination attempt. But I will. I will put an end to this threat against you," Leif said.

"You can't throw stones at Waylon, not yet. An attack on him would only draw attention we don't need right now."

"Not Waylon," Leif said in agreement. "Not yet."

When I didn't respond, he dropped his hands to my shoulders. We both let out deep breaths and separated. I moved to the bed, and he stepped toward the door.

"I need to hit something," I said and slipped my foot under the bed to feel the pommel of my sword there for reassurance.

"Yes," Leif said with a nod. "We should train. You should swing a sword as though each day might be your last."

I nodded, ready to follow him into the hall and toward the sea for one of our lessons when I heard Norelli clear her throat.

"This came for you, Wren," she said and pulled an envelope

with a wax seal from her apron pocket. I met her halfway across the room, my stomach dropping to the floor when I saw the W pressed into the wax. Wendolyn.

I turned from her as I peeled the wax seal from the paper, revealing a formal invitation with my name written at the top in elegant silver.

You are invited to the royal tea party in celebration of Princess Wren Bellator's engagement. Your presence is requested on the thirteenth of August in the royal gardens at the castle of Honor Cove. Afternoon tea will be served at two. Gifts will follow.

Fucking Wendolyn.

14

The news of my engagement tea spread fast, and it was all anyone could talk about at breakfast. This was precisely why I didn't associate with my ladies-in-waiting. Wendolyn Bailey, chief among all three of them, prided herself in having any kind of status at court even if it meant being associated with a rebel princess. She came from a good family, one that produced several priests who served at Aria's altar, and her piety served only herself. She would tattle on anyone unless it meant implicating herself or preventing her promotion. You could call her a missionary of sorts, shoving her own beliefs anywhere where it would result in her gain or at least a boost in her ego.

"I hate her," I muttered to Leif across the table.

"You haven't seen her in weeks," he said.

"I wish it were longer."

"You're lucky the king removed all of your ladies from your direct service."

"It's the only gift he's ever given me," I said and lifted my eyes from the oats I had stirred on my plate until they'd become a thick paste. Leif was looking down at the table where the king had risen from his seat. The entire hall quieted moments later.

"I'm sure you have heard the rumors of an assassination attempt on my daughter's life," he said, sending my stomach plummeting into my shoes. "I would like to make it public knowledge that she is well protected and that anyone who may be connected to the attack or may bring any more threats to her life will be subject to the worst torture. No one will thwart the trial. No one will resist Aria's will and those who try will live long enough to wish they hadn't."

The king scanned the room as though waiting for someone to speak before he sank back into his chair. No one moved for a long moment before a priest from the arena stepped up and began to lead the room in prayer. I bowed my head but kept my eyes trained on Leif who looked back at me with the same concern.

"All anyone has been able to talk about today is the attack on the trial," Norelli said under her breath as we walked into the gardens where most of the members of court were. Women in flowy dresses walked the stone aisles with their arms linked, gossiping while their male suitors walked behind. Dallin and his ever-expanding club of men were gathered around the fountain. One of the men leaned over the side of the pool and pressed his face to the water, raising it to spit a mouthful back into the fountain to mimic the way the stone mermaid in the center of the pool spat a stream of water out of her mouth.

"He spits like a good lady!" Lord Rorik Raust said, his voice loud enough to carry across the gardens. Lord Elias Vonhenson handed a mug of beer back to Rorik before taking a swig of his own.

"That's how I know none of you have any experience," Dallin roared. "A real lady never spits. She swallows."

The group of them descended into howls of laughter that

drew attention from nearly everyone in the garden. Just as they lowered their voices to an acceptable level, Dallin shoved Rorik into the fountain and the group's howling drowned out any pleasant conversation again.

"Yes, the attack on the *trial*," I scoffed and led the way from the balcony to the stairs that led down to the garden. "That, and the damn tea party. That's all that's important, apparently."

"Maybe the trial will start before the tea party," Norelli said as we descended the stairs.

I opened my mouth to agree with her hope, but my thoughts went to the blessing on the ship. Nex had seen right through me. Who's to say Aria wouldn't prolong my torture here as well?

Before I could respond, movement from the left caught my attention. Lord Beau Renault was still dressed in his formal clothes from dinner, a pair of dark slacks and a button-up shirt that only made his blue eyes and blonde hair stand out more than usual. They held my attention a little too long as he rose from his bow and smiled.

"Care for an escort?" he asked.

"I'm in good company. I don't need yours," I said, forcing myself to look into his eyes despite wanting to look anywhere else. He didn't flounder the way I felt I was, however. He shrugged and stepped closer, taking my hand.

"You don't need the company of any man, but would you like mine?" he asked, lacing his fingers with mine. "Because I would very much like yours."

I was so screwed.

The silence in the garden pulled me out of the moment as I pulled my hands from his. I was more dramatic than I needed to be, making a point to step back and send a glare his way despite my heart pounding at the memory of his lips on mine.

"You put a target on your back," I hissed. "You get too close to me, you'll be the first they all try to kill in the trial."

Beau's smile barely dimmed at the words. "It's worth the news I have to tell you."

News? His smile widened. He stepped to the side and nodded his head toward the stone path. It wouldn't make his death any easier, but I walked ahead anyway, Norelli trailing close behind. He kept pace with me, not saying a word as we walked side-by-side until we had moved farther away from the other contestants and down the path toward the trees and rose bushes.

"I think we're alone now," he said as I walked, passing the first row of bushes and continuing toward the taller boxwood shrub that separated the walking path from the open field where games were often held.

"I am never alone," I told him with a snort.

"Only in libraries?" he asked.

I turned to face him, catching the amusement in his expression and feeling the heat rush to mine.

Damn him. Better yet, damn *me*. What was this anyway? If the contestants in the trial or the trial itself didn't kill him, I'd have to. Why was I even here, walking with him despite whatever he might have to tell me?

Beau starting to walk again. I followed despite the shock I was still recovering from. "When the news of your attack spread outside of the castle," he said, "a rebellion sprang up in a village not far from the Mist. It was small. They launched an attack on a road that the king's soldiers use to transport Fallen slaves from the Dark Realm. It was quelled quickly, but they did free some of the captured Fallen men and women and they stopped the slave trade operation in the area long enough."

"Why is this important to tell me?"

"Because this rebellion was near Hap."

Hap. Hap was north. I had to visualize the map from my lessons with Leif to understand just how far north that was. Hap was one of the most northern villages in the Light Realm. That meant that not only had the word of my attack traveled to the farthest parts of the realm, but it had traveled fast. My father didn't want that kind of news outside of the castle. It was why he declared such a severe punishment for anyone caught threatening my life. But I knew it wasn't about me at all. It was about the trial and preserving his claim on the throne, strengthening his ties to power through whatever marriage I would be bound to through Aria. If the word of my attack had spread that far and that fast, then there was a direct channel somewhere of people who opposed him.

It also meant that I was in a very precarious position now.

"Thank you for telling me," I said, noticing the anxious look on Norelli's face just behind him.

"Wren," Beau started. His pace had slowed just enough to keep us in the privacy of a tall shrub at the end of the path. He drew close to me, close enough to steal my breath. "Don't trust your guards."

His words were ice in my veins, chasing away all desire that had flooded my core. He was only a few inches away, his face so close to mine that I could almost brush his nose with mine. Before I could process the moment, he walked ahead. Norelli and I followed, leaving the privacy of the shrub to rejoin the path and start back toward the castle.

"I don't want to pretend like I don't know. I want to figure out which guard is taking orders from Waylon," I said, keeping my voice low.

Leif looked up from his seat at my chamber table with a serious expression that I had grown accustomed to and despised. It was a warning of sorts, telling me that my words had consequences despite whatever action I was willing to take. I didn't plan on interrogating my new guards or anything, but my mouth could get me in just as much trouble. I knew that. It didn't mean I cared, however.

"I appreciate that you both have such respect for me," Norelli said, tossing a final log onto the fire before she joined us at the table. "But most people don't. I can make my way around a room, and most will never notice me."

"What do you suggest?" Leif asked, pivoting in his chair to look at her.

My stomach twisted.

"Send me away," she said.

The room was quiet for a moment, just the crackle of the fireplace filling the room.

"What? No," I said, glancing at Leif who I was glad to see looked skeptical.

Norelli sat back in her seat. "Just for a week. Call it punishment for ruining a dress or something."

I opened my mouth to ask why she would ever suggest I send her away only to pause. The kitchen staff knew who was allergic to what, who enjoyed the company of whom … The laundresses, though, were often present for the gossip, saw the results of an intimate night, and overheard words that were meant to be secret.

"Where should I send you?" I asked with a sigh.

"Send her as a maid," Leif said as I struggled to decide which was worse. "It will be easier to go unnoticed as a maid. They are often in the kitchen. It will give you more advantages."

My chest hurt at all the possibilities for the plan to go awry.

"Sleep here tonight. Tomorrow, go to the servants' quarters," I said.

"How will I let you know what I find?" Norelli asked, leaning her arms on the table.

Leif sat forward in his chair. "I'll come to the kitchens." He sent me a knowing look as he spoke. "Wren enjoys a cup of tea before bed."

His words eased the tension in my shoulders slightly. Chamomile tea with a splash of honey. He'd fetch it for me anytime I was sick or sad or when he could tell I was on edge.

"Good. Now," Norelli said and stood from the table. "If we are finished discussing the details, I'd like to go to sleep. Great Mother knows I won't get any once I join the others."

I tried not to think about what tomorrow would bring as Leif excused himself and Norelli and I got ready for bed. Norelli had insisted on sleeping each night on the couch, which was more comfortable than anything in the servants' quarters, but tonight I made her climb into bed with me after using her own words about a good night's rest against her.

"Norelli"

"Wren," she said, firmly enough that I turned my head to look at her. She was curled up beneath the thick comforter with one arm beneath the fluffy pillow. There was a foot between us in the large bed. "I will be fine. I've endured much worse."

"I know," I said. Silence stretched between us, and I ran my thumb back and forth across the space between us for a moment as I tried to reign in all my thoughts. Part of me thought I might cry if I admitted how I felt. I wasn't used to this. I wasn't used to having friends. I wasn't even sure I'd ever really had one, never any close in age like Norelli. They were always appointed to me in some way, forced to show interest or were doing so in hope of gaining something more. Norelli was so honest and had never insisted on treating me like a princess. I shared some of my deepest thoughts with her while we folded my clothes together at night.

"When you and Leif leave after the trial starts, you don't have to wait for me. The law here may say you serve me, but I don't want to keep you from living the life you should've had."

"The life I should've had died with my parents and my village in the Mist," Norelli said with a sad smile. "I think the best way I can honor them is by helping you to spark change."

"You've already done that. You can leave. You can do whatever you want. I'll help you in whatever way," I said.

Norelli reached out and took my hand, putting an end to my fidgeting.

"You don't need me to tell you this, but you will be fine. I will be fine," she said and removed her hand from mine. She pulled the sheet closer to her chest. "You need to trust us."

"I do trust you!"

"Trust that we aren't just doing this for you and your people. Leif and I want to fight. When we leave at the start of the trial, that's what we want to do."

She held my gaze for a long moment before she let out a deep sigh and closed her eyes. I rolled to my back and did the usual assessment. My riding clothes were layered beneath my night-gown. A dagger was strapped to my right thigh. My small pack with the contraceptive tea and the shell Leif had given me was belted around my hips where my sword was sheathed. It wasn't comfortable to sleep this way, but nothing put my mind at ease more than knowing I was ready.

Part IV

O'Riah

The Goddess Aria and the God Nex were in harmony and so were their creatures within their realms until the day the air grew thick. As time went on, the world grew cluttered from death. The sun cast rays down on the sea and stole water, pulling it to the sky where clouds grew thick enough to hide the sun from the realms below. It grew cold. Aria used her power to bring life, but with no light to survive it quickly wilted. The people of the land were terrified and starving as the earth provided less food and their world grew darker.

Aria and Nex asked the Great Mother for help clearing the air. The Great Mother went to the peak of Mount Sollom and found a dragon. She took with her the body of a warrior from Aria's realm, a man who had died protecting his people. The Great Mother laid the man on the peak on a funeral pyre. She blessed his body and asked the dragon to breathe fire over the man until he turned to ash. Once this was done, O'Riah rose from the ashes.

O'Riah became the God of the Air. With wings of a dragon and the ability to wield fire, he moved clouds and commanded the wind. With fire, he scorched the dead earth so that Aria could bring forth new life. While Nex calmed storms at sea, O'Riah calmed storms of the sky. He brought forth rain from the sky when the land was in need and the world was more balanced than ever before.

15

Norelli was gone when I woke up the next morning. I pulled my nightgown off over my head, leaving on the riding gear I wore beneath it, and went to the training center to meet Leif. He stood at the railing of the balcony, watching the contestants below get stretched and ready for their workouts. Leif glanced my way as I approached and gave me a small smile before looking down at the arena.

"Who is here?" I asked him before looking over the faces on the dirt floor.

"The usual crowd. Loreign isn't here."

"He's probably at the beach swimming in his slacks," I muttered. "I don't know what to do about him in the trial."

"You feel confident that you can handle the others?" Leif asked as Lord Donovan Merry approached a practice dummy with his sword in hand.

"I've watched all but Ezra train each day. Most of them have shown all their strongest skills simply to try and impress me. Dallin is the most skilled in combat, but he hasn't shown anything that I'm concerned I can't hold my own against. The way Ezra tossed him from the ship though ..."

"There are skills yet that only you possess, little bird," Leif said quietly, his jaw tensing. It took me just a moment to realize what he meant. My mind went to the library where I kissed Beau. I felt heat creep into my face at the memory.

"Ezra made it clear that he doesn't want me in that way," I said.

Leif turned from the railing to stare at me, surprise on his face. He was quiet for a long moment, and I knew he was working through the same logic that I had.

"When I questioned his intentions, he tried to compare himself to me. He said that we weren't that different," I said and looked down at the ring. Donovan was much better than he was just a few days ago, but I was trained well enough that I saw each opening as he attacked the dummy. I saw the perfect opportunity to attack when I watched each of these men spar. They were all stronger and bigger than me, but I was quicker, and I knew that all I would need to do was be strong enough to block their attacks until I saw my chance.

Leif let out a low hum as we watched the contestants take to the ring.

"Whatever his intentions are, he kept your secret," Leif noted.

That was the part that frustrated me. I felt like I owed him and while I knew better than to put myself in that position at all, being in debt to Ezra Loreign put me on edge. A part of me trusted him as much as I hated him, but still there was something in the back of my mind that told me there was so much more to him than what I'd discovered. Not knowing your opponent came with risks and minimizing those risks was the entire reason for my daily visits to the ring. Ezra knew that as well as I did or else he too would be among the men below us now. It meant one of two things.

Ezra Loreign had other ways to learn about his opponents.

Or he was skilled enough that it made little difference to the outcome.

Leif let out a deep sigh that pulled me from my brooding. "A messenger approaches."

I looked up from the ring as two armed guards approached me, one of them a member of my newly appointed entourage. Both bowed when they stopped before us.

"Princess." The messenger was a young guard, probably no more than a few years older than I was. He was novice enough that his cheeks reddened, and he lowered his gaze to the floor when he straightened up to address me. "Lady Wendolyn Bailey asks that you join her for brunch this morning."

"Lady Wendolyn Bailey may ask, but that doesn't make her deserving of my answer," I said and turned toward the railing again. I stiffened when my guard stepped forward.

"Forgive me, Your Highness," the messenger said. "She asked that I tell you it is about seeing that your engagement tea is planned to your liking."

My guard leaned in, just close enough so I could hear his low voice.

"The king has ordered your guard to escort you to anything pertaining to the trial, formal or informal." He spoke cooly, the respectful words undermined by his steely tone that failed to hide the threat. Not only was I imprisoned by my own guards, but now I was held hostage to Wendolyn fucking Bailey's will.

"Fine," I said and turned to face them. I sent a glare at my guard before brushing past both men for the exit at the other side of the balcony. I had never visited the nobility wing. It looked much the same as the hall outside my own chamber, with gilded sconces along the trall and tapestries depicting the history of my family going back centuries. I knew the castle well enough to know which door led to Wendolyn's chamber and if it hadn't been for the young messenger darting ahead, I would've burst through the door myself.

My guard was still calling out my introduction as I entered the sitting room where Wendolyn sat before a coffee table of breakfast pastries and fruit, a few Fallen maids surrounding her with fabric samples. There was a man seated in the chair next to her with a small stack of paper resting in his lap. He moved to stand as I entered, but I waved a hand his way, my eyes set on Wendolyn who wore a rare frown.

"I want no part in planning a party that I would rather not attend in the first place," I told her.

"Princess," she greeted and let out a dramatic sigh.

I wanted to snap at her, but my guard's earlier threat still hung in the air around us.

"What do you want?" I asked, keeping my tone as even as I could. It was a task and it was still obvious that I couldn't care less about whatever petty decision she'd spent the morning agonizing over before asking me for a consult.

The man in the armchair cleared his throat. His cheeks flushed when I cast my annoyance his way, recognizing him when I did. He was one of the king's council members, Lord Thomas, a lower-tier member of sorts. I saw him on the outskirts of the room during the few meetings I had attended. He took notes or something of that nature. That would explain the stack of paper in his lap that bore the king's signet.

"His Majesty requested the details of the engagement tea in your honor. Due to the recent events that increased security, he has denied some of the guest list," Lord Thomas said.

Wendolyn groaned and pinched the bridge of her nose. "The king removed well over half of the guests invited. They've already been informed of that."

I felt a little relieved. For once, something my father ordered made things easier for me.

"Who kept their invitation?" I asked as Leif entered the room, moving around my guards so I could see the apology in his expression. He wanted me to play nice. He'd always wanted me to let my guard down with my ladies, telling me that while I did not like them they would likely be the only friends I would be allowed in the castle. To their credit, they had always been kind, some because they were expected to be and others, like Wendolyn, because being close to me made them more desirable. It didn't mean I had anything in common with them or shared the same beliefs in the slightest. If I had expressed what I really thought and felt, there was no doubt that I would bear more scars across my back than I already had.

Wendolyn deflated, sitting back against the couch. "Just your ladies-in-waiting, former ladies-in-waiting," she said in a sigh. "Us and a few other unmarried ladies at court, widows mostly."

She said the last part with the same disgust that most of the nobility did. A widow at court was a rare thing. Most of them married quickly after their husbands' deaths or didn't appear at court again. There were only two currently at court and neither had come with a male escort. They were sisters and came together in hopes of finding new husbands in person rather than through family connections. It was the biggest scandal at court before the announcement of the Trial for Marriage overshadowed it.

"If I could provide some insight," the man in the armchair said and cleared his throat, glancing nervously my way before speaking. "The king and the prince merely removed anyone that might have political motives for attending the tea."

He didn't need to reveal the truth. Women had little say. Married women, however, could be used as political pawns on their family's or husband's behalf. But I knew that it was more than a matter of removing anyone that could be a threat to me. They had stripped what was supposed to be this grand celebration of my upcoming marriage to a gathering of the disgraced. It meant that the kingdom could continue to celebrate me as a prize and my father and brother could keep me isolated from anyone I might influence.

"Cancel the tea," I said.

Wendolyn's mouth formed an appalled O.

"The castle has made preparations, and the king has ordered

that you attend," Lord Thomas said, adjusting in his seat and flipping through his packet of papers when I looked his way.

Wendolyn stood up, pushing her dark braid over her shoulder and smoothing her dress as she waved for the maids with the fabrics to come forward.

"I need to know which color you prefer for décor," she said, her renewed excitement dimming a little when she looked at me. "I promise I won't need you for any other details."

She really was insufferable, but part of me felt sorry for her for being considered a part of this. Wendolyn might have been a status-seeking succubus, but she was cleverer than people gave her credit for. Her looks were deceiving, and she used them as a tool to get what she wanted such as expensive gifts from suitors or, rumor has it, blackmail over powerful men. The morality police she may be, but no one knew the social workings of court like Wendolyn Bailey.

I suppose there are worse people to be trapped in a room with than discarded women of wisdom and individuality.

"The blue," I told her and turned on my heel.

"It's been over a week," I said. Leif had still not taken our swords from the cave, keeping us both shrouded in the shade.

"Norelli hasn't been there any of the times we've agreed to meet."

"Then go find her. Ask one of the maids."

Leif groaned and looked out at the sea before turning his crestfallen eyes on me. "I did. She's been moved to a different post in the castle."

My heart started to pick up pace. There wasn't any time to panic. Norelli needed us. She put her life on the line for me and now we couldn't protect her. That's all that mattered right now. I took a deep breath and focused my attention, thinking through all the posts. How had Leif not been able to figure out where she was?

"I want her reinstated as my maid. Once you find her, you bring her back to my chambers," I said, surprised when Leif pressed a finger to his lips. I froze, not sure what I'd expected. He linked his arm with mine and turned away from the cave.

"Your guards are not far," he whispered and led me toward the shore. We walked in silence along the beach for a while. It wasn't until we'd gone a few yards that I noticed my guards walking quietly behind, creating a wide circle around us that I hadn't noticed from the privacy of our cave. Beau's words floated to the front of my mind, chilling my skin more than the sea air.

"Beau said not to trust my guards," I whispered. "The revolt near Hap."

Leif hummed in acknowledgment. We'd discussed this before. Waylon was behind the assassination attempt. These were Waylon's guards who followed me everywhere. I knew not to trust them before Beau had even warned me, despite how chilling it was to hear him say the words aloud. Still, there was something about the days since the attack that had me unnerved, like there was something we had missed.

"During the trial, there will be a time to kill your opponents and time to spare them," he said, his voice low. "Considering who you may need by your side through the Great Mother's tests is just as important for your survival as knowing who to get rid of."

I was trading one political game for another. I wasn't good at politics. I didn't have the patience to put up with people, especially those whose work was determined only by what they had to gain. What's worse, I knew he was telling me to keep Ezra close. And as much as I wished I had just gutted him during our screaming match on the beach, I knew Leif was right. No one else in the trial would know what to expect from him. I didn't know what to expect from him, but he was keeping my secret.

"I won't combine forces with him, but I won't kill him either," I said as we approached our horses. "At least not at first."

Leif smirked as he pulled his hand free and reached for the reins of our horses. When we got back to my chamber, a team of seamstresses and maids were already there waiting. I bathed while they laid out garments and makeup and I was immediately buttoned and cinched into a blue silk dress that clung to my waist and flowed loose around my ankles. While a maid curled my hair and pinned it up, so it cascaded down my back in long brown waves, I wished Norelli were here instead. A woman slipped a pair of gilded sandals onto my feet, and I was thankfully spared the pinchy heels.

I didn't have the privacy to sneak my dagger, nor would I be able to hide it beneath the silk of my dress. This was a tea party though, so I planned to sneak the first knife I could from the table.

"You look beautiful," Leif told me when I opened the door. I took his hand, and he pressed a kiss to my knuckles while the rest of my guards took their places around us.

"All dressed up just to lounge at some tea party downstairs," I said under my breath, ignoring the gentle squeeze Leif gave my hand before releasing it.

With the guest list consisting of no more than twenty women and a rainstorm moving through since my walk with Leif, the tea party had been moved from the large garden veranda to a drawing room on the first floor of the castle. I could already hear the guests' giggles and gasps as I walked down the hall, the ominous groan of thunder outside mirroring my feelings.

My guards took their places along the wall, two of them reaching for the double doors while I listened to Leif's quick whispers about how I could manage to play nice for a single afternoon. The doors opened at the room filled with cheers and gasps; the women who weren't calling their congratulations about the upcoming trial were fawning over my dress. I was glad when the doors shut and there wasn't a single man in the room to witness the shallow conversation that ensued.

"Any of those men would be grateful to have you as a wife!"

Loura Frey said in such a tone that grated on my ears. "You look absolutely gorgeous, not to mention and the esteem you would bring to any of their families!" I took a few steps away from her with a forced smile and walked right into the arms of three of my former ladies-in-waiting. They all started to gush about the contestants at once and I could hardly tell who was speaking anymore.

I tried to tune them out by looking around the room while they talked, managing to focus on my surroundings enough that their voices blended into a chirps in the background. Just as my mind thought to look for the nearest exit, my eyes landed on a familiar face on the other side of the room. She raised her eyes to me as she took her place by the window with a tray of tarts with raspberries on top.

My muscles relaxed a little knowing Norelli was here. She was safe.

"Let's start with gifts!" Wendolyn yelled over the crowd.

That's all it took to chase away what little reprieve I'd felt.

16

Wendolyn ushered me into the center of the room where an armchair had been placed for me. I sat down and took in the scene around me. Plush couches and chairs were soon occupied by the ladies who all beamed back at me as one of the Fallen maids wheeled a large trolley of wrapped gifts to my side.

"Oh!" Wendolyn exclaimed and swatted the woman's arm with her folded-up fan. "The other trolley! I can't wait any longer."

"There's more?" I asked, eyeing the large stack of gifts that the poor maid was now wheeling away. Instead of addressing me, Wendolyn turned toward the room with flushed cheeks.

"It's customary for each of the suitors to send a gift," she said, sending the room into a fit of giggles that made me want to crawl out of my own skin.

"Yes! This is the one," Wendolyn said when another maid rolled a trolley, thankfully a smaller one, to my left side. Before I could begin to look over the display, Wendolyn lifted a small box from the top and held it up for the room to see.

"This comes from Lord Astor Willow." Wendolyn handed the

box to me as the room went quiet. I pulled the lid off the white box and lifted a pair of white silk gloves. Beautiful pearls were sewn from the wrist to the elbow. I was stunned for a moment by how gorgeous they were before I remembered that all these lavish things were coming from men eager to marry me for status.

"Next," I said and sat the gift aside, ignoring the momentary disappointment that crossed Wendolyn's face before she lifted a large box from the trolley with a groan.

"This one is from Lord Dallin Vondrelle," she said before apologizing for dropping it in my lap. It was heavy. I'd expected a much smaller box from Dallin. Lingerie didn't take up much space, after all. If it weren't for the room of gasping women, I would've tossed what was inside straight into the fireplace in the corner.

"It's beautiful!"

"You have to wear it!"

"Oh, how romantic!"

I was forced to stand to lift all the satin and tulle from the box. Dallin had sent a wedding gown, one that looked to fit perfectly and had surely taken almost a year to produce. Wendolyn took the dress from me and held it higher for the room to see before carefully draping it across an armchair she'd shooed a woman out of.

"And there's still so much more to go!" She practically skipped back to the trolley and continued handing me gift after gift, most of them jewelry, a few clutches, a couple of pairs of glittering heels.

"Of course, he'd send the largest gemstone!" Lady Earnshaw's shrill cry cut through the gasps of the crowd. "His family is the wealthiest."

"Imagine what the diamond on the wedding ring must look like!" Someone from the back of the crowd said as Wendolyn lifted the necklace from the box sent by Beau Renault. The diamond pendant was huge, obscenely so. Before I realized what she was doing, it was resting against my sternum. I looked down at it as the women cheered and I noticed the necklace hadn't been the only gift in that box. There was a bracelet lying at the bottom, a simple silver chain with a small piece of blue sea glass in the middle.

The diamond was from the Renaults, but this bracelet was from Beau alone. His family knew that to impress my father, they would have to play the same game the rest of the contests were playing. Politics and status didn't matter to Beau and it felt a little like this simple gift was a form of protest.

I slipped the bracelet on my wrist while the women were caught up in the excitement. None of them seemed to notice as we moved to the next trolley of gifts that all but one of the contestants had sent a gift.

"I know white is more traditional, but you just look so beautiful in blue," Lady Cotner told me as I sat the bra and panty set in my lap, the fourth in a row I'd pulled from a box or giftbag.

"Don't tell me you're disappointed," Lady Cotner said, her cheeks turning a deep shade of pink. "I can have the tailor send one in white."

"No, it's not that I'm disappointed," I told her and handed the fabric to Wendolyn who sat it with the growing pile of lingerie to the right.

"Oh, the poor thing's nervous!"

"Of course, she's nervous!" The eldest of the Gray widows moved through the crowd, a serious expression on her face. "All of you sit here laughing and gawking as the poor girl exposes her underwear to the whole room. The talk of marriage isn't going to suddenly make a girl comfortable with the idea of sex with some man she barely knows!"

I nearly burst into laughter at her brashness. The ladies were all so taken aback by her words that it gave me a moment to send the widow a small smile, which she returned with an eye roll of disbelief.

"Well, that's what the gel is for, Princess," the nearest woman said, nodding toward the glass jar that had come with a lacy top.

"To make it enjoyable." The moment her eyes met mine she turned bright red and looked away.

For fuck's sake.

Lady Gray spoke before I got the chance. "She doesn't need a gel to enjoy it, nor does she need a man."

"Lady Gray!" Wendolyn chided, turning to glare at the women.

"Don't act so offended," Lady Gray scoffed. "You're in a roomful of widows and unmarried women. Don't pretend like you don't all do some self-exploration during a night alone."

Lady Gray and her sister joined me in laughter. Wendolyn's struggle to maintain control of the party without rebuking me publicly only made the whole interaction that much funnier.

"I forgot to mention that there is a cake!" She clapped her hands and led the way to the long table of pastries. I stood from my chair as the women made their way to the table, not moving as Lady Gray inched her way closer.

"Thank you," I told her as the room filled with conversation again. I was sure everyone was more than happy to forget all about the dirty jokes and the way their princess laughed at them.

Lady Gray smirked, showcasing the wrinkles at the corner of her lips and eyes. "No one knows their way around female pleasure like another woman." The twinkle in her eye confirmed the rumors that swirled around court, a confirmation she meant for me alone.

"I'm sure you're right, but it wouldn't be for me, Lady Gray," I said and patted her arm. She smiled and nodded.

"Then I hope to be friends," she said.

"You are better company than most."

I kept my eyes halfway down the table where Norelli stood before the bowl of peas.

"It can be difficult in the realm, but not nearly as lonely as you would think," Lady Gray said. I had to replay the words in my head, not sure if they meant what I thought they did until I saw the warning look in her eyes. She smiled, giving my left hand a gentle squeeze, before she left me to join the crowd at the table.

No wonder the word traveled so quickly to Hap.

"Princess!"

I looked away from the Gray sisters to where Wendolyn was standing next to a three-tiered cake. My eyes settled on the serrated knife in her hand.

"Would you like to cut the cake?" Wendolyn asked.

"Yes! Of course!" I crossed the room and took the knife from her, holding Norelli's gaze for just a moment before I plunged the tip of the knife into the bottom tier of the cake and lifted a slice away. The room filled with applause.

I looked back down at the cake when someone tapped my forearm. Norelli began pointing to the knife and then the cake, nodding and then pointing to herself before doing the charade all over again.

"She is asking permission to cut the rest of the cake, Your Highness," the maid next to her said.

I opened my mouth to ask why she didn't just ask for herself but stopped. Something was wrong.

"Yes. Go ahead," I told her and extended the handle of the knife to Norelli. She took it, sliding a napkin toward me at the same time. I placed my hand flat on top of it, noticing the way the nearest Fallen maids pretended not to watch as I slipped the paring knife from the napkin and hid it between the folds of my silk skirt. I took my plate with me and moved toward the nearest armchair, using the back of it to conceal myself so I could carefully tuck the blade into the top of my stocking.

"Shall we move on to the next game?" Wendolyn asked the room, lifting a piece of paper from the table before waiting for an answer. Gods, where was the alcohol? I didn't want to endure the rest of this stupid party without it.

As though reading my mind, the double doors opened and two of my guards wheeled in trolleys with glasses of champagne.

"A gift from His Majesty and the prince," one of them

declared. The men bowed before leaving the room, closing the doors behind them to retake their posts.

"Shall we do a round of toasts?" another lady in the crowd suggested as the Fallen maids wheeled the trolley to the side of the table nearest me. The entire crew moved forward to take glasses as the women moved back to their seats. Wendolyn remained standing, the first to accept a glass and determined to be the first to speak. She turned to face me with her glass lifted as she launched into a well-rehearsed story I was sure she intended as a way to show the rest of the women that she was more important than they were.

"Princess Wren and I have known each other since nursery days. Does that sound right?" she asked, waiting for me to confirm.

"Yeah. I suppose," I told her and took a glass of champagne from one of the women.

"Princess Wren may be known as a kind of castle rebel, but she is kind, exactly the sort of strong woman that a future king needs by his side," Wendolyn continued. Only moments in and the envy was painted across the faces of most of the women in the room. I tuned out her words, knowing that she only was so closely acquainted with me because of our families and her being appointed my chief lady-in-waiting so many years ago. We hadn't spoken since my father had dismissed all my ladies months ago. On the contrary, Wendolyn made an active effort to distance herself from my actions so it wouldn't poison her chances at maintaining her status at court.

The fact that not only was she here but was selected to plan my tea party of shame was enough to tell the entire realm that she'd failed to stay in the king's favor.

"And it's for that reason that I am honored to have served you, Princess. I am beyond thankful for your kindness and for allowing me to plan this party to celebrate you," Wendolyn said and raised her glass to me.

"To Princess Wren!" the guests cheered.

I lifted my glass as the women drank, stopping just short of my lips when the light from the window fell across something green among the bubbles. I looked closer to see a single green pea sitting at the bottom of the glass. I lifted my eyes to the long table where Norelli was staring intently back at me. She shook her head, the movement so subtle that it sent chills up my spine.

"Who" Wendolyn sucked in a gasp. I looked back at her. She frowned and pressed a hand to her stomach for a moment.

"Excuse me," she said and forced a smile, her hand now fisting at the fabric across her middle. "W-Who's next?"

I heard a few whispers from the crowd and a quick glance told me that she wasn't the only one feeling ill. Several other women held their stomachs. A few more sat back in their seats.

"Something's wrong. Maybe it's the cake," a woman said and pointed a shaky hand toward the table. The Fallen maids began filing from behind the table to tend to the women, reaching them just as the first woman collapsed to the floor.

Rough hands pulled me back and I shifted my attention to Norelli's wild eyes. She sat the champagne glass on the end of the table as she pulled me toward the nearest window. My heart stopped when I looked back over the room and saw the bodies writhing silently on the floor. Wendolyn's eyes were bloodshot when they met mine, an outstretched hand pleading for help.

"Norelli, what—"

I stopped when I turned to see her shaking her head vigorously. She continued to tug me toward the nearest window, motioning to it with her free hand.

"Tell me what's wrong!"

She let go of me and smashed a fist into the window, sending the shards raining down on us. They hadn't even settled along the floor before she'd pushed me through the window and climbed out behind me. She pulled me toward the garden when I heard the bang of the double doors from the drawing room.

I didn't look back. I ran after her, chasing her toward the

stables where she finally stopped after dragging me behind a cart full of straw.

"What was that?" I asked. She shook her head again, her warm eyes swimming with tears. "Norelli, what's wrong? Tell me!"

She opened her mouth to reveal what little was left of her tongue.

It felt like my entire body had frozen. I wasn't sure what I was looking at. There was no way. Where had she been and who'd done this? I thought I might throw up and then, it felt like fire had replaced the bile in my throat, burning its way out of me.

Before I realized what I was doing, I was already striding back through the castle halls, picking up pace as I went toward that drawing room. The hallway was empty, not a single sound other than my feet as they pounded against the tile. I clenched the paring knife in my hand as I ran for the doors at the end of the hallway, amazed that there wasn't a single guard outside to stop me when I threw them open to reveal the great hall and its room full of political advisors. My father stopped mid-sentence from his throne directly ahead, a frown spreading across my brother's face next to him.

The clanging of armor followed me as men yelled for the king.

"Everyone is dead, Your Majesty!"

I recognized the voice of my head guard, and I turned to see him and my entourage running into the room, their armor bloodied.

"Who is dead?" The king's voice cut through the room and he rose from his throne.

That was the moment I chose to hurl the knife across the room, the tip sinking into the top of his wooden throne where my family's coat of arms was carved.

"Assassins!" I yelled.

No one in the room moved, my voice still echoing off the rafters. I stared straight into my father's tight expression, not intimidated in the slightest by the fury there.

"You mean to gain my attention with this?" he roared, plucking the knife from his throne.

"It worked," I said and stepped closer, only stopping when the guards flanking his platform stepped forward. They froze when the king raised his hands.

"What is the meaning of this?" he asked, raising his eyes to the guards behind me.

"All of the ladies attending my tea party down the hall were delivered poisoned champagne by the assassin you refuse to properly investigate," I yelled over the head guard.

"Everyone is dead, Your Majesty, including the Fallen maids who poisoned the ladies and led the attack," the guard said behind me. I whirled around to face him. He stared straight ahead, dripping blood onto the floor from the sword in his hand.

"*You* killed them," I told him. I was shaking with anger. They were going to pin the entire attack on those poor women, the Fallen slaves who had done nothing but try to reverse the poison after it was too late.

I turned when I heard my father running toward me, facing him just in time to receive the sharp slap across my face that nearly sent me to the ground. My vision blurred, making my stomach churn.

"LOOK AT ME!"

I straightened up and forced my eyes to focus on his scarlet face. I couldn't help myself. I doubted I'd ever get the chance again, so I smiled.

"I am a prize for no man, and I belong to no one," I told him, watching the way his jaw tightened.

"No prize at all," he said, his velvety voice such a contradiction to the anger in his expression that it sent goosebumps over my skin.

I gasped when he grabbed the top of my hair, pulling my back against his chest. My eyes landed on Leif as he ran into the room, coming to an abrupt stop next to the guards. His eyes were wide with fear and I could see the plea ready to fall from his lips before my father spoke again.

"Let me remind you and all who lay eyes on your former beauty who you belong to," he said. He raised the knife before me, pressing it to my face and dragging it slowly down my cheekbone. I clenched my teeth against my scream, tears from the pain blurring my vision of Leif sinking to his knees in the middle of the room.

I clapped my hand to my cheek when he released me, whirling around to face him as the floor grew slick under my feet from my blood. His expression remained neutral, as though inflicting pain on me had brought him peace.

"Sir Folee," he said as he turned and stepped back up the platform to his throne. "Take the princess to her chamber. The rest of the court can bear witness to my tolerance for disobedience."

He took his seat, and Waylon sent a satisfied smile my way as Leif tugged my arm. I ripped it away and stormed from the room, leaving a trail of hot blood after me.

17

I wanted to refuse treatment and let the gash scar as a battle wound. Maybe it would remind the king that despite his every move to cage me, I can still manage to stand against him. If it repelled suitors, even better.

Leif refused to put up with my protest and I decided after seeing the hurt in his eyes that the cut meant something else to him. I wouldn't let him see me like this if it meant feeling what I saw in his eyes. So, the night ended with a visit to the infirmary and stitches.

Norelli was missing and despite the entire castle knowing by the end of the night about the attack and my punishment in the throne room, no one seemed to notice among the dead that one of the maids was missing. Good. I hoped it meant she was safe. I hoped that she'd left Honor Cover entirely and was on her way back to the Mist. Leif swore that he didn't know about how or for what reason she had lost her tongue. The memory of her open mouth would haunt me for a long time and I couldn't chase away the guilt I felt for agreeing to let her leave my employ.

Leif stayed with me overnight and despite my insistence, he

didn't leave when I bathed and got dressed the next morning. I put off going to breakfast as long as I could, accepting that it made things worse in some ways since I'd have to walk into a room of gawking people. I dried my hair as much as I could, piling it into a bun at the crown of my head, and dressed in my favorite riding clothes. If my punishment was meant to put an end to the last bit of allure I held for the crown as their princess, then I was done with dressing the part. Leif didn't utter a word about my appearance when I came from the bathroom. He opened the door and paused, his hand going to the hilt of his sword and mine going to the dagger tucked in the waistband of my pants.

"Apparently, not sending a gift is a faux pas," a deep voice said.

I brushed past Leif in the doorway as Ezra rose from his seat against the opposite wall. He looked as though he'd been there a long time and rose as though his joints were stiff. He lifted a medium-sized box from the floor.

"I told you that the next time—"

"If someone's going to gut me, I'd want them to do it with a proper weapon," Ezra said and shoved the box into my hands. I kept my eyes on his tense expression for a moment before I took a step back and tugged off the lid of the box. I stared down at the weapon inside for a long moment. I'd expected a dagger based on his words and the size of the box, but I hadn't expected anything like this.

The dagger had a hilt made of dark metal, at least I thought it was. It was wrapped in dark leather, only it didn't quite look rough the way leather did. It felt smooth and comfortable to wield. Instead of a blade, a sharp tooth the size of my forearm tapered to such a deadly point that it looked like it would snap with its first use. I lifted the dagger from the box, the strange leather even more comfortable than I had expected, and a closer look at the tooth revealed the most subtle serrated edge. This dagger would easily cut through any opponent and make removing it just as deadly. I wondered if more force would be needed to pull it from a body than any dagger I was used to.

"Where did you get this?" I asked and looked up from the dagger.

Ezra looked unbothered as he adjusted his clothes. He was dressed casually but had his sword belted at his hip. "Bone Breaker of the Mountain," he said looking down the hallway before back at me. "Dragon's teeth are constantly imbibed in dragon fire, making them stronger than steel no matter how old. They remain as sharp as when they were hatched. The hilt is wrapped in a dragon wing. It's nearly impenetrable while feeling like velvet. Easy to grip. Comfortable to hold."

"You know a lot about dragons."

He snorted, a small smirk pulling at the corner of his mouth. "The Bone Breaker of the Mountain rides the biggest dragon."

"You mean *rode*?"

"Rode," Ezra agreed with a nod. "The tooth in that dagger came from a small dragon."

"How would you know?"

"I didn't wander onto that battlefield and decide to kill the Fallen's prince. I've seen my fair share of battles and I've seen enough dragons to know," Ezra said, glancing down the hall again.

"Did you come here for me or are you expecting someone else?" I asked, pulling his attention back. He was annoyed. I could see his broad shoulders tense.

"You ask a lot of questions."

"You give strange engagement gifts to princesses."

"Since when do you give a fuck about gemstones and expensive dresses?"

"Since when do you know me?"

"I've known you long enough, Princess," Ezra said, taking a slow step forward. He kept his challenging eyes on me. After a long moment, he smiled and stepped back again.

"You know nothing," I told him and after a beat, I swung the dagger at him. His movement was so quick that I almost missed it.

He stepped back just far enough that the dagger nearly touched the wisps of his hair around his face.

"I know you're not like them and that's enough," Ezra said, sending me a final curious glance before starting down the opposite side of the hall from the stairs. He wasn't heading to breakfast, that was obvious, and I almost moved to follow him before Leif reminded me that he was still waiting for me to follow.

"You'll want to keep hold of that blade as long as you can, but for now you should leave it in your chamber," Leif instructed.

I stashed the dragon tooth dagger under my mattress with the rest of the things I planned to take into the trial, and Leif and I went down to the hall for breakfast. It was just as busy as I feared it would be and every person we passed either openly stared at my bandaged cheek or did a bad job pretending not to. I didn't want to give Waylon or the king any satisfaction in shaming me, so we took our normal places at the front table, sitting close enough to Waylon that I could hear the annoyance in his voice as he endured Lord Nicholas Fenrick's story about surviving some bear attack in the forest.

No one approached me and Leif and I ate in silence. I was surprised when not even Waylon uttered an insult, finishing his meal and then moving to join the king at his raised table where he listened to one of his advisors read from a piece of parchment. I just happened to be watching them when my father's bored expression turned to intrigue. He pushed the advisor's hands away, sending the parchment fluttering to the floor. I followed his gaze to the end of the hall where the large figure strode into the room with a burlap sack clutched in his right hand.

Ezra moved with ease for someone of his size, crossing the room like a predator stalking his prey. The room quieted with each step he took until the only sound was of his boots across the floor. He tossed the sack on the steps of the podium, the opening of it falling backward and allowing four heads to roll out and settle around him. I recognized one of those terrified expressions as the head of my new guard. Ezra bowed before straightening up.

Waylon stood. "What did you—"

The king extended his arm toward him, keeping him from moving any farther toward the knight.

"Your Majesty," Ezra addressed as he pulled a sliver of paper from his pocket and flattened it out to read. "The note says, *Pass the message on to all those assigned to guard Princess Wren. Allow the poison to work. When the room is silent, ensure everyone there has been dealt with. The rumor of an assassin ends with the Fallen maids.*"

I couldn't believe it. I'd never seen my father or my brother look so surprised before, at a loss. It took a moment for either of them to move.

"Father," Waylon started. Our father lifted another hand for him to be quiet.

"Thank you, Sir Loreign, for ending the threat to my daughter. You may have preserved the sanctity of the Trial for Marriage," the king said, his tone strained.

Ezra bowed again before approaching with the note held out. He handed it to the king and then handed something to Waylon that only made his eyes bulge more with fury. They shook hands and from our distance, anyone except for Leif and I would have interpreted the gesture as gratitude.

As much as I hated him, I had to admit that the move was brilliant. How had he gotten the note? How had he attacked every member of my guard without being caught?

Ezra gave a final bow, though not bending to the full extent, before turning on his heel and leaving the room.

Ezra made appearances for meals alone and only long enough to fill his plate and take it with him. The air was tense around the castle in the days following my second assassination attempt. The king was silent, and I hadn't seen Waylon since his guards' heads were presented to him at breakfast. Neither of them were present when the bodies of the ladies who died at the tea party were blessed by one of Aria's priests and carted away, destined to meet their final resting places back in their home cities.

I had Leif take all of the gifts I'd received and sell them, all but the sea glass bracelet that just seemed too different from the other gifts. I kept it around my left wrist. Something about the cheap bracelet coming from a man who could afford the world reminded me that not everyone was what they seemed. So, I kept the bracelet and divided the money Leif returned with among the families of the deceased who had bothered to attend the send-off.

I looked away from the library window when I heard foot-steps stop behind me.

"Did you find her?" I asked as I turned, my stomach sinking when it wasn't Leif standing there.

"She's gone, isn't she? Your friend?" Beau asked. He was dressed for dinner in a pair of blue slacks and a matching shirt with silver woven throughout. It made his blond hair and blue eyes look so innocent that my stomach hurt knowing he was one among the group of blood-thirsty contestants.

"I hope so," I told him and stood from my armchair.

Beau exhaled deeply as he walked closer. He kept his eyes on the choppy sea past the library windows as he leaned against the bookshelf across from me. "I'm sorry," he said and finally turned those honest eyes on me. They were like ice but in the best way. They cooled the anger that had been smoldering inside me for days, easing the pain of years of solitude and forced obedience. "I'm sorry about your ladies, the maids at that party, your friend, for you ..."

"You're the one who deserves pity, not me," I said and crossed my arms. "Your entire life, everything you are capable of and deserve, squandered on some damn trial for no other reason than to have your family name listed in the history books in association with Aria's blessing."

"I grew up with more than most," Beau said. "My parents were kinder than most of those at court. My village was welcoming and treated me like anyone else, not like some god the way they do here. I had a good life and if my name gets written into the history books it won't be because of Aria's blessing, but because yours will be there with mine. I would rather kneel at your feet than any goddess's who believes some lives are worth more than others."

Something snapped within me at his words, and it felt like the shards of whatever that deep thing was had embedded in dozens of pieces in my chest. My eyes stung as I looked into his face. I took a deep breath, looking for anything that would chase away the tears, anything to still my emotions other than those blue eyes.

"Would you look at me the way you do if I were just the castle whore?" I asked, surprised he didn't wince at the bite in my voice the way he normally did. He kept his expression soft, even giving me a somber smile. He took a step closer to take my hand, his fingers brushing the sea glass bracelet before he looked up at me again.

"You're the most beautiful whore in the realm," he said with a chuckle.

"I want you to treat me like one," I whispered, resting my hands against his chest. I was surprised by the muscles I felt there. He looked up from my hands, mouth parted in shock and cheeks flushed.

"Wren," Beau pleaded despite wrapping an arm around my back. His fingers stilled just short of the cut on my cheek before he traced a finger along my jaw, down to my chin.

"Do you really want to die never knowing what it feels like to be touched?" I asked.

"I could've until I met you," he said, tipping my chin up as his lips brushed mine.

He was sweet, the kiss slow and only deepening when I felt something tense deep in my gut and a moan slipped out between our lips. I pulled his shirt free from his slacks, working my way up the buttons as quickly as I could as he loosened the ties on my riding pants.

Of all the days to wear fucking pants instead of a skirt.

I pushed his hands away and peeled the pants off myself, straightening up as he finished undoing the last of the buttons on his shirt so that it hung open to reveal muscles I was sure hadn't existed until he entered the trial. I pulled my shirt over my head, still wearing my bra when he pressed his body against mine.

He lifted me and I wrapped my legs around him, sliding against the length of him as he backed into the armchair. When he sank into the cushions, and I settled onto his lap, I felt a sharp pinch between my legs and I clenched around him for a moment, his eyes searching my face as his hands brushed my hair from my face.

"Good?" he asked, his mouth parting and his head tipping back when I began to move. "Good. Good. Gods!"

He gripped my hips as I picked up the pace. I relished in the soreness I felt with each thrust. He let out a loud groan that I muted with a kiss, feeling my own desire building only to consume me a moment later. I let out a final moan and pulled back, resting my forehead against his chest as the aftershocks wracked through my body with each heavy breath. I leaned against him as my breathing slowed, listening to the pounding of his heart beneath me. With a single pass of those gentle hands through my hair, I felt my eyes sting again.

Fuck.

I needed just a moment to gather myself, blink away the tears, and then I straightened up. I climbed off of him and found my pants and underwear in a pile a few feet away. I heard him stand behind me as I pulled my clothes on, not looking his way until I'd flattened my shirt.

"Wren, if the trial begins before I see you again," Beau started, halting me in place. I'd taken just a few steps toward the aisle when he'd spoken, hoping to maintain my composure. I kept my eyes on the floor between us, pretending to adjust the hem of my shirt. "You deserve to be loved, deeply so, by someone who deserves you. However this trial ends, don't let everything else end with it."

He'd never sounded so strong before. It was strange. I was so used to the soft, innocent Beau Renault, not this new, hardened version. I glanced up at him, seeing this new strength in the set of his jaw and the roundness of his shoulders.

"So do you." I knew the comment meant little. Days. Another week. It didn't matter how long we had until the trial began. Beau would not survive it to find the happiness he deserved.

I didn't give him a second look before I started down the long aisle of bookshelves.

18

"What are you planning to carry with you?" Leif asked.

I looked up from the swirls I'd drawn in the sand between us with the dragon tooth dagger. We'd been over the same questions so many times, every time that we met for lessons, that I couldn't tell anymore if he was asking me to be sure I was prepared or to assure himself that I was.

"My sword belt. I keep this dagger on it." I held up the tooth by the hilt. As much as I loved the dagger Leif gave me, taking Ezra's me with for the sole purpose of killing him with it was too appealing. "I have my sword. I also keep a pouch with other things I may need."

"What other things?"

"The contraceptive tea, some bandages, and a few doses of tonics for ailments."

Leif nodded. The ocean waves weren't as choppy as normal. They were almost calm, a sight so unusual to Honor Cove that it felt like the entire city had gone silent in reverence.

"There was a maid that Norelli spoke to, a laundress," Leif said.

I let the point of the dragon tooth sink deep into the sand between my knees as I looked up at his relieved expression. The corners of his mouth twitched upward slightly.

"She's okay?" I asked.

He shrugged. "The laundress said that she packed all of her things. That was after the tea party. The woman hadn't seen her since, so she couldn't tell me anything else, just that all of her things were gone."

I imagined her walking through the dark trees of the Mist, heading back to her home village like I'd hoped she would once this was all over. Leif looked just as relieved as I felt. Before I could recover from my daydream, he'd taken the dagger from me and swiped away all the swirls in the sand before us.

"We need to discuss what's ahead," he said and began carving new symbols into the sand.

"We already discussed this when you told me I couldn't just start the trial by hacking all the men apart," I said. I was still a little frustrated by this. I knew I needed to be strategic, but I didn't want to work with any of the other men, especially since I'd have to kill them in the end if the elements didn't kill them first.

"I mean what comes after the trial," Leif said. I realized now that the symbols weren't stand-ins for the contestants like the last time we sat in this cave for lessons. He'd drawn a map of the realm. "The men are fighting to marry you, so chances are that you will survive the trial even as you try to steer clear of them for your own protection."

Leif shot me a warning look before he continued drawing more symbols with the dagger. The plan was that I would ally with as few of the men as possible. Beau Renault was the only one I cared to have by my side, but Leif had insisted that I keep Ezra Loreign close since he had been keeping my entry into the trial secret this whole time. After he'd killed my guards and presented their heads to Waylon, Leif was even more insistent that I use him. He told me that the man was already allied to me and had shown as much despite my protests.

"The trial starts. I keep Beau and Ezra close and get the hell away from the other men until the gods force us all together again. By then, I deal with whoever is left until it's just me," I said. I'd played the scenes over and over in my mind each night before bed just in case the next time I opened my eyes I was faced with fate.

Leif circled a little square in the sand that he'd drawn with the tip of the dagger.

"Winning will be just the beginning. The end of the trial is public. The whole castle will be there to meet the winner at Aria's Stone." Leif drew a line from the square parallel to a wavy line I assumed was the sea before drawing another circle and then sinking the tip of the dagger in the center. He sat back and looked up at me, his serious expression sending chills along my exposed arms.

"I'll meet you in the Mist," I told him. My stomach had already twisted into such a knot that I knew it didn't matter. This wasn't the plan. It didn't make sense to flee the trial and head north along the sea.

"You have sympathizers among the seafaring villages in the north. You've never traveled that way, so no one will recognize you."

"It will take twice as long to get to the Mist if I do that, and Hap is near the border. With the recent rebellions, I'll have much better luck of collecting a following."

"And it will be expected of you," Leif said and pointed to me with his index finger. "Going to Hap is the last thing you should do after the trial. You need to evade capture first. Once the trial starts, I will leave the castle and gather supporters for you near the border. I don't want you anywhere near the fray in the early stages. Once you've left the trial and made your way up the coast, I will have troops waiting for you. As long as everything has gone well, we will have a stronghold established for you so that it is safe for you to join the rebellion."

I was shocked. This wasn't at all what I had imagined. I was going to be at the forefront of the rebellion. I wanted to be the one setting the groundwork, not just the queen. I'd spent my whole life in combat training for battlefields, not throne rooms.

"I don't want to join the rebellion. I want to lead it," I said and snatched the dagger from the sand. I jabbed it back into the hilt at my waist and draped my skirt over the top.

"Wren," Leif said as I got to my feet. I made it as far as the mouth of the cave before he was at my side. "If you don't stay safe in the days following the trial then there will be no rebellion."

How long would I have to wait to act? How much longer would it take to undo all the tyranny, all the death that had ravished my country?

"Your Highness," a man said.

I turned from Leif to see three castle soldiers. They bowed, the man nearest me motioning for us to follow. Three horses waited next to ours just beyond the cave.

"The king has news regarding your assassination attempt that he would like to share with you," the man said.

I glanced at Leif who looked just as surprised as I felt.

"Where are we going?" I asked as we went to the horses. Two of the guards mounted their horses while Leif led mine to me. I didn't move as I waited for the man to speak. He glanced hesitantly at his comrades before he addressed me again.

"He asked that we escort you to his chambers," he said and moved to help me onto my horse.

Before he could touch me, I stepped into the stirrup and swung my leg over the saddle. I peered down at the man as I got adjusted in my seat.

"I know the way," I told him and urged my horse ahead. A smile tugged at my lips as I heard the men scramble behind me to get into formation. Leif was at my side by the time I reached the stables, just long enough for me to see the humor in his expression as I climbed down and allowed one of the stable hands to tend to my horse.

The three soldiers were kinder than most and didn't bother asking me to wait for them. They fell in line behind me, giving me a comfortable distance between them that made me feel less like a prisoner than I normally would. The corridor outside my father's chambers was lined with his usual guards. I slowed when I noticed one staring as I approached. No. Several of them were watching me as though I might do something. There was caution in their eyes.

The room was empty aside from the necessary people. The king sat at his round table and where his battle map usually sat was a stack of papers and a gilded plate covered with a matching cloche. Despite the early hours, he had a glass of wine sitting next to the meal. Waylon lifted his glass to his smug smile before taking a long drink. Two guards stood to one side, neither looking amused to be there.

"They say you have news about my assassin," I said as I joined them. My sharp tone didn't garner a single pointed look. Waylon reached for the bottle and took an extra glass from the bar table along the wall behind him.

"Have a drink, sister," he said as he filled the glass. "There is no more threat to your life. You don't have any guards anymore. It sounds like we all get exactly what we wanted all along." Waylon scooted the glass across the table to me. I left it on the edge while he took a swig from the bottle.

"What do you know?" I asked, looking from my smiling brother to our father. He leaned back in his seat, turning his glass so the red wine swirled slowly.

"You have no ladies, no guard," the king said and glanced at Leif before looking back at me curiously. "Do you feel safe?"

I wasn't sure what he expected me to say. Surely, the point in detailing my lack of entourage was to make me feel alone. I felt less alone now than I did when I was surrounded by people. I was much happier without a team than with one.

"Should I not?" I asked and motioned toward Leif. "I am surrounded by only those I trust. I don't see any reason I can't keep myself safe, especially when those far more qualified in that area have failed."

Waylon's smile dimmed before he took another drink from his glass. My father sat his glass on the table and leaned forward. He raised his eyes to me and though he was sitting down, there was such a shift in the air between us that it felt like he was standing. I hated him for it. I hated the subtle way he managed to shift the tension in the room in his favor. I stilled my racing heart against the hate burning a hole in my chest. I willed myself to focus on exuding the same level of calm that was there in his dead eyes.

"Being the loving father I am, I did launch an investigation into your assassin as you asked," he said and scooted the domed plate in front of him. He tapped the gilded top once so that a metallic hum resonated through the room. "Sir Ezra took care of the assassins. Your brother and I saw to the rest of the investigation."

Waylon laughed, and when our father motioned to him, he plucked the cloche off the plate to reveal a severed head. My stomach turned so violently that I nearly vomited on the table. I kept my eyes focused on a spot at the end of the table, not able to look at her without tasting bile at the back of my throat.

"There's a reason they're our enemies," the king said and slid the plate across the table until it was on the edge just inches from me. I could only muster a single look, a glance over Norelli's strong cheekbones and thick hair. I lifted my eyes to his. The king was standing just a foot away now, such a serious glare on his face that it cooled my skin. "Speak against me, lose your tongue. Act against me, lose your head."

I lunged. A pair of arms wrapped around my middle before I could get within inches of my father.

"Sir Folee, take the princess back to her chambers and see that she remains there," the king ordered.

Leif kept a tight grip on my arm as he led me from the room. He didn't let go, not even when I cooperated and hurried down the hall toward my chambers. He kept pace with me, a hand gripping my bicep so tight that I wondered if it would bruise. After throwing open the door to my room, I ripped my arm from his and kicked the chair away from the round table. It slid into the bar table and a bottle and several glasses shattered against the floor.

"Wren!"

"Fuck you!" I turned to face him, watching as his mouth parted in shock. "I will not survive this trial to bide my time in hiding. I want the country to know when I win. I want every soul in the Light and Dark Realms to know that I stood against my father's tyranny. No."

"Think of the long-term, little bird, and stay your wings for the time being."

"I need to be alone. I need you to leave," I blurted. I raised my hands to push him away but paused. I lowered them to my side without touching him, and let out a deep breath.

Leif raised his right hand as though to touch me and that's when I tasted the salt on my lips. He nodded and lowered his arm.

"Okay," he said. We stayed there for a long moment before he turned and left the room.

It started storming overnight and the rhythmic thunder and churning of the rain on the windows matched my aching heart. The sickness crept into my gut more and more until it finally pulled me from my nightmares. I was freezing. Not only that, I was wet. I ran my hand along the fabric beneath me and found small pools of water. I wondered for a moment if I'd pissed myself before I realized the fabric beneath me wasn't my mattress. It was hard, like I'd rolled onto the floor during my nightmares.

Thunder roared outside and I heard someone groan to my right. It was too dark to see anything as I tossed the sheets back and pulled the dragon tooth dagger free from my hip.

"Who's there?" I asked.

"Show yourself!"

"Wren?"

I recognized the second voice. That was Beau. I crawled to the edge of the fabric, confirming my suspicions that I was lying on the ground. Another roar of thunder sounded around us along with a great creaking sound. The floor swayed beneath me as I climbed to my feet. There was another groaning sound, this one vibrating through the floor before thunder sounded, and I was suddenly tossed off my feet.

I heard several other men yell. I landed hard against someone who let out a groan into my ear. I scrambled away from him and straight into someone else's feet.

"What's going on?" Lord Soren Yonder asked as a series of blue lights flashed through the room from a hole in the ceiling.

I saw the ghostly expressions of a few of the other contestants for just moments, long enough to know that this was the start of the trial, and we were below the deck of a ship.

"All hands on deck!" Lord Dallin Vondrelle barked his orders like the captain he was, prompting everyone to scramble up the steps to the deck as the ship rocked. The rain was so heavy that it was hard to see the men as they raced around the deck. Dallin yelled more orders at the few of us who had never manned a ship, his commands getting lost in the thunder.

"Reduce the sails!" Dallin's call was rough over the thunder.

Lord Rorik Raust and Lord Nicholas Fenrick brushed past me for a bundle of ropes on the deck. We were nearly knocked off our feet as the ship hit a rough wave to the right. Someone yelled to hold on as a wall of water rose over the starboard side. I ran for the main mast, the water hitting me hard and ripping my fingers away from the wood. I gasped and inhaled a mouthful of salt-water as I hit the rail. A scream echoed through the air as a body flew past me.

"One man down!" Dallin let out a laugh from the helm.

"This ship is going to break apart!" Rorik left Nicholas, still fighting to gain control of the ropes, to stride toward Dallin behind the wheel.

"Only if you don't reduce the sails," Dallin said. I saw his gaze move from Rorik to me, his expression slack.

The ship let out a groan and then there was a snap from above. I moved just in time to avoid being smashed by the mast, but not fast enough to avoid the sail. The white fabric settled around me. I knew better than to try fighting my way to the edge. I pulled the dragon tooth dagger free and stabbed it through the fabric above me, easily cutting a hole large enough to wiggle through as the sail settled onto the flooding deck.

"Stupid woman!" Dallin lunged for me. He grabbed the top of my hair and tossed me aside. Before I landed on my back, I swiped the dagger across his chest. A line of red seeped through his shirt as he let out a yell. He'd taken just a few steps toward me when someone slammed into him from behind. The pair of men toppled into the railing next to me.

"Don't touch her, you bastard!" Beau landed a punch on Dallin's cheek before he was gripped by the front of his shirt and hauled to the railing. Dallin punched him repeatedly, his knuckles streaked with red when he moved his hands to Beau's shirt.

"This is for trying to claim what's mine," Dallin said before pushing Beau over the railing. I shoved my dagger into the hilt and no sooner had Beau vanished beneath the choppy water than I dove after him. The roar of the storm was immediately cut off by the eerie calmness of the sea. Beau wasn't far beneath the surface, but he was bleeding and struggling to catch his bearings after the beating he'd taken.

I draped his arm over my shoulders and with my guidance, he was able to help kick to the surface. There was an explosion of sound as we both gasped for air. The sky was lit by a web of lightning and the thunder was so loud that I almost missed the sound of wood creaking and snapping. I looked toward the ship and saw that the remaining masts were crossed, separated from the deck and entwined by their sails. The deck was now so flooded that it was level with the sea and the few men that remained onboard were running across the deck to find a way to safely abandon the sinking ship.

"Princess!"

I felt someone's hand on me. I swung my arm to fight them off, but I was pulled away from Beau and into a rowboat where Lord Magnus Ode and Lord Elias Vonhenson waited.

"Let's get rid of Renault," Magnus said and drew his sword. He raised it above his head, the point positioned above Beau as he bobbed, barely conscious in the water below.

"No!" I threw myself at him, sending the boat just off balance enough that all three of us were sent back into the water. I was pulled under by a pair of arms, held underwater long enough that I knew it was intentional.

"I've got you. You're okay," Magnus said after towing me above the waves.

"Let go of me!"

"You shouldn't be here, Princess."

"Let. Go. Of. Me!" I drove the dragon tooth dagger into his gut, feeling the water warm between us as I stared into his wide eyes. I let out another yell and stabbed his stomach a final time before pushing away and turning to look for Beau.

"Beau!" Panic rose into my throat, closing off my airway as I scoured the waves and saw no one. I shouldn't have been worried about him. I shouldn't have cared. He wouldn't survive anyway. Still, I didn't want to be alone in this yet.

"Hold him or take the boat!"

I whirled around to see Ezra, his dark curls slicked away from his face while he kept Beau's unconscious body afloat. I turned toward the boat just a few feet away from us. Elias was pulling himself back into it from the far side, his eyes landing on me as I began swimming.

"We can be allies, Princess," Elias said as I approached.

I gripped the edge of the boat and rather than pull myself over the edge, I used my momentum to drive the dagger into his chest.

His arms were still extended to help me aboard as he crumpled to the bottom. I willed my aching muscles to pull myself over the edge where I fell into the growing pool of blood at the bottom of the rowboat. When I turned, Ezra was already there with Beau halfway lifted onto the edge. My arms screamed in protest as I helped to pull his limp body the rest of the way, collapsing next to him.

I let my head rest against the wooden floor as I looked at Beau's battered face. His nose continued to leak a slow stream of blood. His lip was split and there was a cut on his cheek. His skin had already started to bruise just below his eye. Other than the injuries, he looked peaceful and that was when I realized how quiet it was.

I looked up at the gray sky, not the same black clouds from before. The waves were not nearly as choppy and the lightning and thunder that remained came from miles west of us. Ezra stood tall above me and I tightened my grip on the dagger when he leaned down, expecting him to reach for me and not Elias. He easily lifted the man's body and tossed it into the sea before taking a seat in front of me. He pulled out a pair of oars from the bottom of the boat and fixed them into the crutches.

"Easy, Princess," Ezra said as he began rowing.

"I just killed two men without your help. I don't need your help rowing ashore."

"I wouldn't have given you that dagger if I didn't trust you'd know how and when to use it," he said with a laugh.

I wanted to do it. It would be one less man in this stupid trial, but Ezra seemed more skilled than the others and surviving this would be much easier with his help than alone. I turned my eyes from the large knight to Beau on the boat's floor. My chest ached as I looked at his bloodied and bruised face knowing there was far worse ahead of us.

Even if I did survive the trial to win my freedom, I wasn't so sure it would feel like I won at all.

Part V

SHE WAS PLUCKED FROM THE SEA

EXCERPT FROM THE BOOK OF THE GREAT MOTHER

While sailing the sea, Aria's ship was attacked by a beast and sank. Aria struggled to the surface where the rough waters clawed at her robes and pulled her under each time she came up for a breath. She called out for help, reaching for Nex, but before he could answer her call, another pulled her from the waters.

O'Riah lifted her from the sea and rose to the sky with her tucked to his chest. She looked up at his handsome face, red-brown wings easily cutting through the salty sky, and horns tapered backward from his temples. She was so captivated by him that she allowed him to take her to his realm, to Mount Sollom where they fell in love and their realms grew warm and life blossomed between the two like never before.

All was well on land, but the seas grew treacherous. Nex was enraged that O'Riah overstepped his authority in his realm. He was angry that Aria would allow O'Riah to save her before him. It was then that the seas grew too dangerous for any of the realms to traverse. All ships in the sea sank and no more attempted to sail the waters again.

While Aria and O'Riah grew closer and their realms strengthened, Nex's anger only grew and so did a plan to separate O'Riah and Aria.

"Are you sure he's alive?" Ezra asked me as he rowed toward the beach. We were the only contestants that managed to get a boat. The others were specks bobbing in the sea behind us. We would have at least twenty minutes before anyone else met us on shore, twenty minutes of a head start that I intended to use. There were more important things now than defeating opponents, like food and water and resuscitating Beau who still lay limp across my lap.

"He's breathing," I said, checking again for a pulse and feeling my muscles relax at the thrum beneath my fingers.

Ezra continued to row, each stroke a powerful pull that only quickened our pace once the tide worked in our favor. He studied me for a moment as he rowed, dark eyes that made reading his thoughts impossible. One more reason he was dangerous.

"You're covered in blood," he said.

The way he said it told me he was commenting on my response and not my appearance. My nightdress was thick enough that the blood didn't bleed through, but I could smell it and feel the weight of it pulling down the front of my dress. The fabric was too valuable and not because it was handmade by the realm's most renowned designer. Once on the beach, the fabric could become a bandage, shade, and more if needed. I knew that. Ezra knew that. He was just testing to see what I knew.

"I'll wash once we reach shore," I said. I looked down as Beau groaned. His eyes grew wide as he looked up at me and then sat up as he noticed Ezra, reaching for the dagger at his hip.

"It's all right, Beau," I assured him. "We are all together."

He winced and pressed a hand to his temple. "What do you mean we're together?"

"If you'd rather take your chances alone, you can get out of our boat," Ezra told him.

I glared his way before turning Beau's face so I could inspect his injuries. The bleeding had stopped a few minutes ago, but the bruise under his eye was swollen enough that he couldn't open it all the way.

"How do you feel?" I asked.

"Like I got beat up," he said with a wince. "My head hurts."

"Do you think he has a concussion?" Ezra asked me. He paused for a moment before going back to rowing. Clearly, I hadn't done a good job of hiding my ignorance.

"I've been worse," Beau said, lowering his hand to mine in my lap. I pulled my hand away. Beau frowned. Ezra looked annoyed and focused on a spot to the right of us.

Fuck me.

"We need to find water," I said and ripped the slit in my dress the rest of the way up my leg, tired of the way it was hugging my hips. I found the slit along the other leg and did the same. "Unless you need medical care, Beau, I think we should head straight for the trees." I pointed toward the thick expanse of palms several yards beyond the beach.

"Should we take the boat with us for shelter or maybe even just firewood?" Beau asked as Ezra dropped the oars into the bottom of the boat. We were close enough to shore now that we could ride the tide most of the way to shore.

"It's not worth the hassle," I told him, standing up when Ezra did. "It's too cumbersome."

"I can do it alone," Ezra said when I stepped over the side of the boat after him. The water rose to my waist. He was tall enough that the water was just above his knee and I could see from the twitch at the corner of his lips that he knew I'd misjudged the depth.

"It's faster with two," I told him and took hold of the side of the boat, making damn sure the tide wasn't going to affect my work. He didn't object, and together we pulled the boat toward the beach until it started to scrape against the sand below. Beau got out and helped us pull it the rest of the way.

"Everyone has weapons, I hope," Ezra said, his gaze landing on Beau.

"I have a sword and a dagger," I said, hoping to distract from the tension between the two as we trudged the last few feet through the shallow water. Now on shore, it was obvious that we were all armed. Ezra was dressed like he was any other day except with more leather. His long hair was pulled back the way it normally was, a small bun at the crown of his head. He wore a pair of sturdy pants and a long-sleeved shirt. The only difference from a normal day was the thick belt around his hips bearing his sword and dagger and the leather bracers along his forearms.

"I have a sword," Beau said despite it being obvious. I was glad. Part of me worried that he hadn't been taking the same precautions. There weren't many details recorded about the Trial for Marriage, but the fact that contestants usually vanished in the night was well documented. Beau was dressed casually, with a pair of pants, a long-sleeved shirt, and a sword that sat at his left hip next to an attached leather pouch.

"Anyone have any ideas where we are? Or where we should go?" Ezra asked and looked over the sea. I followed his gaze. The nearest contestant was kneeling on a piece of the ship and using a jagged plank as an oar. He was too far away for me to identify, but

I could tell from the distance that he was armed and would join us in maybe ten minutes.

"I have a compass," Beau said. He was fishing in his pouch when I looked away from the waves. He withdrew the small device and sat it in his right palm, waiting until the small dial stopped to look up. "East. We should travel west." He nodded toward the trees, wincing a little from the gesture.

The Mist was west of Honor Cove. I remembered the maps Leif made me study. Maybe Aria had dropped us in the east. The goal of the trial was not just to outlive the other contestants, but to find your way back to Aria's stone where you made your blood pledge. Given the Light Realm's reverence for her and Nex, it would make sense that we would need to traverse both land and sea during the trial. It's why we asked for Nex's blessing and tested our worthiness in that pool of blue dragons. I knew there were islands far from the coast, but none of them were habitable. They were too dangerous for any kind of civilization, which was why I couldn't think of the names of any of them now.

"Chances are that heading west will lead us toward the end of the trial," Ezra said, echoing my exact thoughts. He looked to me first for confirmation.

Beau pocketed the compass. "We head west to the other side of the island."

"And we gather supplies to build a boat? Even if we aren't far from Honor Cove, you'd really need Nex on your side to make it across the sea in a makeshift boat," I said, glancing again toward the oncoming contestant. I could see another not far behind the first.

"To those with worthy souls, those who see possibility, those with bold spirits and hearts calmed by bravery, the gods will provide," Ezra said, his eyes trained on the trees ahead. Something about his words cooled my skin, but not in an ominous way. It felt like I'd known the words, but I couldn't recall from where.

"That's not from the *Book of the Great Mother*, is it?" Beau asked.

Ezra smirked but didn't move his eyes from the trees. "The truth isn't printed on the pages of any religious text. It's between the lines."

I was stunned. Words like that could get you exiled from the realm or even executed for blasphemy in some regions. Once the initial shock wore off, I hated that I was impressed. I'd said something similar to Leif a few times only to be ordered to keep such thoughts to myself. It didn't change how I felt. Fuck any god who thought putting their followers through a fight to the death like this made you worthy of anything. Violence for sport never made much sense to me, especially when it was perpetuated by a higher power that could easily decide it wasn't necessary.

"It'll be light soon," Beau said. His eyes were on the coastline where the tide brought in wooden shards from the ship. "We can stay in the tree line on our way to the other side of the island and then move to the beach when it gets dark."

I snorted. "It will take too long."

"It's the safest option if you don't want to fry under the sun on the beach or be eaten by something in the forest," Beau said and turned from the sea to face me. There was concern in his eyes and my heart skipped in my chest knowing that it wasn't for his own life. "If we are east of Honor Cove, we're likely on one of the Spine Islands, which means there are creatures here that don't exist anywhere else. I don't want to be lunch for a wyrm or dinner for a drake."

"Staying close to shore may seem safer, but that makes it more likely a path for the other contestants," I said as I gathered the ends of my split nightgown. The wind had started to whip the cool fabric around my calves. Not only was it a hazard on the island, but it was damn annoying. I tied the front and back pieces on my hip opposite my sword, leaving me in my riding pants from the waist down.

"You would rather choose the path of apex predators over the obvious paths with the rest of the contestants?" Beau asked, moving closer to join Ezra and me.

I groaned. The nearest contestant was close enough to shore that he abandoned his makeshift raft and was swimming now. I turned from the men and started for the trees. Beau was at my side in seconds.

"Nature acts on instinct. It doesn't know any better. Man knows better and still acts. I choose nature," I said with a scoff and forged ahead. Beau was tolerable, but still male. Of course, he hadn't considered the reality.

Neither of them said a word as I walked ahead. Water, food, and shelter—if we could find them—are the priorities right now. I tried to focus on the surroundings, noting the palms and kapok trees that seemed pervasive on the island. It was almost silent, which put me on edge. Leif taught me that silence in nature meant danger. It meant that the smaller animals had gone into hiding from larger predators.

"I think we should hunt," Ezra said. I knew he'd stopped walking because I couldn't hear his footsteps anymore. Beau nearly walked into me when I stopped. The annoyed retort turned to ash in my dry mouth when I saw him. He looked exhausted, but not from sleep. I wondered if the punch to his face had done more damage than just the bruising his skin. It was cold beneath the shade of the forest and while I wished I had another layer on, Beau was shivering.

"Beau needs to rest," I said, looking past the man in front of me to Ezra's tense expression. He looked at us as though we were slowing him down even though he'd been at the back of our group for the last hour. "We can hunt once we find water and a safe place for Beau to rest."

"Once it rains, we will have plenty of water and it looks like it rains here often," Ezra said and pointed to the tree next to him. It was the one kind of tree I hadn't been able to put a name to as we walked, but its thick trunks and giant leaves were everywhere. I shrugged to him, motioning for him to elaborate. He groaned. "Large leaves help trees get maximum sunlight and are common in trees where it rains often."

It was his turn to shrug. He pointed to me, and I felt like I was back in lessons with Leif as he peppered me with survival questions. I hated that he was right. I hated more that I hadn't thought of it first. I'd studied our surroundings so carefully since we left the beach, but I hadn't thought about why the ground even this deep in the forest seemed soaked; why it could be so humid here despite the cool temperatures and lack of sunlight; and why we hadn't seen any animals since we'd arrived here.

"Let's hunt," I said, keeping my eyes on him. "Once the rain starts, we can use the leaves to gather water. We can eat. Maybe we can use parts of the bones for weapons."

Ezra nodded once, satisfied with my answer. I saw the corner of his lips pull upward as though I'd impressed him.

"Have you ever been hunting, Princess?"

"I have," Beau interrupted. "Hunting and fishing is a big part of our culture in the northern sea villages."

"You're too weak to hunt right now, Beau," I said, looking at Ezra for support. Rather than agree, he seemed indifferent. Bastard. I understood. We were all contestants. He didn't need Beau to make it to the other side of the island.

"Fine, but let me do the tracking," Beau said.

"Why?" Ezra asked. "I spent months in the forests, surviving on whatever game I could catch and whatever clean water I could find. I can hunt. From the looks of you, we would all be better off if you were to take a nap beneath a tree or hold a leaf until it fills with rainwater."

The last time I saw that look in Beau's face, he was in the training arena looking up at Waylon. He took a few steps toward Ezra who towered over him. He looked ready to shove him but stumbled aside when Ezra pushed him away with one arm. Beau winced, raising a hand to his temple.

"You're concussed," Ezra snorted. "Hiking the forest the way we have might have been enough exercise to exacerbate your symptoms. You aren't any use to us on a hunt."

Beau was red in the face now, but he didn't protest as he rubbed his temple. "How can you tell?"

"I'm not just some soldier. I'm trained in combat. It's my profession. I'm trained for battle and for tending to the aftermath."

Leif had taught me plenty of first aid, but I wasn't good at it. I'd always focused on prevention rather than treatment.

"There are just three of us and we can't leave Beau alone if he's injured," I said.

Ezra nodded like the answer was obvious. "Then you stay. I'll hunt."

"No way," Beau said and stood taller.

"Beau," I started, feeling a headache forming at my brow from the self-serving idiocy from both of them.

"You'll slow things down," Ezra said.

"You may have strength and skill to your advantage, but you know nothing about hunting in this kind of environment," Beau said. Ezra paused his walk toward the trees to look back at him. He groaned and rejoined us, somehow towering over us more than before.

"I've trained for every environment from the Light Realm to the Dark Realm," he said.

Beau scoffed. "Yes, but I've seen the way you look at the seafood at meals in the castle. You never touch it. You act as though you've never seen a swordfish, let alone have one placed on your dinner plate."

"I'm not planning to go fishing among the trees, Renault."

"I don't think you've ever been near the shore. You've never fought in battles near the coastal cities. I don't doubt you've learned about them, but you've never experienced them. You've lived your whole life in the plains, near the farmlands, where the largest fish you might catch in a stream is a salmon or trout and where all the beasts of the forests have hides of fur rather than scales. You're out of your element," Beau said and took a step forward so they were inches apart. "But for me, I'm the closest to home here."

The two stood for a long moment, Beau's boyish face and blue eyes glaring up at the chiseled soldier who looked well-equipped to kill him in seconds with just his bare hands. It would've been ridiculous had it not been for the truth I saw in Ezra's eyes. Beau was right. It was why Ezra spent no time in the training arena and spent every morning on the beach swimming. He wasn't from the coast and there was so much about seafaring life and the threats here that it would be impossible to learn them all, even with years of study.

Finally, an advantage.

With a growl-like groan, Ezra stepped aside and motioned for Beau to lead the way. I saw the surprise cross Beau's expression for just a moment before he walked ahead. Ezra's eyes met mine, a look almost challenging me to say something. It was as though he was just waiting for my insult or a cheap joke. He gave a curt nod for me to walk ahead and after another moment of glaring, I followed Beau.

I kept a good distance behind him, and it seemed Ezra kept an equal amount behind me, from the single glance behind I'd allowed myself. I slowed my pace when Beau did his and I mirrored his position whenever he crouched. I kept my hand on my sword the way he did and had it halfway out of the sheath when he suddenly stopped.

The air felt charged, and my muscles practically vibrated with anticipation as we crouched. I was ready to take a chance and hurry to join him when he slipped his dagger from his hip. Without looking back, he held a hand out to me, asking me to stay. I heard a crunch ahead. Beau hadn't moved, so I knew he'd been successful in his task. I felt the smile tug at my lips. Not only had he tracked down a meal, but he'd also done it in little more than an hour. I hoped the pride was clawing at Ezra. I was about to look over my shoulder at him but froze at the sudden scratching sound. It was a hiss, a short sound that I'd almost missed. Thunder rumbled in the distance and then I heard a shushing sound as the rain met the tops of the trees overhead, the water coming down on us a moment later.

Beau paused before slowly moving forward, still in his crouch. As he moved from behind a tree, I caught a glimpse of a large boar. It would be more than enough to feed the three of us. My stomach ached at the thought of rest after gorging myself. The animal tripped as it limped toward the next tree. It was hard to make out the injured leg, but I could see the claw marks on its right hip as it stopped to drink from the shallow pool of water at the base of the tree.

Beau pulled his dagger out and I had my sword out before I heard the rush of leaves behind me. I turned, ready to swing at the attacker only to face Ezra's angry expression. He swatted away my half-assed attempt at defense with his own oversized sword and barked, "Lie down!"

I was so surprised to see him charging at me that he'd knocked me off balance and I tripped and fell hard on the tree roots. I was halfway to my feet, insult perched on the tip of my tongue, when a large black shape launched from the left and went sliding into the tree where the boar drank.

"Dumbass!" Ezra raised his sword above his head and launched his attack.

20

The boar let out an ear-piercing squeal and fled, racing straight at me. I scrambled to my feet and brought my sword down, lunging forward as the boar tried skirting away from me. The blade came down on its back with a thud. Its squeal was cut off by Beau's scream of pain, and I left the immobilized prey to help.

The panther was big enough that it obscured my view of Beau pinned at the base of the tree. Before Ezra could swing his sword at the animal, it let out a yowl and sprung away. Beau lay against the tree, eyes wide and dagger coated in blood. My heart stopped when I noticed a pair of yellow eyes trained on me. I tightened my grip on my sword as it took two steps toward me, putting it out of reach of Ezra's sword as it swung inches away from the panther's tail. Ezra let out a war cry that didn't work to deter the animal.

I raised my sword, focusing on where to point the tip as the panther charged. Just as it crouched to spring at me, Ezra threw himself across its back. The panther yowled again and twisted, but Ezra wrapped his arms around its neck and his legs around its middle. I hurried forward, switching my grip on my sword so that I held the tip down toward the head of the giant cat. Before I could give the killing blow there was a sickening crunch and the panther stilled.

Ezra let out a grunt and relaxed, his annoyed expression back when he looked up at me. He wrenched his leg free from the body of the panther and stood up. My heart skipped when I heard Beau groan, and I was kneeling in the shallow pool of water next to him a moment later with Ezra just behind.

Beau grimaced as he sat up, blood leaking down the front of his shirt. He winced when he raised his left arm, sending a fresh wave of blood down his front.

"Stop! You're making it worse," I told him and pulled my dagger from my hip. I carefully cut away the fabric at his shoulder until his shirt hung halfway off him. Ezra knelt on the opposite side of Beau and ripped the shirt the rest of the way off of him.

"You'll live," he announced and reached for the pouch strapped to his sword belt.

"That makes me feel better," Beau said, his sarcasm getting lost when he sucked in a gasp of pain. He closed his eyes and tightened his jaw, letting his head rest against the trunk of the tree.

I lowered my dagger to the knot of fabric at my hip and started cutting away the extra fabric of my nightgown. It was more than enough to create a bandage. I used the first swathe to dab away the blood, cleaning away enough to see the four puncture wounds that arched along his shoulder. I wasn't well-versed in this and cursed myself for not paying more attention to Leif's instructions, but nothing looked seriously wrong. Nothing looked broken. It looked as though the panther sank his claws into Beau's shoulder only to be scared off of him. A moment longer and the cat might've ripped further into the muscle.

"You're right-handed, right?" Ezra asked, ignoring me when I asked why it mattered.

"Right," Beau answered, raising his uninjured hand for good measure.

I lifted the fabric from Beau's shoulder again, glad to see that the bleeding had slowed. I covered it again and looked up at Ezra, anger sending fire through my veins when I saw him pull a small flask from the pouch at his hip.

"You really think this moment warrants a drink?" I asked.

Ezra smirked as he unscrewed the cap. The smell of alcohol was strong, like we were standing in a distillery and not getting soaked by rain in a jungle.

"It's the strongest drink in the realm," Ezra said, plucking the fabric from my hand. He clapped a hand to Beau's mouth and poured a small amount of the dark liquid over the wounds. Beau arched against the tree and gave a muffled scream.

"You could've warned him," I said once Beau had stopped screaming.

Ezra screwed the cap back on the flask and replaced it in his pouch. "That has enough alcohol to knock a man out after a couple of swigs. It can also cure most ailments—or cause them—depending on how you use it."

I looked away from Beau as he recovered. "You're a bastard."

Ezra stood up and removed a dagger from his hip, prompting me to reach for mine. "Relax, Princess." He left us to go to the limp body of the boar. He bent down to clean the kill, leaving me to tend to Beau.

"I'll just slow you down, Wren," Beau said.

There was no use pretending otherwise. I focused on his wounds, which had stopped bleeding thanks to the alcohol and my applied pressure. They were deep, though, and with our limited resources, the only choice I had was to clean the area and bandage it with the fabric I'd torn from my nightgown. Beau let out a deep groan as I finished tying the fabric, settling back against the trunk of the tree.

"I'm an idiot," he said with a sigh.

"You are if you keep talking about a simple scratch like it's the end already," I said. I wasn't going to spend the duration of trial dwelling on the reality. I wasn't sure what I expected. Maybe it would be easier if I let go of Beau now and didn't spend the entire trek across the island trying to keep him alive. I'd approached this entire thing as though I would keep him with me throughout the trial, but I knew that even if he survived that long he couldn't make it to Aria's stone by my side.

Yet he smiled back at me now, and his hand was in mine. My chest grew heavy, and I pulled away, rising to my feet and turning to face Ezra as he finished dragging the gutted boar to the body of the panther.

"We need to cook the meat," he said.

I scoffed. "You'd need a fire and your luck of starting one now is slim."

He smirked. "You want to drag the boar or the panther?"

Fuck. It was hard enough hunting and making the kill. Ezra knelt down and went to work prepping the panther as the rain pounded away at his back. Beau was on his feet now, leaning against the tree to brace himself and looking a little like he might pass out from either exhaustion or pain. We needed shelter, ideally something dry so we could cook our meal before the meat went bad.

I started walking, ignoring Beau as he called after me. I wasn't about to drag dead weight when I wasn't sure there was any shelter to drag it to.

It stopped raining twenty minutes into my walk. The forest was quiet, almost strangely so after the thunderous storm. At first it had me on edge. I wouldn't have heard the trickle of a stream if it weren't for the silence though, and that stream led to a river where I found a tree that was growing into the side of the steep bank. The branches stretched over the grainy bank like a canopy and the ground beneath was drier compared to the soft earth around it.

I retraced my steps to Beau and Ezra, following the smell of pork as I got closer. It was a gamble to cook like this. My stomach growled so fiercely that it hurt and by the time I reached the men I was so focused on my hunger that I gladly took a hunk of meat from Beau when he held it out by the bone. My stomach didn't settle until I'd nearly stuffed it full.

"It's getting dark," Beau said. He was propped up by his elbows in the grass and looked like he might fall asleep if he lay flat. I'd sat long enough to eat so that I could feel the soreness setting into my thighs, so I was sure Beau was struggling to keep rest at bay.

"I found a tree by the river we can use for shelter," I said. Ezra looked up from the panther hide. He'd skillfully removed it in a single piece and had scraped the insides clean. I wasn't sure how he planned to use it when we didn't have any way to preserve it, but I didn't ridicule his efforts no matter how satisfying it may feel.

"Is it saltwater or freshwater?" he asked.

"It didn't smell like the sea," I told him. The truth was that I was excited enough about the shelter that I hadn't paid too much attention to the river. It rained enough around here that safe drinking water wouldn't be hard to come by.

"Let's go," Beau said and let out a deep sigh as he rose to his feet.

I caught the worried look on Ezra's face as Beau started through the trees in the direction I had taken before. We caught up with him easily, Ezra still cleaning the panther hide with his dagger as we walked.

"How do you feel?" I asked Beau after he groaned for the third time.

He hesitated before answering. "I think I might be sick."

"Don't be," Ezra called out from behind.

"We're not far," I told them and placed a hand on Beau's back to keep him from slowing his pace. "I can hear the stream."

Beau made a choking sound and stopped next to me, placing his hands on his knees.

"Swallow it!" Ezra barked when Beau heaved again.

Beau pressed the back of his forearm to his lips, a shudder

going through his body as he straightened up. He groaned and spat on the ground before facing us.

"Disgusting," he said, his pale face suggesting that he might be sick again.

"You don't know when you will get your next meal," Ezra explained.

"If that river is freshwater and I just choked on my vomit for nothing, I swear ..." Beau didn't finish his sentence, seemingly too tired to argue. I worried how much of his exhaustion was from the hike here and how much was from the panther attack and the concussion. The tightness in Ezra's expression told me he was wondering the same thing, though I was sure worry was far from his mind.

"Just up ahead," I prompted, leading the way toward the dip in the path that I remembered from before. A few moments later and we were greeted by the rush of the river. Beau increased his pace, so we were walking side-by-side as he approached the canopy of trees by the bank.

"Thank the Gods," Beau said and ducked beneath the low-hanging branches. He practically collapsed against the wall of the bank, knocking loose a clump of dirt from an exposed root. I turned my back on him as he closed his eyes.

Ezra knelt at the water's edge. I went to stand next to him, waiting as he tasted the water.

"Freshwater," he said and stood up, rising a couple feet taller than me.

"Where do you think the river empties?" I asked, watching the water carry a palm past.

He shrugged. "Don't know, but it's freshwater and it's flowing in the direction we're heading. We should keep following it."

"It's clean drinking water and where there's water there's game to hunt."

"And it's far from the contestants on the beach," Ezra said and looked down at me. "Safe."

Safe for now.

I watched the current carry another palm past us, the water surprisingly swift. It was clear, so clear that I could see the rocky bottom several feet from the bank. The island was far from flat. There were several mountains, and we'd walked a few hills just to get to the stream. The freshwater was likely from the daily rainstorms, flowing down from the mountains. The rain would increase how fast the river flowed after the storms.

"Beau needs to rest before we can keep going," I said, studying the current and wondering just how much faster it might be than walking.

"We don't have the time for more than a night beneath that tree," Ezra said.

I turned from the river to face him, sure now that my plan would work.

"Let's make a raft," I said, holding up a hand to silence him when I noticed the skepticism on his face. "It wouldn't need to be anything huge, just enough for us to sit on so we could ride the current in the right direction. We ditch it if we go too far off course, but it would allow us to rest without losing any time."

He looked over the river again, studying it the same way I had. He was frustrated and not for the obvious reason. If it were up to him, he'd leave Beau behind. If it hadn't been for me, he would've left him to the sea. Still, we kept running into problems that Beau was more equipped to solve. He knew what to look for when tracking game through the island. He also grew up on the coast in one of the largest ports in the entire realm.

Before I could suggest it, Ezra strode right past me and brushed aside the leaves to reveal Beau lounging on the ground. I followed him into the dark shelter, barely able to make out either of their faces.

"Can you build a raft?" Ezra asked.

Beau was quiet for a moment and then sat up, keeping his injured arm curled across his chest. "I can't lift that kind of weight."

"If Wren and I brought you what you needed, could you teach us?" Ezra asked.

Beau didn't speak for a long moment. A cool breeze whipped through the branches, making the leaves brush together and my skin prickle. They both glanced my way when I shivered.

"Beau," I started and moved to sit next to him on the ground, forcing myself to ignore the drop in temperature. It was tempting to slide closer to him. I could already feel the heat from his body, even from a foot apart. "Tell us what we'd need for a raft and we can gather it in the morning while you recover."

I saw the guilt in his blue eyes. He was still working through defeat; I knew he wanted to help. It was like the offer was there on his lips, but he nodded instead and sat back against the sloped bank. I looked up at Ezra. He scowled back at me but gave a curt nod in agreement.

"Bring the largest logs you can find and lots of binding material," Beau said and let out a sigh of relief.

I lay down next to him, not willing to snuggle to his side even though the cold made it difficult to get comfortable. I tried my best to sleep; the sound of the river reminded me a little of being back in the castle with my balcony doors open. It sounded like the tide and even smelled a little like the salt in the air despite the reek of body odor and dirt. Somehow, the visualization made it more difficult to sleep, and I wondered if it was because home never felt comforting, not any more than lying beneath this tree did.

I opened my eyes and saw that Ezra was sitting beneath the branches. He was tall enough that they draped over his shoulders and made it look like he was sitting in a doorway. The moonlight glittered off the river before him as he kept watch. I rolled onto my side, studying the outline of his tense jaw and the strange softness in his eyes. I wondered what he was thinking about that made him look so conflicted.

No matter what the inner turmoil, the sight of him sitting there with his sword across his lap was enough.

21

It was quiet and I was warm.

I sat up, the panther hide falling away from my chest and my hair snagging on a root. Beau remained prostrate a few feet away from me despite my gasp of pain. He breathed deeply, peacefully sleeping with his injured arm draped across his chest and the other stretching toward me. I wondered if he'd reached for me after I'd fallen asleep.

After freeing my hair and deciding against redoing the updo, I extended my hand toward him. I didn't have to move any closer to reach him, my palm just inches from covering his hand before I sat back again with that tightness in my chest. This was fucking frustrating.

Beau didn't move as I laid the panther hide across his body. I ensured I had everything strapped to my sword belt and left our shelter to find Ezra. He'd already brought two thick tree trunks. I wasn't about to wait for him to start my task, so I walked up the bank and into the trees.

In the silence of this unforgiving forest, I relished that no one trailed after me to ensure I was safe. For once, it was all on me.

The breath I released felt so cathartic that the sound of it immediately triggered the rest of my body to let go. My eyes stung, and my next breath caught in my throat.

I was young the last time I was in the forest like this, mostly alone. It was summer, and it was one of two trips I'd ever been allowed on away from Honor Cove, the only one without the king present. Leif and his soldiers accompanied my mother and me on the week-long journey to Brem. My mother had been born and raised there, the only daughter of a merchant whose beloved wife died in the days after her birth. My grandfather had amassed millions through his ships. He was an inventor and entrepreneur. He developed new ways to produce cargo ships, among other navigation tools and nautical discoveries. He was the only famous merchant who saw potential in the dangerous islands off the coast of the Light Realm and had spent time traveling back and forth between one near Brem in hopes of someday developing a new city.

Erik Berg was a name known well along the coast and the crown was eager to develop a partnership with him. It meant that Erik would need to forgo his expansion into the islands. The crown became so desperate to gain his favor that he grew rich from their efforts and after some time, the government demanded repayment. My mother became part of the agreement and though Leif never told me outright, I knew it wasn't my grandfather's desire. Like he did so often to preserve my innocence should I ever need to argue it, he told me just enough for me to know the truth. My mother and father were married to tether the Erik Berg enterprise to the crown and to ensure leverage against my grandfather.

There is no power without control.

We were only allowed to travel to Brem because my mother was the only living relative of the Berg family and the crown wanted her to bring the deed to the estate and the shipping enterprise. My mother rejected my father's lavish plans for our trip and Leif and his soldiers indulged her wishes to travel modestly. We stayed in our tent, visited small villages under pseudonyms, and my mother taught me what she knew of the natural world and how the small villages ran as we went. I remembered how humbling it was to see a berry bush in the forest and to learn how those berries got to our table for breakfast in the great hall each morning. It felt empowering to pluck them from the vine myself and to ride on the back of Leif's horse when he hunted for our dinner.

That trip was the only time I'd ever seen my mother cry. She was usually so stoic, never giving an emotional response even when she stood during the trial and heard her fate of execution read aloud. The image of her in the main room of the Berg estate was burned into my brain. I was meant to be playing outside in the yard, but I could hear her sobbing through the large back window. Leif held her while she cried on the floor of the house, cursing my father and the kingdom entirely.

We weren't there for more than a day before we boarded my grandfather's personal ship and sailed back to Honor Cove. I was too young to know what became of the Berg estate and the shipping enterprise, but I know that Brem was never expanded, and the castle has never discussed exploring the coastal islands.

"Need a lift?"

I turned to face Ezra. His arms were thick with bamboo, his smug expression faltering when I faced him. Damn my one moment of weakness. He didn't comment on whatever sadness he'd seen in my face though, glancing up at the vines in the trees above us before looking back down at me.

"I can climb," I told him and approached the tree next to him. He dropped the bamboo with a clatter and watched as I found my foothold along the trunk.

My fingers ached as I gripped the bark and dragged myself up to the lowest-hanging branch. Thankfully, I caught it with my right hand and didn't slide down the rough trunk despite the knob I used to pull myself up snapping away. I pulled myself onto the branch and then onto the next, which was just close enough that I could tug on the network of vines. After deciding where to cut to get the most length, I withdrew the dragon-tooth dagger and used the serrated edge to slice away the thick vines.

Ezra didn't move as the vines fell to the ground beneath me, a pile growing just a foot before him. He watched me work instead before calling for me to stop. "Jump down. We have enough."

I looked down at his extended arms and laughed.

"I climbed up. I can climb down."

"And skin your hands and maybe your face."

I ignored him and shoved the dagger back into the hilt. I climbed down to the lowest branch and began looking for a foothold along the trunk. The knot I'd used before had peeled away from the tree when I'd pulled my way up to the branch. I'd been lucky to grab hold of the branch just to get up here. The other handhold I'd used was too far away to reach without slipping from my perch and it was the only safe place to grab hold. My face burned as I realized defeat. Ezra was right. The only way down was to hug the trunk and slide to the ground. The trunk was thick enough that it meant raking my palms against the rough bark and likely my cheek along with them.

I glanced up long enough to see Ezra's smirk. There was another way that didn't require cutting my hands or asking him to lift me down.

I leaped from the branch, grabbing on to the front of his shirt. Ezra stumbled backward, and all seven feet of him landed heavily beneath me on the ground. He groaned as I pushed away from his chest, dusting off my knees, which were the only part of me that had even brushed the dirt.

"I thought you'd be stronger than that," I quipped, standing over him a moment longer. I wanted to remember what he looked like after I'd knocked him flat just in case the trial never gave me the chance again.

He scowled back at me and sat up. "I'm trained for more useful things, Princess."

I stepped over his legs and moved to the pile of vines next to the bamboo. "I wasn't aware you needed to train to handle women throwing themselves at you, but I guess that explains your lack of knowledge."

He let out an annoyed groan, almost like the growl the panther made before it pounced, and I was warmed by the satisfaction of knowing I'd hit a nerve. I heard his footsteps behind me, but I ignored them to focus on the task at hand. Gather the vines and bamboo. Get the supplies to Beau. Build the raft. Then, ignore Ezra Loreign as we relaxed on our makeshift boat and floated toward victory.

"If you hate me the way you say then you'll find the balls to just fucking hit me."

I turned around to face him. Rather than grip the vine, my hand closed into a fist, and I lunged. I put my entire body into the punch, but I hadn't considered how much shorter than him I was. The punch meant for Ezra's nose smashed into his chest instead and I felt several of my knuckles pop painfully. He let out a grunt from the force of it and pressed a hand to his chest, massaging the spot while I cradled my hand and tried to keep my expression neutral.

"You have qualms about hitting a woman? Or does your opponent always deal the final punch?" I yelled, channeling the pain in my hand into my response.

His jaw tensed. "Are you really done with your little tantrum already?"

I surged forward, surprised when my other arm was seized before I'd raised it past my shoulder.

"I should've gutted you on that beach," I snarled.

Ezra smirked. "You could've gutted me now, but you threw a punch rather than reach for a blade." He let go of my arm, giving me just enough of a push that I had to take a step back to keep on my feet. I glared back at him, withholding the cheap insults that sprang to my mind that would only confirm I had nothing against him.

"You need me," I told him. This whole trial was for naught if I died. The man who made it out wouldn't have a bride and I doubted the king would award him anything for coming out of the trial without me.

"Yes," Ezra admitted and passed me for the pile of vines and bamboo. "The same way you need me. You're smarter than any of these bastards and have bigger balls. I bet taking down that panther would've meant a disastrous end for most, and I did it without even drawing a weapon. We both know that it will be the two of us racing for Aria's Stone on that beach."

I'd assumed as much from the moment all the contestants were announced.

"We'll see," I said as he lifted the bamboo into his arms. "I would love to see the look on my father's face when I put my sword in your gut, but I'm not sure I can endure you for that long."

He let out a laugh and sent me a scowl over his shoulder. "I don't look forward to taking you as a wife, Princess."

He strode ahead and I followed behind with the vines, imaging what it would look like to wrap them around his neck.

Beau told us how to lash all the wood together with the vines, tying the bamboo to the thick trunks of three trees so that we had a raft big enough that we could sit comfortably in a row. We were already riding the current by the time the sun peeked over the tallest trees, the cool breeze emanating from the water providing a little relief from the heat. I was right; the current did make our journey quicker and it allowed Beau to get some more rest. When we dragged the raft to shore for the night, he looked much better than before.

"Where are you from?" Beau asked.

The crackling from the fire was the only sound for a long moment as Beau innocently looked across it at Ezra. It hadn't dawned on me just how little I knew about Ezra and how he'd been allowed to go so unnoticed at the castle. He managed not only to keep his abilities a secret but also his background. All anyone knew was what he'd told us about killing the Fallen prince on the battlefield and he managed to remain so undetected since then that no one thought to ask any questions.

Ezra looked even more cantankerous than usual thanks to the eerie glow from the fire across his tight gaze. I wasn't sure he was going to answer when he let his eyes fall back on the fish between his hands.

"North."

"I'm from the north," Beau said, his tone almost challenging.

"Northwest," Ezra added.

"I know," Beau said, prompting Ezra to look up from his meal again with raised brows. "It's obvious that you're not from anywhere near the sea."

Ezra took the final bite of his fish and set the bones aside. "There are many parts of this realm that aren't near the sea."

"But you know the Mist, don't you?"

Ezra continued to adjust his position in the dirt. He moved his sword belt into his lap before looking up again.

"I'm a soldier," he said. "If you survive enough battles, you learn your way along the Mist."

"How did you go from being an unknown foot soldier to killing the Bone Breaker of the Mountain?" I asked. He pulled his glare away from Beau to look at me. It was clear he was studying me, as though attempting to read further into my words.

"He sent his dragon away and walked into the land of his enemy," he said, never looking away. It was strange. He owned that he had been the one to kill the Fallen prince but didn't want to share the details. It was as if he felt guilt about the event.

"Are they as big as the stories say?" Beau asked, breaking my attention. "The dragons?"

Ezra nodded to the drago- tooth dagger lying next to me. The dagger was the length of my forearm, a large tooth from a large monster. "The Bone Breaker of the Mountain's dragon is the largest."

Beau shook his head with a bewildered look on his face. "How do you know it's the biggest?"

"Because she was the one he rode," Ezra said. "Even the smallest of dragons could destroy hundreds."

"Why haven't the Fallen fought back with that kind of force? If all it took was a few dragons ... Gods, they have a lot more than just a few," Beau said before something like fear crossed his expression. "Don't they?"

I knew we were alone, but I glanced around our camp anyway. The conversation was taking a dark turn.

Ezra nodded slowly. "What would you do if you won the Trial for Marriage?"

Beau glanced at me for a moment, the look so somber that it made my stomach twist, and I had to look away.

"I would marry the princess and go far away. The king has been public about his son ruling. Wren will never have the throne through the line of succession. We can live quietly, never appear at court, fade into the background, and live the simple lives we deserve."

I released my breath slowly, willing my heart to slow. If things were easier, I would want just that. Maybe I would want that with Beau even, gentle and kind Beau. I chased away the growing panic, but I couldn't forget the blue of his eyes.

"What would you do?" Beau asked Ezra.

"The Fallen have more dragons than the public know about," he said. "They will send them eventually. If I win the trial, I will kill the king and end the war. Let the Fallen be."

That's why he was here. He was part of the rebellion and a valuable one. He was highly trained and had insider knowledge about the king's army; if Ezra won, my father would have ... nothing. I wasn't important to the king unless he could use me to gain something. That's why the Trial for Marriage was so important to him. He could use me to gain Lord Dallin's fleet of ships. He could use me to gain Beau's family fortune and good favor of the public. Every man who'd entered the trial had something to offer the king except Ezra. For Ezra, now that I was a contestant and would be the king's greatest enemy, winning didn't give him an edge at all. He'd entered the trial in hopes that I would be leverage. Now, he was just fighting for his own life.

"Why did you enter the trial?" Beau asked me. He sounded almost like a different person, something in his tone broken in such a way that it pierced my gut. A glance across the fire at him put a name to the feeling. Betrayal.

"To win my own hand," I said.

"And tie it to yet another's?" Ezra asked.

I gripped the hilt of the dragon tooth dagger in the dirt. He stared straight back at me, his face neutral as though he hadn't just casually tossed out the insult he had.

"I know I can't win and stay in Honor Cove. There's an army of rebels waiting for me. I win the trial, I win the legal right to my affairs, and I head north."

"But you're smarter than that, Princess," Ezra said with a laugh. "And that's not your plan, that's your beloved guard's plan. And a bunch of rebels, hell, even a few thousand rebels don't make an army."

I wasn't sure how to respond. He wasn't wrong. It was Leif's plan, and I didn't fully agree with it. It wasn't the accuracy of Ezra's words that had me speechless. Just before the trial, I'd also started to see this path as yet another way for a man to use my position. The way to set my people free from the king's rule was not so narrow that I needed to go through a man to achieve it. I didn't need Leif, and despite his training and his knowledge of the realm's military and politics, my years of quiet observation made me think there were other ways, alternatives outside the possibilities of the Light Realm.

"There is magic in the Mist," I said, carefully watching Ezra's neutral expression and the way the color leached from Beau's.

"Wren," Beau breathed.

"Dark magic," I said, unable to keep my voice as strong as before. It was something I'd only heard about during lessons on the *Book of the Great Mother*. I'd read very little about it, but I knew enough to sense the implications between the lines of text. Magic was the thread that held the world together. It's what bound us to the Dark Realm before the fall of O'Riah.

"What would you do, Princess?" Ezra asked again, this time not using my title in the condescending way he normally would.

I took a deep breath and felt the energy build despite knowing what Leif would say. I knew in my heart that there was no way to put a stop to the tyranny in the Light Realm with what we had available to us. It had always felt like something was missing to me, like we were lacking information on the divide between the Light Realm and the Dark Realm, information about what became of the Dark Realm after O'Riah fell. I didn't like not knowing. I never understood why the leaders in Honor Cove didn't demand to know. Magic was abolished in the Light Realm after O'Riah fell. It was a threat to the gods and goddess. I didn't need the religious texts to know that. Still, sometimes I wondered if magic had not been chased out of the realm but had instead abandoned us.

"I win the right to my affairs. The castle has no legal grounds for my arrest unless I express a threat to the crown. So, I won't be pursued if I leave the realm. I go to the Mist," I said.

"What do you expect to find?" Beau asked, unable to mask his incredulous tone despite trying. "Maybe you do find a witch in the Mist. Do you think they would join you to overthrow the crown?"

I didn't know what I expected from the Mist, but I expected it to be different from what I was taught it was. I didn't believe the Fallen were our enemies and I didn't believe that the Mist and the Dark Realm were these uninhabitable places. The truth was somewhere in the middle.

"The truth isn't printed on the pages of any religious text. It's between the lines."

I knew what Ezra said on the beach stuck with me for a reason. He'd been brave enough to say what would label most as heretics in the Light Realm. There was something out there, something that had bound us together once, and I was sure it could be used to overthrow my father's regime and end the violence between our realms.

"I think we created the enemy," I said, finally willing myself to look at Beau's horrified expression. "I think the truth lies in the Mist."

No one spoke. Beau looked terrified, but something in his eyes connected with mine and told me he understood. The fire let out a loud crack that pulled me from my thoughts and reminded me where we were. We were still stuck on this island, pressing onward for the other side, hoping that Aria would provide a ship home. Still at the mercy of a goddess I wasn't sure I trusted.

22

I woke to near darkness, our campfire smoldering a few feet away. I sat up; any stupor from the early hour was chased away when I realized Beau wasn't there. He was the second watch. Ezra lay on his back several feet from me, holding the hilt of his unsheathed sword in one hand while the other was wrapped around the hilt of his dagger. He looked peaceful despite the position, unaware that we had been unguarded for who knew how long. Long enough to let the fire dim.

I tossed a log onto the fire and unsheathed my sword as I scanned the trees for any sign of him. *Gods, where is he?* He'd trained and had gotten stronger in the days leading up to the trial, but I didn't trust his ability to fight here. I'd promised an easy death, not one alone in the darkness.

My feet found my way to the trees. The moonlight barely shone here, an ominous glow that only further chilled my skin. My heart thundered and as I tried to calm myself, steel myself against the guilt writhing like snakes in my gut, I noticed my breathing become haggard. I gripped my sword. I felt for the dagger at my hip to make sure it was there. I jogged in a circle around our campsite, checking the perimeter until I recognized the trees again as those I'd started among.

Gods, fuck him. What a damn idiot.

"Wren."

My body stopped. I whirled to face him, dropping my sword and cupping his face before I realized the movement. He held my wrists, bringing his forehead to mine so I could fall farther into the calm reprieve of those blue eyes.

"What's the matter?" he asked, hands moving to my face next and swiping away moisture. Tears. When had I started to cry? When had I lost my resolve in all of this?

I backed away, letting his fingers linger a moment longer on my cheeks before I took that final step.

"Where were you?" I asked, taking a deep breath.

He gave a bashful smile. "I needed to use a bush."

We'd traveled this far together. We were all desensitized to the basics of our bodily functions. It was almost funny how embarrassed he still was about it until I remembered the way the fire had waned and how long it had taken to find him.

I shoved his chest, and he stumbled backward a few feet. "You were gone longer than that."

"Well, I needed longer than a few minutes," he said, the blush visible even in the dim moonlight.

I moved to shove him again but couldn't bring myself to do it. As soon as my hands found his chest, it was like that damn broke all over again and I was running through the forest alone, like my fingers were touching him for the first time. I looked him over, glad to see that he at least had enough sense to bring all his weapons when I felt his fingers pry mine loose from his shirtfront. He pressed them together, rubbing soothing circles along the back of my hands until I relaxed.

"I could kill you for being so stupid right now," I said.

He smirked and pressed a kiss to the back of my hand that made my heart leap in my chest. "I'm counting on that. How else would you take over the realm?"

Together.

The word came to mind so fast that it felt like a slap. I could take Beau Renault with me to the end, let him win, marry him. We could run away together like he said, and ... The ache in my chest only intensified as the vision of the future faded. If I let him win, we'd be swept up in the excitement of the marriage. The castle wouldn't give us a moment alone for days or even weeks. The plans were already in place for each of the men, should they win. The alliance with his family would form. I wasn't sure when we'd get the chance to run away. If we did, I knew I wouldn't be happy sitting still. I couldn't, not while the rest of our realm was under my father's rule. I couldn't let them suffer. The thought of even one more shipment of captured Fallen crossing from the Mist, even one more person living the life that Norelli had, clawed at my insides. And Beau wasn't made for the life of a soldier.

If I had him, I wasn't sure I could leave him.

"Let's get back. We've been gone too long," I said, slipping my hands from his and leading the way back toward camp. He kept a respectable distance from me as we walked, just enough that I was aware he was still there. I could hear his footsteps, heard the deep breath he took, and remembered the way his chest rose and fell beneath my hands. The memory helped to calm me, stirring something else within me that took me back to that day in the library.

I came out of my thoughts when his hands gripped my hips from behind. The heat that pooled in my core was chased away a moment later when I realized why he'd stopped me.

"Shit," I whispered, reaching for my sword.

Three men were gathered around our camp. Ezra was on his knees, the tallest man standing behind him with one hand fisted in his hair and the other positioning a dagger to his throat. One stood guard while the other rifled through the few things we had.

"Is that Lord Jakob Somerled?" I asked as Beau drew his sword.

"No. The one with Ezra is Donovan Merry. The one

searching our camp is Astor Willow. That man standing watch is Soren Yonder."

I could see that now. Lord Soren Yonder was easy to recognize. He was one of the more skilled swordsmen. It made sense that Lord Merry would be with them. He was one of the least skilled of the entire competition. Lord Willow wasn't a great fighter by any means, but he was cunning the way that Lord Dallin was. He would fight dirty, maybe even off his own men if they won this fight.

"What do we do?" Beau asked, crouched next to me now with his sword out.

"They're waiting for us to come back," I said and straightened up.

"We can't just walk into that."

"If they weren't waiting for us then they'd have killed Ezra already. He's too much of a threat, which means they are hoping to bargain."

"No," Beau said as the logic caught up with him. It was too late. I'd already gone far enough from the trees that the men noticed me. Willow stood up to watch as we approached, but Yonder moved to the front of the pack. The clear leader.

"Your Highness," Yonder greeted though didn't move an inch to bow.

"What do you want?" I demanded.

He laughed and glanced back at Willow and Merry before returning his gaze to me. "Not even going to put up a fight for your man?"

"He's no more mine than I am yours," I said, catching the smirk that pulled at the corner of Ezra's lips.

Lord Yonder turned, aiming a punch at Ezra's face. Ezra caught his fist in his palm instead, twisting it hard and making the man yell in pain. Yonder backed away, cradling his hand, and Ezra let out a groan. His teeth clenched against the pain as Merry dragged the dagger across his back. Ezra kept his eyes on me, the fire there encouraging me to hold my position. Do not yield.

"What do you want, Lord Yonder?" I asked as he turned to face me, his face flaming from the failed attack. He straightened up and took a few steps forward. I could feel Beau close in behind me, and saw the way Yonder glanced his way. I raised my sword between us, the point nearly grazing his chest.

He smiled. "I mean no disrespect, Your Highness, but you know what I want."

I lowered the tip of my sword between his legs, using the flat side of it to gently lift the most sensitive length of him. He raised his chin, and I mirrored the response, smiling. "I see," I said soft enough that only he could hear.

If it hadn't been obvious before, it was now as I positioned the point of my sword to his chest again. His smile changed, a wry look that reflected in his eyes.

"What do *you* want, Your Highness?" Yonder asked.

I pulled the dragon-tooth dagger from its sheath, waiting to see how he'd react before I spoke. His eyes went from the dagger back to mine. He was on alert, but clearly too curious about my answer to end the conversation yet.

"No one has ever asked me that question," I said and moved my sword so that it rested on his shoulder.

"That's a shame," Yonder said and took a step forward. I raised the dagger now, the tip of the razor-like tooth just an inch from his chest. He glanced down at it before looking up at me again, smiling once I did.

"I don't like being told what to do," I told him, turning the dagger in my hand so I could press the full length of it against his chest when I stepped closer.

"I don't like fragile, pretty things," Yonder retorted, licking his lower lip.

"Good thing I'm not fragile," I said as he inched closer. "I'm in this trial to choose my own man. No one chooses for me. Not even the gods."

"You disavow the will of the gods to bear witness to this death?"

I closed the distance between us, my right arm now resting on his shoulder rather than my sword. "A little bloodshed has never bothered me. I am a Bellator, after all."

I traced the tip of the dagger down his chest and belly as I stepped against him, careful not to cut him. His grip on his sword loosened as he moved his hands over my hips, one hand squeezing my ass. I smiled at him in response, my stomach turning when I saw the lust in his eyes and felt the tightness of his pants against me.

"Two weapons between us," I said and tapped the dragon-tooth dagger against his gut. I tightened my grip on my sword behind him. "One of pain and one of pleasure."

He let out a chuckle and pulled me tighter to him, making it even easier to sink the dagger into his abdomen. He barely uttered a sound, leaving Merry none the wiser when I swung my sword for him. They both fell at the same time, Yonder bouncing off my shoulder and landing on my left and Merry falling behind Ezra just feet from his own severed head.

There was a stunned silence around the campfire before Lord Willow turned and ran for the trees. Halfway there, Ezra launched Merry's dagger across the clearing where it sank into the man's back. He let out a scream and collapsed.

"Gods," Beau said in an exhale.

Ezra rose from the ground, not giving us a second look as he lifted his sword from his makeshift bed where he'd left it. He tossed the sheath aside as he stalked across the clearing for Lord Astor Willow's body, crouching over him to make sure he was dead.

"Are you all right?" Beau asked when I turned. I knelt down over Soren Yonder to pull my dagger free from his gut. I used his pants to clean the dragon tooth.

"Fine," I said. His words tugged at my heart. I was sure it had been an impressive performance, but I hated how it has happened. I should've bolted across the clearing and ran at the men, sword swinging. It felt cheap the way I hung off Yonder's arm. Cheap, but probably more effective and less risky. It was far less satisfying. All it served was to kill two more contestants and further remind me of my sex.

"Pack up," Ezra said as he returned to our group. "Let's go."

He finished buckling his sword belt around his hips and bent over to retrieve the last of his things, revealing the blood-stained back of his shirt.

"You're bleeding," I said as Beau finished gathering our things.

Ezra was already walking toward the trees. Beau and I had to jog to catch up to him.

"You don't even know how bad the wound is," I called to him. I was eager to travel too, but an early start wasn't worth him bleeding out along the way.

Ezra didn't slow his pace until he reached the river. He tossed the weapons he'd taken from the men onto the raft and then turned to face us, shoving Beau so hard that he was tossed to the ground in a heap.

"You were supposed to be on watch!"

"Leave it, Ezra!" Slapping his chest was like slapping a boulder.

"I only left for a moment to find a bush," Beau said, wincing as he stood up.

"I woke to a knife at my throat because you needed to take a shit. Great," Ezra scoffed, turning toward the raft.

"I'm sorry. I didn't think a few minutes would make a difference," Beau said.

Ezra whirled around again to grip the front of his shirt, giving Beau a shake. "You wake someone for relief," he said. "Or next time it might be a knife at her throat. We all know that would make the difference."

Ezra let him go, but Beau wasn't finished. He was red in the face as he followed Ezra to the raft.

"I'm not like those men," Beau told him before looking at me as though reassuring me as well. "I'm not like those men, here for a diamond on my arm at parties or a father-in-law to grant my every wish. I'm not that kind of man."

"We know, Renault," Ezra said and approached Beau with our makeshift oars in his hands. "Your own family sacrificed you to the cause. They see the king's power as more valuable than their only son. Fuck them. That's not family. I know it hurts, but that relationship isn't worth mourning. Not now. Not when there's hope to overthrow the entire system and make sure that millions of others don't suffer the same."

Ezra shoved the oars into Beau's hands. Beau was shaking, his tone laced with anger. "If you believe that then why don't you just fucking kill me?"

Ezra hesitated. I could tell he didn't want to answer, but Beau stood firm. My stomach sank when Ezra looked at me, the words sinking into my soul before he even said them.

"Because I made a promise," he said.

Ezra cast me a final apologetic look before he went to the raft. I could feel Beau's gaze on me, feel the understanding fill the distance between us. He didn't need all the details to know the truth. I was getting out of the Trial for Marriage alive. He wasn't coming with me.

23

Beau sat at the front of the raft, navigating and steering us around the growing number of boulders in the river. I moved to the back of the raft to join Ezra. He gathered his dark curls into a bun at the crown of his head while I sat the supplies, including the last of the fabric from my skirt, in my lap behind him. Even seated he was tall, my eyes level with his bloody shoulder blades.

"I can tell it's not that bad," he said, hesitating with his hands at the hem of his shirt. "It doesn't matter if the wounds are anyway because—"

"Shut up and take off your shirt," I snapped. The river was loud around us for a moment and I could sense Beau's eyes on my back. I expected Ezra to shoot one of his famous cutting retorts, some cheap joke about wanting to get him naked, but he didn't. He sighed, lifted his shirt over his shoulders, and balled the bloody fabric in his lap.

The gash stretched from the bottom of his left shoulder blade to his right shoulder. Any other circumstances and he'd have it stitched, but we didn't have the medical supplies and as I stared at the slowly bleeding cut, I felt so stupid and useless that I sat paralyzed. While he stood his ground against the men and endured the attack like the soldier he is, I flaunted my curves and got groped so I could take off Lord Donovan Merry's head with a cheap shot.

"I know you don't get squeamish at the sight of a little blood," Ezra said, keeping his voice low enough for just me to hear. There was a small trail of blood that rolled down the length of his spine. I staunched it before it could soak into his pants, noticing for the first time the tattoos beneath the gore.

It wasn't unheard of for soldiers of the realm to have tattoos, but it also wasn't common. It especially wasn't common to see them and never this many. A line of markings, an old language maybe, stretched from the base of his neck down his spine. The longer I stared at it, the more enraptured I felt. It told a story, that much I knew somehow, though one I couldn't fully read. It felt like I was back in lessons with Leif studying the lines of the *Book of the Great Mother*. I could sense the words down his back meant something significant, but I wasn't educated in the way I needed to understand.

"Do you understand it?" Ezra asked, his voice low. He kept his gaze on the shirt in his hands.

"I can't read it," I told him.

"I didn't ask if you could read it. Do you understand it?"

Fuck if I knew the difference. That was, until I bit back my retort and looked over the markings again. I knew they were words without needing to know the language. I knew they weren't of the Light Realm, at least not the culture of it that I had been brought up in. It felt neither native nor foreign. It felt like the truth was swirling around my mind and I couldn't yet grasp it.

"The truth isn't printed on the pages of any religious text. It's between the lines."

"I think so," I told him.

"Trace it," he said. He glanced over his shoulder, his dark eyes the softest I'd ever seen them. All of the usual hardness was gone. A different version of Ezra Loreign sat inches from me and seemed powerful in a way that had nothing to do with physical strength. "See if it feels familiar."

I'd been eager to touch the tattoo, so my finger easily rose to the first marking at the top of his spine. The patterns felt natural. I traced the calming swirls and angles down his back. It felt relaxing even to me, less like I was writing and more like a relief. The farther down his back I traced, the more emotion gathered heavily in my chest. It was both difficult and reassuring to finish tracing that final marking. I let out a deep sigh. Ezra's shoulders relaxed like he had as well.

"I should clean your wound," I said, my hands finding their way to the fabric in my lap.

"It's going to get rough!" shouted Beau.

I turned toward the front of the raft where he was steering, his expression serious. He tossed one of the oars onto the raft between us and before I could take it, Ezra brushed past me with his shirt back on to take his place to my right. I looked ahead of the men at the river. The water had been choppy as Ezra and I sat together, but several more boulders were ahead and the farther I looked the worse it got.

"How do we navigate?" Ezra asked.

"We don't," Beau said, adjusting his grip on the oar and taking hold of the vines we'd used to bind the raft together. "Use the oar to push away from the large rocks. We ride it out the best that we can."

No sooner had the words left his mouth did he do just that. Beau had to let go of the raft to push us away from the first boulder, not able to keep us from scraping over the top of another and nearly sending me sliding into the water. I held on to the vines in the middle of the raft like he had, remembering the fabric in my hand.

As soon as we passed that first boulder, I lunged for the front of the raft. Before Beau could question what I was doing, I looped one end of the fabric through his sword belt and the other around the vine. I tied it tight, hoping it helped provide him better footing to propel us away from the jagged rocks and farther down the river.

I let out a scream when we hit another bump, and I was tossed off the raft. I came down hard on the raft, Ezra keeping me from sliding farther toward the edge with a hand against the small of my back. I looked up at him as the raft lurched to the right with a creak.

"Shit!" The oar bowed in his hands but held firm. He shoved us away from the boulder.

"Hold on!" Beau's voice was nearly lost among the roar of the waves, just loud enough to warn us of the steep drop seconds before we were upon it. I held tight to the vines with both hands, Ezra's hand still planted to my back while the other barely gripped the vines to my right. I could feel my body rising, gravity fighting to separate me from the safety of the raft before I smashed into it again.

Ezra let out a groan in my ear, half of his body draped across my legs from the force of the fall. A wave washed over us, leaving me spluttering. The river was narrower here, surrounded on both sides by tall boulders. I could hear the raft bumping and scraping over the rocks below. Beau lifted his oar to push us away from the left boulder, planting the end of the oar against it. Before he could push away, the raft shifted heavily to the right, and the long pole caught on a rock. The resistance set him off balance and knocked him off his feet.

His legs slid into the rough water. I caught his arms, struggling to hold on. The longer I did, the more my arms ached against the battering of the water. Ezra moved away from me, taking Beau's place as he tried steering us around the next of the boulders.

"Let go of me, Wren!" Beau said. "I'm just dragging us down."

"No!"

"It'll be okay," he said, blue eyes nearly shattering my resolve. I held tight to his wrists, arms shaking, sure he would be ripped from me at any moment. Whatever he said next was lost when Beau's back smashed into a rock. I held firm to him as I was wrenched from the raft, both of us plunging into the water. I looked toward the gray sky and took a deep breath before I was pulled under, like another piece of driftwood among the waves for the tide to take.

I held Beau with just my left hand, bumping and twisting beneath the waves as the water tossed us along the riverbed. Our hands wrapped around a rock underwater, and the undertow forced me to let go of him. I wasn't sure which direction I was facing as the water churned around me. My lungs ached for air, and I focused on feeling for the bottom of the river or a rock, something to push against so I could break through the surface. Something found me instead.

A pair of hands gripped my hips from below, shoving me until I was caught in the flow of the river and found myself slowly rising. Rain pounded down on my face as I emerged with a gasp, my scream lost in the rumble of thunder.

"Take my hand!"

I caught sight of Beau's outstretched hand, a good foot or so out of my reach, as I felt the next pull from beneath. I was sucked beneath the water again before I could attempt to grab his hand, and tossed over a rock that scraped my back. I hit the next boulder hard enough that I inhaled a mouthful of cold water. My heart raced in a new way like it was aching to escape my body before it suffocated.

His hands were on me again, gripping my waist and pulling me upward by my left bicep. My nose burned and it felt like my chest would explode once my head surfaced again. I was breathing hard, so hard that I wheezed and coughed from the panic and shock.

"Deep breaths. Fill your lungs," Beau said next to me, struggling to hang on to the front of my shirt.

"Grab on!" Ezra wasn't far ahead, kneeling at the back of the raft with the broken end of his pole stretched toward us. I took deep breaths like Beau told me to, easing my panic and clearing my head enough to have the sense to grab on to his sword belt. My back hit another rock, propelling me into him and making him lose his grip on me.

"Hold tight. I'm going to reach for him," Beau said, extending a hand toward Ezra's oar now instead of me. The boulders got smaller as we floated farther down the river, making it easier to see the sky above. Beau's hand slipped on the end of the oar. He lunged a second time, his hand grasping the tip. Ezra pulled. I held on tight as he towed us toward the raft, neither of them faltering despite the choppy water. We were nearly there when my back hit a rock. Ezra had grabbed Beau's hand and pulled him onto the edge of the raft, the water rushing between my body and Beau's, nearly pulling me under again. I nearly lost my grip, keeping my right hand fisted around his leather belt while the current ripped away the other.

Then my head smashed into something hard.

It felt almost like lying in bed, ensconced in warmth and the feeling of being rocked to sleep. There was a thumping in my ear, the rhythm soothing until it vanished and my body recoiled as it was placed on something hard and cold.

"Wren," Beau said, his voice filled with such worry that I opened my eyes. I could see the outline of his body leaning over me and could feel both his hands cupping my face before the second figure shoved him away. There was shouting as I was turned onto my right sight. My stomach churned and my throat burned as I vomited onto the ground. My knee slipped from beneath me when I rolled to all fours and vomited again, nothing but water splattering between my hands.

Once I was sure I'd emptied my entire stomach, I sat back. My head ached and my muscles were sore. Ezra and Beau both sported several new bruises and looked as tired as I felt. Beau sent

Ezra a challenging look as he scooted closer to me, worry overtaking his face as he took mine between both of his hands again. His eyes roved over me before reaching my gaze, sapphire eyes so bright that I could see them despite the dim light of our cave.

"Where are we?" I asked, my voice hoarse.

"You hit a rock in the river. Knocked you out," Beau said and brushed away the wet hair that had stuck to my cheek.

"The river got smoother by the time we got you on the raft. The storm got worse though," Ezra said quietly. "The river widened and there was this cave."

I looked around us. We were sitting on a kind of shelf of overlapping rocks next to the pool at the mouth of the cave. The rain came down in sheets outside, blurring the outside world. It was surprisingly calm and quiet in the cave despite the storm. It was peaceful, almost too peaceful to bear. It was much easier not to think about the reality when we were on the move.

"We should keep going once the rain lets up," I said.

"No."

They spoke in tandem, glaring at each other. Beau broke the tension to address me, turning his back on Ezra. "You need to rest."

"I'm fine."

"I'll scout the area," Ezra interjected and stood up, his tall frame shielding the last bit of light from the mouth of the cave and making it easier to see the way he looked at me. I'd expected annoyance like before, maybe even anger for allowing the river to take Beau and me. But there was something else in his eyes. He looked at me as though studying a chessboard before making the next move halfway through the game. Was he nervous?

"Try not to drown while I'm gone," he said before turning and diving into the water. He swam toward the mouth of the cave, his broad shoulders cutting through the water with each stroke like a shark's fin. I hadn't realized I'd balled my fists until Beau had taken my hand, massaging the tension away.

"We've all relied on each other so far," he said and offered a small smile. "I'd say we are all even."

I pulled my hand free to push a strand of hair from my face, realizing how matted it had become since I'd last done it. I wasn't sure I knew how to weave the braids anymore. I'd barely gotten it right the last time, but now ... Norelli could never teach me again.

"It'll be okay," Beau said, brushing away a tear as it fell.

I raised my hand to wipe my face, and he captured it in his. He held my gaze for a moment, assessing, before placing a gentle kiss on my knuckles. My heart thumped in my chest, and I looked away before I could allow myself to fall any deeper into his blue gaze. I looked over the still water, almost clear enough to see the bottom. I closed my eyes and imagined floating along the surface. I wanted to be weightless for once, washed of the dirt of the trial, and enjoy what the gods had created rather than think about how much I detested them.

"Swim with me," I said and opened my eyes.

He nodded when I looked at him, resting my hand against his cheek. "Okay."

I untwisted my hair, releasing the last piece of myself that grieved for Norelli and thought instead about emerging from the water the way I wanted. I would braid my hair the way I knew how. I would be clean from the past of this trial and what was behind me at the castle. I would never come to this island again and the next time I set foot in the castle at Honor Cove, it would be because it was mine.

I removed my sword belt from around my hips and pulled what was left of my nightgown over my head. I'd stripped off my riding pants before Beau made a sound, tossing them aside and leaping in before he could finish his protest. The water was cool and when I emerged, long hair fanning out around me, I felt somehow better than before. I turned to look back at Beau as he stood on the edge. He smiled, a bashful look that only made me feel sexier and more powerful.

"Swim with me," I repeated.

Beau smiled wider, hands resting on the buckle of his belt. I sent a splash his way. He laughed and took a step back before the water could wash over his boots.

"You don't like to play fair, do you?" he said with a laugh.

I resisted the urge to send another wave his way. "Fair is a different matter. I don't play by others' arbitrary rules." I kicked my feet against the depths, arching my back so I could float, the air cooling my exposed breasts.

"Rules be damned," Beau said, his face flushed as his eyes moved up to my face again. He hesitated before unbuckling his belt and letting the weapons clatter to the stone. He lifted his shirt over his head and tossed it behind him, pausing when he looked at me again.

My gaze fell on the burn on his torso first before noticing how different the rest of him looked now than when I first saw him shirtless in the infirmary. There were more angles to his body now, ridges along his stomach that were a testament to his preparation for the trial. His biceps were larger, shoulders rounder. He blushed under my gaze and lowered his eyes as he began to slip out of his boots. With a deep breath, he unfastened his pants and let them fall.

He was beautiful, everything about him so pure and almost unhuman. Instead of feeling desire, sadness tugged at my heart. He deserved to escape this trial and escape to the outskirts of the realm and live that quiet life he dreamed of. He deserved to be loved so deeply by someone softer than me. He should be free from the coming war and pain. He'd been through enough already.

My heart pounded in my chest when he dove into the water, swimming closer beneath the surface until he emerged just a foot away. He smiled as he took my face between his hands, and I hoped he mistook the moisture on my face for river water and not for what it was.

"You are so beautiful," he said. I saw how his eyes glistened.

I pulled him flush against me, pressing my lips hard to his.

When he responded, softening the kiss and slipping his hands around my waist, I wrapped my legs around his. He kept us afloat as we kissed. I bit his lower lip and he pulled back a fraction, raising a hand to softly stroke my face. My back met stone. His lips met mine again, the kiss slow and gentle, as though he was savoring every moment, accepting that this might be the last kiss he ever got. My stomach twisted with guilt, my eyes burning from the pain of fate and anger at him for not fighting, for entering into this damn trial already knowing he would die, for not asking me to protect him or to stand by my side at Aria's stone at the end.

I angled my hips and tightened my legs around him. His mouth went slack as he sank into me, a gasp slipping past his lips. I used the stone behind me and my legs to twist us around, placing his back against the stone. I gripped the edge of the stone behind his head and pressed my knees to the wall, pinning him between the cool surface and my body.

He moved a hand between mine to hold himself up, placing the other against my right cheek and shattering the last of my resolve with those blue eyes. They were reassuring and I knew he was promising me that whatever would happen, the last of the terrible things to come in this trial, this moment, and how it felt to be with him like this made everything else easier to bear.

I rolled my hips as the tears fell, focusing on the feel of him between my legs and the sound of his heavy panting. His forehead rested against mine and his hand on my face moved to my right hip where his grip only grew tighter until his entire body relaxed beneath me with a deep groan. Beau's breathing slowed and his hand moved back to my cheek, his thumb stroking back and forth with each inhale and exhale.

"I'm sorry," I said, barely holding back the sob building in my chest.

He continued to stroke my cheek and pressed a kiss to my forehead. "My life to this point, this trial ... The gods may decide fate, but this moment will always be ours."

My body melted against him, relaxing in a way I wasn't sure it ever had or ever would again.

Part VI

A Love that Created Mountains

Aria willingly stayed at Mount Sollom. She stayed because that's where O'Riah was and that's how her realm would grow stronger. As she fell for him, he was equally enraptured by her. Their bond was strong, as immovable as Mount Sollom itself, and as a result, their realms bloomed. O'Riah was no longer alone in his realm and the heat and sun from his powers only enabled life to thrive in Aria's realm despite her absence.

Together, they were stronger. The world was stronger. Their realms began to blend together as their boundaries blurred and their people grew more familiar with the new lands. Aria's people began to migrate into O'Riah's realm and life came with them, bringing new plants and new lifeforms that never before walked there. All was well in the realms, and more was to come between the god and goddess.

Their love only grew deeper with each moment they shared together. Their bodies became one and Aria brought new life to the mountain and it thrived, spreading until more and more of their mortal children lived within their realm together. The new tenants were alive in all the ways Aria provided, but quickly grew in their knowledge of life in O'Riah's realm. A new era of life was started and it completed Aria and O'Riah. It was a full circle, binding O'Riah, Aria, and the mountain together in a way that only the worst of tragedies would separate.

24

Not long after we dressed, Ezra returned to the cave. He looked angrier than before. A quick look over him as he climbed out of the water told me that he hadn't been injured. There were no signs that he'd been in a fight or he'd had any trouble wherever his scouting had taken him.

"I found our raft, a few pieces of it anyway," he said and squeezed the excess water from his dark curls.

"Well," Beau said and sat a little straighter across from me. "Is there any good news?"

Ezra sent him an annoyed look before he spoke. "We are maybe a day from the coast."

"How do you know?" I asked, getting a stern glare in return.

"I may not have grown up among the merchants but I can recognize a seabird," he sneered and turned away from me.

If Beau didn't look so relaxed reclining against the wall of the cave then I might have lunged for Ezra. I was so tired of his comments that I almost welcomed returning to the shore with the other contestants. At least he'd have someone else to annoy him than whatever it was about me that did the trick.

"What other predators roar like dragons?" Ezra asked. The cave went quiet and my skin cooled when I saw the fear in Beau's expression. Ezra didn't seem effected by his reaction as he waited impatiently for either of us to answer him.

"Probably the closest thing here to a dragon," Beau said quietly. "A drake."

"You mentioned drakes when we reached the beach. What do you know of drakes?" I asked, remembering a photo from a geography book Leif made me read several years ago. Drakes looked like dragons only much smaller. They didn't have wings, and they were far less intelligent, which is what made them dangerous. They were known to chase prey to their detriment.

Beau sat up, his eyes darting to the mouth of the cave before his shoulders relaxed. "I know they don't swim."

Ezra nodded. "I know they prefer to hunt at night. Can they breathe fire?"

"If they grow large enough," Beau snorted.

"Did you see one?" I asked. There was no other reason Ezra would mention it.

He didn't bother looking my way when he answered. "I heard them."

"Them? More than just one?" I asked, ignoring the way Beau's face paled.

Ezra nodded and sat down between us with a sigh. "That's a problem for tomorrow. I'll take the first watch."

He didn't look at either of us as he pivoted to look toward the mouth of the cave, unsheathing his sword and setting it in his lap. Either something had pissed him off or he was just tired of Beau and me and the fact that he'd saved us both and nearly gotten killed because of us. It made my stomach hurt. The panther attack might have ended differently if it wasn't for Ezra Loreign. Because of him, I made it to this cave alive rather than dying at the river's bottom. It only made me hate him more.

I dreamed of Beau Renault. I dreamed we were together in the house my mother had grown up in, that house that overlooked the port where my grandfather's ship sat ready to explore the islands. I imagined we lived there together, that I visited my grandfather's grave there and that I told two blond children about how he'd discovered an island and embraced Nex's sea. I saw Beau riding the waves, the ocean uncharacteristically calm and I knew it was because he was at the ship's helm. Beau and the sea. Beau and I together. No kingdoms and no monarchies to determine our futures.

I was wide awake. The dream was just that, a fantasy that would never be and couldn't be. I couldn't live that life knowing what the rest of the realm faced and how the people suffered.

"I can take over," I told Ezra.

He was sitting at the far side of the rocky shelf with his sword in his lap, his hair hanging loose around his shoulders instead of tied at the crown of his head like normal. Something about the way he looked seemed mediative, and I immediately wondered if I had interrupted.

"No," he said without looking my way. "You need your rest."

"So do you."

"I didn't nearly drown today."

I was already halfway there with my sword in one hand and the dragon-tooth dagger in the other.

"I don't have a hole in my back like you."

"And I've been focused on conserving my energy since," Ezra said and looked up at me. "Not on having my holes filled the way you have, Princess."

I slammed my fist into his face. He groaned as the blood flowed down his mouth and chin, but he didn't look phased at all by the attack. It was like he'd expected nothing less from me and that almost prompted me to punch him again. He leaned over the edge of our stone shelf and spat a mouthful of blood into the water.

"I do what I want and I won't be shamed for what I did

today," I told him and pushed the hair that had fallen free from my poor attempt at braids back over my shoulder. "You can think what you want, that I should've let go and let Beau die in that river today—"

"No. I don't think you should let him die, even though it makes keeping you alive more difficult," Ezra snorted, lowering his hand from his face as the bleeding from his nose slowed.

"I can keep myself alive," I said.

"None of us would be alive right now if it weren't for the other," Ezra said, his tone razor-like. He sent me a challenging glare before dipping his fingers into the water and rinsing away the last of the blood from his chin. He wasn't a great swimmer. I wondered if he'd drown if I pushed him in now. He'd learned enough that it would probably take me holding him under and I knew I wasn't strong enough for that. He'd probably just climb out of the cove angrier than before and I'd have to put up with worse glares and retorts on the way to the beach than I already was.

I tossed my sword and dagger onto the stone behind him, gaining his attention.

"Stop with the self-pity, Ezra. You didn't make any promise to me. Stop pretending like you can't kill Beau. The fact that I won't kill him, let him die, and that I nearly drowned to save him doesn't make me any different from you. We are both prolonging the life of a man who's destined to die. You can say that you're doing it just because of some promise, but I have no reason for saving Beau's life except that he deserves better. I curse the gods and their fucking games. I won't be controlled by them. Aria may say it's Beau's fate to die, but I won't let her take him without a fight. What does that make me?"

"Worthy of a crown, Princess," Ezra growled, his jaw tight. After a beat of silence, he smirked and looked back at the water. "Sit."

"You don't have to pretend to like me," I said and started for my weapons.

"Not pretending," he said, making me stop halfway bent over so my face was level with his. "At least let me fix your shitty attempt at dragon braids."

"Dragon braids?" I asked.

He raised his brows, making it clear that he wouldn't say anything until I sat. I let out a groan and sunk the rest of the way to the stone, moving my dagger and sword to my side.

"So?" I prompted.

"Easy, Princess," Ezra snorted. He moved behind me, and I nearly scooted the dagger closer. "Take your hair down."

I was beginning to loathe letting my hair down. It reminded me that I was still just a girl in Honor Cove, in the Light Realm where my greatest power was determined by whom I married. I pulled my hair free from the ties and ran my fingers through it to try loosening the knots that had formed. Ezra's hands replaced mine as he combed through my locks.

"So?" I repeated.

He chuckled. "You're a stubborn pain in the ass."

"With bad hair, according to you. What are dragon braids and how do you know how to do them?" I asked, not willing to make light of the subject. I needed to know as much as I could find out about the man, even if that meant something as shallow as hairstyles.

"I'm a soldier. It's my job to know about the Fallen," he said, combing my hair so gently that I'd almost forgotten he was doing it. "Dragon braids are only worn by Fallen riders."

"What's a rider?"

"A Fallen soldier that has a dragon. It's the top military force. If a soldier is worthy, a dragon will hatch for them. That's what makes them a rider. The dragon chooses the rider, not the other way around. The braids are meant to represent the spines along a dragon's back. Riders wear the braids to honor their dragon," he said as he moved his hands to my forehead and started the first braid along the top of my head.

Soldier.

I could feel the meaning of the word in my bones. That's what I was: a soldier.

"How do you know how to do dragon braids?" I asked again. He was nearly finished with the first braid, fingers easily weaving my hair together.

"I've seen enough riders to know."

We sat in the silence. I felt like I was back in my chambers in the castle. I was sitting at the vanity again, watching in the reflection of the mirror as Norelli braided my hair. Only, I wasn't in my chambers, and I was looking at my own tired reflection in the pool of water in front of me.

"I knew who you were the first day I saw you wearing the braids," Ezra said. He finished the last of the three braids and was gathering all of my hair into a ponytail at the crown of my head.

"What do you mean you knew who I was?" I asked as he finished the hairstyle.

He let out a deep breath. "I knew you didn't belong. You may not have known what the braids were, but Norelli did."

It felt like my heart had torn a little.

"I'm sorry," Ezra said. His tone had changed. This was the first time we conversed without the subtle layer of condescension. There was no tension between us now, just his gentle hands in my hair, combing the length of my ponytail. Part of me wanted to scoot away, but the touch felt comforting.

"She warned you about my guards, didn't she?" I asked, turning so I could look at him.

He released the end of my ponytail, and it fell over my shoulder. I could see the guilt in his expression.

"She overheard Waylon talking to your head guard and made an assumption that they were part of a larger plot. It didn't take her long to intercept the notes," he said. I remembered how Ezra had approached the king and Waylon at breakfast after he'd tossed the severed heads on the floor. He'd read one note allowed before handing it to the king. The other he had given to Waylon.

"What did the second note say?" I asked, not needing to specify.

He snorted in disbelief. "I read the first aloud that had the plot to murder everyone at your tea party. The second note was to your head guard. After you survived the tea party, Waylon sent a vial of poison to the man with a note. The dumbass signed his name to it. It didn't say specifically what to do, but just to use it when the time called for it. Norelli intercepted the note and the poison before it ever got to the guard. I was unaware of that. If I had known that then I wouldn't have given the note over to Waylon."

I could tell from the serious look on his face that he blamed himself for Norelli's murder.

"You didn't kill her, Ezra," I said with a sigh. I was at a loss. Maybe I never should've gotten her involved. I could've asked her to bring those shoes from my room and then let her go back to serving hors d'oeuvres. She would have been better off. At least, she'd have been as well off as any other Fallen slave in the castle.

"Neither did you, Wren," Ezra said with a supportive nod.

It didn't matter. She was gone. She was one of the only friends I'd ever had and in another day or two, maybe even a matter of hours, I would kill the only friend I had left.

25

There was a gasp next to me.

I opened my eyes as the large sword dragged across the stone beside me, releasing a grating scrape as Ezra fumbled to grip the hilt. I rolled to my back, my hand wrapping around the hilt of my sword as Ezra dropped his at the edge of the pool and vanished beneath the water.

"Beau!" I yelled as the spikes along the scaly creature dipped below the water after Ezra.

"What was that?" Beau yelled at my side with his sword in his hand a moment later.

"I don't know," I said and stepped to the edge.

"Wait!" He grabbed my arm tight, pulling me back from the edge. My heart thundered in my chest. There was no telling how far that thing would drag Ezra beneath the surface, how long it would keep him there. Beau sent me a somber look, almost begging me to listen. "This is a trial, Wren."

I knew what he meant. It could be the two of us at the end. I could take Beau with me to Aria's stone. I could even let him win. Just a minute longer, if that, and that dream I had could be reality.

Just a little longer and I could walk away. I could pretend the rest of the realm didn't exist and live with him, maybe even fall in love with him.

I couldn't pretend though.

I pulled my arm free and dove into the water with my sword in my hand. My heart skipped in my chest when I saw the beast. A wyrm. It was at least a yard long and had a spiky ridge along its back. It had an almost dragon-like head, with sharp teeth that were snagged on Ezra's clothes. His eyes met mine as he attempted to twist and stab the wyrm, the blade coming feet from his mark.

I swam hard toward him, aiming the point of my sword at the wyrm's eye. My stomach lurched when that eye shifted to focus on me, prompting me to kick harder and make my move, hoping I was close enough to stab flesh. The water rumbled around us as the beast recoiled in pain. The water between Ezra and I turned red as I pulled my sword free and reached for him.

I was propelled into Ezra's chest by the force of the wyrm's tail cutting through the water as it swam away. Wrapping my arms around him, I kicked for the surface only to slowly sink. Ezra's eyes were closed and his head lolled in the water like a doll. I kicked harder, my efforts doing nothing to move us upward and making my muscles scream in protest. My heart thumped hard in my chest as I fought, pushing away the thought that I might have to leave him there to save my own life.

The water broke above us and as the bubbles cleared, Beau wrapped his arms around Ezra's thick chest from the other side. He gave me an encouraging nod and we swam together, rising until we were able to push Ezra's head above the surface. I gasped, using my free hand to keep Ezra's head from drooping into the water.

"The river," Beau said, guiding us toward the mouth of the cave while I focused on keeping Ezra afloat. We moved back into the river, which was mercifully calm, and dragged Ezra the rest of the way to shore once we'd reached shallow water. I ignored Beau as he told me that there wasn't any more we could do and climbed on top of the large knight. I did the chest compressions just as Leif had taught me, pressing my lips to Ezra's and filling his lungs with air from mine. I'd only done a single round when Ezra stirred. He shoved me off by my hips and rolled to his side, vomiting water over the rocks.

"Thank the gods," Beau said under his breath.

Ezra sat up with a deep breath, looking at me in shock. "You should've let me drown."

"Yes, but I'm not an idiot."

"Just honest, apparently," Ezra grumbled and took another deep breath.

"Are you okay?" Beau asked, moving closer so he could rest his hand on my shoulder. Ezra glanced up at him before replying, probably to be sure he was speaking to him and not to me.

"Give me a moment," Ezra said, his hands slipping to his sword belt. He felt along the leather for the weapons, looking down when he reached the spot where his sword should be.

"Oh. Here," Beau said and moved away from us. I watched as he went back to the river's edge. He lifted the large sword with two hands, holding it a little like he'd never held a sword before due to its size. "I snagged it before it could slip into the water." He laid it on the rocks next to Ezra who immediately lifted it to inspect it before sheathing it at his hip.

"Thank you," he said. It was strange, the sincerity in his tone clearing the air between us. There was a moment when we all exchanged glances, almost like we were testing to see that we all agreed, that we were all tired of pretending to be enemies.

"Fuck this trial," I said and stood up, extending a hand to Ezra. "Are you ready?"

He grasped my hand, making me feel small and only making me accept the fact once he stood to full height again. I was small in his eyes, but so were most.

"Let's go."

It didn't take long to see the evidence of the predators. We picked up our pace and decided not to rest mid-day when heard the yowl of a monkey, and several more following. There was a roar that shook the ground around us. It was like a battle was taking place and we had unwittingly stumbled among the trenches.

The forest was unnervingly quiet after the sounds from the attack, keeping us on edge for signs of another. We relaxed a little when the birds returned with their brightly colored feathers and their unique songs, venturing closer to the river now that it seemed we were safe from attack.

"How did you get your start in the army?" Beau asked Ezra.

I saw the tightness in Ezra's jaw and I wondered if he would answer. It was a bold question from Beau, one that could reveal things about his skills and his weaknesses.

"My father," Ezra said in a clipped tone.

"He was a soldier then?" Beau asked.

Ezra snorted. "The best."

His response caught my attention and pulled my eyes away from spot along the river where I'd just seen a fish leap from the water. If his father was one of the best soldiers, he would have had a high rank. Leif would likely know him. Ezra would've been the son of a knight, but no one at the castle recognized him and you wouldn't forget Ezra once you'd laid eyes on him.

"Who is your father?" I asked, watching him carefully.

He didn't give anything away. He smirked, a brief glance letting me know that he knew exactly what I was doing.

"He was forced to retire, nearly died for his realm, and was left disabled," Ezra said, that gravely tone back in his voice. He was very good at controlling his emotions. They never showed in his face unless he wanted them to, not even when you looked deep into his eyes for a glimmer of them. Still, there was something so subtle about the way he spoke that gave it away. I could tell Beau hadn't caught on, but I knew that there was a story there that deeply affected him.

"I'm sorry," Beau said, keeping his eyes on the river. "Which battle?"

"No battle," Ezra said, his tone like the edge of a sword. "The stupidity of youth. Another's mistake."

He tightened his grip on the hilt of his sword and I searched the trees to be sure he hadn't seen anything. He didn't relax as we walked, not until Beau stopped a while later. He hesitated before going to the riverbank.

"What are you doing?" I asked, looking back at Ezra before I followed him.

Beau held a hand up to silence me as he watched the water. I stood next to him, not seeing the fins beneath until he began slowly wading almost knee-deep into the water. He knelt, his hands just above the water. I hadn't noticed Ezra join me, a smirk spreading on his face as he watched him. I almost asked him what he was doing when I heard the smallest splash of water.

Beau turned to us with a large fish in one hand and a boyish smile on his face. He tossed it to the bank where it flopped along the rocks. I retrieved it before it could rejoin the others upstream.

"It will be dark soon and we haven't eaten in over a day," Beau said, keeping his voice low. "Wade in like I did and follow my lead."

He returned to his crouched position while Ezra and I moved away from each other. I slowly walked through the water the way Beau had, chasing off the nearest fish as I moved. I wondered how Beau managed it, because I couldn't avoid creating ripples and noise. I nearly slipped on the rocks once. Ezra was already knee-deep in the water, putting him several feet farther out than Beau was, and was mirroring his movements.

I crouched, losing my balance and splashing around the water until I got my footing again. Ezra shot me an amused look that sent all thoughts of fishing and dinner from my mind. I watched him more than I focused on my own efforts, not satisfied until I saw the humor leave his face and the irritation return at his third failed attempt.

Beau caught two more fish in the time it took us to figure out the technique. Ezra was getting better, managing to snag the fish with his large hand, but not quite contain its squirming before it wriggled free. I, on the other hand, was absolute shit at this. How was I supposed to move slow enough not to scare off the fish, but quick enough to capture them?

"Wren, you can go back," Beau said. "I think we almost have enough."

Ezra let out a groan, shoving a fist into the water and sending a wave over his legs. He straightened up with a smile directed at me, the largest fish yet held in his right hand. I turned back to the river as he tossed his catch ashore, determined to contribute more to the meal than just gathering wood for the fire.

I focused on the river, letting the sound of it over the rocks quiet the blood thundering in my ears. The fish started to swim closer again, carving a path between my legs and over the tops of my boots. I crouched lower, keeping my hands in front of me and waiting until one swam close enough, determined to wait for the perfect strike rather than the largest catch. A medium-sized fish paused just in front of me and I shoved my hand beneath the surface, grabbing on to the fish and pulling it from the water. My grip was too tight though and the fish shot from my grasp, flying over the middle of the river where Ezra was. I lunged forward, catching it in both hands, but feeling my back foot slide on the rocks. I took another step forward as I tried containing the fish with both hands, my foot sinking deeper than I'd been prepared for.

I held on to the fish, too stubborn to let go until my body was submerged in the water. Before I could pull myself up, Ezra hauled me up by the back of my shirt. I'd never heard him laugh before. It was a deep, booming sound. He smiled with those too-perfect teeth that made him look even more handsome. It only made me hate him more. My cheeks were hot and there was no hiding my embarrassment. They'd both seen it on my face and I could tell it only fueled Ezra's laughter now that I was out of the water.

"Didn't think I'd be the one with the largest catch," he said.

I shoved him, but he didn't budge, and I nearly lost my balance again instead. He smiled wider.

"We have enough," Beau said, trying to diffuse the tension. "We should start on dinner before it gets too dark."

"We provided the meal," Ezra said to me with a shrug. "Least you can do is clean the catch."

I ripped my arm away from him when he patted my shoulder.

"I'll help. It will be quicker with two," Beau offered.

I didn't look his way, keeping my glare on Ezra. "I don't need any help."

I trudged through the river, almost losing my balance again before I made it to shore where the fish were. I did my best to ignore Ezra's laugh as he joined us, volunteering to man the fire.

"Let me help," Beau said again, waiting until Ezra was out of earshot. Those blue eyes were like ice to flames, dimming the anger churning in my gut. "Please?"

I let out a sigh and nodded, still not willing to admit that I needed his help. I didn't know how to gut a fish and Beau was kind enough not to further tank my ego. Instead, he talked himself through the steps, moving at a slower pace until I had caught on and we worked in tandem. Ezra dropped some logs not far behind us and by the time we finished preparing the fish, our backs were warmed by the flames.

"I thought you didn't need any help, Princess," Ezra smirked when Beau asked him to help carry the fish to the fire.

I whirled around and shoved his chest, this time hard enough that he at least seemed surprised.

"Say another word and I'll bloody your nose again!"

"Wren!" Beau shouted, grabbing my arm. I pulled free only for him to grab my wrist again, this time holding tighter. "Stop."

"You're bold for a woman your size," Ezra said as he looked me over. "Even with a sword."

"Yeah? Keep at it and I'll show you what I can do with it."

"Wren," Beau said again and tugged on my wrist. Once he'd gained my attention, he looked past me at Ezra just long enough to tell him to take the fish. He did, leaving us alone again on the bank. He let go of me and clasped his hands on top of his head, letting out a deep breath.

"He's an ass," I said.

"And he's liable to kick yours and mine if you provoke him enough," Beau snapped, the anger in his face softening when he faced me again. "You are strong. You are capable of winning the trial and walking away with everything you've dreamed of, but if you don't it will be because of your temper."

I opened my mouth to argue, ready with my usual response when I realized he wasn't Leif. I wasn't at the castle in one of our usual lessons and there was no knowing where Leif was or if he was safe. Still, his warning managed to find me through Beau Renault who looked back at me with soft eyes and concern. And just like with Leif, it was that look that quieted the roar of sound within me.

I inhaled, letting the night air fill my lungs entirely before I let the breath out. I gave him a nod and he stepped closer, a hand brushing along my lower back. He lingered at my side, pressing his lips to my temple. I hadn't been expecting it and when I looked up, he was already walking toward the fire. Ezra lowered his eyes from mine to the skewer in his hands, turning it twice before holding the fish over the flames.

26

It was quiet as we cooked our meal over the fire, the birds the only sound until the darkness took over. We kept our weapons unsheathed and ready in case we needed them, the possibility of attack chasing away the last of the tension between Ezra and me. We focused on our meal instead, eating all of the fish and allowing our travel-weary bodies to bask in the warmth from the fire.

I was still hungry and a look at Beau and Ezra told me they likely were too. I wondered how much longer this trial would last. My stomach twisted so much I thought I might lose my dinner. How much longer would they all survive? How much longer until I would need to kill again?

I tried thinking about anything else, fidgeting with the clasp on the small pouch at my belt when I remembered the items inside. It had been several weeks since I'd last made the tea, long enough that if I didn't drink some soon, monthly events would complicate what was next for me in the trial.

"What's that?" Ezra asked and nodded toward the container. I looked around us for anything I could use to gather water from the river, not seeing a single item that would work as a cup.

I stood up with a groan. "I'm going for a drink."

"You can't go alone," Beau said, reaching for his sword. Ezra was quicker, already on his feet with his sword in hand.

"I won't be attacked alone by the fire again," he said and pointed to Beau. "I'll go."

I ignored him and focused on the goal. Get to the river. Find a leaf or something to hold the water. Mix the tea. That was it. I could put up with Ezra for however long that took as long as he didn't talk or get in my way.

"Where are you going?" Ezra asked as I walked along the bank, the moonlight providing just enough light for me to see that there weren't any leaves at all along the river. I ignored him and turned around, glad that he had enough sense to at least move out of the way and let me continue my search.

"What the fuck do you need, Wren?"

"I need water," I told him, looking up at him.

He let out a deep sigh and moved to the river, cupping his hands and dipping them into the water. His hands were large enough that they carried several mouthfuls of cool water toward me. I wanted to reject the offer but I knew I wouldn't find anything better. I opened the container and eyed the water again, thinking through how much I needed to make a full dose.

"I'll have to do this twice," I said.

"Why are you adding that?" Ezra asked curiously.

Why couldn't he just let me do this without an explanation?

"The alternative wouldn't be pleasant for anyone."

"I didn't ask about the alternative," Ezra said and moved his hands away from me, a few drops of water slipping past his fingers. "What's the powder?"

"Worried I'm going to poison myself?"

I heard that grumble of annoyance in his throat. He dropped his hands and stepped toward me, close enough that the water splashed against both our boots. He gripped my hand around the vial, holding it still and lowering his nose to the uncorked top to give it a sniff. He looked up at me, dark eyes meeting mine and I knew then. Just like I knew from the subtle change in his voice. He could read the truth in me too.

"Are you bleeding?" he asked.

"No," I said, feeling my face heat.

"How long?"

I had to think about how many nights we'd endured to know. "Maybe two or three more days."

He nodded and stepped back, lowering his eyes from mine to reach for the pouch at his sword belt. He pulled out a small piece of cloth tied together with a piece of twine. He held it to me and after a moment, I took it in my free hand.

"Save the tea. Eat that instead," he said, taking the vial from me and stoppering it. "You won't bleed for another twenty-eight days. Assuming."

He said it with compassion but also so matter-of-fact that it stunned me. I knew before now that he was different from any Light Realm soldier and he didn't treat me like any other man would either. My heart was beating fast, emotion thick in my throat though I wasn't sure what for. It wasn't anger or sadness. I wasn't even all that embarrassed anymore, not after he so casually said the words. Still, he'd known what to do and had the means. *He's prepared for this. He planned ahead for me.*

"Were you a doctor before the army?" I asked, removing the cloth from around the tiny root. It looked like ginger but was bitter when I placed it on my tongue. Thankfully, it was easy to chew and didn't taste that bad.

He smirked. "No, but I understand why you would think that. Most men would run the other way at the mention of a woman's monthly bleeding and most women in the realm wouldn't know what to take to stop it."

"So, why do you?" I asked after swallowing the last of the root. He handed the vial of tea to me and I secured it in the pouch at my waist.

"I grew up differently," he said and started back toward our camp, walking slowly until I joined him.

"Everything okay?" Beau asked, looking from Ezra to me before I nodded.

"Fine. Just needed some water," I told him.

Ezra tossed another log on the fire and it crackled in response. I watched as the flames licked the wood and it slowly turned black.

"How much longer until we reach the beach?" Beau asked. His tone was somber despite his neutral expression. I caught Ezra watching me before I turned my attention back to the fire.

"We may be there this time tomorrow," Ezra said. Beau already knew as much. He said the same thing early this morning. He'd spent his entire life by the sea. It was getter harder for him to mask the anxious in his expression as we got closer to the beach.

"How did you know how to fish like that earlier?" I asked, hoping it chased away the heavy feeling.

Beau smiled. "I spent most days surrounded by merchants and fishermen."

"I thought you spent them in the stables with the horses," I said with a chuckle.

"I did until I could sneak off on a horse to visit the docks," he laughed. "I'd ride to the docks and watch the ships come in, watch the way the men worked, and listen in on their stories. I'd watch the women prepare the day's catch before taking the fish to the markets. When I could get away with it, I'd sneak into the pubs and the fishermen there would teach me their trade."

"You weren't like every other teenager, were you?" I relaxed a little, leaning back on my hands. Beau laughed and I noticed that even Ezra smiled a little.

"I was no different than most. I mean, sneak out of the house, get drunk in the pub when no one questioned my age, and sneak back home before my parents noticed I'd been gone," he said and nudged my foot with his. "What kind of trouble could a princess get into?"

I scoffed. "Very little. Well, it depends on who you ask. My father would say I'm the definition." I could tell from their faces that they didn't care about what the king thought. It was refreshing and promising to know that I wasn't the only one in this trial against the king's intentions. I thought about what my upbringing was actually like outside my royal obligations, about the ways I would play card games with Leif and the ways I would often push his buttons. "Leif would say it's my mouth that gets me into trouble. I rarely did anything to get into trouble. I've always been surrounded by so many eyes that there were rarely opportunities to do anything. He would get so mad at me because when I did get myself into trouble it was never for him to punish."

I was so used to the reality that I didn't know the weight of it until I saw their faces, the tightness that had set into Ezra's jaw. Beau looked sad again, his hand halfway extended to me before he decided not to touch me. I knew he wanted to touch the scar across my cheek, brush away that single moment of violence when there were so many before it that couldn't be.

"I've never regretted a word I've said though," I said, trying to keep my tone light.

"What do you regret?" Beau asked after a moment. The fire cracked loudly between us. His expression faltered for a moment as we stared at him, giving away the hint of sadness.

"There's no time to dwell on regrets while we're in this trial; every second is focused on surviving," Ezra said, moving his sword into his lap as though making a point.

"I think that's exactly why it's a good time to talk about it," Beau said and sat up a little straighter. "We could die tomorrow or maybe the next day. The point is that I don't want to die without letting go first."

"Then what is it you regret?" Ezra asked him.

Beau paused as though weighing the words before setting his eyes on me and then looking over the fire. "I regret going to the docks on the days my sister asked me to stay with her."

The story of the fire flashed through my eyes, the burn on his abdomen. Time was not something you could ever get back and it stung as I thought about Norelli and Leif.

"I told Norelli and Leif to leave," I said, blinking back the tears in my eyes. Fuck. I should've pushed harder. I should've forced them to leave.

Ezra let out a deep breath, the kind that I felt in my bones. It chilled my skin to see the serious look on his face.

"I wish I had stayed put like he told me to. I put my pride before my position and now my father is so disabled he can barely talk," he said, his voice shaking with emotion. "He has given me everything and still does."

I wondered what it was like to have a father who loved you so deeply that they would not only die for you, but endure a life of pain so that no harm came to you. I felt deeply about my father, but my voice did not shake with love. My body ached from the hate I had for my father and the terror I'd endured and the horror he openly talked about inflicting on others.

"I'm sure he's proud of you," Beau said.

Ezra smirked. "Not if he knew where I was." He let out a single laugh. "My mother would take on Aria herself to be here."

"Wow," Beau said under his breath. I could tell he was thinking the same thing I was. Most families would be honored to have a son in the Trial for Marriage no matter the end result. It was a religious thing that was equal in esteem to sainthood for most. That alone made me scoff.

"Your mother is a rarity," I said. I felt like I understood her from the statement he said alone. She defied what was acceptable for a woman in our culture, was willing to fight for what she wanted.

Ezra's serious expression was back on his face, back to the always alert version of himself I was used to. Still, there was a slight smile that pulled at the corners of his lips as he gave a curt nod. "She's a lot like you, Princess."

"Is that a compliment or a slight at your mother?" I asked and sat up, making a point to cross my arms over my chest.

"Depends on how you look at it," Ezra said and pinned me with a stare so intense that I knew I'd talked myself into a corner. "My mother never settles for less than what she's determined to take."

His expression was neutral, almost kind even, but the words cut deep. I thought about every lingering glance, every innuendo, the brash comment he made back in the cave ... I wasn't an idiot. I knew then that he'd either been at the mouth of the cave when Beau and I were entwined in the water or when we were lying naked together afterward. Ezra Loreign was smart. You would've thought he'd been brought up in the intricacies of court politics and scandal and not recently given a title. The man had only spent a few weeks in the castle, and he knew more than most of the gossips that roamed the halls.

"So, it was a compliment," I said.

He smiled and gave me a knowing nod.

If I didn't need him to get back to Aria's stone, I would plunge my dagger into his gut. The dagger that he gave me. The dagger he said I needed.

"If someone's going to gut me, I'd want them to do it with a proper weapon."

Fuck him. I'm an idiot. Fuck me.

"I'll take the first watch," Beau said with a forced smile. I wanted to offer. It was technically my turn, but I could tell that he wanted to be alone. Maybe he'd read into the conversation the same way I had. Ezra must have sensed the same finality, because he was already lying flat on his back, eyes focused on the stars above.

I lay down. The stars were so bright against the dark sky, something about them soothing despite the mix of emotions that made my stomach churn.

I wished the end of the trial would come sooner. All the same, I wanted to lie beneath those stars forever, far away from the horrors of the realms and away from the ambitions of the doomed men on the beach.

I ended up with the morning shift. Seeing the orange glow of the sunrise creep into the normally gray skies was almost worth the early-morning grogginess until I heard the uncomfortably close roar. It was unlike any sound I'd ever heard, clearly not mammal or bird and yet not reptilian either. The sound was deep, enough so that the trees seemed to shudder around us.

Beau stirred and rolled to his back, fumbling for his sword. Ezra lay peacefully on his back, with one hand around the hilt of his sword and the other around his dagger. The drake roared again, this time closer, and yet he still slept.

I stalked over before Beau could reach him, kicking Ezra in the side and wishing we had enough time that I could relish in the pained sound he made.

"There's a drake not far off," I told him. "We need to move."

Beau had already put out the last of our smoldering campfire.

"Which direction are they?" Ezra asked as he got to his feet, unsheathing his sword in case he needed it.

I scoffed. "You can't tell?"

"You're the one who heard them."

"Yes. How did *you* not hear them?"

He ignored the question and walked ahead of us, leaving Beau to cast me a look of disbelief before we hurried after him.

"Wait!"

The firmness in Beau's voice was enough to give me pause. Ezra let out a groan that was more of a growl as he stopped a few feet ahead of us, turning to face Beau who didn't look intimidated in the slightest the way he would've before. The two men exchanged glares for a long moment, as though waiting for the other to lunge.

"What?" Ezra asked.

"What happens when we do reach that beach and run into the other contestants?"

"What do you mean?" I asked.

Beau's expression softened a little when he looked my way, but not the same way I'd expected. This wasn't the look of a man facing the bitter end. My skin went cold at his concerned gaze, and I understood that his worry was meant for me.

"We're better together until we're not," Ezra said simply.

Beau scoffed. "What does that mean?"

"It means we face the others as a team," I said, sending them firm looks. They'd both made it clear already that I was the only reason they hadn't had a go at each other. If I wasn't here only one of them would be. None of the contestants would be surprised to see Ezra arrive on the beach, despite their hopes. No one would expect all three of us. That's what would keep Beau alive a little longer. That's what would prolong the inevitable. We would face them together until we were forced apart. Then, and only then, would I give Beau Renault the easy and honorable death he deserved.

Beau and Ezra maintained their glares for a long moment before Beau nodded. He looked at me, the acceptance in his blue eyes making my heart skip. I looked away, catching Ezra's eye. He didn't look at me with disdain or judgment. This time, he looked sad and it felt like something clicked into place among the three of us.

"Together," Ezra said with a nod to me before looking at Beau. "Fuck the gods."

Beau shook his head in disbelief and for a second I thought he would push back against the comment. Instead, he extended his hand to Ezra. "The truth is between the lines."

For a moment we were transported back to the beach after we'd barely survived the sea, none of us happy to be with the other. I didn't feel that different from the person I was then, but even admitting that there was more truth than what was written on the pages of the religious texts marked Beau as someone new. As they shook hands, it was like we were solidifying ourselves as more than allies. It was an agreement that it was us against the gods. We might not walk away, probably wouldn't if we faced them. This trial wasn't about winning the hand of a princess. It was about power. I would not be the steppingstone to something more, something closer to the gods, a kind of power Aria relinquished.

The truth was between the lines.

The truth was between the Light Realm and the Dark Realm.

The truth was in the Mist.

The two men parted, and Ezra turned on his heel and forged the path ahead. The foliage around us had changed before I realized how quiet we were. Everything was somehow greener here, lusher than before. The birds sounded different, reminding me of when we'd rowed ashore several days ago.

"We're close, aren't we?" I asked as we walked. None of us slowed our pace.

"A few hours," Beau said, looking skyward where a bird briefly appeared against the dark sky before disappearing before the treetops. As if on cue, thunder rumbled, and it began to rain. It didn't take long for the weather to turn tumultuous, the rain pounding down on us and making it difficult to see far ahead.

"It will wash away our scent," Beau shouted over the sound.

The wind tugged at my braid and the rain seemed to pick up, battering us harder than before. I hoped he was right. If we had to endure the storm, the least bit of fortune would be that the drake behind us would be forced to slow its pace as well.

"We go as long as we can," Ezra said, glancing over his shoulder at us before continuing ahead.

My fingers were wrinkled from the downpour. I kept my head bowed, trudging ahead until I walked right into Ezra's back. I looked up to discover that I'd actually walked into his chest, and I was only inches away from his face. Most of his curls were plastered to his face, and what wasn't whipped behind him in the wind. His eyes moved from mine, prompting me to turn to look for Beau.

He wasn't there.

My heart leaped into my throat, and I felt my body tense. I had to remind myself of the reality to keep from sinking to the ground.

"Where is he?" I asked loud enough for Ezra to hear.

"I don't know any more than you."

I started to backtrack, taking only a few steps before I heard him.

"Stop!"

I froze, looking toward the sound and seeing him several feet away in the brush with his sword ready. That's when I realized why he'd vanished. He'd been hunting, not abandoning us, and we were in over our heads.

It was like time stood still for just a moment, all of us poised for attack. Beau stood frozen with his sword raised, a drake only a few feet in front of him with its eyes set on me. Just to the left of him, another drake had its red eyes set on Beau, crouched low as it prepared to spring. The low grumble to my right told me there was another just behind me, likely preparing to leap at Ezra.

My gaze met Beau's for just a second before that loud roar shook the ground beneath us. I ripped my sword from the sheath and lunged for the drake behind Beau, ignoring the beast that ran for me. I felt its claws brush my shoulder, not feeling the sting of the cut until after I'd sliced my sword across the drake's snout in front of me. Beau drew close to me, letting out a yell in my ear as he protected my back just as I had protected his.

There was a roar from behind that surprised me enough that I'd nearly allowed the drake in front of me to land a blow to my shoulder. I screamed and lunged, swinging my sword for the beast once and then twice before it drew back. I screamed again, slicing my sword through the space in front of me when the drake launched its next attack; sending a cascade of gore across the greenery around us. The beast gave a hollow cry, and I scurried forward, raising my sword above me and letting out a yell as I drove it into the drake's skull.

I had to press my foot to its head to pull the blade free, turning just in time to see the third drake bearing down on Ezra. It lowered its head and roared, Ezra standing his ground just a few feet in front of it and screaming right back. I didn't hesitate. I whirled around, my hand pulling the dragon-tooth dagger from my hip and launching it toward the drake. Ezra had prepared an attack of his own and I got lucky as the dagger barely missed his shoulder, whizzing dangerously close to his ear before it lodged in the drake's forehead.

Its roar was cut off, though the echo of it remained and shook the trees around us. Ezra turned slowly as the beast fell, looking back at me in astonishment before his jaw tightened and he closed the gap between us.

"The third drake!" Beau took a few steps in the direction of the retreating beasts before giving up, turning instead in time to watch as Ezra charged toward me.

"You nearly took my head off," he said.

"But I didn't," I told him as he came to a stop a foot away. "You're welcome."

I saw a muscle twitch along his jaw and his grip on his sword tighten.

"You are infuriating," he said and sheathed his sword. His eyes lingered on me for just a moment before he turned toward the dead drake, easily pulling my dagger free. He cleaned it using the rain and the leaves around us before handing it back by the blade. All it would take is a single thrust and I could sink that sharp edge into his gut. He knew as much. Still, he drew in close with the hilt extended toward me without a moment of hesitation.

"Thank you," he said low enough so only I could hear. I took the dagger from him, hesitating a moment before I sheathed it at my hip.

"Wren," Beau said, the fear in his tone sending a chill over my skin. "You're bleeding."

I could tell from the way the color leached from his face that there was more than a little blood. My muscles felt weak, and my vision blurred.

I heard them arguing before that swimming feeling dulled the pain in my shoulder and garbled the sound of their voices. I couldn't see a thing, and I could only hear them between the silent moments. That was until the burning started.

My eyes flew open, a pair of terrified eyes greeting me as pain seared through the cut along my shoulder. I screamed, trying to pull his hands away only for them to vanish a moment later. The first breath caught in my chest as I scrambled away, resulting in a coughing fit that made my stomach twist.

"She's fine," Ezra said. "You're fine."

I swallowed the bitter bile in my throat and looked up at him, catching sight of the anxiety in his expression for the split second it was there. Beau moved to my side, taking my face between his hands. I gasped when something pressed to the cut, but Beau kept hold of my face.

"He's just bandaging you," he said.

"It's not that bad. You probably passed out from the shock of it," Ezra snorted.

I sat up to glare at him. "I've seen much worse than a little cut. I did not pass out from shock."

"We're all exhausted, dehydrated, malnourished," Beau cut in, looking between the two of us like a parent chiding two children. "Our bodies can only take so much before it needs rest."

Ezra went back to wrapping the last of the white cloth around my bicep. The wind had died down and the rain was lighter than before. The two drakes were lying a few feet away, prompting me to scan the trees for any sign of the third.

"We should keep moving before the other one comes back," I said as Ezra finished with my arm.

"You just passed out, Wren," Beau said.

"I'm fine," I said as I got to my feet. My vision blurred and I heard them both scramble. I was horizontal before I realized I'd fallen again, my vision nothing but a mess of hazy colors as my body fought to stay conscious.

"She's right," Ezra said next to me. "We can't rest here with the rotting beasts around us and if we don't get the beach as soon as we can, we may miss our opportunity for an advantage over the other contestants."

"Let me carry her," Beau said as my vision cleared. Ezra easily scooped me off the ground before he could reach me.

"I've got her," Ezra said. He adjusted me in his arms. If I didn't feel so weak, I would've made him put me down. "Find something to collect the rain. She needs water," Ezra said before walking ahead.

Despite feeling embarrassed, it was hard not to be grateful. He was strong and his size made lying in his arms more comfortable. My head was pounding, so I closed my eyes and let it rest against his chest.

"Don't get too comfortable with your competition, Princess," Ezra said, his voice low. I heard a deep laugh. "Unless getting comfortable with the men is the strategy, then by all means"

I pinched his chest through his shirt, and he let out a grunt. It was a weak action and left me wishing I could've done more, but I was tired, and my headache only got worse the more I leaned into my anger.

"I don't need to get comfortable to have a competitive edge. I can stand against any man here in a fight because I was trained in secret since I was a kid. I know more than any of you know." Gods my head hurt. I raised a hand to my forehead, shielding my eyes from the light and the rain as much as I could.

"I know that."

"You don't have to play nice to make me feel better or make yourself look like less of an asshole."

"No, I know that you're capable. I knew it as soon as I saw you at the ball," Ezra said. He spoke the words with such assurance that it made me lower my hand to look up at him. I felt less faint, so I could see the truth in his expression. His chest rose and fell with his sigh, almost feeling like a hug around me.

"How could you tell that I can hold my own in battle?" I didn't need to imply what I meant. I was a woman in the Light Realm. Battle was not a place you would ever find us and no one ever expected a woman to be able to defend herself physically. Not only would it be strange for him to notice my skill, but to so easily recognize it as formal training was strange.

Ezra lifted his eyes to look at the trees. "The way you moved."

"The way I moved?"

He nodded. "The men at court see it as alluring and graceful, the way you weave through a crowd and so easily skirt their blatant attempts to brush against a beautiful princess. Everyone at court talks about your dancer-like qualities. That and your other assets, of course," he scoffed. "I recognized the way you place your feet. The way you adjust your arms to keep them close to the dagger you would keep strapped to your left thigh. The way you would carry your arms higher when you wore your hair up because you had a tiny dagger concealed among the pins.

"Was that a compliment?" I asked with a snort, barely getting the words out past the shock of him knowing exactly where I concealed my weapons.

He smirked. "You are a rose deep in a thorn bush, Princess, and I can't say that I blame you for it."

Looking up at his dark eyes, seeing something like pity within them ... Normally a reaction like that from him would set my body aflame, but it didn't. I knew that as much as I wanted to blame it on my dehydration and exhaustion that it was more than that. I wasn't angry that he had so easily read me. I was interested in him. He was so different from anyone else I'd ever met, far from anything like the other men at court. It was obvious and often discussed before the start of the trial. Still, I could tell that there was still so much I didn't know about him that I was sure only set him further apart.

Ezra Loreign was not just some recently knighted man who came to win the hand of a princess.

"Wren," Beau said, appearing in front of us with a leaf full of water between his hands. I gladly took it, downing the entire thing before holding it steady to collect more rainwater. Beau kept close with his sword drawn as we walked. Ezra remained silent. It was a test of my thin patience to wait for the leaf to fill with enough water to drink. As much as I wanted to walk on my own, I knew I needed food and water before I was in any shape to keep up with them.

By the time I felt like I could walk what little there was left of our trip, judging by the lack of sunlight, the trees began to change and the dirt beneath our feet was more sand than mud.

"We're here," Beau said and gave a laugh. He looked back at us with a smile on his face. "The beach."

It was still far enough ahead that I couldn't see it through the trees, but I could smell the salt and hear the waves. I heard Ezra's relieved sigh as he lowered me to my feet. I walked ahead, joining Beau as we continued at a quicker pace until we could see the shore.

The ocean looked the most peaceful I'd ever seen in the light of the setting sun. The tide washed over the untouched beach, marking us as the first of the contestants to arrive. I scanned the waves for a sign of a ship. Maybe there would be one once the other contestants arrived. My stomach twisted as I thought about the gods and how perfect it would be for a ship to appear only after everyone had met on the beach to face their differences head-on.

"Time to make camp," Ezra said as he caught up to us. The air grew thick around us. The others couldn't be far behind. This would likely be the last time we sat around a campfire together. It might be the last time we were allowed to be anything but rivals. It could even be the last night Beau had, the last time he would lie next to me beneath the stars and hold my hand.

It felt like my heart had fallen to the sand. If only I could bury the burden of it.

Part VII

The War of Land and Sea

Excerpt from The Book of the Great Mother

Nex was so enraged by Aria's betrayal that he made the sea a constant storm. Aria's people were confined to the land and his anger grew so intense that it clouded the sky across all the realms. It made even the skies over Mount Sollom thick. It was the stormy skies that sparked O'Riah to action. Concerned for his dragons and his people in the sky, he went to the coast to speak with Nex.

Their meeting was full of bitterness and only worsened the relationship between the two gods. When Aria went to calm the seas herself, Nex ordered the waters to take her and she was pulled from the shore and into the sea. O'Riah was beside himself with worry and attempted to fly over the sea despite the tumultuous air. When he threatened Nex and began conjuring waves of fire at the sea, Nex pulled Aria under the waters and attempted to drown her.

A war between the creatures of the sea and the beings on land began, which resulted in catastrophic loss of life and angered the Great Mother. She brought an end to the battle when she broke through the sky and forced Aria to the shore once more. O'Riah took Aria back to Mount Sollom where they both met the wrath of the Great Mother. In order to keep the peace among all the realms, she ordered Aria to return to her realm and O'Riah to remain in his. Aria began the journey to her realm the same day and O'Riah was distraught, left broken and alone once more on Mount Sollom.

28

We watched the sun descend into the water as we sat around our campfire, not worried anymore about being seen. An orange-red hue lingered in the sky as we finished the last of our fish and tossed the bones into the flames. I was exhausted, but I couldn't turn my mind off as I watched the sunlight fade. I could see the same struggle on Ezra's face. Beau looked peaceful, as though he was considering the sunset putting him closer to the end of the trial. Maybe he was. Maybe the end would be a relief.

Part of me envied him. Nothing would be the same once we faced the others and went back into the sea. Once back on the shore of Honor Cove, my entire life would change. My heart was pounding at the thought of running across the beach, of reaching Aria's stone to claim the right to my own life. I tried to swallow the thickness growing in my throat as Ezra rose to disappear into the trees again. I took a deep breath, nearly calming my panic when the words slipped from my lips in a whisper.

"Come with me," I said, pulling Beau's attention from the sea.

His brow wrinkled. "What do you mean?"

"I want you to reach the stone with me, win the trial by my side." Tears rolled down my cheeks and the weight of the last few days fell from my shoulders. "We can escape Honor Cove and go to the Mist."

A smile slowly tugged at the corners of his lips, his blue eyes lighting up in that way I loved. "You would let me win?"

I nodded as my mind was flooded with thoughts of him running into battle beside me. We could develop a plan against my father together. He had the diplomacy I lacked to create connections. He could help me build an army.

"You would marry me, Wren?" Beau asked, taking my face between his hands and resting his forehead against mine.

"Yes," I said and raised my hands to his chest, gripping the front of his shirt as though he might be ripped away from me at any second. He would be, if I hadn't said the words.

He laughed in disbelief, and then he kissed me, soft at first. I could taste the salt of my tears on his lips before I realized he was crying, too. We rose to our knees, and he pulled me tight to his chest, holding my face to his by the back of my head while the other wrapped around my lower back.

"We need a plan," he said and pulled away, brushing the last of the moisture from my face.

"Stay close to me. I won't let anything hurt you," I told him. I pressed my hands flat to his chest, feeling the lean muscle beneath his shirt that I was sure hadn't be there months ago. This whole time I'd worried about his ability to stay alive in the trial, but maybe the fact that he was still here and still faced the dangers ahead without wavering made him more a soldier than many. He was selfless to a fault, willing the sacrifice himself for honor for his family and for always stepping in to comfort me. I could get him out alive, and he could live that quiet existence he craved. And deserved.

He took my hand and pressed my knuckles to his lips. When he let go, we sat down in the sand. It was dark enough to see the stars and yet I still couldn't calm my mind enough to sleep. Ezra returned a few minutes later and sank into the sand a few feet to my right. He unsheathed his sword and laid it across his lap before looking at me.

"Sleep. I'll take the first watch."

I glanced at Beau to my left. He lay on his back with his hands resting on his sword belt, his expression calm.

"I'm not tired," I said and turned back to Ezra.

He snorted. "You are. Lie down."

"Don't talk to me like I'm a damn child."

"I wouldn't if you knew what was good for you," he said with a groan. "You nearly passed out from exhaustion today. You need to rest."

He wasn't entirely wrong about being tired. I was too tired to argue with him anymore. I lay on my back the way Beau had, keeping my hand around the hilt of my sword and the other around my dagger. "Wake me up in a few hours. I'll take the next shift."

"No," Ezra said with a laugh. "I'm waking him up."

I could tell from the look he gave me that he expected me to argue, hoped for it even. I lay the rest of the way down instead, focusing on the stars straight above me instead.

"Fine."

"Fine."

After a second I heard that grumble of annoyance to my right and I felt the smile pull at the corner of my lips.

I was surprised to wake up on my own rather than to the clamor of battle. Beau was snacking on the berries we'd collected along the hike here. When he noticed me, he held out a handful.

"Thanks," I said and accepted them. The red ones were tart, so much so that it was hard to continue eating them as my mouth puckered. I glanced toward Ezra as I heard the swish of sand beside me.

"Finally," I said and kicked his boot. "You know you snore like a boar, right?"

"I know that I don't," he said without missing a beat. "But you do when you sleep on your back, which is why I rolled you onto your side."

He sat up with a grin as my stomach twisted. I'm normally a light sleeper and it was a little embarrassing that I hadn't woken up. It must've shown because Ezra only smiled wider.

Beau reached across me, extending a handful of berries toward Ezra.

"Any changes?" Ezra asked as he took the berries.

Beau shook his head and tossed the last of the berries into his mouth.

Most people would've thought the extra time a blessing. I was just bored. It had me more on edge knowing that any moment would be the one that set everything in motion.

"What's that?" Beau asked.

I looked at his curious gaze and followed it toward the ocean. I didn't see what he had. Maybe it was something swimming in the water. I kept my eyes on the waves so I wouldn't miss it when I noticed something protruding from the water several yards out. It continued to rise, clearly not the fin of any fish, until the large mast was revealed along with two smaller ones. All bore sails prepared for sailing. The belly of the ship burst through the waves with a loud *poof* that sent a wave rushing to shore. The ship sat several yards at sea, a swimmable distance, ready for its crew.

"Gods," Beau gasped.

I was just about to suggest that the rest of the contestants must not be far off when a loud roar echoed through the trees behind us. Ezra tugged on my arm as he drew his sword.

"To the beach," he told us a moment too late.

A drake burst through the trees behind us, charging straight at Ezra who took a step aside to keep from being trampled. I pulled my sword from my hip as the beast turned in the sand to face us and gave another roar, revealing all of its pointed teeth.

"On your right!" Beau yelled.

Ezra turned just in time to place a cut along a second drake's snout. It screeched in pain and recoiled. I looked just long enough to notice the beast in front of me lunge. I raised my sword and it hesitated before swiping at the weapon with its talons.

I deflected the attack, pulling my dagger free and launching it at its exposed chest. The dragon tooth sank deep, eliciting a cry from the monster. The sound hadn't died out before I swiped my blade across its throat. Blood splattered across the sand and the drake fell, nearly knocking me over on the way down.

I heard a man yell. I didn't recognize it as Ezra or Beau. Past the spot where Ezra and Beau were fighting the second drake, the rest of the contestants fought three more. I wrenched my dagger free, and I sprinted past Beau to reach the five men, coming to Lord Vonhenson's aid as a drake snapped its massive jaws inches from his right ear. The drake's eyes flicked to me, giving Vonhenson the moment he needed to stab the drake in the side. I shoved my sword into the drake's neck, pulling it free when it fell at my feet.

Vonhenson's eyes widened when he saw me, but he paused for just a moment before racing to help Lord Raust. The two remaining drakes were pressed tail to tail, making it difficult to get a good opportunity to attack either without taking a risk of being impaled by the spiked tail of the other. The drake in front of me swiped at Raust's feet, missing him but causing him to stumble to the ground. The beast lunged, teeth sinking into the sand as Raust rolled onto his side. Before the drake could attack again, Ezra let out a guttural cry and sliced off its head.

"That's the last of them!"

Lord Dallin turned from the body of the last drake to face us. A pair of arms wrapped around my middle. Before they could fully restrain me, I threw my head back. I heard the crunch and pushed away, turning to face Lord Somerled. Ezra tackled Vonhenson around the stomach and they both hit the sand hard.

"Stop!" Dallin yelled. "You're going to get us all killed!"

Ezra sent a final punch to Vonhenson's face, knocking out a few teeth in the process. Dallin stood with his sword pointed at Beau in warning, giving him a challenging look before he smiled back at me.

"You must be a sturdy thing to make it this far," he said with a laugh.

"What did you say about us all getting killed?" I asked. I saw his eyes move past me where the ship was bobbing among the waves. That's why it hadn't appeared before. We were all meant to sail together. There was no way three of us could manage it alone. The ship needed a crew.

"It will take all of us to sail that ship," I answered for him. His smile only widened until he was laughing like he'd planned the ordeal himself.

"For fuck's sake," Ezra said behind me and slammed his sword into the sheath. Beau's shoulders slumped, and he sheathed his sword before moving to my side. Dallin's smile dimmed as he noticed the movement, prompting me to take a step away from Beau. The damage was done, though.

"I see," Dallin said, looking me over before looking at Beau again.

"How do we get on the ship?" I asked, forcing him to look at me again.

"Swim out. There should be a ladder portside," he said and pointed to the ship.

Ezra swore again and turned toward the beach, storming ahead so quickly that I had to jog to keep remotely close to him. The others followed behind, sloshing through the shallow water until we were all deep enough to swim. It took more effort than I anticipated to make it past the waves, my muscles aching by the time I caught up with Ezra. He was a weak enough swimmer that I passed him and made it to the ladder first.

The water was choppy, and I was so short that the first rung was just out of reach. Without asking, Ezra lifted me so I could take hold of the ladder. I ignored the feel of his big hands on my thighs and pulled myself up, the effort much easier once I could reach the rung with my feet. I had just climbed aboard when he started up behind me, the others finally gathering beneath us.

"We better hope it's a short trip," Ezra muttered under his breath, jaw tight as he peered down at Vonhenson who was at the bottom of the ladder.

"I need you to help me with something," I said, watching to make sure we would be alone a few seconds longer. Ezra looked back at me, the tension in his expression softening. He looked like he was going to question me for a moment.

"What?"

"It's Beau," I started. Ezra groaned and shook his head, interrupting before I could finish.

"He dies on your terms and your terms only, I know."

"And you will protect him, if needed."

He was back to his stony self as the words left my lips, but he gave me a curt nod.

"On my life, Princess," he said, the words tight. I held his serious gaze until Lord Vonhenson joined us and forced us to step apart.

29

The ship was almost too large for our small crew of eight. I didn't need to know anything about sailing to know as much, nor did I need Dallin's remarks as he looked over the mast and rigging like I'd seen him look over women at court.

"A crew of twelve would be best," he said and turned to face the group. "Eight will have to do."

"You can't be serious," Lord Somerled said and moved away from the railing to stand next to him. "It's us against them."

I placed my hand on the hilt of my sword as he nodded toward Ezra, Beau, and me. It was clear the way his gaze lingered on Ezra that he didn't consider me a threat. They all seemed glad to see me alive, but none of the men acted as though I was a part of the trial at all. I was merely a companion to them.

"Which is why they won't do anything," Dallin said with a smile directed at me. It made my stomach turn and I could taste the bitter bile rising in my throat.

"You touch her and you're dead," Beau said and spat on the deck between us.

The other men laughed. Dallin pointed a stubby finger at Beau and said, "You?"

"Try anything and I'll toss you overboard," Ezra said, his tone even. "I wouldn't count on the seas being as kind to you as the last time."

The laughter died as Dallin's smile faded. His frown only made his wrinkles more obvious. One step, then another, and Dallin was just a couple of feet from Ezra.

"All this time you've been her guard dog, Loreign," Dallin said, taking one more step forward that put the two men almost a foot apart. Dallin did not look concerned by the fact that Ezra was at least a foot taller and wider than he was. "Even if you won, you have nothing to offer the king. No power. No fortune. No estate that I could find or even a plot of land to your name. You can't expect to be rewarded if you survive this. The gods may award the winner with a bride, but the real prize is the power bestowed by the king. Everyone knows that power only comes to those who can afford it."

Ezra laughed. "Real power cannot be bought. Over time, all the people you control, even those whose lives you paid for, will see your power for what it is: a bunch of paper and tin. And without any real substance or care behind it, they will see how easily paper burns and tin melts. They may even bear the torch themselves. And they'll see that behind your meaningless wealth and lack of responsibility for what you've bought that you're just a man who discards pretty things when they no longer shine just for him."

The sound of waves filled the silence as the two men glared at one another. Finally, Dallin let out a huff and took a step back. Then he glanced at me, a sinister smile spreading on his face.

"We'll see just how much my fortune is worth once I win," Dallin said. He turned and started toward the bridge. Beau took a few steps after him and I followed, worried he was going to attack before I saw the confusion on his face. He looked at me and then at the rest of the crew.

"You're all just going to let him command the ship?" he asked.

His words seemed to thaw the stunned silence on deck. The men cast each other cautious looks before the whole group of us had hurried toward the stairs to join Dallin on the bridge. He'd already taken his place behind the wheel by the time Beau was the first to arrive.

"You're not going to just take over the ship," Beau told him and pulled on his shoulder. Dallin had no choice but to turn from the wheel.

Dallin gave a chuckle. "I don't know that any of you pretty boys are up to the challenge."

"I studied navigation charts, spent every day with merchants at the dock. I'm more knowledgeable about how to prepare a ship than you are," Beau said, glancing at the rest of us as though making sure we supported him.

"You've never sailed a ship, have you?" Dallin asked, laughing again when the truth showed in Beau's expression. "Face it, boy. Only one of us here is seasoned enough to get us through these waters; the same man who spent over twenty years on the bridge."

I opened my mouth to argue, wanting more than anyone to rip him away from that damn wheel. But he was right. He had spent a great deal of his life sailing the sea, seeing more of the realm and doing more manual labor than most of the men here, other than Ezra. I believed Beau when he said that he'd been educated, but he had not put his knowledge to the test and this far into the trial we needed someone who could guarantee our safety.

"Renault," Dallin started as he grasped the wheel. "You may command the deck."

Beau shook his head in disbelief as Dallin ordered all of us back to the deck. We waited for Beau to join us, clearly trying to wrap his head around being in charge. He drew in a deep breath as he looked around before picking two men out of the crowd.

"Somerled and Raust can lower the sails. Fenrick and Loreign, keep watch of the waters," he said before turning to face me. "You and I will see what lies below deck."

He gave the orders so easily, as though it was second nature, but I could see from the glimmer in his blue eyes that he'd been strategic. He wanted to speak with me privately, and from the waiting look on his face, it was serious.

Ezra hesitated before joining the others to man the ship, leaving Beau and me to move to the stairs below the bridge. They opened up to a large room. Hammocks were strung along both sides. There were gun ports along the walls but no cannons. Near each hammock was a wooden chest. Just behind the stairs was a single compartment. I moved to that room while Beau started toward the nearest chest.

The back room was empty, other than a wooden table that was bolted to the floor. It looked like it was meant to be a storeroom. I unlatched and opened every cupboard along the far wall, only to find each empty. When I moved back into the main room, Beau had moved on to a fourth chest halfway down the room.

He slammed the lid shut on the chest and looked at me as he straightened up, shaking his head. "All empty."

"The storeroom is too," I said and moved farther into the room. He sat down on the top of the chest and held a hand out toward me. I crossed the distance between us to take it, moving into the space between his knees so I could drape my arms on his shoulders.

"So, this is why you wanted to get me down here alone," I teased and pressed a kiss to his forehead. He smiled and moved his hands to my hips. "What is it you want to tell me, Beau?"

His hands stilled at the shift in tone. His blue eyes flicked up to meet my gaze, studying me as though trying to decide if he should continue.

"What is it?" I asked again.

His shoulders tensed beneath my arms. "I think it's time to stop trusting Ezra."

My heart skipped a beat, and I pulled back from him. "Why?"

"He's a contestant in the trial just like the rest of those men, Wren."

"He always has been, and he's never hidden the fact."

"True, but he wants to win."

"And for us to make it out of the trial alive, you must win. I was meant to be in the trial as much as I am meant to win it now. I either win the trial and set off for the Mist alone, or you can win, and we both escape. I can search the Mist for answers, and you get your life outside the control of the court and your family," I said, giving him a gentle shake. I didn't understand why there was still an issue with this. Why did he not seem to understand that we could both have our freedom?

"Do you want to be my wife, or do you want to set me free?"

It felt like he'd slapped me. "What do you mean?"

"The minute we reach the shore, the second I step foot on that stone, we are wed under Aria's will. Husband and wife," he said, holding my hands tight now.

I pulled my left hand free. "I refuse to be of value only because I'm something to someone."

He managed to grab my hands again, this time holding them tighter and pinning me with such an intense stare that it kept me from moving. He stood up and drew close, tears glistening in his eyes.

"I refuse to be yet another man who cages you, Wren. I can be loving and kind and you can be valuable because you are with or without me, but in our realm, marriage is just another way to bind you. So, I'm asking again, do you want to be my wife, or do you just want to set me free?"

He held my hands firm, not allowing me to brush the tears that fell on his cheeks. My stomach was in knots. My chest ached. I wanted to turn away and press tight to his chest at the same time, whatever would keep me from looking back at him like this.

"What changed?" I asked. "We can leave the realm together, we can both be free of the Light Realm."

He shook his head. "You can, Wren, if you win alone. If you let me win and become my wife, you will always be in the shadow of the kingdom. You may never inherit the throne, but you will always be fodder for it, and even if we join the rebellion, I'm not a soldier. I am a liability, a weapon to be used against you or a distraction to slow you down, and I refuse to be either."

"Beau—"

"You don't want to marry me, Wren. And even our marriage wouldn't free me."

As his tears fell, he released his grip and allowed me to embrace him. I clung to him for just seconds, resisting the urge to kiss him so I wouldn't have to look into his eyes again. I brushed the moisture from my face and allowed the anger to consume me, burn me from the inside out so I could face the others ready to destroy them however I needed so I could win this fucking trial.

I left Beau below deck and hurried upstairs, planning to go as far as I could, only to find Ezra standing watch at the bow. I put several feet between us as I placed my hands on the railing and focused on the horizon. I wondered how long before we would see land again and how much longer after that it would be until we reached it. How many of us would survive to set foot on the sand?

"Did he tell you, or did you finally get wise, Princess?" he asked, moving so he was just inches from my left side.

"I don't trust you," I blurted. I didn't need to explain anything to him. It wasn't like he didn't already know. He was thankfully silent, even seemed relaxed as he stared over the waves. I looked up when he finally stirred, reaching into the pouch at his belt to remove the smallest vial I'd ever seen. Clear purple liquid sloshed within, no more than a teaspoon.

"The poison Norelli intercepted from your guard," he said quietly before sliding it along the railing. I took the vial and quickly stashed it in my pouch. "It's gentle. If you were to slip it to someone before bed, they would think they were simply going to sleep. They wouldn't suffer. That's why it's a common poison used by wives."

Ezra took another step away from me, turning so he could lean his back against the railing. "Wren," he said before I could take more than a step away. "It's only enough for one. So, reserve the mercy for someone who deserves it."

I didn't bother answering him before I moved further away. Ezra may know more than he should, especially where Beau and I were concerned. What he didn't know was that Norelli had also given me a vial of poison.

Beau remained below deck for nearly an hour. Once the sails were ready and we caught the wind, everyone but Dallin was free to keep watch of the waves. There was still a clear separation between our groups. Ezra and I kept eyes on each other and the other men. The other contestants would whisper to each other in passing, staring at me when they didn't think I was looking. I tried to ignore the glances and smiles they sent my way, but even when I turned from them, I could feel their eyes roaming my body.

A chill ran over my skin and not just from the cool air and the waves that splashed over the railings. My hair was damp and what was left of my nightgown, mostly the top half, was pasted to my body, leaving little to be imagined for the watching men. It might have been the reasons for their unabashed stares even. A part of me felt ashamed, but I wouldn't cover myself. The longer they stared, the sooner they realized they all were. Nothing drove men wilder than knowing that what they wished to possess was already beheld by another. It didn't matter than none would have me. It only mattered what they believed.

My stomach twisted from the sick reality, trying to forget what it would mean for the duration of this trip. I would play the part. That's what would get me through this trial and would make eliminating the competition the quickest and easiest.

I heard his growl of annoyance just behind me. "You're freezing."

I turned just a fraction to scowl at Ezra, his hands working at the buttons of his shirt. "I know what you're doing, and it doesn't matter."

"So, you're aware that every man here can see just how cold you are," he said, getting the final button undone. My stomach turned for a new reason now, anger burning through my gut and making it that much more enticing to stick to my plan.

"I know that my body makes for an easy distraction, maybe my best weapon," I said, unable to hide the sarcasm in my tone.

Ezra scoffed. "Don't cheapen your skills just because the fools do."

"I know how they see me and I won't waste my energy trying to convince them otherwise when they will all be dead soon," I said and turned fully from the rail to face him.

"I know how it pissed you off to let Lord Merry grope you just so you could get a cheap shot. It's the same reason you're in such a foul mood now, catching all these men staring at your soaked-through shirt when no one cares that they're every bit as drenched."

"It doesn't matter what I say or what I do—"

"What you do is *all* that matters," he spat, drawing the attention of the nearest men. "These men only see your tits and want you for nothing else than that and your title. To them, you are here in this trial as a pretty little companion and not as a threat. Now, you can continue letting them believe that you are nothing else, or you can show them that you're a soldier worthy of respect."

I glanced at the men around us. The entire group of them had turned from their posts to watch, all wearing the same look of jealousy, most of them eyeing Ezra now rather than me. It was a challenge, like they were waiting for the right time to step in, sizing up the clear alpha of the pack before deciding it was safe to take his place. That's how these men functioned, always fighting to be the richest in the room. I was just a rare jewel to add to their fortune, to make the rest of the men glare at them the way they were all looking at Ezra now. The truth is that I'm not the prize. I'm the alpha.

"The realm will know that once I'm standing on Aria's Stone," I said and straightened up.

"Fuck the stone," Ezra said. He wrapped an arm around me, gripping my ass with one hand and encompassing my breast with the other.

I shoved him hard, putting enough distance between us so that I could kick him in the gut. When he doubled over, I swung for his head. My fist landed against his jaw, once, twice, and then I smashed his nose and sent a rush of hot blood over my hand. Ezra drew his sword, but I was quicker, drawing in close and positioning the dragon-tooth dagger at his throat.

"Drop it!"

The deck was quiet, the clatter of Ezra's sword hitting the ground. I moved his sword behind me with my right foot. I saw movement to my left. Beau had his sword drawn and was charging toward us.

"Stop! Beau, stop!"

Beau froze but kept his eyes trained on Ezra. Once I was sure he would stay put, I looked back at Ezra again and saw the smallest twitch at the corner of his mouth. He'd orchestrated this whole thing. He knew exactly how to push my buttons, and I'd played right into it.

"On your knees," I said. I kept the dagger at his throat as he held his hands up in surrender, slowly sinking to his knees. Even in this position, he wasn't much shorter than me. He did look vastly different somehow, his eyes warm rather than cold like I was used to and his expression soft instead of set with that rebellious tight jaw. He was surrendering to me, even tipping his chin upward to expose the soft hollow of his throat to me. I could tell that he was prepared for a killing blow if I decided to administer it. I focused my eyes on the curve of the dagger, the weapon he'd given me, remembering what he'd said as he'd gifted it to me.

"If someone's going to gut me, I'd want them to do it with a proper weapon."

There were so many reasons I hated him. He got under my skin like no one else. He was stronger, bigger, and not to mention annoying as fuck. But he stood against my father, my brother, refused to play by the rules of court, and he'd taken out my assassins when no one else cared to so much as investigate the threats. All of that and he didn't give a damn about marrying me. He didn't enter the Trial for Marriage to win a wife or any riches from the crown. Not only did I want to kill him fairly and not because he willingly knelt before me, but he didn't deserve to die before the rest of these men.

I would kill him with the dragon-tooth dagger like he'd asked me to, but not yet.

"Give me your shirt," I told him.

The dagger was still so close to his skin that a thin line of blood dripped from the shallow cut I'd made as he shrugged out of the shirt. The fabric wasn't much thicker than what was left of the nightdress I wore, but together they would better hide my curves. He held out the shirt to me and my eyes fell on the tattoos on his arms, remembering the strange swirls and characters across his back. As much as I wanted to inspect those marks again to try deciphering them, I lifted my eyes from his arms to his face. I moved the tip of the dagger from his throat to his chest, placing a shallow cut across the spot where his heart lay pounding beneath.

He winced but didn't budge, keeping his eyes on mine.

"Touch me again and I will carve your heart out," I said and lowered the dagger. I looked up at the men who had gathered around us, every one of them watching in shock. "If I catch any of you leering again, I will gouge both your eyes out and feed them to you."

I shoved the dagger back into the sheath at my hip and I crossed the deck for the stairs, sending a glare at Dallin as he stood at the bridge above me. For once, he didn't smile back.

It was warmer below deck, just another perk of leaving the crowd. I pulled on Ezra's shirt over my own, the fabric baggy enough to hide my body beneath. It was like a dress on me. We must have reached calmer waters, because the ship did not sway beneath my feet and it was easier to cross the hull of the ship as I thought about what had just happened.

Ezra's grip on my body. My hands shoving his chest. The warmth of the blood, now washed away from the spray of the sea, running down my fingers. It was how he'd looked up at me from his knees that stuck with me.

I pushed the thoughts away and instead looked over the hammocks, weighing the pros and cons of choosing the one closest to the stairs. Once I'd settled on it, I went to try it out. I had never sat on a hammock before, and I was glad now that I'd decided to do so in the empty room. The first time I attempted to sit on it I found myself flipping over and lying flat on the floor. Two more times and a few bruises later and I'd figured out how to lay down in the bit of fabric. It was awkward, but more comfortable than sleeping on the hard earth back on the island. I only hoped that the ship wouldn't rock too hard overnight so I wouldn't get seasick.

I nearly fell out of the hammock again when I was ready to return to the deck, using the chest next to me to steady myself. Something told me to open it and I was glad when I did. Sitting in the bottom of the chest was a pair of riding pants, fresh socks, a new pair of boots, and a long-sleeved shirt. They were all women's cuts and looked to be my exact size. I almost ran to the next chest to check if my suspicions were correct about there being clothes inside of it as well, but I decided to use the rare alone time to change.

I was right. The clean clothes fit me perfectly. I noticed as I slipped into the boots that the door to the storeroom was open. I was hopeful as I passed the stairs and relief washed over me so intensely that I could've cried. The storeroom was stocked with fresh fruit, nuts, and even cuts of meat ready to be cooked.

Maybe the gods weren't vengeful after all.

It was pitch black outside by the time we'd finished preparing our feast. The only light was from the lamps hung around the deck and the moon above. We were all so thankful to find food below that the tension in the air thinned, and we stuffed our bellies and lounged on the deck without fear of being gutted.

A few of Dallin's men were tipsy from the ale we'd found, Lord Jakob Somerled drunk enough that he finally gave up standing with a few other men and sat down on the floor with his mug in his hand.

"Ah! Look what I found," Vonhenson said from the stairs. He'd gone back down to refill his mug and had returned with a guitar. "The gods didn't just bless us with a meal. I'd say the ale and guitar are a sign that they want a celebration!"

"Who's the soft-hearted bastard who can play the thing?" Dallin said, eliciting a roar of laughter from most of the men that only grew louder when Lord Somerled raised his hand from his seat on the ground.

The guitar was passed around the group, finally reaching Somerled who immediately played an impressive opening to a song so upbeat and technical that the deck went silent. The laughter returned when he began to sing, the lyrics so obscene that Beau turned bright red when I caught his gaze across the group. He looked down at his mug and then raised it to his lips, taking a long drink as I skirted the group to join him.

"Come to gouge my eyes out?" he said with an awkward laugh. He let out a sigh and looked up from his mug. "I'm sorry. That was in poor taste, and I hope you don't think that I ... I didn't mean to stare."

"I will gouge your eyes out if you don't stop stuttering like a schoolboy," I laughed, glad to see him smile in return. I looked down at my mug between my hands, the outline of my reflection mirrored in the dark liquid. I'd been nursing the drink since the night began, not taking more than a few sips to keep up the charade.

"You entered the trial to win your freedom, lead the revolution. You reject all these men, emphatically so. Yet you've worn my gift all this time," Beau said. My eyes went from the ale to the sea glass bracelet. I wondered then as I did now if wearing the bracelet was a form of self-torture. I knew I would kill Beau. He knew as much. We may have had a brief moment of hope for something else, a life we could have if we could both forget about the rest of the realm and the horrors the people faced. It would make us no better than the rest of the lords of the court.

"It reminds me of you, and you give me hope that there's still good in this realm," I said and looked up at him. "I think that in another life, I would have loved you."

A boyish smile spread on his face and lit up his eyes. "I am so glad that I was fortunate enough to love you in this one."

My eyes stung. I wanted to hit him. It enraged me how easily he accepted his fate. I swallowed the emotion along with several mouthfuls of ale, lowering my almost empty mug to look up at him again.

"I may only have hours left to live," Beau said as Somerled held the final note of the salacious song. "I want to celebrate with the girl who leaves fancy parties to get drunk with her maid and the runt of the court."

The memory of the night made it hard to hide the smile pulling at the corners of my lips. I laughed. "To Beau Renault," I said and lifted my mug. "Good Person."

He chuckled and raised his mug. "To Wren Bellator." His mug clanked against mine. "The Queen of Honor Cove and the Light Realm."

I felt the words in my bones, and I happily drained the last of my mug, waiting until Beau had done the same to offer a refill. I took both of our mugs below deck and into the storeroom. Much of the barrel was gone, but the sound of the men on the deck could've told me that. I dipped our mugs into the barrel and sat them on the table in the middle of the storeroom. I meditated on Ezra's words from earlier as I pulled the vial of poison from the pouch at my hip.

"It's gentle. If you were to slip it to someone before bed, they would think they were simply going to sleep. They wouldn't suffer."

I took a deep breath before tipping the vial and dumping the entirety of it into Beau's mug. I used the end of the vial to swirl it around before stashing it back in my pouch and carrying the mugs back upstairs.

"You're telling it wrong," Beau shouted over the group.

"What was that?" Dallin asked, the humor on deck diminishing as he glared at Beau. "Why are you interrupting the greatest tale to have happened at sea?"

Beau didn't hesitate, not at all effected by the cautious gazes the rest of the men were sending him. "Because you're telling it wrong."

"Am I?" Dallin snorted and motioned to Beau with his mug, sloshing ale onto the deck. "How could you know the story of Beck better than a sailor?"

"Because I studied it with the priests back in Scout Sea. That story comes from The Law of the Sea, the religious text of the God Nex."

No one spoke. Dallin's face was red, the wrinkles across his brow more pronounced as he glared at Beau. Maybe it was the fact that it was late, or maybe Dallin was too drunk to challenge Beau like he normally would. He gave him a curt nod instead.

"Go on. You tell it then."

Beau nodded and walked to me. He took his mug from my hands and moved up the stairs to the bridge until he was raised high enough for the whole group to see. He rested the mug on the railing and looked over us as though it was the first time he'd ever addressed a roomful of people. Maybe it was. He took a deep breath.

"This is the story of Beck, the Man Blessed by the Sea."

31

I'd never heard the entire story. I'd spent my entire life in Honor Cove and my lessons were filled with the teachings of the *Book of the Great Mother*, but aside from Aria's teachings, I hadn't studied much about Nex. Most of us hadn't unless you lived in a seaside village where Nex's priests lived in their temples. Of all the parables from Nex's Law of the Sea, Beck's was the most famous.

Beau set the scene immediately. Beck was a young man, barely out of his teenage years, when he left his village to join a crew to sail the sea. His life had not been a happy one. His mother had been found guilty of conspiring to kill her husband. She was hanged in the center of town and it disgraced the family, which only worsened the beatings and starvation that Beck endured at his father's hands.

Beck's father became a drunk and gambled much of their money in the taverns. Beck worked at the docks during the daytime, fishing to feed himself and his father and selling whatever extra he caught to pay their debts. A storm beat against the shores one day and well into the night, tossing the ships in the port and leaving his nets empty. He went home hungry, hoping his father would return too drunk to notice. Instead, his father came back in a fit of rage after losing all his money at the tavern.

When he saw that their pockets were empty and there wasn't a thing to eat, he beat Beck. The boy was used to these nights and he endured the blows, waiting for the beating to end so he could clean up the mess and help his father into bed where he would pass out for the night. The end did not come though and the blows grew harder and more blood gathered on the floor of the drafty shack until he was begging for his father to stop and trying to resist the blows. Something snapped within Beck and when his father swung for him the last time, he placed a kick to his stomach that sent him staggering into the kitchen counter.

His father was enraged and snatched a butcher knife from the counter. He was too drunk to wield it, however, and instead fell on the blade and died.

Beck didn't know what to do. No one would believe that he had been defending himself. No one had ever cared to help poor Beck, so he left the shack without a single possession and went to the docks. By day, the merchants would come and go with their goods. Most nights the port was empty. The sea was a dangerous place at night, and the sailors who'd endured it would return with their ships battered and bearing tales of monsters and ghostly visions among the waves.

There was a ship of explorers at the docks that night who were preparing to set sail. The captain hoped to discover new land in the name of the king. The crew was full, but Beck convinced him to take him on without pay. He told the captain that he wanted to see the sea and learn how to sail. The captain sensed he was on the run, but most of the men who crewed these explorations were men with little to lose. So, Beck was invited aboard and they set sail shortly after.

Beck spent his days at sea swabbing the deck, preparing meals, and doing the manual labor that not even the lowest of deckhands wanted to do. He found it to be a welcome distraction and an easier burden than the life he'd left behind. He quickly gained the respect of the crew and even the captain himself was happy to impart his years of skills on the young sailor.

As they encountered uncharted waters, the crew grew excited and anxious about what may lie ahead. They celebrated one evening after the captain finished updating his records with descriptions of the new creatures they'd seen. As the night went on, most of the men passed out from drink and the captain entrusted Beck to keep watch. As the party dispersed and the captain went to his quarters, Beck climbed the mast to sober up and keep watch from the crow's nest.

The moon shimmered along the water. Beck saw shapes gliding along the waves, almost like figures dancing, something swirling beneath the surface. He could hear the distant sound of singing and a soft voice calling out for him. He saw a woman among the waves, skin like porcelain and hair like moonlight. She smiled at him, and Beck knew that the woman was singing for him, the song stirring something in his heart. As he watched her glide along the waves, he received her message without needing to hear her words. If he kept this secret, told none of the crew what he had seen, and bared his heart to the sea then in three days he would be marked by the God Nex and gifted the power of the sea.

Beck woke the next morning in the crow's nest. The captain was angry that he'd fallen asleep on watch and had him whipped. Beck bore the lash and told no one what had happened during the night, promising to make up for his mistake by keeping watch the next night. The captain agreed and that night, Beck climbed up to the crow's nest again.

That second night as he kept watch, Beck saw the woman again among the waves. She called him down to the side of the ship, and he went, meeting her at the railing where the sea lifted her so he could look into her blue eyes. She told him of his future as a powerful captain. She shared the secrets of the sea, the creatures that dwelled beneath the surface, and the magic it possessed. She was the sea, Nex's power and heart, and Beck fell in love with her as soon as she kissed him at the railing, a touch that showed him everything he could possess.

Beck was instilled with a new desire to sail the sea and as the hours passed after that first day, he felt stronger and closer to Nex. He could feel the god's presence in the wind. The captain was pleased with Beck's new enthusiasm and offered to raise his position in the crew. Beck denied the promotion and asked to remain in the crow's nest at night. His wish was granted and on the third night, when he climbed the mast, the woman of the sea returned and beckoned him to the railing.

This time, the woman took Beck into the waves where their hearts became one. Beck made love to the sea and even when he returned to the deck of the ship, he could feel the tide ebb and flow in his soul and he ached to be back with the woman. The captain was worried about Beck's sudden shift in mood. Many a man had gone mad at sea and was never the same once he reached the shore.

Beck promised that he was perfectly sane and that he only felt more passionate about sailing the sea and their mission for discovery. Still, Beck's obsession concerned the captain and rather than turn in for the night, he stayed awake to keep an eye Beck as he took to the crow's nest to watch for the woman.

It was the fourth night, and the woman came to call Beck to the railing. This time, she pulled him beneath the waters. Beck struggled to breath until she kissed him and breathed the life of the sea into his lungs. She took him to the bottom of the sea where he faced a great blue dragon. It had several webbed arms with razor-like talons and fangs that it flashed at the sailor. But Beck was not afraid. He knew not to be afraid. He could feel the power of the sea deep within him, breathed it in with each inhale, and knew as he'd bonded with the sea that they were one and Nex had given him a blessing bestowed upon no other man.

Nex blessed Beck, leaving the marks of a tentacle swirling from his wrist to his elbow, and allowed him to return to the surface with the woman. Nex told him to command the ship and sail west, a message he passed on the next morning to the captain when he showed him how he'd been marked. The crew was astounded, but the captain didn't believe that he'd been touched by Nex. He believed that Beck had been driven mad by the horrors they'd heard about the sea during the night. Beck tried to fight back, demanded that the captain do as he say. Instead, the captain had him detained and he cut off Beck's arm that bore Nex's mark.

Beck passed out from the shock of the amputation and when he woke on the deck, the ship was under siege. The captain and crew walked the deck as though possessed, lured to the railing by the songs of dozens of sirens, where they were pulled into the sea to never surface again. Beck was left with the ship alone, Nex sending the wind to fill his sails and the waves to guide his ship west where he discovered the Spine Islands.

"The history I know says Beck was an old captain that brought riches to Nex's temples along the coast, not some scrawny boy who fell in love at sea," Dallin scoffed, spitting on the deck near the stairs Beau had ascended.

"He did," Beau said and made his way back to the main deck. "Beck told the first priest that he came from the sea on a great blue dragon. He was an old man by this time, gray-haired and frail, but rich from his travels. He made his way up the coast, giving his fortune to Nex's temples with the message to honor the sea."

Dallin let out a booming laugh. "And the old captain left the last of his fortune to the king in Honor Cove before he died."

"Vanished," Beau corrected. "The priests say that Beck told stories at the temples about traveling as far up the coast as he could before he would walk into the sea and let the waves take him."

"So, the captain was crazy after all," Dallin said, getting a laugh out of Fenrick and Raust on either side of him.

"The stories never say anything about him having a tentacle mark on his arm when he visited the temples," Vonhenson spoke up. I saw the way Ezra shook his head in disbelief, downing the last of his ale before setting his mug down next to Lord Somerled, who looked into it as though hoping he'd been given another round.

"One of the temples has a painting of Beck with the tentacle mark," Beau said and lifted the mug to his lips. My heart leaped into my throat, and I felt my body go slack. I had taken a step toward him when Dallin let out a roar of a laugh, making Beau hesitate.

"You think the old captain just toured the coast and happily walked into the sea to his death?" Dallin asked.

It didn't take much effort to take the mug from Beau. He was too focused on the story to think much of it. He explained what had been left at the various temples as I moved back into the crowd. I sat the mug down next to Ezra's, ignoring the curious look he sent me.

"I hope you don't regret that," he said under his breath.

"Shut up," I said. He moved his foot before I could stomp on it, my boot smashing Somerled's fingers instead. The man was so drunk that all he did was grumble in his sleep.

"You either grant him the mercy now or you save him so that he can die at the hands of the coming war," Ezra scoffed before eyeing me. "Even if you win the trial, entering against the king's wishes, twisting the rules of Aria's game is an act of treason. The king will order you to be executed as soon as you reach the stone. You may be able to fight your way out of Honor Cove, but Beau Renault can't. You can't escape the city unscathed and watch his back at the same time. There are worse fates than dying with honor in this trial."

"I know that," I said, keeping my voice even.

"He has accepted his fate," Ezra said, turning to face me. "Why are you still questioning yours?"

The words stung. He didn't wait for my response. He turned his back on me and walked toward the stairs.

PART VIII

A Wall of Darkness

Excerpt from The Book of the Great Mother

When Aria left O'Riah's realm, the Great Mother spread darkness throughout the border. The darkness destroyed any life between the two realms, making the region the most dangerous to cross as it sucked all the light from the world. The border separated Aria from O'Riah and as soon as the border went black, a sorrow so deep tore through Aria and O'Riah as they realized they would never be allowed together again.

The humans remaining in O'Riah's realm were forced to a world so dimly lit that they nearly starved and the only life that prevailed was that which could survive the damp earth and in the air. Aria's humans began to wither and die from disease and starvation and her people were forced out of the sea by Nex and into the cities where they developed a new society that was often unkind and cruel to one another.

Nex slowly grew sympathetic to Aria and allowed her people back into the sea, but it only helped to separate her people as only those most fortunate could afford to traverse the sea. A hierarchy developed among her people that caused harm to most all, setting rules that never existed under her realm before and allowed many people to be harmed in her name and for the sake of monetary gain.

The Wall of Darkness only grew more dangerous and fewer people attempted to cross as the likelihood of survival grew less and less. Aria would never see O'Riah again.

Lord Fenrick discovered Lord Somerled at the bottom of the stairs the next morning. He was dead and the men assumed that he drank too much and had fallen down the stairs on his way to bed. I remembered as they carried him up to the deck that I'd set the poisoned ale next to him the night before. Dallin asked Nex to bless his soul and then he, Fenrick, and Vonhenson tossed the body over the railing and into the waves.

"Make ready to sail!" Dallin barked and made his way up the stairs to the bridge.

Every time that man took command, I wanted to sink my dagger in his chest and watch that smug smile fade. He caught me glaring and gave me a wink, prompting me to turn away and see what I could do to help.

"Ezra," Beau spoke from his spot in the middle of the deck. "Could you help raise the anchor?"

Ezra didn't respond. He passed Beau for the windlass where Fenrick and Raust stood. Beau turned to look at me, a small smile spreading on his face, and motioned for me to follow him. He led me toward a series of ropes on one side of the ship where he showed me which ones to release and how to fasten them again once the sail was set. I left him for the other side of the ship to take care of the remaining sail, barely getting the ropes tied before a gust of wind filled the sails and we moved forward.

"Where did you get all those tattoos?" Raust asked.

I turned around to see Ezra dismantling the windlass and tying the planks of wood down on the desk. All of the contestants had found clean clothes in the chests below deck, but there was a brief period when I'd worn Ezra's shirt that left him shirtless before the men.

Ezra didn't look up from his work, still bent over to tie the final plank as he spoke. "While at war."

"I'm from Coleus. Soldiers pass through all the time. I've never seen one with any tattoos," Raust said with a snort.

Ezra stood from the planks. I saw the way both men looked over him as he rose to his feet. "You didn't see mine until yesterday."

"You weren't born with them, right?" Fenrick asked. Raust did a double-take and that's when I noticed the curiosity on Fenrick's face. His cheeks were tinged pink once he'd realized we were all staring.

"I've never heard about tattoos. Is it a coastal thing?" he asked, looking to Beau for reassurance. Beau shook his head, clearly no more eager to enter into the conversation than I was. He followed after me as I went to sit on the stairs to the bridge where I could better see the waves.

"Tattoos are permanent," Raust said in disbelief. "They don't just wash off."

"I know that!" Fenrick punched Raust's shoulder and lifted himself to sit on top of the windlass. "I just wanted to know how you get them."

"How else do you think you blacken the skin like that?" Raust asked and pressed his palm to his forearm. He let out a loud hiss, which prompted Ezra to face them with a groan.

"It's ink. You dip a needle in ink and pound it deep into the flesh so it will stay."

"Ink?" Fenrick's eyes went wide. So had Raust's, but he quickly masked his surprise.

"That still doesn't answer my question, Loreign," he said and leaned against the windlass next to Raust. "What are they for?"

"I don't owe you an answer," Ezra said simply, tone even, but expression tight.

Raust was offended and Fenrick let out a mocking laugh next to him.

"Maybe they're to show assholes like you that he can sit for hours while someone pounds a needle over and over into his back," I said loud enough for the whole group to hear. "Snakes bear marks to tell you which are poisonous."

"And convicts bear marks as well," Raust sneered at me before looking at Ezra. "Maybe that needle was a punishment and the marks are a reminder."

Ezra punched Raust so hard that he fell into the windlass and knocked Fenrick off. Both men lay on the deck in a tangle. Fenrick began to shout for him to get off, cursing him for dragging him down.

"You think I want to touch your unwashed ass?" Raust spat a mouthful of blood onto Fenrick's shoes as he rose to his feet.

"I think you wanted an excuse to start a fight," Fenrick said and aimed a kick between Raust's legs. Raust moved out of the way before he could attack, opening his mouth at the same time as a loud squawk sounded from above. There came another and another and when I looked up, dozens of seagulls were flocking around the masts. There was a ripping sound, several more, and the seagulls began tugging at the top of the sails until long rips had formed.

"Stop them!" Dallin yelled from the wheel.

We all hurried to the masts, yelling at the seagulls. They paid no attention to us as they continued shredding the sails until pieces started to rain down on us.

"STOP THEM, YOU BASTARDS!"

"It's a lost cause!" Beau yelled, turning to face Dallin, the only contestant who hadn't attempted to do something. "The sails are gone. We can't even repair them, they're destroyed."

Before Dallin could finish screaming his insults a loud *thunk* sounded on the deck. I turned to see a strange-looking sword lying on the deck in front of Lord Fenrick. He stared down at it in astonishment and then looked up at the sky.

"Is that yours?" Raust asked, looking down at the weapon. It looked like a short oar only there were shark's teeth lining the sides of the flat wood.

Fenrick looked at us all in turn and shook his head. "No."

"Then where did it come from?" Raust barked just as another *thunk* sounded. This time, I saw what had happened. Another shark-tooth sword fell from the gray clouds and settled on the deck in front of Lord Vonhenson who had been keeping watch from the bow. He pushed away from the railing, eyeing the sword as he stepped around it. A scraping sound came from behind him as he walked across the deck to us and it wasn't until he was halfway across that he stopped to look down at the sword that had followed him. He backed toward the starboard side and the sword slid along the deck after him. Fenrick looked down at the sword in front of him before he jogged portside. The sword skidded along behind him.

Fenrick pointed at Ezra. "Those marks must be demonic!"

"This isn't me," Ezra said and pointed at the sky. The clouds were darker and thunder rumbled not far away.

Dallin let out a single laugh. "Looks like the gods are ready to speed up this trial!"

Fenrick and Vonhenson eyed each other carefully. Vonhenson was the first to bend for his sword, prompting Fenrick to snatch his off the deck and charge.

Vonhenson stepped to the side and swung at Fenrick as he ran past, missing his back by inches. Thunder clapped from above as though cheering on the men. Fenrick spun around and swung across his body wildly, a back-and-forth motion as he advanced that forced Vonhenson to take several steps back before he could assume the offense.

Vonhenson swung the sword toward Fenrick's head, changing direction mid-swing and aiming for his free arm instead. Fenrick pivoted, but not far enough. He let out a yell of pain and brought his left arm to his chest, four of his fingers landing on the deck in front of Beau and me a second later.

"It's a fight to the death," Vonhenson said with a smile. "And I won't lose to a prick like you."

Fenrick lunged, swinging hard with little strategy. The force played in his favor though, making Vonhenson work to block each attack. The men were both red in the face from their efforts and when Vonhenson shoved Fenrick away by their swords, both men took a moment to catch their breaths.

Lightning lit the sky and a roar of thunder made the ship shudder under my feet. The waves were rougher now, making us all sway and forcing Fenrick to abandon his attack to keep on his feet. He staggered to the side, Vonhenson taking a swing at his face and leaving behind a shallow cut across his cheek.

"You're a dead man, Vonhenson!"

Fenrick regained his footing and ran across the deck. The ship rocked and Vonhenson couldn't get his sword raised in time. The men collided, Faust's sword missing its mark and slicing along the side of Vonhenson's neck instead.

Vonhenson shoved Fenrick just far enough that the shark's teeth along his sword ripped through flesh as he swiped across the man's midsection. Blood poured onto the deck between them as the men staggered. Neither were able to keep their footing this time and they collapsed, Vonhenson trying to staunch the bleeding at his throat while Fenrick pressed both arms to his stomach.

Vonhenson let out a roar and swung his sword. Fenrick yelled in pain as he rolled to his hands and knees, Vonhenson's sword hitting the deck to his right. Fenrick screamed as he brought his sword down on Vonhenson's chest like an axe, hitting him twice before he collapsed to his hands and knees again, leaving the sword stuck in Vonhenson's chest as he pressed his hands to his stomach.

Vonhenson's eyes remained open, his empty stare on the storm clouds above. Fenrick rolled onto his back, sobbing. He called out for Aria and then Nex, telling them how he'd completed their task. He stopped screaming and lay back on the deck, hands trembling over the mess of his gut before they stilled.

The rumble of thunder was more distant now. We were all silent as the ship road a final wave, the waters calm enough now that I left the stairs to check the men. Ezra went to Fenrick while I went to Vonhenson. I didn't need to kneel beside him to know he was dead and the same must have been true for Fenrick as I looked back at Ezra as he stood over the man.

I turned my attention to the railing, grabbing hold as the ship lurched and we were propelled forward again. There were no sails left above us and no wind to fill them anyway. This was yet another act of the gods, a reward for the death onboard. Dallin started to laugh, adjusting his grip on the wheel.

"Blessed be the gods!" he cried, waving a fist at the vanishing clouds above.

33

Beau and Lord Raust heaved Lord Fenrick's body to the port side of the ship. I offered to help with Vonhenson, but Ezra scooped the limp body into his arms with little effort. I followed him to the railing and watched as he tossed the body over the side. Vonhenson bobbed face-up in the wake of the ship and I watched until I couldn't see him anymore.

"We don't matter to them," I said under my breath.

"Who?" Ezra asked, turning from the railing to look at me.

I scoffed. "Us. We don't matter. To the gods."

Ezra smirked. "I matter because I say I do. Gods be damned."

He patted my shoulder and moved back to the stairs to the bridge and took a seat. He removed his dagger from his hip and looked down at it, turning it a few times before he looked up again and caught me staring. I looked away, watching Lord Raust instead as he slowly walked toward the bow. He stood with his hands on the railing, staring at the waves. His shoulders rose and then fell with a sigh, Raust moving his hands to his sword belt. Raust's hands went to his dagger and then his sword as though he was ensuring that they were there. He relaxed his stance and turned around to continue his slow walk back across the deck.

Beau sat a bucket next to the last of the blood on the floor. He lifted the bucket and dumped the water onto the wood, picking up a mop next and washing the blood toward the edge of the ship. Once the worst of it was cleared, he looked up at me and offered a small smile.

"You're angry," he said, smile fading a little as he leaned his forearms on the railing.

"At the gods, yes," I said and mirrored his position, watching as the sun set on the horizon. It was the only time we ever saw it at sea, as it slowly sank into the water, almost taunting us that it might be the last time we ever looked at it. No one had said a word about it, but I think we almost believed that it was. All work on the ship stopped and everyone stood still each day to watch, hoping we would be alive to see it rise again. It was maddening to me.

Not to Beau, however. He looked peaceful as he stared over the waters. That look alone made my chest heavy and made me wish to turn my back on the sun entirely in protest.

"Don't be," he said.

I did turn my back. I stepped closer to him, pushing on his chest so he had no choice but to straighten up and look at me. "I am not supposed to be in the trial. I went against Aria's intentions, the king's intentions. I've committed treason by being here. The gods did not want me here."

"You belong here, Wren."

"Listen!" I slapped his chest once. "Nex blessed you before the trial. Those blue dragons embraced you, but I was stung by them. I was stung by them during a storm at sea. It's a curse on my entering the trial."

"But you're still here," Beau said, grabbing my hand. He held it for just a moment before I pulled free, part of me wishing I hadn't. "If it was Aria's will, she wouldn't have accepted your offering. Nex may not have blessed you, but Aria did."

"The gods don't work like that. It's the gods together."

"Who's to say they don't work separately? This is Aria's trial. She let you enter. She has blessed you," Beau said and pressed a hand to his chest. "I think the gods do work separately and when my heart stops, it will be because one of the gods allows it, maybe Aria as the goddess of this trial or maybe Nex as the God of the Sea"

"When your heart stops it will be because *I* allow it," I said, only realizing how loud the words came out after I felt the eyes on me. I sucked in a deep breath, trying to calm the anger raging within me. "When I lose you, it will be on my terms," I whispered.

He smiled. This time, I let him take my hand. I didn't care that everyone was watching. I didn't care that it put a target on his back. I would protect him as I had through this entire trial.

"It will be okay," he said and kissed my knuckles. He smiled again and let go of my hand. He picked up the mop and bucket from the deck and started toward the stairs. I turned just in time to see the last of the sun slip beneath the water.

The storeroom of food was nearly empty. When the five of us went below deck for our meals, we found only enough for one sitting on the table. A brawl between Raust and Dallin nearly broke out as we debated how to divide the meal. Raust argued that at least one of us could be dead at any moment and it would be a waste of food, leading Dallin to ask who he thought that person would be.

After a lot of shouting, it was decided that no one could be trusted. It was Beau who finally settled the debate, pointing out that no one planned on killing me or hoped that I would die. Everyone would protect me because without me at the end of the trial, there was no winner.

The food tasted like ash in my mouth as I ate. I knew it would be foolish to waste the food, and it only ensured that I could survive just a little longer now that the storeroom was barren. So, I ate the entire meal and downed the final mug of ale while the men sat in silence.

We all survived the night and when we raised the anchor the next morning, the waves carried us on our way just as they had the day before. Dallin remained at the wheel, though he likely didn't need to. We all knew it was a matter of his ego. The clouds were dark most of the day and I nearly fell asleep as I sat on the stairs until I heard a crack of thunder.

I realized that the ship had stopped moving and we were rocking slightly. Thunder rumbled closer and the air around us felt charged as we waited for the swords to fall. The first did, landing at Raust's feet where he sat with his back against the railing on the starboard side. He stared at it for a moment before he stood, picking up the shark-tooth sword by the hilt and testing the weight of it in his right hand.

My heart skipped when the second one hit the deck just to my left. Ezra let out a sigh. He looked annoyed as he knelt to pick up the weapon. He moved away from the stairs and into the middle of the deck to face an anxiously waiting Raust. I looked at the wheel behind me. Dallin didn't look as amused by the duel as he had yesterday. Raust had spent the whole trial in his pocket. If he died, it meant that it was the three of us against him.

"Let's get this over with," Ezra said. I looked back at the pair, Raust the only one to raise his sword at the ready.

"You think you can kill me so easily?" he snorted.

"I have no patience for fun and games," Ezra responded, still not making a move. "Let me know when you're ready."

"Cocky bastard," Raust said. He paused for just a moment before he lunged. Ezra didn't just block his attack, he batted his sword aside. It set Raust off balance and would've made for an easy jab to his chest, a single blow to end the duel. Ezra didn't take it. He waited for Raust to recover and launched a second attack, blocking all three of his swings with ease before the man backed away to recoup.

I realized after I saw the second missed opportunity for a kill what Ezra was doing. It was a kind of mercy. He was allowing Raust to stand and fight, die with a good fight rather than be struck down so simply, brutally. Ezra blocked attack after attack, the fight starting to wear on Raust's stamina as his attacks grew more erratic. The longer they went on, the more obvious it was how ill-matched they were. Raust's breathing was loud and heavy. Ezra remained calm, barely a sheen of sweat on his brow.

Raust had begun to notice the fact not long after we had and it made him sloppy. The ship swayed under us, and he barely focused on his footwork, losing balance twice as he swung at Ezra. His sword beat against Ezra's hard, the sound piercing the air and several shark teeth flew from the weapons.

"You think this is a game, Loreign?" Raust yelled, his arms and legs shaking and his eyes wide. "You are no better than the rest of us. You're a lowly soldier, not worthy of a princess. You wouldn't know what to do with the fortune the king offers."

Raust attacked again and still Ezra blocked without much effort, evading a blow to the head and another aimed for his shins. It wasn't until Raust was too exhausted and had to back away that the attack stopped.

"Even if you were to win, you would be nothing," Raust said, spit flying from his lips, "The king wouldn't grant the fortune to a man like you. You're just a soldier, fodder for battle. You can put on borrowed suits and go to balls, but you will always be fodder in someone else's war."

He ran at Ezra, swinging for his head. Ezra blocked the first attack, but let Raust disarm him with the second. He stepped aside when Raust swung for his chest, using the opening to move behind him. Ezra needed only a second. He grabbed Raust's head with both hands and twisted. There was a stomach-turning crunch and Raust collapsed on the deck. Ezra stood there for a long moment as the storm died out and the sea stilled.

Once the waves sent the ship lurching ahead again, urging us closer to Honor Cove, Ezra lifted Raust into his arms and walked toward the railing. He paused for a moment, as though he considered delivering a eulogy, and then tossed the body into the sea. A chill ran over my skin when he turned from the railing, catching my gaze before he looked away. Raust was one of the best swordsmen among the contestants, yet Ezra had made him look novice. I understood why Ezra Loreign had never appeared in the training ring before the trial. It made sense why he would hide such great skill.

It did not make sense for Lord Dallin Vondrelle to choose that moment to leave his post at the wheel, sword drawn as he stalked straight for Ezra.

34

"I know who you are! I know why you are here!" Dallin swung at Ezra and was blocked, swords braced against one another. "You aren't here for the king; you're not even here to marry the princess. You are here to dismantle the crown. You're part of the rebellion."

Ezra pushed him away and took a step back, lowering his sword. He was almost unbothered by the outburst, maintaining a relaxed stance and keeping his expression even.

"Why do you think I'm here?" I interrupted and stepped between the two men. I sensed Ezra take a step to move me, but I adjusted to keep him at my back. Dallin looked between us before focusing his attention on me, my stomach twisting at the way his eyes roved over me.

"I don't care why you are here," he said and let out a laugh of disbelief. "In this realm, you won't get anywhere in a rebellion without a man. Even if you are giving the orders, it will have to be through a man. No army will respect you, not even those rebel bastards who share your every thought and idea. How can you possibly understand how to lead an army?"

I didn't care that he held a sword, I charged for him anyway and Ezra didn't stop me. By the time Beau was at our side, I held the front of Dallin's shirt in both my hands.

"Because Leif trained me," I said and shook the front of his shirt. "Every day. During our lessons. I learned all the skills taught to soldiers. I understand battle strategy. Since I was seven, I was trained in these things, swordsmanship included, and I don't care that men won't believe me capable. I will show them I am and challenge anyone who questions that. I do not ask, Lord Vondrelle. I demand."

I could see the horror in his eyes. It lasted just a moment before the anger set into his wrinkles, but it was there, and I clung to the fact. I would see that look on the faces of every man I encountered who challenged me. I would make them see how serious I was and the truth in my skill. I am worth respecting. I will be respected. I will accept nothing less, especially from men with a lesser education and skillset than my own.

I released the front of his shirt. Beau took a step to intervene, but he froze. His gaze went past me, likely in answer to Erza. His body tensed, but he took a step back, keeping a hand on his sword while I waited for Dallin's reply.

"You trust your guard dogs not to muzzle you once the time arrives?" he asked. I must have paused too long because his smile widened. "I hope you have a strong leash."

"If it wasn't for Wren, Ezra and I wouldn't have survived the jungle," Beau said.

Dallin looked over me again, but his eyes didn't linger on the curve of my waist or my chest. This time he looked at my legs and my arms and I wondered if this was how Ezra felt. It was empowering, like I had the upper hand for once.

"Pity," Dallin said, looking at Ezra and Beau in turn before he sheathed his sword. He had taken just one step when a *thunk* sounded behind him. Dallin nearly tripped over the shark-tooth sword. Another one landed to my right. I'd never been so glad to face a fight in my life. Dallin's cheeks were red as though he'd just been turned down for an investment. He snatched the sword from the deck and adjusted his grip around the hilt, keeping his eyes on me as I did the same with him.

My fingers scraped the wood of the deck. Reluctantly, I looked away from Dallin at the sword a few inches away. The closer I reached, the farther the sword slid. My heart sank in my chest and I felt sick when I realized it wasn't meant for me. I looked up at Beau as he knelt down, fingers closing around the hilt of the sword.

Dallin began to laugh as Beau and I straightened up. "You've touched my bride for the last time, Renault."

I started toward him only to be scooped up from behind. I brought my elbows against Ezra's firm chest, but his arms remained vice-like around my middle. He growled in my ear when I attempted to kick him between the legs.

"It has to be this way. You can't intervene," he said.

"The fuck I won't."

"He's fine," Ezra said, raising his voice so Beau could hear now. "Lord Vondrelle is skilled, but he has slowed with age. He relies on misdirection and distractions."

Beau didn't turn his gaze from the old man when he gave a nod meant for us. Dallin held his position, the sword held at hip height in his left hand. Beau adjusted his footing and raised his sword at the ready, sucking in a quick breath that gave him away immediately. Dallin switched his sword to his right hand, causing Beau to stutter his step just enough that it gave Dallin the second he needed to rake the shark teeth across Beau's shoulder.

Shit.

Beau let out a yell but regrouped quickly to parry. His sword went wide, swinging past Dallin's head. Before Dallin could counterattack, Beau was able to land a punch on his jaw with his free hand. It was just hard enough to make Dallin stagger backward, enough of an advantage that Beau rushed him before he had fully gained his footing.

"Don't get sloppy, Renault!" Ezra barked the words as though it was normal, like he was back in his battalion leading a training session. Beau abandoned the attack to get his feet set beneath him and it was just enough time for Dallin to reset so he could block Beau's next attack.

"Let go of me," I growled to Ezra, pushing his arms around my stomach as Beau struggled to block the battering Dallin sent his way.

"If you kill him, it might piss off the gods enough to take it out on us."

"You're pissing *me* off enough that I might kill you," I said and reared my head back, hoping to smash his nose and instead looking straight at the sky. He kept me pinned to his chest with one arm. He had a hand around my braids, keeping my gaze raised above the fighting so I couldn't see anything other than the lightning. My heart beat at my chest like the wings of a moth caught in a spiderweb. The sounds of the fight were all I could focus on, every nerve in my body reacting whenever I heard Beau grunt or groan.

"He's fine," Ezra said, his tone annoyed. It was laced with something more than just his usual annoyance and it set me on edge, made my chest hurt like my heart might burst through my body. Beau screamed in pain and tipped me over the edge, panic taking hold of my body as I gripped the hilt of my dagger. I pulled it free and turned the blade toward me, plunging it just past my right hip to reach Ezra. I missed my mark but must've nicked him enough. He yelled in pain, releasing his grip on my hair enough that I was able to lower my gaze. He held firm to my waist, but I'd rattled him enough that I could bash the back of my head into his face. He let go.

Beau was nursing a bloody nose, a cut across his jaw and cheek along with the one on his shoulder. He'd managed to stab Dallin in the leg just as I broke free. Beau took a step out of reach so he could swipe away the blood running down the side of his face, allowing me to attack. I ran past Beau, Dallin not looking up at me until I was just feet away, too close for him to do anything about it. I gripped the dragon-tooth dagger tight and jabbed it hard into the man's abdomen, shoving him backward until we were pressed to the wall next to the stairs of the bridge.

Dallin let out a raspy breath in my ear, screaming when I twisted the dagger in his gut.

"This is for all your wives, the pain they endured while alive, and for their deaths. This is from me." I pulled the dagger free and moved it to his throat, not hesitating before I split the skin there and sent a wave of red flooding the front of his shirt. Dallin's eyes went wide, and his mouth parted.

"Wren!" Beau gasped.

I took a step back, watching as Dallin Vondrelle slumped to the ground with that look of fear frozen on his face. I was ripped out of the moment by Beau as he turned me around by my bicep, gripping both of my arms as he looked me over.

"I'm fine."

"It wasn't your fight," he said, cupping my face. "You shouldn't have ... The gods ..."

I moved his hands from my face and held them between us. "I couldn't just watch."

"Wren"

"No!" I shoved his chest, and he staggered backward, nearly slipping into the bloody pool that had gathered on the deck. "I can't."

As though reading my thoughts, those dreaded swords fell from the sky again. My heart sank as I heard the sound behind me, knowing that the second sword wasn't meant for me. It was like the gods were making the choice for me, forcing me to watch Beau meet an end by someone else's hand. He pulled me to his chest and released a deep sigh in my ear.

"You cannot protect me from what I've fully embraced," he said. He cut off my retort with his lips, pressing them hard against mine. He stepped away from me before I was ready, scooping the sword from the deck and swiping the blood away from the cut on his cheek.

I looked across the deck at Ezra as he slowly straightened up with the second sword in his hand. He noticed me staring. I could see the heaviness in his expression as he stared back at me, twisting the shark-tooth sword in his palm. I looked away as a crack of thunder pierced the air, the sound so close that it rang in my ears. Rain began to pour down on us.

"I won't blame you," Beau called to Ezra over the storm. "But I want to go down fighting."

Ezra shook his head and tossed the sword onto the deck, sending it skidding into my boots. No sooner had I reached for it did the blade start sliding back toward him. Ezra stomped on it and sent it sliding back to me.

"I won't be ruled by any god who asks me to cut down someone like you!" Ezra yelled at Beau. "I don't kill the innocent, not even when the gods order it. Let Aria drain my life. Let Nex drown me. I will not fight for them."

"We don't have a choice in this, Ezra!" Beau said, his voice strained. He glanced at the choppy sea and then at me, stopping my heart for a moment. If they didn't fight, we might all die. If none of us were willing to stand for the gods then what was the point in blessing a winner in this trial? If I died, there would be no revolution. My father would continue to rule the Light Realm and the Fallen would continue to become slaves to us. Waylon would ascend the throne eventually and likely be worse. He may even press farther into the Mist and seek to destroy the Fallen entirely. There would be nothing left, no one to stand against him if he took the throne.

I could see the truth in Beau's eyes. He'd already worked out where this would leave us. He managed to stand his ground as the boat shifted beneath us, the waters growing rough enough to require an effort to stay upright. Ezra was like a mountain, unmoved as he lifted the shark-tooth sword from the deck for the second time. He let out a great yell and launched it into the air, sending it whizzing from the ship.

"You can't keep doing this, Ezra," Beau told him and looked

away from me. "Nex will sink the ship. Wren will never get to shore, never lead the rebels."

Ezra opened his mouth to speak, but no words came out. His eyes widened and he raised his right hand in front of him.

"Beau, duck!"

Beau did without question and the shark-sword returned, flying hilt-first at Ezra who had no choice but to catch it. Rather than argue, Beau ran. He charged straight at Ezra with his sword raised. The sound of thunder drowned out my scream of anger, a sound that ripped at my throat as I cursed the Great Mother herself for allowing her children to pit their creations against one another in this stupid trial.

Ezra caught Beau's sword with his own, pausing for just a moment before he shoved him away and launched his counterattack.

35

Ezra used the flat side of the shark-tooth sword to try batting Beau away. It worked, forcing him to fall into the railing where he clung as a wave rocked the ship. Ezra remained on his feet despite sliding several feet closer to Beau. I fell into the windlass and bounced off. I caught myself against the deck, rolling to my back just as a wave crested the nearest railing and flooded the deck.

"I know what you can do!" Beau yelled.

"The storm has only pushed us closer to shore! Just give it more time and we'll be close enough!" Ezra held his hands out to his sides, not raising them again until Beau swung his sword at his head.

I coughed from the salt water I'd inhaled, feeling my stomach roll with nausea. Ezra blocked Beau's sword as he swung for his middle and then again for his legs, making it look so easy that there was no denying that he was preventing the inevitable, sticking to the promise he'd made me. I drew my sword and attempted to climb to my feet, another wave sending the ship lurching to the left and forcing me into the windlass again. This time, I wrapped my arms around it, bashing my mouth against it hard enough that the metallic taste of blood filled my mouth.

Ezra blocked another swing before he kicked Beau in the gut, sending him into the railing again hard enough that the wood shook behind him.

"The ship will sink!" Beau yelled as he propped himself up on the railing with one arm.

"If we wait until we're close enough, we can swim," Ezra replied. Lightning lit up the gray sky. He noticed me struggling to maintain my footing. I was sure these waves were meant for me more than them, like Nex himself was trying to keep me from interfering. I gripped my sword tighter and pushed away from the windlass, enduring the sway of the ship the best as I could and willing my feet forward no matter how unsteady I was.

"I know those blue dragons stung her," Beau said when he noticed me. He groaned as he stood from the railing, shark-tooth sword still held in his right hand. "I know they stung you, too. If this ship sinks, Nex won't be merciful."

"Then I'll face him swinging," Ezra said and tossed his sword onto the deck again.

Beau shook his head as the weapon only slid to Ezra's feet again. "I won't let you take her with you."

Shit! Damn him. Damn him for being right. It was like the gods knew he had to die here on this ship.

Ezra didn't have to lean all the way down. The sword rose to his hand like a magnet. He tightened his grip on it as Beau steadied himself against another wave as it rocked the ship, forcing me to stagger to the right and force me to use my sword like a cane to keep from falling. Ezra remained stoic, looking away from Beau as he slowly advanced to meet my gaze.

"Fight me!" Beau yelled, landing a punch to Ezra's jaw that was hard enough to make the man stagger. Once he'd gained his footing, he looked up at me again. He sent me a curt nod and that single gesture silenced the panic in my chest, eased the thickness that had gathered in my throat.

"No," Beau said, finally noticing why Ezra had stopped. "Wren, please."

"Not her," Ezra interjected, drawing the attention back to him. "My word. My promise."

"It's not a promise you can make," Beau said, his tone almost pleading as he looked back at me. "My death isn't your burden to bear, Wren."

Before I could say a word, the ship hit a wave with such force that all three of us were tossed onto the deck. My head smashed into the wood as seawater flooded the deck, burning my nose and choking me as I struggled to push myself onto my hands and knees. Part of the railing in front of me was in splinters, shards of the wood scattered between Beau and me. Ezra scrambled away from the railing at the bow of the ship in time for the section he'd landed against to break off with a crack.

Thunder roared in the sky along with a new sound, something more sinister that made me very aware that I'd dropped my sword in the fall. I looked away from Beau's panicked expression to search the deck for my sword, finding it halfway across the deck. The ship hit another wave as I crawled toward it, forcing me to move faster as the ship tipped and the sword began sliding toward the opposite railing. The dragon-tooth dagger was still safely sheathed at my hip, but I couldn't guarantee I'd be able to face what came next without my sword.

The weapon slid tip-first toward the railing, perfectly positioned so that it could slide right off the edge of the ship and into the water. I launched myself toward it, sliding the extra few inches I needed on my stomach to grab ahold of the hilt in time for the dark shadow to fall over us. I rolled onto my back with my sword poised above us and froze.

The creature looked like the wyrm back in the cave on the island, only this beast was much larger. The spines along the top of its head stood tall and unlike the wyrm, this sea serpent had a frill of webbing around its head that stretched wide as it opened its jaw to flash its rapier-like fangs down at us. It lowered its head, coming straight for me. I rolled onto my side, throwing myself toward the stairs to the bridge before I realized it was merely diving over top of the ship.

Its body was snake-like, spikes taller than most men standing erect along its back as it slunk over the deck, the last of its body taking out the railing and part of the starboard side with a loud crunch. My heart slammed against my chest as I scrambled to my feet, racing to meet Ezra and Beau in the center of the ship before the monster could emerge again.

"I told you the gods—"

"The gods don't concern us now!" Ezra snapped, sharply cutting Beau off and snatching the shark-tooth sword from his hand. He held both swords now, pivoting so he could see both sides of the ship just as the sea serpent erupted from the waters ahead of the bow. He waited until its head was several meters above us to launch the first sword at it, finding his mark just below the creature's head. It let out an ear-splitting screech as Ezra sent the second sword spiraling through the air, this one sticking into the monster's snout and cutting off the horrible screeching.

The serpent sank head-first into the water again, the wake it left bloody as it sank beneath the surface.

"We have to kill it," I said and tightened my grip on the sword. "We have to let it get close enough. We can't lose any more weapons."

"It will take down the whole ship," Beau said.

The ship suddenly spun, the back of the serpent cresting the top of a wave as it rocked the ship again. I took a deep breath, pushing aside the panic to search for the shore and found it ahead, thankfully in the direction we were slowly heading. If we could just endure this a little longer. If we could kill the beast, we might be safe to ride what was left of the ship to the beach, swim the distance if we had to.

"It will sink us regardless," Ezra said and pulled his sword form his hip. "But we won't survive the sea if it's there with us."

Beau looked almost calm, something missing from his expression when those blue eyes met mine that chilled my skin. Defeat. Acceptance. He drew his sword and extended a hand toward me, but before I could take it the sea serpent burst from the water again. This time, it came straight for us with its mouth stretched wide. We ducked, all three of us wrapping our arms around the center mast in time to avoid those long fangs that sank into the wood above us. The mast cracked, shards of wood raining down on us as the serpent shook the ship with the force of its head shaking side to side.

"Wren!" Ezra yelled from where he was pinned beneath the creature's snout. I realized what he meant for me to do a second later. I raised my sword as the beast finally snapped the mast in half, sinking the tip into the bottom of its jaw. When I wrenched the blade free, hot blood poured over me and the serpent reared back before I could take another jab. It released the mast in its jaws and the thick pole crashed into the bow, all of the rigging and ropes sliding along the deck around us like snakes. Wooden slats flew into the air from the front of the ship, the largest hole yet forming.

The cry of the sea serpent cut off in a pitiful screech and its great head lolled skyward, limp body arched backward as it fell onto the ship. Ezra shoved me toward the bridge before reaching back for Beau as the weight of the fallen monster tipped the bow beneath the water. I wrapped my legs around the mast and looked down to see Ezra's hand slip through Beau's. I heard the zip of the ropes across the deck. There was another crack from my left and I turned in time to see one of the large pullies slide down the deck, pulled by a tangle of ropes that had been attached to the downed mast. The ship let out a creak as the serpent rolled toward the sea, wrapping itself in the ropes from the mast.

"Shit!" Ezra yelled. Beau wasn't sliding anymore but being dragged, his foot now wrapped in the tangle of ropes. I pushed from the mast as the bow continued to descend, catching Beau's outstretched hand. Ezra's sword arm wrapped around my waist, the other holding on to the last piece of the mast still erect in the center of the ship. The ropes left sprawling along the deck were pulled across the flooding ship and emitted a soft shushing sound as they, too, sank into the water after the dead serpent. Panic flooded my veins, firing every nerve in my body to the point that it was difficult to point my sword.

"I've got you," I told Beau as I tried angling the tip of the blade for the ropes cinched around his left ankle, the damn rigging sliding around too much to give me an easy cut. If I missed, I could slice Beau's entire leg off at the calf. I might anyway if I couldn't control my shaking hand. If he lost a leg, he'd still be alive though. Maybe we could get him back on deck with enough time to staunch the bleeding. We could help him swim to shore. Maybe I wouldn't miss. If I could calm myself, I wouldn't miss. If I wasn't in such a damn panic ...

"Wren," Beau said, his voice so calm it only worsened my panic. I held on to him tighter, silently willing him to cling tighter to me.

"I've got you," I said and focused on the ropes again, catching the last of them sliding into the water in my peripheral. "I'm almost there."

"Wren," Beau said again. He changed his grip, and my heart leaped in my chest as I feared he might let go. My eyes found those blue ones and they sparkled with that innocence that drew me in initially. He'd loosened his grip on me so he could slide both of his thumbs along the sea glass bracelet around my wrist.

"Hold on to me. Please, Beau! I can't hold you alone," I begged. I almost moved my sword hand to hold him, but I was worried I might cut him. I knew better than to drop the sword.

"It'll be okay," he said. I'd heard those words before, back in the river. I thought I was going to lose him then. My heart shattered as I looked into his blue eyes and saw the reassurance there. The corner of his mouth ticked upward in a small smile as he said the words again, stroking his thumbs across the sea glass at my wrist.

"It'll be okay."

The last of the rope was pulled under and Beau was tugged from my grasp, barely above the surface long enough for me to see those blue eyes and boyish cheeks before he vanished into the dark water.

He did not resurface.

Part IX

Death of Flame and Wings

Excerpt from The Book of the Great Mother

O'Riah would have died if he could the moment the darkness took hold in his realm. All life within his realm began to fade and there was little he could do to save it. He was the God of Air and life on land was not something he had the power to save. He watched the suffering from the mountaintop and wept for them, for the love he'd lost, and the death of his realm. He'd been so enraptured by love that he was unable to rule his realm, leaving the air barren. He was so distraught that he couldn't maintain his own realm, his powers fading and the air growing thin from his waning existence.

His realm was new, barely started when the war broke out with the sea. He couldn't survive without Aria, so he decided to try and reach her. He prepared his realm for his absence and gave the last of himself to the poor communities that were making the most of the small amount of life left in the realm. Once he had given everything he had to his people, he prepared for what awaited in the Wall of Darkness between his realm and Aria's.

The skies grew dark despite his resolve, the Great Mother warning him of her punishment should he defy her. He ignored her commands and spread his wings. O'Riah flew into the darkness and fought against the pain as the dark magic of the Mist ate away at his wings, searing holes in the thin membrane and tearing at the sensitive skin as he flew farther and farther from the mountains.

At last, he'd flown too far to question his decision. He was determined and the pain in his wings grew so great that every beat was agony. Still he flew closer to Aria. His fate was sealed. Even if he wanted to turn around, it was too late. His wings, barely aloft from the holes the dark magic had torn asunder, finally failed him and he fell to the earth. He fell to the ground and the darkness enveloped him.

He cried out from the agony of the wings he'd lost and the love he'd never reclaim. The Great Mother punished him further by stealing his holiness, leaving him on the earth in his mortality as he crawled back to the mountain blind. O'Riah never made it back to his realm. He didn't continue his rule and the realm floundered. His people were left in darkness, barely surviving, kept alive only by the brave souls who made it through the darkness of the land by the Great Mother's grace.

36

The sea went silent. The ship creaked around us, water reaching my knees.

"The ship's sinking. We need to move," Ezra said, patting me on the shoulder. I looked away from the water and down at my hands, noticing that the sea glass bracelet was gone. There was a small tan line around my wrist with a rectangular patch of lighter skin where the sea glass had sat.

"Get up, Princess."

"I will burn this realm."

"Get your ass up now if you want his death to mean something!"

I pulled my legs beneath me, whirling around with my sword raised so fast that I hadn't fully formed a plan. Ezra caught the blow with his, putting our faces inches apart. He opened his mouth to speak, but I wasn't done. The deck groaned under our weight as I shifted my feet, pulling my sword back and striking him again. Once. Twice. The sound pierced the air, and the force vibrated up my arms. On the third blow, he angled his sword so mine was deflected to the right. I reached for the dragon tooth dagger at my hip, slicing the blade across his chest.

"Don't let your anger cloud reality!" Ezra said, not raising his sword until I swung again. Our blades met between us. Our faces were so close that I could feel his hot breath on my face.

"Beau's death was the only honorable one in this trial. He fought not to gain power or my hand, but to offer me something I can never have," I said, my stomach churning with anger. Ezra adjusted his sword, sliding it so the guard was pressed against mine. I knew it was a strategic move, but he'd gripped my other wrist before I could work out what kind. With a simple turn of his sword and a firm push, my sword was pulled from my grip. My feet came out from under me and lights flashed before my eyes as I hit the deck.

Ezra pinned both of my legs to the ground with his, both of my arms restrained above me by his. I spat at him, saliva sliding down his cheek and clinging to the stubble of his jaw. He shot me an annoyed look before moving my hands so he could pin my wrists with one of his. It was that day on the ship all over again, that day we all walked into that crate of blue dragons to be blessed by Nex.

"His death is not on your hands. He didn't die because of you. He died *for* you, Princess," Ezra said with an edge to his tone. He slid my sword back into the sheath at my hip before wiping the spit from his face.

"We could've all made it out of this," I said. If I'd just freed him from the ropes ... We were in the clear to swim to shore. We could've reached Aria's stone together and escaped Honor Cove. Three made for a stronger team than just one.

"Listen," Ezra said, patting my face hard enough to pull me from my thoughts. He stared down at me with intense eyes, as the man who'd commanded soldiers, the knight who had killed the Bone Breaker of the Mountain. He left his hand against my cheek, drawing his thumb across the scar there as though making a point. "You will win this trial. I will see to it. I will cover you the moment we reach the shore, make sure no one can stop you getting there. You get to the stone, win your freedom, and then you get the hell out. Do you understand me? I took down several men at once on the battlefield, the castle guards will be easy. But I can only buy you a little time. If you want any of this to matter—Beau, Norelli, all the Fallen the king has tortured and enslaved, all your people who deserve better—you will do as I say, so I can support your escape."

"Why do you care so much?"

"Because if you die, nothing else matters," he said and pressed the pad of his thumb against my scar. "No one deserved what you've endured and no one deserves to wear a crown as much as you do."

He kept me pinned a moment longer, the ship's creaking and groaning only growing louder. I knew the water had reached us thanks to how cold my feet in my boots were. Finally, he let out a deep breath and released me. He lifted his sword from where he'd sat it next to us and stood, sheathing it at his hip as he looked toward the shore.

I could see the beach, the cove where Leif and I trained. The castle stood tall at the top of the cliff and I wondered how many people knew we had returned. That thought alone pulled me off the floor. We needed to swim ashore fast, before many others could gather at the stone. Once they discovered I was in the trial, if the king didn't already know, we would have a very short window of opportunity.

"Swim to shore. Get to the stone. Flee the city." I said the words with conviction, keeping my eyes focused on that small gray spec that was the arena.

"I'll see that you get there, Princess."

I dove into the cool water, hearing a splash from behind as Ezra did the same. I focused on strong strokes, trying to ignore the nagging feeling in my gut that told me this wouldn't be so straightforward.

Swim to shore. Get to the stone. Flee the city.

Ezra wasn't as quick a swimmer. He was still a yard away when I reached the shore. I eyed the arena down the beach and decided to wait for him. The sound of sand to my right made me turn around in time to see a guard charging at me with his sword raised. I stepped out of the way, his blade slicing the air to my left and sinking into the sand. A pair of arms wrapped around my waist, and I threw my head back, hearing the crunch of a nose before the man yelled in pain.

I pulled my sword free and spun to face the second guard.

"She trained with Sir Folee! Stay on your guard!" a man yelled.

I didn't give him a moment to prepare. I swung for his head, batting his sword away as he raised it halfway to defend himself. I heard Ezra join the fight behind me, more guards shouting around us. I sank my sword into the gut of the man before me before I turned to face the next guard who had stormed the beach.

"Behind!" I yelled to Ezra when I saw a guard run for his turned back. Ezra ducked to the left, forcing both of his opponents to pause when they noticed each other. It gave him the opening he needed to spill open the gut of one with his sword and the other with his dagger.

"We need reinforcements!" one of the guards to my left yelled. I finished with my second attacker, slicing off his sword arm before doing the same to his head.

"We can't let them alert any others!" My words hadn't been necessary. Ezra was already chasing down the two retreating guards. I focused on the man who had given the orders, an older man I'd recognized from the king's personal guard. He looked me over, hesitation in his eyes before he lunged.

I dodged his attack, remembering how Leif had taught me to keep on the balls of my feet. I was at the advantage here. I'd only ever trained on sand. Leif told me it would make me stronger and faster on flat land, which was his reason for not moving our training elsewhere. This man wasn't as fast as I was and he hadn't expected my skill. I blocked his attacks rather than dodged them this time just to get an idea of his next move, to anticipate the next opportunity. He was a broad man, and it was clear he was used to his strength being his advantage. I endured his heavy swings, watching as he grew more frustrated and put more of his weight into his attacks.

His shoulders tensed, and he pulled back his sword, preparing to slice at my stomach with more force than before. Instead of blocking this time, I took a step back out of reach and let the blade whoosh before me, waiting until he was forced to pivot to keep from spinning around. I jabbed my sword into his side and backed away before he could parry.

I glanced up the beach where Ezra stood with the limp bodies of the remaining guards between him. I looked back at the man lying on the sand in front of me, his eyes lifeless as they stared at the sky.

"They were sent to stop me," I told Ezra as he ran to join me, blood splattered across his shirt. "The king knows."

"Get to the altar before they do!"

I ran as fast as I could in the sand, Ezra easily falling into step beside me. My heart raced faster when I reached the stone path, my feet pounding so hard against the stones that my legs ached. My panting sounded loud in my ears, so loud that it wasn't until I reached the arena that I realized how quiet it was. It sounded as though the sacred place was completely empty.

I skidded to a stop outside the stone arches. I saw nothing but the sandy floor of the arena and the dark stone of the altar. Ezra stopped just ahead of me, anger in his eyes when he looked at me.

"Time isn't on our side here," he said and motioned for me to follow.

"Something is wrong."

"It will be if you don't fucking move!"

"No! I can feel it. Something is off," I said as I followed him, taking the lead into the arena as I drew my sword.

I was right.

The arena was empty except for the small crowd of people at the far side. The king stood dead center in his finest robes. Waylon stood beside him, wearing the crown he reserved for special occasions. I saw their wrath from across the arena. The way the king's faced turned a deep shade of red. The way Waylon had stiffened.

The six guards that surrounded them and the men of the court drew closer, away from their posts along the stone walls with the swords drawn in preparation for the king's orders.

"Wren Bellator!" The king's voice echoed around the arena. "You are stripped of your titles. You are guilty of treason to the crown, conspiracy to usurp the throne, and you will be executed!"

I tightened my grip on my sword.

Ezra stood firm beside me as he raised his. "Run."

I'd gone just a few feet across the sand when there was an explosion from the left and sand rained down around the arena. A snake large enough to make the arena look like its nest rose from the sand, its giant hooded head turning downward and its yellow eyes set on me.

37

"Wren!"

I skidded in the sand, falling onto my ass before I could catch my bearings. The snake stood tall, tongue flicking out of his mouth before it gave a hiss and opened those jaws just wide enough for me to see a pair of fangs and a mouthful of needle-like teeth. The snake lunged with such speed that it was a wonder I'd raised my sword at all. The pommel smashed into my chest and I sank into the sand, the snake hissing angrily and recoiling.

Blood seeped down its snout as the last of its body emerged from the sand, coiling around its head in preparation for another attack. I scrambled to my feet, barely standing when I felt the snake lunge again. It brushed my back as I stood to run, spinning me around and forcing me back to the sand on my hands and knees. I slid into the stone archway.

Ezra let out a battle cry and jabbed at the snake's tail, piercing the scales for just a moment before he threw himself to the side to avoid its large jaws. The snake smashed into the archway behind Ezra with a bang that shook the arena. Ezra ran toward me, yelling for me to move as the gray walls around the snake began to rain down in large pieces. They rolled off the snake's powerful body, settling in the sand like the boulders on the beach.

"Move!" Ezra's sword dripped a trail of blood behind him as he ran.

I kept close to the wall as I sprinted, feeling like a mouse searching for shelter. I found it in the next archway when I saw that giant shadow above me. The snake darted past the archway after I'd passed to the other side. I ran ahead, hoping to get close enough to the altar so that I could dart back through before the snake could turn around to face me.

The snake darted through the archway instead, cutting me off and forcing me to turn and run back to the archway I'd left from. It hissed loudly behind me and I felt its tongue flick just past my ear when I rounded the corner and flung myself to the side. The snake took out the side of the archway with a boom. I threw my arms over my head and turned from the wall, breathing a sigh of relief when no more than palm-sized bits of stone fell onto my body.

The snake slithered into the middle of the arena, sending the remaining guards racing for the outer arches. It was obvious now that the snake was here for the trial alone. It acted as if the onlookers and guards peering around the arches weren't there at all, its yellow eyes for Ezra and me only as it looked between the two of us. When it looked at Ezra, I took my opportunity to run.

"No!"

My heart leaped in my chest at the warning, giving me just enough time to duck behind a piece of fallen archway to avoid the jaws of the snake. I pressed myself against the stone as the teeth surrounded me, those long fangs clamping down around my makeshift shield and trapping me there like iron bars on a prison cell. I searched around me for anything fleshy to stab, but there was nothing but teeth until the debris was lifted.

"Go!"

I obeyed. I glanced over my shoulder long enough to see the

snake with the piece of wall in its mouth before it tossed it aside, sending a spray of sand over Ezra, who stood several yards away.

"Run, Ezra!"

"The stone!" he called in response, already facing off with the snake as it poised to spring. I turned to the dark platform wrapped around the snake's tail. If I reached it and won, would the snake vanish? I looked back at Ezra when the snake let out a hiss of pain, blood streaked down the front of its body. What about Ezra?

He told me he'd cover me, help me escape the arena. He meant that he would stay behind, be killed in the fight or captured and executed for treason. He was a traitor to the crown as much as I was, a member of the rebel forces despite killing the Fallen prince.

I ran for the stone, nearly slipping in the sand. My legs ached as I struggled, moving slower than I'd planned for. My heart raced in response as though aware that I'd made a mistake. The snake lunged for Ezra again but missed. It turned its massive body, pinning Ezra to the stone wall. Its yellow eyes were like a drink of cold water on a hot day. I was relieved that it gave up on crushing Ezra, but shocked as it turned and began to slither toward me.

I ran to the stone, just a yard away, then a few feet. I knew it was too late. The snake was just behind me, and I was forced to turn from the stone just as that giant head came down on me. I jumped, managing to evade those long fangs and landing on its snout. I slid down its head and onto its back. It reared back, taking me up with it until I was too far above the arena to survive the fall. I gripped my sword with both hands and plunged it into the snake's back. The hiss sent a shiver down my body as it dove for the sand, dragging me with it until it took a sharp left turn, and my blade slid free.

I rolled onto my back, moving to get to my feet as the snake turned to face me again. My foot slipped, and my free hand only sank deeper into the sand. My stomach churned, bile at the back of my throat as the snake slithered quicker, tongue flicking out once before it opened its mouth wide. Ezra let out a yell, stepping over me so he was straddling my legs to face the monster. He dropped his sword tip first into the sand and raised his open hands to the snake. His shoulders tensed, and his scream changed. It was primal, a raw sound like he was putting every bit of strength behind him, and he likely was. Because fire exploded from his hands and surrounded the head of the snake.

The snake coiled tighter, a furious hiss combining with the searing of flesh. Black spots began to spread across its tan body until Ezra dropped to one knee with a yell. The snake drew back, hissing and curling around itself as it recovered. Ezra was still on one knee, panting and hands vibrating as though the task had expended the last of his energy.

The snake hissed again, flashing those long fangs at us as it prepared to strike. I pulled my legs to my chest, finally able to get to my feet as the snake lunged. I grabbed the hilt of Ezra's sword, the weapon heavy enough that it took both of my hands to lift it just in time to send it into the snake's nose. It pulled free, sending a wave of blood over the sand as it drew back, swaying from left to right as though finally feeling the extent of its wounds. It hissed, drawing back for another attack slow enough that I was able to lunge forward, stabbing it in the chest twice.

The snake fell to the sand, spilling dark blood around my feet as I looked back at Ezra. He straightened up, chest rising and falling with deep breaths.

"Magic!" Waylon yelled. He led the way back into the arena, the guards following him as the king and the rest of the court trickled in. "He's a sorcerer!"

I looked back at Ezra, part of me expecting an answer before I decided I didn't need one.

"Are you okay?" I asked him, handing over his sword as I joined him.

He gave me a nod of reassurance as he took the weapon, adjusting his hold on it as he raised his attention to the guards that had started to move away from the arches and onto the sand, spread out as though planning to surround us.

"The altar," I said and looked back at him.

"Yeah. The altar," he said and took a step away from me. A strange feeling came over me, an unease that made me raise my sword. I hadn't expected that it was Ezra who would attack.

He caught me off guard, not swinging with his full strength. This wasn't an attack to kill, the way he'd faced the other contestants. He didn't intend to kill me, and the realization settled deep in my bones a moment too late as he twisted his sword with such skill that I could do nothing to maintain my grip. My sword fell from my hands and into the sand and he snatched it up with his free hand before I could so much as bend over.

He ran for the altar, and I sprinted after him, the guards running to meet us. Ezra dropped my sword at the bottom of the dark pedestal, and I was quick to catch it by the hilt before it hit the stone, barely slowing my pace as I made it to the bottom step after him. I swung my sword but missed, a haphazard.

"Fuck!"

Ezra reached the top of Aria's Stone just seconds ahead of me and I had my sword raised halfway when he turned to face me, grabbing the wrist of my sword arm above us and pulled me tight to his chest.

His lips crashed onto mine, and it felt like the world around us spun immediately. He held me tight, but another force had us frozen, as though the gods held time in their hands, and we were at its center. My sword arm burned, the pain growing until it felt like hot needles were stabbing their way from my wrist to my elbow. Thunder cracked through the dark sky. Lightning flashed so bright it made my eyes hurt as I pulled away from the kiss to stare into those dark eyes, an apology there that ignited a new anger deep in my chest.

Ezra Loreign stole the trial away from me.

The guards finally reached us. It took two of them to shove Ezra off Aria's Stone, sending him tumbling in a whirl of darkness. I didn't have time to figure out what that darkness was before one of them lifted me from the stone, another prying my sword from my fingers. Ezra started to yell the same time as the gasps and cries of shock came from the onlookers.

"Execute her! Kill her! Kill them both!" The king's screams were unlike any I'd ever heard from him. Not anger. Fear.

The guard behind me held my arms at the small of my back and another gripped the back of my head. I turned to look at the crowd of court members to avoid having my nose smashed into the stone. I felt the cool axe lining up against the back of my neck, the screams growing more frantic around me as I sucked in a calming breath, determined to stare down my father and brother as they both screamed, waving their arms at the guards as the lords around them backed toward the safety of the wall.

Something was off, but before I could figure out what I was tugged from behind. I gasped, sure I'd feel the blade sever my head and instead hearing it smash into the stone. My hair caught for a moment before another tug from behind freed me and left me on my hands and knees on the steps of the podium.

"Arm yourself, Princess!"

I was alive. My once-long hair now hung loose just below my shoulders. The two guards who had restrained me were lying not far away on the steps, blood flowing down the dark stone from their wounds. I found my sword lying at the bottom of the podium and I scrambled to retrieve it as the sound of metal on metal rang around me.

"Kill them both! Traitor! Fallen bastard!"

I turned in time to sink my blade into the gut of an advancing guard. I let him fall at my feet and looked toward Ezra in time to see him incinerate the remaining two guards before him. I shielded my eyes from the sudden brightness, not lowering my arm until their screams had died out and the arena was silent.

"Someone alert the castle!" Waylon yelled as I lowered my arm. Ezra wasn't standing on the sand like before. He stood on

Aria's Stone and had black bat-like wings stretching far from his back, both easily seven feet long.

"You bastard!" Despite Waylon's attempts to stop him, the king took several steps forward. "You Fallen piece of shit! You spit on the gods, maybe even the Mother herself in the name of a god she struck down! This entire time, you obscured your identity like a coward!"

"I never lied about who I was or where I came from. I did come from that battle," Ezra said. I glanced at the archways for any sign of more guards. I could hear shouts outside the arena. They had to be close.

"You think you can steal what is mine for your lawless king?" My father was red in the face, visibly shaking.

Waylon stepped up next to him, putting on a brave face despite the tremors I saw shoot through him. "You really are just a lowly foot soldier gone rogue. Your own people sent you to be massacred on that battlefield."

Ezra spread his wings wide. "My name is Ezra Loreign, Prince of the Dark Realm, Bone Breaker of the Mountain, and I am ruled by no god."

The air was sucked from the arena. I heard the shouting of guards just beyond the arches, calls for soldiers to get into position. I clenched my sword tighter. I wouldn't die here without spilling blood first.

"Wren," Ezra said. I looked up at him on the pedestal, one large hand extended toward me. "Come with me or stay and let your revolution die with you."

Fuck.

Anger burned in my gut, eating away the last bit of hope I had felt as we fought side-by-side on that beach.

I took his hand.

38

Ezra held me tight to his side with both arms, those strong wings carrying us high fast. I heard a whistle, and he groaned. A scream flew from my lips as we fell, nearly hitting the top of the arena wall before he was able to extend his wings. He let out a yell as the wind filled his wings, carrying us over the surrounding buildings. The arrow impaled through his right wing nearly jabbed my face as we safely descended.

I heard more arrows whistle through the air but no more seemed to hit their marks until we were down the cobblestone street and had reached the top of a two-story inn. Ezra groaned and we plummeted. He held me tighter and those large wings surrounded us. We hit the roof and skidded. I braced myself for the fall to the ground that never came.

"You'll have to jump," Ezra said and pushed me off of him. "I'll catch you."

He crawled to the edge of the roof, dangling his feet down first before dropping to the ground. I saw the people in the streets begin to run as he adjusted his wings. I moved to the edge like he had, trying not to pay too much attention to the twenty-foot drop before I pushed myself off.

He caught me and placed me on my feet beside him, drawing his sword and looking around for anyone who might challenge us.

"Leave them be," I told him and drew my sword, leading the way into the street. "We have to get to the gate."

"I'm too injured to fly."

"The guards there are young. We can take them," I said as I heard the sound of horses hooves from the approaching side street. I turned left into an alley, slowing my pace when I saw the wooden fence at the end.

"Climb it," Ezra snarled behind me, his hands already on my waist and lifting me onto the fence. I scaled the last of it, dropping to the ground as he climbed over with ease. We ran for the end of the alley, making it to the street and nearly getting knocked down by a soldier riding a horse.

Ezra pulled me away from the horse and turned to face the four guards just behind.

"Get to the gate!" one of the soldiers yelled, prompting the man who nearly trampled me to race ahead toward the town wall. Ezra wasn't intimidated by the cavalry and charged at the nearest man. The horse was spooked by him as he extended the wing that didn't have arrows protruding from it, tossing its rider into the street where Ezra drove his sword through his chest.

These were castle horses, not military horses. The remaining three skittered about anxiously, leaving the soldiers on their backs to try regaining control. I used this to my advantage and attacked the next man, slicing into his thigh as he tried turning his horse toward me. His yell had barely escaped his lips before I stabbed him in the gut, leaving him to fall from his horse as it raced down the road to safety.

Ezra ducked to avoid a soldier's sword, leaving him for me so he could take on the last rider of the pack. I charged for the soldier, planning to spook his horse like I had the last. This man had learned from the others though and slid from the saddle instead to engage me head-on. I blocked a swing for my head, then my right thigh, stepping aside to avoid being impaled in the gut. My hair fell around my face, obscuring my vision just long enough to feel the soldier's blade slice my left thigh before I could pull away.

I ignored the pain and jabbed at his middle, stabbing him in the side before he backed out of range. I took a step toward him to deliver the killing blow, but the end of a sword shot through his stomach before I could make a move. The man fell, sliding off the tip of the sword to reveal Ezra behind him in his bloodstained clothes.

"Let's go," he said, already jogging ahead of me with his sword still out.

We ran down the next few streets, most of the townspeople darting inside or moving away out of fear when they saw us coming. Ezra had been an intimidating sight before he'd sprouted wings, so the Fallen prince likely looked like hell on legs to them now. It was an effort to keep up with his pace, the cut on my leg only aching worse the longer we ran.

"We won't make it to the border like this," I said between breaths.

"I know," he said, leading me on until I was sure my leg would give out, and then going to the door of a small house on the corner of the street. When the door held firm, he took a step back and kicked it open. He pulled me inside and slammed it shut.

"Mommy!"

We whirled around to see a blond boy no older than three with two babies lying on a blanket next to him, both of them screaming as the boy stared up at us with wide eyes.

"Who is you?" the little boy asked me, bursting into tears when Ezra moved farther into the room. A woman appeared in the doorway from the next room, freezing for just a moment when she saw us.

"Shit!" I said as she ran for her children, dragging the blanket across the room with the babies still screaming as they were towed along with it.

"What do you want?" the woman yelled, snatching up the little boy and practically tossing him into the hallway with his siblings.

"We won't hurt you. We just need help," I said quickly, hoping the crying babies wouldn't draw any attention from the street.

"What do you mean?" she asked, eyeing the arrows sticking from Ezra's wings. Her face paled and she took a few steps back to shield the three children from view.

I moved in front of Ezra, bringing her eyes back to me. I sheathed my sword and held my hands up in surrender. "Clothes. We need a change of clothes and we'll be gone."

"Stay in your house and don't say a word to anyone," Ezra added.

The woman eyed us again, looking toward the small kitchen across the room as though deciding if she could reach the knives along the wall in time to make a difference. She didn't speak until the little boy called for her again.

"Fine. I'll bring you both clothes. Stay here."

She hurried into the hall, scooping the crying babies into her arms and shuffling her toddler into the bedroom. I heard her trying to shush the children.

"Quickly!" Ezra ordered.

I kicked him, letting out a hiss at the sharp pain that shot through my thigh. I turned from him when I saw the way he looked down at the gash.

"Anything that will cover us is fine," I called to the woman. "Robes, cloaks, a blanket"

"We need *clothes*," Ezra sneered under his breath.

"You'll be damn lucky if she finds anything in your size," I shot back, turning away from him when I heard her return to the room. She surged forward just long enough to shove two thick traveling cloaks into my arms.

"Please, go," she said with a whimper.

I pulled the cloak over my shoulders and fastened the clip on the front. "Thank you."

"Is there a back door?" Ezra asked, allowing me to help him drape the cloak over his wings. Thankfully, it made him look less conspicuous.

The woman stepped aside and pointed through the hall. Ezra darted ahead, leading the way to the back of the house, where a door opened into the back alley. We walked slower than what felt necessary as we reached the next street. I fanned my hair over my shoulders, hoping it would hide my facial features and make me blend in with the other women walking the street with their baskets full from the market a few streets over.

"We need to get to the gate and leave the city," Ezra said, his voice low and gravelly.

"Where do you think I'm taking us?"

He ignored the comment and kept close to me. Even with him standing at least a foot taller than the crowd, few paid us any attention. The street grew busier with men and women, making it that much easier for us to become lost from the castle guards. We saw only a few as they went from door to door, questioning the people for any sign of us. These men likely didn't know what Ezra even looked like. They didn't wear the mark of the castle guards on their armor. The word must have spread, and soldiers had been called in.

"The gate is just a few more blocks," I said after the nearest couple had passed us with two children in tow.

"There's a crowd," Ezra said, nodding ahead of us. I was too short to see, but I could read the meaning in his expression. He let out a growl, jaw tensing as he moved from the street to the sidewalk. "A guard. I can see the gate. We can't get through, not now."

"Can you fly?" I asked, already sure of the answer. It was our last hope, to fly over the wall and make a run for the trees. I looked around us, taking in where we were. I didn't leave the castle often, but I knew Honor Cove. We'd gone far enough to be on the poorest streets of the city. The attire alone of the people around us should've told me that.

"I have an idea," I said when I noticed a castle guard leaning against the building across the street. His armor hung loose, his weapon's belt low along his hips as though he'd missed a notch in his belt while putting it on. Or, like he'd dressed in haste judging from the way he staggered and the red welt across his cheek.

I made sure not to rush as I carved a path through the growing crowd. I felt Ezra move closer as we passed the drunk guard, only to see another pair entering the building ahead. I'd never been to this place. I wasn't even sure if this was it, but I'd heard the castle guards and their gibes enough times to assume what that S on the door stood for.

I pushed through the door and found myself in a sea of men, all sitting at round tables to be in compliance with the rules posted on the wall above the bar at the back.

Must be seated for service!

1. *Barmaid*
2. *Bed*
3. *Stahl*

I slipped into one of the few empty tables near the wall. Ezra slid into the seat next to me, eyeing the nearest table of guards who were too drunk and focused on their barmaid to notice us. One of the men tried slipping his hand up her short skirt and she scooted away, turning to chide him with a coy smile on her face. Movement at the next table drew my attention. A man lifted a single finger and kept it there until one of the barmaids came to sit a mug on his table.

I looked over the room again. It was obvious that this wasn't like any other tavern. There were stairs in the corner. The barmaids all wore the same short skirts and ruffled tops that scooped low enough to show the tops of their breasts. Another hand shot into the air from a table in the middle of the room, this man holding up three fingers.

It didn't take long for a woman to appear at his side. She was much older than the others and didn't wear a uniform. Her dress was floor-length, black, with a high neckline. As she leaned over to speak to the man a necklace fell from the top of her dress, the charm a silver S.

I turned to instruct Ezra to call her over, but he already held three fingers in the air. My stomach twisted with nerves as another group of guards came in, this threesome sober unlike the rest in the room.

Madam Stahl sauntered over with a walk that could melt even the most egotistical men into a puddle, I was sure. She was fully in charge without needing to demand it, warping the rules of the realm in the only way available to a woman.

"Madam Stahl," Ezra greeted with a handsome smile that had even me pinned to my seat.

She smiled, eyes wandering over both of us before she turned to address him again. "You can't bring your own into my establishment, doll."

"My wife," Ezra said, firm but still calm. My body heated with anger at those words. It made me very aware of the dagger beneath my cloak.

Madam Stahl looked to me next. "My apologies. We don't offer rooms for travelers."

Ezra leaned forward so his lips were inches from her ear as she looked at me. "We would like your room, Madam."

The woman pulled away, the sinful smile faltering. "I don't offer my services, but I have a room and a girl who could be happy to entertain you both."

"You'll want to entertain us yourself," I said and pushed my hair back to show off the scar along my face as I began to recite the rhyme I'd grown up hearing the lords and ladies sing at court.

"Madam Stahl, who serves them all, will steal a young lord's money—"

"And what is a lady of the court doing debasing herself by—" The madam froze with her mouth open for a moment, looking me over again before she pressed her lips together. She straightened up, nodded toward the back of the bar, and started walking toward the padlocked door.

"There are dozens of soldiers here. What do you think you're doing giving us away to that bitch?" Ezra hissed in my ear, gripping my shoulder to keep me from standing.

I made sure no one had noticed us before I replied. "Hiding right under their noses."

He released me and with a final glance toward the drunk guards a table away, he stood and we followed Madam Stahl through that locked door.

39

Behind that padlocked door was another that opened to a room more luxurious than I'd imagined for such a simple brothel.

"I've harbored many fugitives, but never one who may inherit a crown," Madam Stahl grumbled as she moved into the large room. It was far more glamorous than the dusty bar in the front of the building. This sitting room had three red couches in the middle with a chandelier hanging above. There was a gilded bar in the corner and to the right was a door that was open to a bed big enough for four.

"So, what they say is true," I said as she moved to the bar.

She looked up at me with a scowl on her face. "May I ask which part, Your Highness?"

"You don't have to pretend to tolerate my title, especially when I wish to reject what comes with it," I said and moved to the nearest couch. "I know that you steal from your patrons, and I have an idea why."

"Oh?" She continued to fill three glasses with wine at the bar, not at all phased by my cutting tone. She'd been through much worse, I was sure. "I don't see how I could steal what they are willing to give."

"I don't think it's the money that you steal from them," I told her, finally getting the reaction I'd hoped for. It was a subtle one, the way she gripped the wine bottle tighter and ran her thumb along the stem of the glass. "Young lords are focused most on money and are happy to be acknowledged for it. They aren't afraid yet of politics though. I'm sure they divulge more than they should."

"Secrets," Ezra scoffed.

Madam Stahl smiled and sat the three glasses on a mirrored tray before carrying it to the sitting area. Ezra remained standing next to me even as the woman sank into the couch across from me. She kicked her heels off and pulled her feet beneath her before taking a glass of wine and lifting it to her lips for a drink.

"The sons of the richest lords will loosen their lips as long as I will loosen mine," Madam Stahl said with a laugh.

"You bed the sons, get the father's secrets, and tell them to ..." Ezra said, waiting for the woman to answer.

"I know you're on the run from the crown, accused of treason for entering the Trial for Marriage, I'd assume. The king might have wanted to keep your entry a secret, but the men closest to him were an exception. I found that secret out not long after the trial began."

"You're the line to the rebels, aren't you?" I asked. My leg had started to ache, and I wasn't interested in relaxing with a glass of wine the way she was.

She smiled and sat her glass down on the coffee table. "What gave me away?"

I hadn't come to the brothel knowing she was giving information to the rebels. I hadn't put that part together until after. I knew it was a place where secrets were kept, and I had hoped she would keep ours while Ezra and I tended our wounds and worked out a plan to get out of Honor Cove.

"There are closer places in better neighborhoods for men to

get sex," I told her and took the wine at last, hoping the alcohol would take the edge off the pain in my leg.

"Is that all?" she said with a laugh.

I downed the glass and sat it back on the table. "You're the only one with a song. I took a guess that it meant something more."

"Lucky guess," she mused and stood from the couch to retrieve the bottle from the bar. "I see the young lords. They divulge their family secrets, sometimes big ones involving their fathers' business with the king, to me or my girls. Eventually, they grow older and are required to stay closer to the castle. They forget what they've told me as they become more focused on gaining their fortunes and the politics of court. The king keeps close watch on your guard, Sir Folee's comings and goings. However, no one suspects his visits to the neighborhood whore to be anything of import, so they don't report them to the king."

Ezra scoffed. "It's brilliant."

"I tell the secrets to Leif, and he uses them to keep you safe and informed about the rebellion. I take his instructions and the secrets and tell them to my contact. They then take those down the chain and to the rebellion in the north," Madam Stahl said, glancing at Ezra. "There was a great commotion today regarding the trial. There are rumors of a Fallen man flying through the sky. Many townsfolk swear that they saw this, and some say that a woman was with him."

"Let them make of it what they will," I said as she refilled my glass. "But keep it secret that the princess is as alive as the rebellion."

She sat the bottle aside and smiled. She stood from the couch, took her half-empty glass, and started for the door. "You may have the room and anything else you need. I'll have one of my girls come tend to your wounds."

"No," Ezra said, and Madam Stahl paused in the doorway. "Leave the supplies at the door."

The woman nodded and then shut the door behind her.

A knock came at the door not long after the madam left, alerting us that the medical supplies had arrived. While we were waiting, it was decided that my leg took precedence. I sat on the floor with my legs extended in front of me. Ezra opened the door to retrieve the bowl from the floor. The supplies were rolled inside a pair of towels. He sat them next to me and went to the bar to fill the bowl with water before returning to kneel beside my injured leg.

"Can you heal it?" he asked as he dipped a rag into the bowl.

"What do you mean? I'm not a starfish. No, I can't heal myself."

He looked up at me like I was the crazy one.

"You bear Aria's mark." He nodded to the vines that now wrapped up my right forearm. I hadn't gotten a good look at them until now. Black vines intertwined, circling my arm from my right wrist to my elbow. It looked like a tattoo, like one of Ezra's along his spine.

"Is that what your marks are, from O'Riah?"

He ignored me and dipped the rag into the water again, saturating it only to wring it out and then submerge it again. It took him a moment to respond as he looked over the tools spread on the towel, not really looking at them from the way his hands twisted the rag.

"The one down my spine is from O'Riah," he said and looked up at me. "It's a connection to him, to an ancient magic."

"Is that why you can conjure fire?" I asked as he again submerged that rag in the bowl of water. He didn't answer. He moved his hands from the rag to my pants, carefully slipping his fingers into the hole above the cut and easily ripping the fabric so that it split farther up my thigh and down to my knee. He picked up the rag and began mopping the blood from my skin.

I clenched my teeth and threw my head back from the initial sting of it, focusing on breathing as he pressed on the cut to clean it.

"I need to stitch it unless you want another scar like the one on your cheek," Ezra said. The pain lessened, and I lowered my head to look at him as he prepped a curved needle.

"Do you know what you're doing?" I asked, not caring that I sounded condescending, and he held a sharp object he intended to stab me with more than once. He wasn't fazed by my comment as he continued to prepare the needle.

"Yes. I'm a soldier. I'm trained to dress battle wounds," he answered and lifted a small bottle from the towel. A green liquid swirled within as he held it to me. When I didn't take it, he groaned. "It's for the pain. It will make the process easier for you to bear."

"It will dull my senses."

"It will dull your pain."

"We can't afford to have our judgment clouded."

"That didn't stop you from drinking that glass of wine before," Ezra said with a laugh.

Gods, how did I endure this man before? Now that I knew the truth, his harsh words were even more maddening. He was right. It was just one glass of wine, and I did drink it because of the pain, but I wasn't about to admit that to him. It was just one glass. I was hardly impaired.

"We'll save it for you then," I told him and leaned back on my hands.

Ezra raised a brow and smirked, setting the tonic aside and picking up the needle. He didn't give me any warning before he set to work. Tears pricked my eyes immediately, and I held my breath against the pain of the first stitch. I was flat on my back now, eyes pressed shut and teeth clenched tight as he continued his work, never saying a word or slowing his pace. I didn't release a deeper breath until I felt the bandage wind around my thigh, knowing then that the worst was over.

"If you overexert yourself too much when we finally escape this place, I'll have to redo these stitches," Ezra said. His words felt like a foreshadowing because I wasn't sure how we would escape without some kind of fight.

"Fuck off," I told him and sat up. "You still have arrows in your wing."

He laughed and adjusted his position, spreading his left wing so I could better inspect it. It was a little surprising that both arrows were still embedded in the dark webbing. The first had gone in at an angle and it was the arrowhead that kept it from slipping from the puncture wound. The way it was positioned made me wonder how he hadn't shown the pain on his face before. It looked as though the edges of the arrowhead would've scratched the wing with the smallest movements, and further inspection confirmed the fact. The back of his wing was covered in scratch marks around the wound, none of them deep enough to require stitches, thankfully.

The second arrow had gone almost entirely through, and I followed the trajectory by pulling it the rest of the way through the wound. He barely flinched at the motion. His shoulders tensed when I did the same with the first arrow and sat it on the hardwood floor beside us.

"There's another rag there," Ezra said, nodding to the large towel that held the instruments. The rag was of the same color and blended in so well that it took me a moment to spot it. I dipped it in the water like he had before raising it to his wing to clear away the blood and dirt.

"The webbing is thin. I don't think stitches will hold," I told him as I brushed the dark blood from the wing.

He flinched and pushed the supplies closer to me. "It's dragon hide, not webbing. It may look thin, but it will hold, and it must. Do it properly and we can fly out of this place, if we have to."

"Then you do it."

"I can't get the right angle," he said and picked up the supplies. I sat back with the rag in hand and watched as he began to prepare the needle.

"You said you're a soldier …" I started, not able to form my thoughts into words before he spoke next.

"Anyone who dons a crown is for their people," he said and finished with the needle. "For the Fallen, ruling the realm is less about blood and more about being worthy. The rulers of the Dark Realm consider themselves less as kings or queens and more as protectors. The realm is our responsibility. Caring for the people and creatures within it is our responsibility. We honor the old magic and learn the ways of O'Riah. If we are worthy of protecting the realm, we are chosen by a dragon and we serve the skies. If we are worthy of serving sky and land, ruling over the realm, we are gifted by O'Riah."

"I thought O'Riah was a fallen god," I said, ignoring the needle as he scooted it closer to me on the towel. "How can he still bless you if he isn't a god?"

"Because O'Riah embraced and respected the old magic and when he died, he became one with an ancient power provided by the Great Mother, a power the Light Realm has forced into the Mist and declared heresy," he said and sat the towel in my lap this time. "Get to work, Princess."

I sucked in a deep breath, partly from nerves about the possibility of fucking this up and the other part annoyance. "Here." I held out the tonic.

He smirked. "Wouldn't want to cloud my senses."

"Fine," I said and set it aside, not in any mood to indulge his snide comments. "So, you're the prince because you're somehow worthy, not because you're the king's son?"

"A happy coincidence," he said as I lifted the needle from the towel. "I had the privilege, if you want to call it that, of learning and understanding early on. I excelled in training. A dragon hatched for me, making me a soldier. We trained often, and she became the strongest dragon and I the strongest rider. That's when I became the prince."

I hadn't watched him as he tended to my leg. Leif had taught me the basics of survival and first aid, so I knew the processes, but

I'd never put it into practice before. All of my skills were based on treating human skin, not Fallen wings.

"It's no different than for humans," Ezra said, likely reading into my hesitation. "Just make sure the stitches are close and tight in case we need to fly."

I ignored my concerns and set to work. His body tensed as I pierced the wing, but he didn't move. He was right. The dragon hide was thin but strong. It took a little force to pierce it with the needle. He endured the process with no more than a deep groan. I dropped the bloody needle on the towel and shoved it all aside. I stood up with a little help from the arm of the couch and went to look at the bedroom.

I'd never seen a bed so large. It had to be custom, a four-poster bedframe with sheer red curtains that would hide nothing when pulled closed. The attached bathroom had a tub big enough for three. As heavenly as a bath sounded, I didn't want to risk it. I didn't want to rely on Ezra to keep watch. I didn't want him out of my sight. Even now, I was aware of his movements in the other room as he cleaned up the medical supplies and I was sent running back into the main room when I heard the door to the apartment open.

Ezra lifted a tray from the floor and closed the door, locking it in place.

"Dinner," he said and took the tray to the coffee table.

Madam Stahl had sent a generous helping of stew and bread, and we devoured it all.

"We'll check the gate in the morning," Ezra said, standing up from the table. "They'll likely redirect some of their soldiers to scour the city. They know we haven't left. If we are lucky, it will mean that there are fewer soldiers posted at the gate. It would be ideal if we could just go through. Flying would draw too much attention."

"It might not. There's not much around the gate, not many onlookers," I told him as he started for the bedroom. "Where are you going?"

He turned to face me, that annoyed look back on his face as his large frame took up the entirety of the doorway. "To bed, and you should too."

"I'm not sharing a bed with you."

He groaned. "You had no problem lying beside me before."

"You hadn't betrayed me then."

"I got us both out of that arena."

I stood from the couch, ignoring the twinge in my thigh. "I entered this trial to free myself from the crown, to lead an army against my father and brother. I've trained my entire life in secret for just that and I was doing perfectly fine on my own, so don't act like you're doing me any favors."

"I entered this trial because I thought your people might give a damn if their princess was wed and captured by the Fallen prince," Ezra said, pointing toward the door. "They don't, but I saw an even better opportunity. You don't care about the crown the way it is. You don't care about the power. You want to dismantle it and the harm your father's rule has inflicted on your people and mine. You are stronger with me than you are alone and as much of a pain in the ass as you are, the Fallen are better served if we join your leadership."

I was stunned. My heart stopped dead in my chest for a moment.

"I knew that day we met that you were something different and I knew you had strength that the others were too stupid to see. They see what they want. I see what you are, Princess. I know that you are capable of leading the rebellion and enacting change. I'm telling you that I can make that easier if you would just—"

"Do what you say?" I jumped in, crossing my arms. "Place myself beneath yet another man?"

"Trust me," Ezra said, finishing his sentence with a deep breath. It was the softest he'd ever looked, almost a plea in his expression. It made my insides twist, and I wasn't sure with what emotion. Anger? Disappointment that he wouldn't continue to stand up to me? Frustration because I was entertaining the idea that maybe he was right?

"You are the most stubborn woman I've ever met," he said under his breath. He moved into the bedroom for just a moment, returning with two blankets. I tried not to think about what they had been through when he tossed one to me.

"You told me once that I was a rose buried deep in a thorn bush," I said as I unfolded the blanket and took it back to the couch. I was a rose buried in a thorn bush, a woman surrounded by armor. I wasn't easily attacked, and I defended myself well. He should've expected nothing less.

"Did that bother you, Princess?" Ezra said with a snort as he took the couch opposite me. "It must've for you to remember it."

I could've defended myself, but the truth was I knew he hadn't meant the words that way. He knew that I was aware of that and I'd paused long enough already that no response would be enough to hide the truth. I lay down on the couch and I reached for my sword belt on the floor for where the dragon-tooth dagger was still in the sheath. I pulled it free and kept it in my right hand over the blanket as I rested my head against the pillow and tried not to listen to Ezra's soft breathing just feet away.

Part X

Trial of Flame and Wings

Excerpt from The Codex of the Fallen

O'Riah's realm was dying and he couldn't bear to watch as the life beneath him faltered. The loss of Aria was agony enough, but watching everything she'd created die was too much to bear. He gave all that he had to his people as he prepared for the journey, sure he would never return.

As he flew through The Wall of Darkness, he felt holes tear in his wings and his skin burned from the effort. He fought as long as he could to remain airborne and when he fell, he ran and then walked, and then crawled as far as he could toward Aria's realm. He knew it was a result of the Great Mother's wrath for venturing outside his realm. He knew she was punishing him for stepping into Nex's role by saving Aria and he didn't care. He continued toward the border knowing each step forward would hurt. Pain was worth getting to Aria. He loved her more than the depth of any cut, more than the agony of any burn. So, he ventured on until he'd nearly reached the edge of darkness.

That's when the Great Mother burned his wings from his back and sent him spiraling toward the earth. He crashed and found himself in agony, more than agony, he was left mortal. His life was bound with constraints, limits of time and physical barriers that made taking a step closer to Aria a death sentence for his realm. O'Riah was distraught and he was left to die in anguish amidst the darkness like so many lost souls after him have since.

But O'Riah was not alone in his final days. The Great Mother did not create him. He was born from the old magic of the realms, born from a dragon's flame and given the body of a fallen soldier. When he took his final breath and his mortal body decayed, that old magic became one with the Wall of Darkness and touched the lives of all those who resided in the Dark Realm. Those brave enough to look within, to resist their darkest desires, face their greatest fears, and endure pain beyond death itself were deemed worthy enough to receive O'Riah's power and entrusted to care for his realm after his death.

40

We made sure to check our wounds when we woke up to ensure they would withstand a fight. We got up before the sun, but Madam Stahl had risen earlier still. We found breakfast sitting at the door, along with some food packaged for the trip. We ate what we could and tucked the rest into the pouches at our waists.

"You say we won't attract much attention?" Ezra asked. He'd already asked the question in various forms throughout the morning, and my answer was always the same.

"Yes. Even if there's a big fight, it won't draw much attention outside of the block." I wasn't concerned with being noticed. I was more concerned with our ability to fight off the soldiers. We couldn't guarantee how many there would be, and we could only hold off so many. The plan was to get as close to the gate as we could without being seen and then try to create a strategy once we got a better view.

I finished strapping my sword belt around my hips. Ezra was making do with the traveling cloak we'd taken from the mother down the road, but I'd donned a new pair of pants and simple top from Madam Stahl's closet. The top hung lower on my chest than

I cared for, revealing the tops of my breasts, but I double-knotted the strings holding the top together and hoped everything would stay put. I would hide myself beneath the cloak like Ezra would until the fight broke out.

"Hold on," Ezra said as he pulled on his boots last. "Come sit."

"We don't have time to sit," I told him as he sank onto the couch. I could hear that low groan rumble in his chest from my spot near the door. He showed me the strips of fabric lying on the coffee table.

"You're a warrior," he said. "You should look like one."

Rider braids. The way he'd told it before, they were a symbol reserved for soldiers with dragons. I was neither.

"We don't have time."

"It will be a message for anyone who might see that you aren't just running from the king, but rebelling against what he stands for."

The words felt powerful as he said them, reminding me of how Norelli had tied my hair the day I went to the ship, a small symbol that I did not agree with the trial. She'd tied my hair that way after I'd entered, making sure I was ready to enter the trial as a warrior and not a princess.

I crossed the room and sat on the couch next to him, turning my knees so my back was to him when he raised his hands to my hair. We sat silently as he combed his fingers through my hair, gently weaving the three braids away from my face and tying the last of my hair in a ponytail at the crown of my head.

"Thank you," I said. He was silent for a moment, maybe because it was the nicest I'd been to him since the arena and a part of me regretted the act. He stole that from me. He didn't need to win the trial for us to be here now. He didn't need to kiss me.

I pushed away the thought and stood up, leading the way back to the door and opening it without asking if he was ready. I didn't bother stopping to talk to Madam Stahl who was at the bar with a tray of eggs. I pulled my hood on and crossed the room for the entrance, feeling Ezra just behind me.

It was still dark outside when we moved onto the street, only a few men there on their way to work. I kept my hands close to my weapons as we passed the storefronts. I was right. There were no homes on the block leading to the gate, just businesses that sat empty and waiting for the start of the workday. If we moved quickly, we could avoid any bystanders.

"It looks clear," Ezra said, his voice low.

Near the corner of the street sat a small produce market with barrels and wooden boxes that we could hide behind. I kept my eyes on the street as we approached before crouching behind a box and allowing space so Ezra could hide behind the largest barrel. Thankfully, our cloaks were simple enough that we might pass for a couple of burlap sacks to anyone who might cast a glance our way.

"I can't tell how many there are," I said and peeked over the box again. I rarely traveled this far through the city, but it seemed strange that there weren't any more guards than what I saw. A pair of soldiers stood in front of the wooden doors, and another pair stood inside a small stone building where the mechanism to open the door surely was.

"How fast we open that door will determine our success," Ezra said. He shifted next to me, and I knew he was testing his injured wing. Even if he could fly us over the wall, the soldiers posted there had swords and bows. We were close enough that we would be an easy target if we tried to escape by air.

"We'll have to take out at least half of them to get near the gatehouse," I said, watching the two men inside laugh.

"We'll draw them out and make quick work," Ezra said.

"They won't leave their posts," I said, drawing his gaze away from the surrounding buildings. We were so close that I could see the small regrowth of a pair of horns poking through his dark hair.

"They won't if anyone approaches. Their jobs are to defend,

not to attack. They won't be expecting a fight. They expect someone to approach them," he said.

"Then we'll do something they won't expect."

"Yes, we will," he said and turned away from me. He held a hand out toward the street and before I could ask what he was doing, there was a loud whoosh and heat washed over us. Flames burst from his palms and smashed into the store across the street, sending glass shattering on the sidewalk and immediately engulfing the small building in fire.

"Shit, Ezra!"

"Arm yourself," he said and pulled his sword free, rising from our hiding spot as all of the guards ran into the street to face the blaze. He charged, and I ran just behind with my sword held high.

Ezra easily cut down the first soldier he engaged before the group realized what was happening. I swung for the second soldier, my attack blocked, as the remaining two ran for the gate, shouting. They hadn't even reached their posts ,and the clang of a bell filled the air. Someone was in the top of the tower.

I thrust my sword into the soldier's gut, pulling it free just as something whooshed past on the left.

"Archers!" Ezra yelled, pulled his next opponent to his chest in time to shield himself from several arrows. He let go of the man and let him drop to the ground and ran for the gatehouse. I followed, ice shooting down my veins when I saw the line of archers along the wall. The bell rang so loud that my warning to Ezra was lost.

Something hit the ground to the left as I ran. A man. A soldier. He lay on his stomach with an arrow in his back.

"Go!" Ezra yelled just before the gate gave a loud creak. The doors began to swing outward, and I didn't wait for him to join me. I slipped past through the opening to find the real fight.

The soldiers that hadn't remained along the wall had descended the stairs to face at least a dozen men and women. They weren't dressed for battle, and a few of them weren't equipped. A woman to my right used a pitchfork to bludgeon a soldier before sinking the prongs into his stomach. There were a couple of men on the backs of horses that fired arrows toward the top of the gate, slowly picking off the archers there as their companions fought below.

I rushed to join them, piercing a soldier's back before he could bring his sword down upon a man lying below him. I was onto the next before the man could even get to his feet, let alone utter his thanks. I noticed Ezra join us, his cloak gone now and wings setting him apart from the rest and serving as a target for the soldiers.

They fought their way closer to him, the archers focusing their aim on him and making it easier for the men on horses to shoot the last of them down. I followed the crowd, attacking the soldiers from behind until they caught on that they were surrounded by our small group. It was too late for them to escape, so they stood their ground as the men and women attacked.

"You all right?" Ezra asked, moving around a fighting pair to reach me. His shirt was soaked with blood, but he looked uninjured.

"Yeah. I think so," I told him. It felt like my body had finally caught up with my mind as the last two soldiers met their end to our right. My muscles ached and I felt the dull burn grow in my leg, forcing me to shift my weight off of it.

"You popped the stitches," Ezra said. I looked down to see the blood soaked into the fabric around my thigh.

"Later," I told him and looked up, noticing the group around us staring.

"Get to your horses!" One of the men shouted.

The group began to stir, only a few taking their eyes off of us to run toward the trees. I heard the whinny of a couple of horses and the thunder of hooves as they escaped into the forest around us. The two men on horses remained, both stowing their bows at their backs. They looked like hunters, and if anyone were to stumble upon them even just a mile away, no one would question their motives in the forest. The older man had his horse packed with satchels while the other man was packed much lighter. Both men had dark hair, although the elder's was speckled with gray throughout.

The older man dismounted from his horse and led him by the reins closer to us. "My son and I are far enough from home that we can't spare both."

"Who are you?" I asked as he handed the reins to Ezra.

He turned his eyes on me and inclined his head in a casual bow. "Madam Stahl sent a girl to me last night. She said you could use someone on the other side of the gate."

More rebels. The tension in my chest eased.

"We need to get away from here before more troops get to the gate," Ezra told me, moving a hand to my shoulder that I pushed away immediately. All three men noticed the gesture.

"Good luck," the younger man called out as his father settled into the saddle behind him. The spurred their horse forward and were lost between the trees before I could open my mouth the thank them.

"Get on," Ezra said, moving the horse closer so I could step into the stirrup.

"Watch the way you talk to me."

"Get on the fucking horse," he said and lunged for me. He lifted me so easily into the air that I had no choice but to comply. I hooked my left leg over the back of the horse and pulled myself the rest of the way into the saddle, adjusting myself as he mounted behind me and tugged the reins from my hands.

I held on when we lurched forward, moving at a fast enough speed that I was too jostled about to fling all the curses at him that I wanted to. They built in my chest, heavier and heavier and burning a hole in my stomach so intense that when we finally stopped to let the horse rest I jumped from the saddle ready to face him.

He slid from the saddle, taking just a few steps away from the horse to face me. He held his hands out by his side and said, "Do your worst, Princess."

I launched my fist as hard as I could at his nose, relishing in the crunch I felt beneath my fingers and the warmth of blood that flooded his face. He stumbled back for just a moment before he straightened up, still not raising his hands to defend himself.

"You are a lying piece of shit!" I told him. "You stole the trial from me in a cheap shot. What's the plan from here? You going to hold me captive and take me to the Dark Realm?"

"You're coming with me," he said with a snort.

"Like hell I am." I charged, shoving him and then slapping him across the face hard enough to leave behind a red mark. He endured the attack, allowed me to punch and slap until it wasn't satisfying just to hurt him anymore. I wanted him to fight back. "Hit me, you asshole!"

He was quick, grabbing ahold of my biceps and pinning my back to the nearest tree. "You're coming with me because you will want to. Think about what I told you last night, Princess. You will lead the rebels, but I can promise you that they aren't waiting by the hundreds in an encampment for you. Did you see those men and women back there?" He pressed me harder against the tree for emphasis. "They aren't ready and you aren't ready."

"How can you know that?"

"Because I'm the leader of the Fallen army," he said and released me.

"Then come with me. I'm going north to meet Leif and the rebels. Come with me and help us."

"No," Ezra said firmly and took a step back. "We're headed west to the Mist, to the Dark Realm, and finally to Mount Sollom."

I almost punched him again, but I stopped. He asked me to think about what he'd said before. He told me what had changed after he'd met me, how different he knew I was. I believed him when he said I would lead the rebels and take the Light Realm. I could see it in his eyes. He begged me to trust him.

"What's in Mount Sollom?" I asked.

He relaxed a little. "An army. My kingdom. The rebellion in

your realm is larger than many realize, but it will take many more to stand against trained soldiers. You stand for so much more than just your people, you stand for mine. You stood for Norelli."

"We have no right to hurt our people or yours," I said.

"And that's why you're coming with me," Ezra said, that plea back in his tone, making his voice shake as he set his deep eyes on mine. "Compassion bridges the realms and cuts down hate the way even the greatest power cannot. Because people are united not by kingdoms but by empathy and kindness. Come with me, train with riders, and soon you will lead your rebels from the back of a dragon. Together, we will burn the hate your father has spread in your kingdom."

Tears stung my eyes. I could see it clearly, and I knew he wanted this as much as I did. We could free the Light Realm from my father's oppression and free the Fallen as well, blend our realms the way they once were.

"Come with me," Ezra said again and extended a hand.

I placed my hand against his large palm. He closed his hand, and I laced my fingers with his. He gave mine a tight squeeze and tears fell onto my cheeks, rolling down the scar left there by a man who never deserved the title of father, let alone king. I took a deep breath and squeezed back.

"Yes."

ACKNOWLEDGMENTS

This book has lived in my head for several years and it feels bittersweet to finally have it out in the world. My family and friends have always been my biggest support system, so I owe so much to them. To my husband, Alex, thank you for cheering me on and listening to me fangirl about all my ideas. I love you. To my son, Finn, I hope that I've taught you that you are capable of greatness and can do anything you set your mind to. Dream big. Dad and I will always be there to watch you win and help you through the tough times. We love you so much.

I am thankful for the friends who show up to signings, share my books, and encourage me to chase my dreams. Jill, thank you so much for reading all my books and letting me know when you find those typos or weird sentences. I appreciate all your feedback and support. You're the best. Whitney and Amanda, thank you for sharing my books. You are both some of the first people to shout to the sky when I have book news and it means a lot to have you by my side.

Of course, thank you to all the people who have read my books, left a review, shared my books with friends, and more. I appreciate it and hope you all loved my books as much as I loved writing them. I have a lot of big goals and more stories to write. I can't wait to get them down on paper and share them with the world.

ALSO BY AMY PROKOPIS

Visit my website to subscribe to my newsletter!

www.amyprokopis.com

Follow me on social media!

A girl on the run for her life.
A boy searching for a better future.
Two nations on the brink of war.

Guardians of the sixth gate.
Complete the circle.
Find your match.

He's a 500-year-old vampire looking for the cure.

She's a college girl with a traumatic past.

She has all the answers he's looking for.

She just doesn't know it yet.

Winter Romance
with a witchy twist!

ABOUT THE AUTHOR

Amy Prokopis is a fiction author from Oklahoma who writes fantasy books. She loves writing everything from science fiction and fantasy to contemporary romance. She graduated from Oklahoma State University with a bachelor's degree in English and a minor in German before obtaining a master's degree in school counseling. Besides writing, Amy enjoys distance running and spending time with her husband, their son, and their Havanese, June.

www.ingramcontent.com/pod-product-compliance
Lightning Source LLC
Chambersburg PA
CBHW020225010826

48973CB00006B/1375